The Complet
Volume

The Complete Works
Volume 12

Letters and Journals
Vol. V

by

Lord Byron

The Complete Works, by Lord Byron

This book in its current typographical format first published 2009 by

Cambridge Scholars Publishing

12 Back Chapman Street, Newcastle upon Tyne, NE6 2XX, UK

British Library Cataloguing in Publication Data
A catalogue record for this book is available from the British Library

ISBN (10): 1-4438-0602-1, ISBN (13): 978-1-4438-0602-2

Cover images: portrait of Byron from a drawing by J. Holmes, and engraving of Newstead Abbey. Taken from *The Works of Lord Byron* (13 vols.), London: John Murray, 1895.

CONTENTS

CHAPTER XX. APRIL–DECEMBER, 1820

1094.—To Lady Byron.

Ravenna,
April 3, 1820.

I received yesterday your answer dated March 10. My offer was an honest one, and surely could be only construed as such even by the most malignant Casuistry. I *could* answer you; but it is too late, and it is not worth while.

To the mysterious menace of the last sentence—whatever its import may be—and I really cannot pretend to unriddle it,—I could hardly be very sensible, even if I understood it, as, before it could take place, I shall be where "nothing can touch him farther." I advise you, however, to anticipate the period of your intention; for be assured no power of figures can avail beyond the present; and, if it could, I would answer with the Florentine—

> "Ed io, che posto son con loro in croce
> ...e certo
> La *fiera moglie,* più ch'altro, mi nuoce."

BYRON.

1095.—To Lady Byron.

Ravenna,
April 6th 1820.

In February last, at the suggestion of Mr. Douglas Kinnaird, I wrote to you on the proposition of the Dublin investment, and, to put you more in possession of his opinions, I enclosed his letter. I now enclose you a statement of Mr. Hanson's, and, to say the truth, I am at a loss what to think or decide upon between such very opposite views of the question.

Perhaps you will lay it before your trustees. I for my own part am ignorant of business, and am so little able to judge, that I should be disposed to think with them, whatever their ideas may be upon the subject. One thing is certain; I cannot consent to sell out of the funds at a loss, and the Dublin House should be insured.

Excuse all this trouble; but as it is your affair as well as mine, you will pardon it. I have an innate distrust and detestation of the public funds and their precarious [?];

but still the sacrifice of the removal (at least at present) may be too great. I do not know what to think, nor does any body else, I believe.

Yours, BYRON.

I rec[d] yours of March 10th, and enclosed an answer (to Mr. Thomas Moore) to be forwarded to you.

1096.—To John Hanson.

Ravenna,
April 6th 1820.

DEAR SIR,—

I have just received yours dated March 22[d]. Your *January packet* only arrived last Sunday, so that I shall put off replying to it for the present (as there is a witness wanting for the Scotch deed, etc.), and answer your March epistle, which, as you yourself say, is of much more importance.

But how shall I answer?

> Between the devil and deep Sea,
> Between the Lawyer and Trustee—

it is difficult to decide. Mr. Kinnaird writes that the Mortgage is *the most advantageous thing possible*; you write that it *is quite the* contrary. You are both my old acquaintances, both men of business, and both give good reasons for both your opinions; and the result is that I finish by having no opinion at all. I cannot see that it could any way be the interest of either to persuade me either one way or the other, unless you thought it for my advantage. In short, *do settle* it among you if you can, for I am at my wits' end betwixt your contrary opinions. One thing is positive. *I will not agree to sell out of the funds at a loss,* and the *Dublin House property must be insured*; but *you* should not have waited till the Funds get low again, as you have done, so as to make the affair impracticable. I retain, however, my bad opinion of the funds, and must insist on the money being one day placed on better *security somewhere.* Of Irish Security, and Irish Law, I know nothing, and cannot take upon me to dispute your Statement; but I prefer higher Interest for my Money (like everybody else I believe), and shall be glad to make as much as I can at the least risk possible.

It is a pity that I am not upon the Spot, but I cannot make it at all convenient to come to England for the present.

I am truly pleased to hear that there is a prospect of terminating the Rochdale Business, in one way or the other: pray see *it out.* It has been hitherto a dead loss of time and expences, but may I suppose pay in the long run; and if *you could for once* be a *little quicker about that,* or anything else, it would be a great gain to me and no loss to you, as our final Settlement naturally will depend in some measure upon the result. If the claim could be adjusted, and the whole brought to the hammer, I could clear every thing, and know what I really possess.

Pray write to me (direct to Ravenna). I do not feel justified in the present state of the funds, and on your statement, of urging the fulfilment of the Blessington Mortgage, and yet I feel sorry that it does not seem feasible. At any rate, see Mr. Kinnaird upon it and come to some decision. Let me hear about Rochdale.

Yours ever truly, BYRON.

P.S.—Advance old Joe Murray whatever may be necessary and proper, and it will be deducted from my Bankers acc[t]

1097.—To Douglas Kinnaird.

Ravenna,
April 6th, 1820.

MY DEAR DOUGLAS,—

I have received the enclosed letter from Mr. Hanson, which I confess "*doth give me pause*"

> Between the devil and deep sea,
> Between the Lawyer and Trustee.

I am sadly bested. What *can I decide*?

> Or this way, or that way, or which way I will,
> Whate'er I decide, *t'other* bride will take ill.

I love six per cent.—if *six* it be (but it seems *six* means *five* in Ireland)—but I can't sell out at such a thundering loss in the funds at present; and then the *housen* maun' be insured, otherwise the security would be like George Faulkner's burglary—

> "Last night an empty house on Ormond quay."

In short, I can't consent, and can't dissent—what the devil is to be done? Do pray decide anything, and I'll agree, if you will but set the example. But my feelings overpower me.

Yours ever and most truly, BYRON.

P.S. I can't come to England till after the Coronation, because of family matters; my spouse and I could not march together at it, and I have no great inclination.

1098.—To John Murray.

Ravenna,
April 9, 1820.

D^R S^R,—

In the name of all the devils in—the printing office, why don't you write to acknowledge the receipt of the second, third, and fourth packets, viz. the Pulci—translation and original, the *Danticles,* the *Observations on,* etc.? You forget that you keep me in hot water till I know whether they are arrived, or if I must have the bore of recopying.

I send you "a Song of Triumph" by W. Botherby, Esqre, price sixpence, on the Election of J. C. H. Esqre for Westminster (*not* for publication);

> Would you go to the House by the true gate,
> Much faster than ever Whig Charley went;
> Let Parliament send you to Newgate,
> And Newgate will send you to Parliament.

Have you gotten the cream of translations, Francesca of Rimini, from the *Inferno*? Why, I have sent you a warehouse of trash within the last month, and you have no sort of feeling about you: a pastry-cook would have had twice the gratitude, and thanked me at least for the quantity.

To make the letter heavier, I enclose you the Cardinal Legate's (one Campeius) circular for his Conversazione this evening: it is the anniversary of the Pope's tiaration, and all polite Christians, even of the Lutheran creed, must go and be civil. And there will be a Circle, and a Faro-table, (for shillings, that is—they don't allow high play) and all the beauty, nobility, and Sanctity of Ravenna present. The Cardinal himself is a very good-natured little fellow, Bishop of Imola and Legate here,—a devout believer in all the doctrines of the Church. He has kept his housekeeper these forty years, for his carnal recreation; but is reckoned a pious man, and a moral liver.

I am not quite sure that I won't be among you this autumn, for I find that business don't go on—what with trustees and Lawyers—as it should do, "with all deliberate speed." They differ about investments in Ireland.

> Between the devil and deep Sea,
> Between the Lawyer and Trustee,

I am puzzled; and so much time is lost by my not being upon the spot—what with answers, demurs, rejoinders, that it may be I must come and look to it. For one says do, and t'other don't, so that I know not which way to turn. But perhaps they can manage without me.

Yours ever,

B.

P.S.—I have begun a tragedy on the subject of Marino Faliero, the Doge of Venice; but you shan't see it these six years, if you don't acknowledge my packets with wore quickness and precision. *Always write, if but a line,* by return of post, when anything arrives, which is not a mere letter.

Address direct to Ravenna; it saves a week's time, and much postage.

1099.—To John Murray.

Ravenna,
April 11th 1820.

Dear Murray,—

Pray forward the enclosed letter to a fiddler. In Italy they are called "Professors of the Violin." You should establish one at each of the universities.

Yours, B.

P.S.—Pay forward it carefully with *a frank*: it is from a poor fellow to his musical Uncle, of whom nothing has been heard these three years (though what he can have been doing at Belfast, Belfast best knows), so that they are afraid of some mischief having befallen him or his fiddle.

1100.—To Douglas Kinnaird.

Ravenna,
April 14th, 1820.

My dear Douglas,—

The hopes of the termination of this interminable mortgage, and the breaking of my carriage (not the travelling one) by an overturn (I was upset a month ago), have induced me to solace myself with a new one, ordered at Florence (a landau), and to which I have appended a pair of brand new horses, harness, and the like. All this, besides cutting a formidable figure in francs, and in scudi, will look not less repugnant in pounds sterling; so that you will make a fearful face, as becomes a banker, trustee, and particularly as a friend, who is privileged to look as disagreeable as possible. But then, as a set-off, I have despatched sundry packets of poeshie to Master Murray, of that ilk, cantos of "Donny Johnny," and translations from Pulci, and "Visions of Dante," and a brief translation from the same, &c.—the which, added to my *fee* from the funds, viz., half my year's income in July, will or ought to bring us right again, to say nothing of a handsome sum in ransom epistles, and circulars, yet itching in my breeches pockets.

It rejoices me to see that Hobhouse is at last an M.P.; his former fate reminded of the lines on Guy Faux—

> "Guy Faux turpis erat, voluitque cremare Senatum
> Ast hoc invento, Ille (the Constable understood) *recepit eum* (took him up)."

But now, as Garshattachin says, "I'm glad you're a Baillie," though he passed through a queer sort of a turnpike to his preferment.

> Would you go to the house by the true gate,
> Much faster than ever Whig Charley went,
> Let Parliament send you to Newgate,
> And Newgate will send you to Parliament.

Pray are you in Parliament this time? or only as far as Newgate, on your way there? The return, or close of the poll for Bishops Castle is not given in the "Pas de Calais," nor in "Galignani," so that I am in ignorance of your proper success.

We are in expectation of a *row* here in a short time. The Spanish business has set all Italy a constitutioning, and they won't get it without some *fechting,* as we Scottish say. Now this being likely, I shall stay to see what turns up, and perhaps take a turn amongst them, instead of coming to hear so much, and to see so little done, as seems to be your Anglo-fashion at present.

Here, you may believe, there will be cutting of thrapples, and something *like* a civil buffetting, if they once begin, and there are all the dispositions. You can have no idea of the ferment in men's minds, from the Alps to Otranto.

As I have been inoculated among the people rather, within these last four years, if matters wax serious, I should not like to sit twirling my thumbs, but perhaps "take service," like Dugald Dalgetty and his horse, on the savage side of the question. But I must say no more just at present, except desiring you to write now and then, as long as the communications are open.

I desire to be remembered to that Hobhouse—whom I perceive characterized in the "Courier" as a coldblooded conspirator, full of mischiefs—Guy Faux again —"callidus, a hot-headed fellow; frigidus, a cold, determined villain"—and to all the respectable part of your people, in whose principles, however, I do *not* fully concur.

Believe me, yours ever, &c.,

B.

P.S. I enclose to *you* some rhymes of last year, which I have just copied out. I wrote them on passing the Po, in June, 1819—the subject of them being that at Cavanelli sul' Po, nearer the sea, and I much higher up.

I send them to you, instead of to Moray, as a sign of my high displeasure; and so tell him, in future, I shall enclose everything to you, since he neglects to answer by return of post, when I send him nonsense by packets.

As a reward for his rudeness, *bleed* him in the *jugular,* when you treat for the MSS. I have a drama, too, upon the anvil—*not* for the stage.

1101.—To John Murray.

Ravenna,
April 16, 1820.

Dear Murray,—

Post after post arrives without bringing any acknowledgement from you of the different packets (excepting the first) which I have sent within the last two months, all of which ought to be arrived long ere now; and as they were announced in other letters, you ought at least to say whether they are come or not. You are not expected to write frequent or long letters, as your time is much occupied; but when parcels that have cost some pains in the composition, and great trouble in the copying, are sent to you, I should at least be pit out of Suspense by the immediate acknowledgement, per return of post, addressed *directly* to *Ravenna.* I am naturally —knowing what continental *posts* are—anxious to hear that they are arrived; especially as I loathe the task of copying so much, that if there was a human being that could copy my blotted MSS. he should have all they can ever bring for his trouble. All I desire is two lines, to say, such a day I received such a packet: there are now at least *six* unacknowledged. This is neither kind nor courteous.

I have, besides, another reason for desiring you to be speedy, which is, that there is THAT brewing in Italy which will speedily cut off all security of communication, and set all your Anglo-travellers flying in every direction, with their usual fortitude in foreign tumults. The Spanish and French affairs have set the Italians in a ferment; and no wonder: they have been too long trampled on. This will make a sad scene for your exquisite traveller, but not for the resident, who naturally wishes a people to redress itself. I shall, if permitted by the natives, remain to see what will come of it, and perhaps to take a turn with them, like Dugald Dalgetty and his horse, in case of business; for I shall think it by far the most interesting spectacle and moment in existence, to see the Italians send the Barbarians of all nations back to their own dens. I have lived long enough among them to feel more for them as a nation than for any other people in existence; but they want Union, and they want principle; and I doubt their success. However, they will try, probably; and if they do, it will be a good cause. No Italian can hate an Austrian more than I do; unless it be the English, the Austrians seem to me the most obnoxious race under the Sky.

But I doubt, if anything be done, it won't be so quietly as in Spain. To be sure, Revolutions are not to be made with Rose-water, where there are foreigners as Masters.

Write while you can; for it is but the toss up of a Paul that there will not be a row that will somewhat retard the Mail by and bye.

Address right to *Ravenna.*

Yours, B.

1102.—To Richard Belgrave Hoppner.

Ravenna,
April 18, 1820.

Dear Hoppner,—

I have caused write to Siri and Willhalm to send with *Vincenzo* in a boat, the camp-beds and swords left in their care when I quitted Venice. There are also several pounds of *Manton's best powder* in a Japan case; *but unless* I felt sure of getting it away from V. without seizure, I won't have it ventured. I *can get* it *in* here, by means of an acquaintance in the Customs, who has offered to get it ashore for me; but should like to be certiorated of its safety in leaving Venice. I would not lose it for its weight in gold—there is none such in Italy, as I take it to be.

I wrote to you a week or so ago, and hope you are in good plight and spirits. Sir Humphry Davy is here, and was last night at the Cardinal's. As I had been there last Sunday, and yesterday was warm, I did not go, which I should have done, if I had thought of meeting the Man of Chemistry. He called this morning, and I shall go in search of him at Corso time. I believe, to-day being Monday, there is no great conversazione, and only the family one at the Marchese Cavalli's, where I go as a *relation* sometimes; so that, unless he stays a day or two, we should hardly meet in public.

The theatre is to open in May for the fair, if there is not a row in all Italy by that time,—the Spanish business has set them all a-constitutioning, and what will be the end, no one knows—it is also necessary thereunto to have a beginning. You see the blackguards have brought in Hobhouse for Westminster. Rochfoucault says that "there is something in the misfortunes of our best friends not unpleasing to us," and it is to this that I attribute my not being so sorry for his election as I ought to be, seeing that it will eventually be a millstone round his neck, for what can he do? he can't take place; he can't take power in any case; if he succeeds in reforming, he will be stoned for his pains;—and if he fails, there he is stationary as Lecturer for Westminster.

Would you go to the House by the true gate,
    Much faster than ever Whig Charley went;
Let Parliament send you to Newgate,
    And Newgate will send you to Parliament.

But Hobhouse is a man of real talent however, and will make the best of his situation as he has done hitherto.

Yours ever and truly, BYRON.

P.S.—My benediction to Mrs. Hoppner. How is your little boy? Allegra is growing, and has increased in good looks and obstinacy.

1103.—To Richard Belgrave Hoppner.

Ravenna,
April 22[d] 1820.

My dear Hoppner,—

With regard to Gnoatto, I cannot relent in favour of Madame Mocenigo, who protects a rascal and retains him in her service. Suppose the case of your Servant or mine, you having the same claim upon F[letche]r or I upon your Tim, would either of us retain them an instant unless they paid the debt? As "there is no force in the decrees of Venice," no Justice to be obtained from the tribunals,—because even conviction does not compel payment, nor enforce punishment,—you must excuse me when I repeat *that not one farthing of the rent shall be paid,* till either Gnoatto pays me his debt, or quits Madame Mocenigo's service. I will abide by the consequences; but I could wish that no time was lost in apprizing her of the affair. You must not mind her relation Seranzo's statement; he may be a very good man, but he is but a Venetian, which I take to be in the present age the *ne plus ultra* of human abasement in all moral qualities whatsoever. I dislike differing from you in opinion; but I have no other course to take, and either Gnoatto pays me, or quits her Service, or I will resist to the uttermost the liquidation of her rent. I have nothing against her, nor for her; I owe her neither ill will, nor kindness;—but if she protects a Scoundrel, and there is no other redress, I will *make* some.

It has been and always will be the case where there is *no law.* Individuals must then right themselves. They have set the example "and it shall go hard but I will better the Instruction." Two words from her would suffice to make the villain do his duty; if they are not said, or if they have no effect, let him be dismissed; if not, as I have said, so will I do.

I wrote last week to Siri to desire *Vincenzo* to be sent to take charge of the beds and Swords to this place by Sea. I am in no hurry for the books,—none whatever,—and don't want them.

Pray has not Mingaldo the Biography of living people?—it is not here, nor in your list. I am not at all sure that *he* has it either, but it may be possible.

Let Castelli go on to the last. I am determined to see Merryweather *out* in this business, just to discover what is or is not to be done in their tribunals, and if ever I cross him, as I have tried the law in vain, (since it has but convicted him and then done nothing in consequence)—I will try a shorter process with that personage.

About Allegra, I can only say to Claire—that I so totally disapprove of the mode of Children's treatment in their family, that I should look upon the Child as going into a hospital. Is it not so? Have they *reared* one? Her health here has hitherto been *excellent,* and her temper not bad; she is sometimes vain and obstinate, but always clean and cheerful, and as, in a year or two, I shall either send her to England, or put her in a Convent for education, these defects will be remedied as far as they can in human nature. But the Child shall not quit me again to perish of Starvation, and green fruit, or be taught to believe that there is no Deity. Whenever there is convenience of vicinity and access, her Mother can always have her with her; otherwise no. It was so stipulated from the beginning.

The Girl is not so well off as with you, but far better than with them; the fact is she is spoilt, being a great favourite with every body on account of the fairness of her Skin, which shines among their dusky children like the milky way, but there is no comparison of her situation now, and that under Elise, or with them. She has grown considerably, is very clean, and lively. She has plenty of air and exercise at home, and she goes out daily with Me Guiccioli in her carriage to the Corso.

The paper is finished and so must the letter be.

Yours ever, B.

My best respects to Mrs. H. and the little boy—and Dorville.

1104.—To John Cam Hobhouse.

Ravenna,
April 22nd, 1820.

Dear Hobhouse,—

By yesterday's post I had yours of the 31st ulto. The papers told me that you had got *out,* and got *in*; I am truly glad of both events, though I could have wished the one had had no connection with the other.

I beg your pardon for confounding you with Hunt and Cobbett, but I thought that the Manchester business 1 had effected a reconciliation, at least you all ('bating Cobbett) attending one meeting soon after it, but I am glad to hear you have nothing to do with those scoundrels. I can understand and enter into the feelings of Mirabeau and La Fayette, but I have no sympathy with Robespierre and Marat, whom I look upon as in no respect worse than those two English ruffians if they once had the power. You will hardly suppose that I should deny to you what I said to another; I *did* use such an expression on the subject of Bristol Hunt, and I repeat it. I do not think the man who would overthrow all laws should have the benefit of any; he who plays the Tyler, or Cade, might find the Walworth, or Iden; he who enacts the Clodius, the Milo, and what is there in Bristol Hunt and Cobbett *so* honest as the former, or *more* patriotic than the latter? "Arcades ambo," blackguards both. Why, our classical education alone should teach us to trample on such unredeemed dirt as the *dis*-honest bluntness, the ignorant brutality, the unblushing baseness of these two miscreants, and all who believe in them.

I think I have neither been an illiberal man, nor an unsteady man upon politics; but I think also that if the Manchester yeomanry had cut down *Hunt only,* they would have done their duty; as it was they committed murder, both in what they did, and what they did *not* do, in butchering the weak instead of *piercing* the wicked; in assailing the seduced instead of the seducer; in punishing the poor starving populace instead of that pampered and dinnered blackguard, who is only less contemptible than his predecessor, *Orator Henley,* because he is more mischievous.

What I say thus I say as publicly as you please; if to praise such fellows be the price of popularity, I spit upon it as I would in their faces.

Upon reform you have long known my opinion; but *radical* is a new word since my time, it was not in the political vocabulary in 1816, when I left England, and I don't know what it means—is it uprooting?

As to yourself, it is not in the power of political events to change my sentiments. I am rejoiced to see you in Parliament, because I am sure you will make a splendid figure in it, and have fought hard to arrive there, and I esteem and admire Burdett, as you know; but with these, and half a dozen more exceptions, I protest, not against *reform,* but my most thorough contempt and abhorrence of all that I have seen, read, or heard, of the persons calling themselves *reformers, radicals,* and such other names. I should look upon being free with such men as much the same as being in bonds with felons.

I am no enemy to liberty, however, and you will be glad to hear that there is some chance of it in Italy. The Spanish business has set the Italians agog, and if there turns up anything, as is not unlikely, I may perhaps "wink and hold out mine iron" with the rest; or at any rate be a well-wishing spectator of a push against those rascally Austrians, who have desolated Lombardy, and threaten the rest of the *bel paese.*

I should not like to leave this country in case of a row; but if nothing occurs, and you come out during the recess in autumn, I might revert with you, though only four years of the usual term of transportation are expired.

I wrote to you last week about my affairs, which are puzzling; Dougal says the Irish thing is excellent; Hanson says it is ruinous—decide between them.

I have sent lots of poeshie to Murray, who has not condescended to acknowledge but two, of half a dozen packets; *bleed him in the jugular,* as they did our char-a-banc driver in the Simmenthal in 1816.

Believe me, yours ever and truly, B.

P.S.—I have written in great haste, and it is bedtime; my monkey, too, has been playing such tricks about the room as Mr. Hunt at his meetings; so that I have hardly had time to be common-sensible, but never mind.

1105.—To John Murray.

Ravenna,
April 23, 1820.

DEAR MURRAY,—

The proofs don't contain the *last* stanzas of Canto second, but end abruptly with the 105th Stanza.

I told you long ago that the new Cantos were *not* good, and I also *told you a reason*; recollect, I do not oblige you to publish them; you may suppress them, if you like, but I can alter nothing. I have erased the six stanzas about those two impostors, Southey and Wordsworth (which I suppose will give you great pleasure), but I can do no more. I can neither recast, nor replace; but I give you leave to put it all into the fire, if you like, or *not* to publish, and I think that's sufficient.

I told you that I wrote on with no good will—that I had been, *not* frightened, but *hurt* by the outcry, and, besides that, when I wrote last November, I was ill in body, and in very great distress of mind about some private things of my own; but *you would* have it: so I sent it to you, and to make it lighter, *cut* it in two—but I can't piece it together again. I can't cobble: I must "either make a spoon or spoil a horn,"—and there's an end; for there's no remeid: but I leave you free will to suppress the *whole,* if you like it.

About the *Morgante Maggiore, I won't have a line omitted:* it may circulate, or it may not; but all the Criticism on earth shan't touch a line, unless it be because it is *badly* translated. Now you say, and I say, and others say, that the translation is a good one; and so it shall go to press as it is. Pulci must answer for his own irreligion: I answer for the translation only.

I am glad you have got the *Dante*; and there should be by this time a translation of his Francesca of Rimini arrived to append to it. I sent you a quantity of *prose* observations in answer to Wilson, but I shall not publish them *at present*: keep them by you as *documents.*

Pray let Mr. Hobhouse look to the *Italian* next time in the *proofs*: *this time,* while I am scribbling to you, they are corrected by one who passes for the prettiest woman in Romagna, and even the Marches, as far as Ancona—be the other who she may. I am glad you like my answer to your enquiries about Italian Society: it is fit you should like *something,* and be damned to you.

My love to Scott. I shall think higher of knighthood ever after for his being dubbed. By the way, he is the first poet titled for his talent in Britain: it has happened abroad before now; but on the continent titles are universal and worthless. Why don't you send me *Ivanhoe* and the *Monastery*? I have never written to Sir Walter, for I know he has a thousand things, and I a thousand nothings, to do; but I hope to see him at Abbotsford before very long, and I will sweat his Claret for him, though Italian abstemiousness has made my brain but a shilpit concern for a Scotch sitting *inter pocula.* I love Scott and Moore, and all the better brethren; but I hate and abhor that puddle of water-worms whom you have taken into your troop in the *history* line I see. I am obliged to end abruptly.

Yours, B.

P.S.—You say that *one half* is very good: you are *wrong;* for, if it were, it would be the finest poem in existence. *Where* is the poetry of which *one half* is good? is it the *Æneid*? is it *Milton's*? is it *Dryden's*? is it any one's except *Pope's* and Goldsmith's, of which *all* is good? and yet these two last are the poets your pond poets would explode. But if *one half* of the two new Cantos be good in your opinion, what the devil would you have more? No—no: no poetry is *generally* good—only by fits and starts—and you are lucky to get a sparkle here and there. You might as well want a Midnight *all stars* as rhyme all perfect.

We are on the verge of a *row* here. Last night they have overwritten all the city walls with "Up with the Republic!" and "death to the Pope!" etc., etc. This would be nothing in London, where the walls are privileged, and where, when somebody went to Chancellor Thurlow to tell him, as an alarming sign, that he had seen "Death to the king" on the park wall, old Thurlow asked him if he had ever seen " * " chalked on the same place, to which the alarmist responding in the affirmative, Thurlow resumed "and so have I for these last 30 years, and yet it never * * * *." But here it is a different thing: they are not used to such fierce political inscriptions, and the police is all on the alert, and the Cardinal glares pale through all his purple.

April 24, 1820, 8 o'clock, p.m.

The police have been, all Noon and after, searching for the Inscribers, but have caught none as yet. They must have been all night about it, for the "Live republics —death to popes and priests," are innumerable, and plastered over all the palaces: ours has plenty. There is "down with the Nobility," too—they are down enough already, for that matter. A very heavy rain and wind having come on, I did not get on horseback to go out and "skirr the country;" but I shall mount tomorrow, and take a canter among the peasantry, who are a savage, resolute race, always riding with guns in their hands. I wonder they don't suspect the Serenaders, for they play on the guitar all night, here as in Spain, to their Mistresses.

Talking of politics, as Caleb Quotem says, pray look at the *Conclusion* of my Ode on *Waterloo,* written in the year 1815, and, comparing it with the Duke de Berri's catastrophe in 1820: tell me if I have not as good a right to the character of "*Vates,*" in both senses of the word, as Fitzgerald and Coleridge?

"Crimson tears will follow yet"—

and have not they? I can't pretend to foresee what will happen among you Englishers at this distance, but I vaticinate a *row* in Italy; in whilk case, I don't know that I won't have a finger in it. I dislike the Austrians, and think the Italians infamously oppressed; and if they begin, why, I will recommend "the erection of a Sconce upon Drumsnab," like Dugald Dalgetty.

1106.—To Douglas Kinnaird.

Ravenna,
April 30th, 1820.

My dear Douglas,—

I have to congratulate Hobhouse on his election, but I do not know whether I have yet to pay you the same compliment.

I must now trouble you with a small bit of "booksale and backshop" business. Jno. Murray was very impatient for some more of Juan, so I sent him *two* Cantos; that is, *one long* Canto cut into two; but expressly *stated* and *stipulated* by me to *reckon* (in money matters) *only* as *one,* in fairness to him, as well as from this having been the original form; in fact, the two are not so long as *one* of those already published, which are both very tedious.

It seems that *one* half of these Cantos do not please the said John and his Synod, and they are *right*; I *know,* and said to him always, that they were *not* good, but he was very eager, so I sent them. Now I am by no means anxious for the publication, and have written to say so; I have also sent him various things, verse and prose (the *prose* I *don't* mean in any case to publish just now), so that you may let him off if he likes. I don't care about the money, only do you let me know in time, that I may not calculate upon any extra sum beyond the income funds in July next. I had made no bargain with him, leaving all that to you, and he has behaved very fairly, and I wish to do as much by him as I would whether he had or no. If he chooses to decline, let him, and let the thing rest in abeyance; I don't want any other publisher nor publication. If he wishes to publish he may, and you may settle as seems fair to both.

I enclose you his letter to me for you to go upon; you will, I think, agree with him, that the trash is not very brilliant this time; but I can't alter, I can't cobble; I have struck out a few stanzas, and that is all I can do, except suppressing the whole new Cantos, to which I have no objection.

News I have none to send, except that we expect a rising in Italy for a Constitution. I sometimes think of going to England after the Coronation, and sometimes not. I have no thoughts, at least no wish, of coming before, and not much after; but I am very undecided and uncertain, and have quite lost all *local* feeling for England, without having acquired any *local* attachment for any other spot, except in the occasional admiration of fine landscapes, and goodly cities.

It is now turned of four years since I left it, and out of the last eleven I have passed upwards of six years a-gipsying. You tell me nothing of the whereabouts of Scrope, our old crony, nor does Hobhouse; you worldly gentlemen make excellent friends, however; you lent him money, and I daresay it was that, more than your memory that he liked; but he was a fine fellow, and as he never had any of *my* cash to authorise me to forget him, I should be glad to know what hath become of him.

Yours ever very truly, BN.

P.S. I want to ax Hobhouse a question; in his last letter he denies that any reconciliation has taken place between him and *Hunt,* and yet I see Hunt at *the dinner,* and an eulogium from Burdett on the blackguard who called Hobhouse an ape, or a monkey at the last election. I wish to know why he sate down to table with him? I don't mean that such a fellow could merit a gentlemanly resentment, or give either satisfaction or apology, but why *eat* in his company?

1107.—To John Murray.

Ravenna,
May 8, 1820.

DEAR MURRAY,—

From your not having written again, an intention which your letter of ye 7th Ult^o^ indicated, I have to presume that "*The Prophecy of Dante*" has not been found more worthy than its immediate precursors in the eyes of your illustrious Synod. In that case, you will be in some perplexity; to end which, I repeat to you, that you are not to consider yourself as bound or pledged to publish any thing because it is *mine,* but always to act according to your own views, or opinions, or those of your friends; and to be sure that you will in no degree offend me by "declining the article," to use a technical phrase. The *Prose* observations on J[n] Wilson's attack, I do *not* intend for publication at this time; and I sent a copy of verses to Mr. Kinnaird (they were written last year, on crossing the Po) which must *not* be published either. I mention this, because it is probable he may give you a copy. Pray recollect this, as they are mere verses of Society, and written upon private feelings and passions. And, moreover, I cannot consent to any mutilations or omissions of *Pulci*: the original has been ever free from such in Italy, the Capital of Christianity, and the translation may be so in England; though you will think it strange that they should have allowed such *freedom* for so many centuries to the *Morgante,* while the other day they confiscated the whole translation of the 4th Canto of *Childe H*[*arol*]*d,* and have persecuted Leoni, the translator—so he writes me, and so I could have told him, had he consulted me before his publication. This shows how much more politics interest men in these parts than religion. Half a dozen invectives against tyranny confiscate *C*[*d*] *H*[*d*] in a month; and eight and twenty cantos of quizzing Monks and Knights, and Church Government, are let loose for centuries. I copy Leoni's account:—

"Non ignorerà forse che la mia versione del 4° Canto del *Childe Harold* fu confiscata in ogni parte: ed io stesso ho dovuto soffrir vessazioni altrettanto ridicole quanto illiberali, ad arte che alcuni versi fossero esclusi dalla censura. Ma siccome il divieto non fa d'ordinario che accrescere la curiosità così quel carme sull' Italia è ricercato più che mai, e penso di farlo ristampare in Inghilterra senza nulla escludere. Sciagurata condizione di questa mia patria! se patria si può chiamare una terra così avvilita dalla fortuna, dagli uomini, da se medesima."

Rose will translate this to you. Has he had his letter? I enclosed it to you months ago. This intended piece of publication I shall dissuade him from, or he may chance to see the inside of St Angelo's. The last Sentence of his letter is the common and pathetic sentiment of all his Countrymen, who execrate Castlereagh as the cause, by the conduct of the English at Genoa. Surely that man will not die in his bed: there is no spot of the earth where his name is not a hissing, and a curse. Imagine what must be the man's talent for Odium, who has contrived to spread his infamy like a pestilence from Ireland to Italy, and to make his name an execration in all languages.

Talking of Ireland, Sir Humphry Davy was here last fortnight, and I was in his company in the house of a very pretty Italian Lady of rank, who, by way of displaying her learning in presence of the great Chemist then describing his fourteenth ascension of Mount Vesuvius, asked "if there was not a similar Volcano in *Ireland*?" My only notion of an *Irish* Volcano consisted of the Lake of

Killarney, which I naturally conceived her to mean; but, on second thoughts, I divined that she alluded to *Ice*land, and to Hecla—and so it proved, though she sustained her volcanic topography for some time with all the amiable pertinacity of "the Feminie." She soon after turned to me and asked me various questions about Sir Humphry's philosophy, and I explained as well as an Oracle his skill in gases, safety lamps, and in ungluing the Pompeian MSS. "But what do you call him?" said she. "A great Chemist," quoth I. "What can he "do?" repeated the lady. "Almost any thing," said I. "Oh, then, *mio Caro,* do pray beg him to give me something to dye my eyebrows black. I have tried a thousand things, and the colours all come off; and besides, they don't grow: can't he invent something to make them grow?" All this with the greatest earnestness; and what you will be surprized at, she is neither ignorant nor a fool, but really well educated and clever. But they speak like children, when first out of their convents; and, after all, this is better than an English blue-stocking.

I did not tell Sir Humphry of this last piece of philosophy, not knowing how he might take it. He is gone on towards England. Sotheby has sent him a poem on his undoing the MSS., which Sir H. says is a bad one. Who the devil doubts it? Davy was much taken with Ravenna, and the *primitive Italianism* of the people, who are unused to foreigners: but he only staid a day.

Send me Scott's novels and some news.

P.S.—I have begun and advanced into the second Act of a tragedy on the subject of the Doge's Conspiracy (i.e. the story of Marino Faliero); but my present feeling is so little encouraging on such matters, that I begin to think I have mined my talent out, and proceed in no great phantasy of finding a new vein.

P.S.—I sometimes think (if the Italians don't rise) of coming over to England in the Autumn after the coronation, (at which I would not appear, on account of my family Schism with "the feminie") but as yet I can decide nothing. The place must be a great deal changed since I left it, now more than four years ago.

May 9th, 1820. Address directly to Ravenna.

1108.—To John Cam Hobhouse.

Ravenna,
May 11th, 1820.

My dear H[obhouse],—

You were not "*down*" but 700 ahead in the *poll* when I lampooned you. I had scrawled it before the election began, but waited till you were, or at least appeared, sure (in the *Gazetteer*) before I sent to *you* what would have been a sorry jest had you *failed*; it would then have been ill-natured; as it is, it was buffoonery, and this, you know, has been all along our mutual privilege. When I left England *you* made those precious lines on Murray, and Douglas, Kin[d] and y[r] humble servt., and in 1808 you put me into prose at Brighthelmstone about Jackson, and W. W[ebster], and Debathe, and wrote mock epitaphs upon my poor friend Long, when he was lost at sea, all for the joke's sake.

Do you remember Capt. Bathurst's nautical anecdote of the boatswain shooting the Frenchman who asked for quarter while running down the hatchway, "No, no, you —, you fired first"?

As for the Moray, he had no business whatever to put the lines in peril of publication. I desired him to give them to *you,* and their *signature* must have showed you in what spirit they were written. And I am very glad that you have given him a lecture on the subject; having the greatest delight in setting you all by the ears.

If you *will* dine with Bristol Hunt, and such like, what can you expect? But never mind, you are in, and I can assure you that there is not a blackguard among your constituents half so happy as I am in seeing your triumph. I never would have forgiven you the use of such instruments, except in favour of success. And pray don't *mistake me*; it is not against the pure principle of reform that I protest, but against low, designing, dirty levellers, who would pioneer their way to a democratical tyranny, putting these fellows in a parenthesis, I think, as I have ever thought on that point, as it *used* to be defined; but things have changed their sense probably, as they have their names, since my time. Four years ago *Radical* was unknown as a political watchword.

I am sorry to hear what you say of Scrope; it must have been *sore* distress which made that man forget himself. Poor fellow, his name seems not fortunate; there was Goose Davies, and now there is a Captain (who has planted his servant and run away for mistaking signatures) of the same nomenclature; but what can have become of Scrope? Does nobody know? He could hardly remain at Bruges; it is hard that he should "point a moral and adorn a tale," unless of his own telling, and his loss is the most "ill-convenient for my Lord Castlecorner" that could have occurred. I shall never hear such jokes again. What fools we were to let him go back in 1816, from Switzerland. He would, at least, have saved his credit and money, and then, *what* is he to do? He can't *play,* and without play he is wretched.

You have, by this time, seen all my *-prose* and poeshie. I don't think of publishing the *former,* but I wish you to read it. From Murray I have heard nothing lately.

I sometimes think of going to England in autumn, but it is a project so repugnant to my feelings, that my resolutions fade as the time approaches.

Yours, ever truly, B.

1109.—To John Murray.

Ravenna,
May 20, 1820.

Murray, my dear, make my respects to Thomas Campbell, and tell him from me, with faith and friendship, three things that he must right in his Poets: *Firstly,* he says Anstey's *Bath Guide* Characters are taken from Smollett. 'Tis impossible:—the *Guide* was published in *1766,* and *Humphrey Clinker* in *1771—dunque,* 'tis Smollett who has taken from Anstey. *Secondly,* he does not know to whom Cowper alludes, when he says that there was one who "built a church to *God,* and then blasphemed his name:" it was "Deo erexit *Voltaire*" to whom that maniacal Calvinist and coddled poet alludes. *Thirdly,* he misquotes and spoils a passage from Shakespeare, "to gild refined gold, to paint the lily," etc.; for *lily* he puts *rose,* and bedevils in more words than one the whole quotation.

Now, Tom is a fine fellow; but he should be correct; for the 1st is an *injustice* (to Anstey), the 2nd an *ignorance,* and the third a *blunder.* Tell him all this, and let him take it in good part; for I might have rammed it into a review and vexed him—instead of which, I act like a Christian.

Yours, B.

1110.—To Richard Belgrave Hoppner.

Ravenna,
May 20th 1820.

My dear Hoppner,—

Let Merryweather be kept in for *one week,* and then let him out for a Scoundrel. Tell him that such is the lesson for the ungrateful, and let this be a warning; a little common feeling, and common honesty would have saved him from useless expence and utter ruin.

Never would I pursue a man to Jail for a mere *debt,* and never will I forgive one for ingratitude such as this Villain's. But let him go and be damned (*once in though first*); but I could much wish *you* to see him and inoculate him with a moral sense by shewing him the result of his rascality.

As to Mother Mocenigo, we'll battle with her, and her ragamuffin. Castelli must dungeon Merryweather, if it be but for a day, I don't want to hurt, only to teach him.

I write to you in such haste and such heat; it seems to be under the dog (or bitch) Star that I can no more, but sottoscribble myself,

Yours ever, B.

P.S.—My best respects to the Consolessa and Compts. to Mr. Dorville.

Hobhouse is angry with me for a ballad and epigram I made upon him; only think —how odd!

1111.—To John Murray.

Ravenna,
May 20th, 1820.

Dear Murray,—

First and foremost, you must forward my letter to *Moore* dated *2d January,* which I said you might open, but desired you *to forward.* Now, you should really not forget these little things, because they do mischief among friends. You are an excellent man, a great man, and live among great men, but do pray recollect your absent friends and authors.

I return you the packets. The prose (the *Edin. Mag.* answer) looks better than I thought it would, and *you may publish it*: there will be a row, but I'll fight it out one way or another. You are wrong: I never had those "*two* ladies," upon my honour! Never believe but *half* of such stories. Southey was a damned scoundrel to spread such a lie of a woman, whose mother he did his best to get and could not.

So you and Hobhouse have squabbled about my ballad: you should not have circulated it; but I am glad you are by the ears, you both deserve it—he for having been in Newgate, and *you* for not being there.

Excuse haste: if you knew what I have on hand, you would.

In the first place, *your packets*; then a letter from Kinnaird, on the most urgent business: another from Moore, about a communication to Lady B[yron] of importance; a fourth from the mother of Allegra; and, fifthly, at Ravenna, the Contessa G. is on the eve of being divorced on account of our having been taken together *quasi* in the fact, and, what is worse, that she did not *deny* it: but the Italian public are on our side, particularly the women,—and the men also, because they say that *he* had no business to take the business up now after a year of toleration. The law is against him, because he slept with his wife after her admission. All her relations (who are numerous, high in rank, and powerful) are furious *against him* for his conduct, and his not wishing to be cuckolded at *threescore,* when every one else is at one. I am warned to be on my guard, as he is very capable of employing *Sicarii*—this is Latin as well as Italian, so you can understand it; but I have arms, and don't mind them, thinking that I can pepper his ragamuffins if they don't come unawares, and that, if they do, one may as well end that way as another; and it would besides serve *you* as an advertisement:—

> "Man may escape from rope or Gun, etc.
> But he who takes Woman, Woman, Woman," etc.

Yours, B.

P.S.—I have looked over the press, but Heaven knows how: think what I have on hand and the post going out tomorrow. Do you remember the epitaph on Voltaire?

> "Cy gît l'enfant gâté," etc.

> "Here lies the spoilt child
> Of the World which he spoil'd."

The original is in Grimm and Diderot, etc., etc., etc.

1112.—To Thomas Moore.

Ravenna,
May 24, 1820.

I wrote to you a few days ago. There is also a letter of January last for you at Murray's, which will explain to you why I am here. Murray ought to have forwarded it long ago. I enclose you an epistle from a countrywoman of yours at Paris, which has moved my entrails. You will have the goodness, perhaps, to enquire into the truth of her story, and I will help her as far as I can,—though not in the useless way she proposes. Her letter is evidently unstudied, and so natural, that the orthography is also in a state of nature.

Here is a poor creature, ill and solitary, who thinks, as a last resource, of translating you or me into French! Was there ever such a notion? It seems to me the consummation of despair. Pray enquire, and let me know, and, if you could draw a bill on me *here* for a few hundred francs, at your banker's, I will duly honour it,—that is, if she is not an impostor. If not, let me know, that I may get something remitted by my banker Longhi, of Bologna, for I have no correspondence myself at Paris: but tell her she must not translate;—if she does, it will be the height of ingratitude.

I had a letter (not of the same kind, but in French and flattery) from a Madame Sophie Gail, of Paris, whom I take to be the spouse of a Gallo-Greek of that name. Who is she? and what is she? and how came she to take an interest in my *poeshie* or its author? If you know her, tell her, with my compliments, that, as I only *read* French, I have not answered her letter; but would have done so in Italian, if I had not thought it would look like an affectation. I have just been scolding my monkey for tearing the seal of her letter, and spoiling a mock book, in which I put rose leaves. I had a civet-cat the other day, too; but it ran away, after scratching my monkey's cheek, and I am in search of it still. It was the fiercest beast I ever saw, and like * * in the face and manner.

I have a world of things to say; but, as they are not come to a *dénouement,* I don't care to begin their history till it is wound up. After you went, I had a fever, but got well again without bark. Sir Humphry Davy was here the other day, and liked Ravenna very much. He will tell you any thing you may wish to know about the place and your humble servitor.

Your apprehensions (arising from Scott's) were unfounded. There are *no damages* in this country, but there will probably be a separation between them, as her family, which is a principal one, by its connections, are very much against *him,* for the whole of his conduct;—and he is old and obstinate, and she is young and a woman, determined to sacrifice every thing to her affections. I have given her the best advice, viz. to stay with him,—pointing out the state of a separated woman, (for the priests won't let lovers live openly together, unless the husband sanctions it,) and making the most exquisite moral reflections—but to no purpose. She says, "I will stay with him, if he will let you remain with me. It is hard that I should be the only woman in Romagna who is not to have her *Amico*; but, if not, I will not live with him; and as for the consequences, love, etc., etc., etc."—you know how females reason on such occasions.

He says he has let it go on till he can do so no longer. But he wants her to stay, and dismiss me; for he doesn't like to pay back her dowry and to make an alimony. Her relations are rather for the separation, as they detest him,—indeed, so does every body. The populace and the women are, as usual, all for those who are in the wrong, viz. the lady and her lover. I should have retreated, but honour, and an erysipelas which has attacked her, prevent me,—to say nothing of love, for I love her most entirely, though not enough to persuade her to sacrifice every thing to a frenzy. "I see how it will end; she will be the sixteenth Mrs. Shuffleton."

My paper is finished, and so must this letter.

Yours ever, B.

P.S.—I regret that you have not completed the Italian Fudges. Pray, how come you to be still in Paris? Murray has four or five things of mine in hand—the new *Don Juan,* which his back-shop synod don't admire;—a translation of the first canto of Pulci's *Morgante Maggiore,* excellent;—a short ditto from Dante, not so much approved: the *Prophecy of Dante,* very grand and worthy, etc., etc., etc.:—a furious prose answer to Blackwood's "Observations on *Don Juan,*" with a savage Defence of Pope—likely to make a row. The opinions above I quote from Murray and his Utican senate;—you will form your own, when you see the things.

You will have no great chance of seeing me, for I begin to think I must finish in Italy. But, if you come my way, you shall have a tureen of macaroni. Pray tell me about yourself, and your intents.

My trustees are going to lend Earl Blessington sixty thousand pounds (at six per cent.) on a Dublin mortgage. Only think of my becoming an Irish absentee!

1113.—To Richard Belgrave Hoppner.

Ravenna,
May 25, 1820.

A German named Ruppsecht has sent me, heaven knows why, several Deutsche Gazettes, of all which I understand neither word nor letter. I have sent you the enclosed to beg you to translate to me some remarks, which appear to be *Goethe's upon Manfred,*—and if I may judge by *two* notes of *admiration* (generally put after something ridiculous by us) and the word "*hypocondrisch,*" are any thing but favourable. I shall regret this, for I should have been proud of Goethe's good word; but I shan't alter my opinion of him, even though he should be savage.

Will you excuse this trouble, and do me this favour?—Never mind—soften nothing —I am literary proof—having had good and evil said in most modern languages.

Believe me, etc.

1114.—To Thomas Moore.

Ravenna,
June 1, 1820.

I have received a Parisian letter from W[edderburn] W[ebster], which I prefer answering through you, if that worthy be still at Paris, and, as he says, an occasional visitor of yours. In November last he wrote to me a well-meaning letter, stating, for some reasons of his own, his belief that a re-union might be effected between Lady B. and myself. To this I answered as usual; and he sent me a second letter, repeating his notions, which letter I have never answered, having had a thousand other things to think of. He now writes as if he believed that he had offended me by touching on the topic; and I wish you to assure him that I am not at all so,—but, on the contrary, obliged by his good nature. At the same time acquaint him *the thing is impossible. You know this,* as well as I,—and there let it end.

I believe that I showed you his epistle in autumn last. He asks me if I have heard of *my* "laureat" at Paris,—somebody who has written "a most sanguinary *Epitre*" against me; but whether in French, or Dutch, or on what score, I know not, and he don't say,—except that (for my satisfaction) he says it is the best thing in the fellow's volume. If there is anything of the kind that I *ought* to know, you will doubtless tell me. I suppose it to be something of the usual sort;—he says, he don't remember the author's name.

I wrote to you some ten days ago, and expect an answer at your leisure. The separation business still continues, and all the world are implicated, including priests and cardinals. The public opinion is furious against *him,* because he ought to have cut the matter short *at first,* and not waited twelve months to begin. He has been trying at evidence, but can get none *sufficient*; for what would make fifty divorces in England won't do here—there must be the *most decided* proofs. * * *

It is the first cause of the kind attempted in Ravenna for these two hundred years; for, though they often separate, they assign a different motive. You know that the continental incontinent are more delicate than the English, and don't like proclaiming their coronation in a court, even when nobody doubts it.

All her relations are furious against him. The father has challenged him—a superfluous valour, for he don't fight, though suspected of two assassinations—one of the famous Monzoni of Forli. Warning was given me not to take such long rides in the Pine Forest without being on my guard; so I take my stiletto and a pair of pistols in my pocket during my daily rides.

I won't stir from this place till the matter is settled one way or the other. She is as femininely firm as possible; and the opinion is so much against him, that the *advocates* decline to undertake his cause, because they say that he is either a fool or a rogue—fool, if he did not discover the liaison till now; and rogue, if he did know it, and waited for some bad end to divulge it. In short, there has been nothing like it since the days of Guido di Polenta's family, in these parts.

If the man has me taken off, like Polonius "say, he made a good end,"—for a melodrame. The principal security is, that he has not the courage to spend twenty scudi—the average price of a clean-handed bravo—otherwise there is no want of opportunity, for I ride about the woods every evening, with one servant, and sometimes an acquaintance, who latterly looks a little queer in solitary bits of bushes.

Good bye.—Write to yours ever, etc.

1115.—To John Murray.

Ravenna,
June 7, 1820.

Dear Murray,—

Enclosed is something which will interest you, (to wit), the opinion of *the* Greatest man of Germany—perhaps of Europe—upon one of the great men of your advertisements, (all "famous hands," as Jacob Tonson used to say of his ragamuffins,)—in short, a critique of *Goethe's* upon *Manfred.* There is the original, Mr. Hoppner's translation, and an Italian one; keep them all in your archives,—for the opinions of such a man as Goethe, whether favourable or not, are always interesting, and this is moreover favourable. His *Faust* I never read, for I don't know German; but Matthew Monk Lewis, in 1816, at Coligny, translated most of it to me *vivâ voce,* and I was naturally much struck with it; but it was the *Staubach* and the *Jungfrau,* and something else, much more than Faustus, that made me write *Manfred.* The first Scene, however, and that of Faustus are very similar. Acknowledge this letter.

Yours ever, B.

P.S.—I have received *Ivanhoe;—good.* Pray send me some tooth powder and *tincture* of Myrrh, by *Waite,* etc. *Ricciardetto* should have been *translated literally, or not at all.* As to puffing *Whistlecraft, it won't do*: I'll tell you why some day or other. Cornwall's a poet, but spoilt by the detestable Schools of the day. Mrs. Hemans is a poet also, but too stiltified and apostrophic, and quite wrong: men died calmly before the Christian æra, and since, without Christianity—witness the Romans, and, lately, Thistlewood, Sandt, and Louvel —men who ought to have been weighed down with their crimes, even had they believed. A deathbed is a matter of nerves and constitution, and not of religion. Voltaire was frightened, Frederick of Prussia not: Christians the same, according to their strength rather than their creed. What does Helga Herbert mean by his *Stanza*? which is octave got drunk or gone mad. He ought to have his ears boxed with Thor's hammer for rhyming so fantastically.

1116.—To John Murray.

Ravenna,
June 8th 1820.

Dear Murray,—

It is intimated to me that there is some demur and backwardness on your part to make propositions with regard to the MSS. transmitted to you at your own request. How or why this should occur, when you were in no respect limited to any terms, I know not, and do not care—contenting myself with *repeating* that the two cantos of *Juan* were to reckon as *one* only, and that, even in that case *you are tut to consider* yourself as bound by your former proposition, particularly as your people may have a bad opinion of the production, the whilk I am by no means prepared to dispute.

With regard to the other MSS. (the prose will *not* be published in any case), I named nothing and left the matter to you and to my friends. If you are the least shy (I do not say you are wrong), you can put the whole of the MSS. in Mr. Hobhouse's hands; and there the matter ends. Your declining to publish will not be any offence to me.

Yours in haste, B.

1117.—To Thomas Moore.

Ravenna,
June 9, 1820.

Galignani has just sent me the Paris edition of your works (which I wrote to order), and I am glad to see my old friends with a French face. I have been skimming and dipping, in and over them, like a swallow, and as pleased as one. It is the first time that I had seen the Melodies without music; and, I don't know how, but I can't read in a music-book—the crotchets confound the words in my head, though I recollect them perfectly when *sung.* Music assists my memory through the ear, not through the eye; I mean, that her quavers perplex me upon paper, but they are a help when heard. And thus I was glad to see the words without their borrowed robes;—to my mind they look none the worse for their nudity.

The biographer has made a botch of your life—calling your father "a *venerable old* gentleman," and prattling of "Addison," and "dowager countesses." If that damned fellow was to *write my* life, I would certainly *take his.* And then, at the Dublin dinner, you have "made a speech" (do you recollect, at Douglas K.'s., "Sir, he made me a speech?") too complimentary to the "living poets," and somewhat redolent of universal praise. I am but too well off in it, but * * *

You have not sent me any poetical or personal news of yourself. Why don't you complete an Italian *Tour of the Fudges*? I have just been turning over *Little,* which I knew by heart in 1803, being then in my fifteenth summer. Heigho! I believe all the mischief I have ever done, or sung, has been owing to that confounded book of yours. In my last I told you of a cargo of "Poeshie," which I had sent to M. at his own impatient desire;—and, now he has got it, he don't like it, and demurs. Perhaps he is right. I have no great opinion of any of my last shipment, except a translation from Pulci, which is word for word, and verse for verse. I am in the third act of a Tragedy; but whether it will be finished or not, I know not: I have, at this present, too many passions of my own on hand to do justice to those of the dead. Besides the vexations mentioned in my last, I have incurred a quarrel with the Pope's carabiniers, or *gens d'armerie,* who have petitioned the Cardinal against my liveries, as resembling too nearly their own lousy uniform. They particularly object to the epaulettes, which all the world with us have on upon gala days. My liveries are of the colours conforming to my arms, and have been the family hue since the year 1066.

I have sent a trenchant reply, as you may suppose; and have given to understand that, if any soldados of that respectable corps insult my servants, I will do likewise by their gallant commanders; and I have directed my ragamuffins, six in number, who are tolerably savage, to defend themselves, in case of aggression; and, on holidays and gaudy days, I shall arm the whole set, including myself, in case of accidents or treachery. I used to play pretty well at the broad-sword, once upon a time, at Angelo's; but I should like the pistol, our national buccaneer weapon, better, though I am out of practice at present. However, I can "wink and hold out mine iron." It makes me think (the whole thing does) of Romeo and Juliet—"now, Gregory, remember thy *swashing* blow."

All these feuds, however, with the Cavalier for his wife, and the troopers for my liveries, are very tiresome to a quiet man, who does his best to please all the world, and longs for fellowship and good will. Pray write.

I am yours, etc.

1118.—To Richard Belgrave Hoppner.

Ravenna,
June 12th 1820.

My dear Hoppner,—

The accident is very disagreeable, but I do not see why *you* are to make up the loss, until it is quite clear that the money is lost; nor even then, because I am not at all disposed to have you suffer for an act of trouble for another. If the money has been *paid,* and not accounted for (by Dorville's illness), it rests with me to supply the deficit, and, even if not, I am not at all clear on the justice of your making up the money of another, because it has been stolen from your bureau. You will of course examine into the matter thoroughly, because otherwise you live in a state of perpetual suspicion. Are you *sure* that the *whole sum came from the Bankers*? was it *counted* since it passed to you by Mr. Dorville or by yourself? or was it kept unmixed with any cash of your own expences?—in Venice and with Venetian servants any thing is possible and probable that savours of villainy.

You may give up the *house* immediately and licentiate the Servitors, and pray, if it likes you not, sell *the Gondola,* and keep that produce and in the other balance in your hands till you can clear up this matter.

Mother Mocenigo will probably try a bill for breakables, to which I reckoned that the new *Canal posts* and *pillars,* and *the new door* at the other end, together with the year's rent, and the house given up without further occupation, are an ample compensation for any cracking of crockery of her's in *aflitto.* Is it not so? how say you? the Canal posts and doors cost many hundred francs, and she may be content, or she may be damned; it is no great matter which. Should I ever go to Venice again, I will betake me to the Hostel or Inn.

I was greatly obliged by your translation from the German; but it is no time to plague you with such nonsense now, when in the full exasperation of this vexatious deficit.

Make my best respects to Mrs. Hoppner, who doubtless wishes me at the devil for all this trouble, and pray write.

And believe me, yours ever and truly, BYRON.

P.S.—Allegra is well and obstinate, much grown and a favourite. My love to your little boy.

1119.—To Charles Hanson.

Ravenna,
June 15th 1820.

MY DEAR CHARLES,—

After a mature consideration I decided to agree to the mortgage, and sent my consent addressed jointly to Mr. Kinnaird with your father, a few days ago.

The contents of the January packet have not been returned, because I presume that *both* the witnesses must be Britons, and the only one here besides myself is my servant Fletcher. Upon this point let me be avised.

It would have given me pleasure that the Rochdale suit could have been terminated amicably, and without further law, but by arbitration; but since it must go before a Court, I resign myself to the decision, and wish to hear the result.

I shall not return to England for the present, but I wish you to send me (obtain it) my summons as a Peer to the Coronation (from curiosity), and let me know if we have any claims in our family (as connected with Sherwood Forest) to carry any part of the mummery, that they may not lapse, but, by being presented, be preserved to my Successors.

It will give me great pleasure to hear further from you on these points; and I beg you to believe me, with my best regards to your father and family,

Yours ever and truly, BYRON.

1120.—To John Cam Hobhouse.

Ravenna,
June 22nd, 1820.

The papers announce the Queen's arrival and its consequences. They have sent a message to our House. What the opinion in England may be, I know not, but *here* (and we are in her late neighbourhood) there are no doubts about her and her blackguard Bergami. I have just asked Madame la Comtesse G., who was at Pesaro two years ago, and she announces that the thing was as public as such a thing can be. It is to me subject of regret, for in England she was ever hospitable and kind to me.

I have never seen her since. If you see the Davys, give my regards, and tell Lady Davy that I shall answer her letter the moment I am aware of her arrival in England.

Yours ever and truly, B.

1121.—To John Murray.

Ravenna,
July 6th 1820.

Dear Murray,—

My former letters will prove that I found no fault with your opinions nor with you for acting upon them—but I do protest against your keeping me *four months* in suspense—without any answer at all. As it is you will keep back the remaining trash till I have woven the tragedy of which I am in the 4th act. With regard to terms I have already said that I named and *name* none. They are points which I leave between you and my friends, as I cannot judge upon the subject; neither to you nor to them have I named any sum, nor have I thought of any, nor does it matter—But if you don't answer my letters I shall resort to the *Row*—where I shall not find probably good manners or liberality—but at least I shall have *an answer of some kind.* You must not treat a blood horse as you do your hacks, otherwise he'll bolt out of the course. Keep back the stuff till I can send you the remainder—but recollect that I don't promise that the tragedy will be a whit better than the rest. All I shall require then will be a *positive* answer but a *speedy* one—and not an awkward delay. Now you have spoken out are you any the worse for it? and could not you have done so five months ago? Do you think I lay a stress on the merits of my "poeshie." I assure you I have many other things to think of. At present I am eager to know the result of the Colliery question between the Rochdale people and myself. The cause has been heard—but as yet Judgement is not passed—at least if it is I have not heard of it. Here is one thing of importance to my private affairs.

The next is that I have been the cause of a great conjugal scrape here—which is now before the *Pope* (seriously I assure you) and what the decision of his Sanctity will be no one can predicate. It would be odd that having left England for one Woman ("Vittoria Carambana the White Devil" to wit) I should have to quit Italy for another. The husband is the greatest man in these parts with *100000* Scudi a year—but he is a great Brunello in politics and private life—and is shrewdly suspected of more than one murder. The relatives are on my side because they dislike him. We wait the event.

Yours truly,

B.

1122.—To John Cam Hobhouse.

Ravenna,
July 6th, 1820.

My dear Hobhouse,—

I am [in] the 4th act of Marino Faliero; you may keep back the rest of the trash till I have shaped the new Sooterkin. I regret nothing but the *fee*; but even the fee in such cases should be a secondary consideration. "The Adversary" (Vittoria Corombona—the White Devil, that is); *there,* I grant you, I am vulnerable, and when a person has made you pass through the pretty reports that this one strewed my path with, you will sympathize with my insanity upon that topic; why don't you also take such another wife?

How is my *Shild*? You never name her.

I have got a motto for my Doge conspirator, Eccolo—"*Dux* inquieti turbidus Adrise,"—ain't it a good one?

I see by the papers you prosper in Parliament,—go on. As to autumn and Switzerland, that is as hereafter it may be,—"*who knows?*" The *mortgage,* eh? and the suit with the counsellors at law? tell me. I am in a scrape on all sides, at home and abroad.

Yours very truly,

B.

P.S.—When the Pope has decided on Madame Guiccioli's business (it is actually before him), I will tell you whether I can come to England (via Switzerland) or not; the relations *for* her, and the husband against her, are stirring up the whole conclave. You may suppose, as pugilistic Jackson says, that I have " a pretty time of it." I can't settle anything till I know the result, which will probably be a separation; he is trying to prove the adultery—which in Italy is no easy matter to prove to a tribunal. There has not been such a row in Romagna these hundred years on private matters, and we expect on one side or the other a fair *stillettata.* It is the fashion: they killed a carabineer the other day, and wounded another—that is, some country gentlemen did, because they had been shut out of the theatre.

1123.—To Thomas Moore.

Ravenna,
July 13, 1820.

To remove or increase your Irish anxiety about my being "in a wisp," I answer your letter forthwith; premising that, as I am a "*Will* of the wisp," I may chance to flit out of it. But, first, a word on the Memoir;—I have no objection, nay, I would rather that *one* correct copy was taken and deposited in honourable hands, in case of accidents happening to the original; for you know that I have none, and have never even *re*-read, nor, indeed, *read* at all what is there written; I only know that I wrote it with the fullest intention to be "faithful and true" in my narrative, but *not* impartial—no, by the Lord! I can't pretend to be that, while I feel. But I wish to give every body concerned the opportunity to contradict or correct me.

I have no objection to any proper person seeing what is there written,—seeing it was written, like every thing else, for the purpose of being read, however much many writings may fail in arriving at that object.

With regard to "the wisp," the Pope has pronounced *their separation.* The decree came yesterday from Babylon,—it was *she* and *her friends* who demanded it, on the grounds of her husband's (the noble Count Cavalier's) extraordinary usage. *He* opposed it with all his might because of the alimony, which has been assigned, with all her goods, chattels, carriage, etc., to be restored by him. In Italy they can't divorce. He insisted on her giving me up, and he would forgive every thing,—even the adultery, which he swears that he can prove by "famous witnesses." But, in this country, the very courts hold such proofs in abhorrence, the Italians being as much more delicate in public than the English, as they are more passionate in private.

The friends and relatives, who are numerous and powerful, reply to him—"*You,* yourself, are either fool or knave,—fool, if you did not see the consequences of the approximation of these two young persons,—knave, if you connive at it. Take your choice,—but don't break out (after twelve months of the closest intimacy, under your own eyes and positive sanction) with a scandal, which can only make you ridiculous and her unhappy."

He swore that he thought our intercourse was purely amicable, and that *I* was more partial to him than to her, till melancholy testimony proved the contrary. To this they answer, that "Will of *this* wisp" was not an unknown person, and that "*clamosa Fama*" had not proclaimed the purity of my morals;—that *her* brother, a year ago, wrote from Rome to warn him that his wife would infallibly be led astray by this *ignis fatuus,* unless he took proper measures, all of which he neglected to take, etc., etc.

Now he says that he encouraged my return to Ravenna, to see "*in quanti piedi di acqua siamo,*" and he has found enough to drown him in. In short,

> "Ce ne fut pas le tout; sa femme se plaignit—
> Procès—La parenté se joint en excuse et dit
> Que du *Docteur* venoit tout le mauvais ménage;
> Que cet homme étoit fou, que sa femme étoit sage.
> On fit casser le mariage."

It is best to let the women alone, in the way of conflict, for they are sure to win against the field. She returns to her father's house, and I can only see her under great restrictions—such is the custom of the country. The relations behave very well:—I offered any settlement, but they refused to accept it, and swear she *shan't* live with G. (as he has tried to prove her faithless), but that he shall maintain her; and, in fact, a judgment to this effect came yesterday. I am, of course, in an awkward situation enough.

I have heard no more of the carabiniers who protested against my liveries. They are not popular, those same soldiers, and, in a small row, the other night, one was slain, another wounded, and divers put to flight, by some of the Romagnuole youth, who are dexterous, and somewhat liberal of the knife. The perpetrators are not discovered, but I hope and believe that none of my ragamuffins were in it, though they are somewhat savage, and secretly armed, like most of the inhabitants. It is their way, and saves sometimes a good deal of litigation.

There is a revolution at Naples. If so, it will probably leave a card at Ravenna in its way to Lombardy.

Your publishers seem to have used you like mine. M. has shuffled, and almost insinuated that my last productions are *dull.* Dull, sir!—damme, dull! I believe he is right. He begs for the completion of my tragedy of *Marino Faliero,* none of which is yet gone to England. The fifth act is nearly completed, but it is dreadfully long—40 sheets of long paper of 4 pages each—about 150 when printed; but "so full of pastime and prodigality" that I think it will do.

Pray send and publish your *Pome* upon me; and don't be afraid of praising me too highly. I shall pocket my blushes.

"Not actionable!"—*Chantre d'enfer!*—by * * that's "a speech," and I won't put up with it. A pretty title to give a man for doubting if there be any such place!

So my Gail is gone—and Miss Mah*on*y won't take *mo*ney. I am very glad of it—I like to be generous, free of expense. But beg her not to translate me.

Oh, pray tell Galignani that I shall send him a screed of doctrine if he don't be more punctual. Somebody *regularly detains two,* and sometimes *four,* of his Messengers by the way. Do, pray, entreat him to be more precise. News are worth money in this remote kingdom of the Ostrogoths.

Pray, reply. I should like much to share some of your Champagne and La Fitte, but I am too Italian for Paris in general. Make Murray send my letter to you—it is full of *epigrams.*

Yours, etc.

1124.—To John Murray.

Ravenna,
July 17, 1820.

DEAR MURRAY,—

Moore writes that he has not yet received my letter of January 2^{d} consigned to your care for him. I believe this is the sixth time I have begged of you to forward it, and I shall be obliged by your so doing.

I have received some books, and quarterlies, and *Edinburghs,* for all which I am grateful: they contain all I know of England, except by Galignani's newspaper.

The tragedy is completed, but now comes the task of copy and correction. It is very long, (42 *Sheets* of long paper, of 4 pages each), and I believe must make more than 140 or 150 pages, besides many historical extracts as notes, which I mean to append. History is closely followed. Dr. Moore's account is in some respects false, and in all foolish and flippant. *None* of the Chronicles (and I have consulted Sanuto, Sandi, Navagero, and an anonymous Siege of Zara, besides the histories of Laugier, Daru, Sismondi, etc.) state, or even hint, that he begged his life; they merely say that he did not deny the conspiracy. He was one of their great men,—commanded at the siege of Zara, beat 80,000 Hungarians, killing 8000, and at the same time kept the town he was besieging in order. Took Capo d'Istria; was ambassador at Genoa, Rome, and finally Doge, where he fell for treason, in attempting to alter the Government, by what Sanuto calls a Judgement on him, for, many years before (when Podesta and Captain of Treviso), having knocked down a bishop, who was sluggish in carrying the host at a procession. He "saddles him," as Thwackum did Square, "with a Judgement;" but does not mention whether he had been punished at the time for what would appear very strange even now, and must have been still more so in an age of Papal power and glory. Sanuto says, that Heaven took away his senses for this buffet in his old age, and induced him to conspire.—*Però fù permesso che il Faliero perdette l'intelletto,* etc.

I don't know what your parlour boarders will think of the drama I have founded upon this extraordinary event: the only similar one in history is the story of Agis,

King of Sparta, a prince *with* the Commons against the aristocracy, and losing his life therefor; but it shall be sent when copied.

I should be glad to know why your Quarter*ing* Reviewers, at the close of *the Fall of Jerusalem,* accuse me of Manicheism? a compliment to which the sweetener of "one of the mightiest Spirits" by no means reconciles me. The poem they review is very noble; but could they not do justice to the writer without converting him into my religious Antidote? I am not a Manichean, nor an *Any*-chean. I should like to know what harm my "poeshies" have done: I can't tell what your people mean by making me a hobgoblin.

This is the second thing of the same sort: they could not even give a lift to that poor Creature, Gally Knight, without a similar insinuation about "moody passions." Now, are not the *passions* the food and fuel of poesy? I greatly admire Milman; but they had better not bring me down upon Gally, for whom I have no such admiration. I suppose he buys two thousand pounds' worth of books in a year, which makes you so tender of him. But he won't do, my Murray: he's middling, and writes like a Country Gentleman—for the County Newspaper.

I shall be glad to hear from you, and you'll write now, because you will want to keep me in a good humour till you can see what the tragedy is fit for. I know your ways, my Admiral.

Yours ever truly, B.

1125.—To Richard Belgrave Hoppner.

Ravenna,
July 20th 1820.

My dear Hoppner,—

On Vincenzo's return I will send you some books, though the latter arrivals have not been very interesting you shall have the best of them.

You do not mention that *Vincenso* delivered to you a paper with *sixty francs*; he had it; did you get it? they were for the tickets.

Lega tells me that the Mocenigo *Inventory* was delivered last week; is it so? I made him send to Venice on purpose.

With regard to Mrs. Mocenigo, I am ready to deliver up the palace directly; with respect to *breakables* she can have no claim till *June next,* the rent being stipulated as prior payment (and paid), but not the articles missing till the whole period was expired. I have replenished three times over, and made good by the equivalent of the doors, and Canal posts (to say nothing of the exorbitant rent), any little damage done to her pottery. If any articles are taken by mistake, they shall be restored or replaced; but I will submit to no exorbitant charge, nor imposition. You had best state this by Seranzo, who *seduced* me into having anything to do with her, and who has probably still something of the gentleman about him. What she may do, I neither know nor care: if they like law, they shall have it for years to come, and if they gain, what then? They will find it difficult to "shear the Wolf" no longer in Lombardy. They are a *damned infamous set,* and, to prevent any unpleasantness to you with that nest of whores and scoundrels, *state my words as my words;* who can blame *you* when you merely take the trouble to repeat what I say, and to restore what I am disposed to give up,—that is her house,—a year before it is due, thereby losing a year's rent?

I can hardly spare Lega at this moment, or I would willingly send him. At any rate you can give up the house, and let us battle for her crockery afterwards.

I regret to hear what you say of yourself, if you want any cash, pray use any balance in your hands (of course) without ceremony. I am glad the Gondola was sold at any price as I only wanted to get rid of it.

I am not very well, having had a twinge of fever again; the heat is *85* in the Shade.

I suppose you know that there is a Revolution at Naples.

Yours ever and truly, in haste, BYRON.

P.S.—I have finished a tragedy in five acts, *Marino Faliero*; but now comes the bore of copying, and in this weather too.

Comp[ts] to Madame Hoppner.

1126.—To John Murray.

Ravenna,
July 22nd 1820.

DEAR MURRAY,—

The tragedy is finished, but when it will be copied is more than can be reckoned upon. We are here upon the eve of evolutions and revolutions. Naples is revolutionized, and the ferment is among the Romagnuoles, by far the bravest and most original of the present Italians, though still half savage. Buonaparte said the troops from Romagna were the best of his Italic corps, and I believe it. The Neapolitans are not worth a curse, and will be beaten if it comes to fighting: the rest of Italy, I think, might stand. The Cardinal is at his wits' end; it is true that he had not far to go. Some papal towns on the Neapolitan frontier have already revolted. Here there are as yet but the sparks of the volcano; but the ground is hot, and the air sultry. Three assassinations last week here and at Faenza—an anti-liberal priest, a factor, and a trooper last night,—I heard the pistol-shot that brought him down within a short distance of my own door. There had been quarrels between the troops and people of some duration: this is the third soldier wounded within the last month. There is a great commotion in people's minds, which will lead to nobody knows what—a row probably. There are secret Societies all over the country as in Germany, who cut off those obnoxious to them, like the Free tribunals, be they high or low; and then it becomes impossible to discover or punish the assassins—their measures are taken so well.

You ask me about the books. *Jerusalem* is the best; *Anastasius* good, but no more written by a Greek than by a Hebrew; the *Diary of an Invalid* good and true, bating a few mistakes about *Serventismo,* which no foreigner can understand or really know without residing years in the country. I read that part (translated that is) to some of the ladies in the way of knowing how far it was accurate, and they laughed, particularly at the part where he says that "they must not have children by their lover." "Assuredly" (was the answer), "we don't pretend to say that it is right; but *men* cannot conceive the repugnance that a *woman* has to have children *except by the man she loves.*" They have been known even to obtain abortions when it was by the *other,* but that is rare. I know one instance, however, of a woman making herself miscarry, because she wanted to meet her lover (they were in two different cities) in the lying-in month (hers was or should have been in October). She was a very pretty woman—young and clever—and brought on by it a malady which she has not recovered to this day: however, she met her *Amico* by it at the proper time. It is but fair to say that he had dissuaded her from this piece of amatory atrocity, and was very angry when he knew that she had committed it; but the "it was for your sake, to meet you at the time, which could not have been otherwise accomplished," applied to his Self love, disarmed him; and they set about supplying the loss.

I have had a little touch of fever again; but it has receded. The heat is 85 in the shade. I remember what you say of the Queen: it happened in Lady Ox—'s boudoir or dressing room, if I recollect rightly; but it was not her Majesty's fault, though very laughable at the time: a minute sooner, she might have stumbled on something still more awkward. How the *Porcelain* came there I cannot conceive, and remember asking Lady O. afterwards, who laid the blame on the Servants. I think the Queen will win—I wish she may: she was always very civil to me. You must not trust Italian witnesses: nobody believes them in their own courts; why should you? For 50 or 100 Sequins you may have any testimony you please, and the Judge into the bargain.

Yours ever, B.

Pray forward my letter of January to Mr. Moore.

1127.—To John Murray.

Ravenna,
July 24th, 1820.

Dear Murray,—

Enclosed is the account from Marin Sanuto of Faliero, etc. You must have it translated (to append original and translation to the drama when published): it is very curious and simple in itself, and authentic; I have compared it with the other histories. That blackguard Dr. Moore has published a false and flippant story of the transaction.

Yours, B.

P.S. The first act goes by this post. Recollect that, without previously reading the *Chronicle,* it is difficult to understand the tragedy. So, translate. I had this reprinted separately on purpose.

1128.—To John Hanson.

Ravenna,
July 27th 1820.

Dear Sir,—

I have received from Mr. Kinnaird the intelligence of the Rochdale decision. It has not surprized me, and there is no more to be said. Even if a further question could arise, I am not disposed to carry it higher. What I desire to be done, and done quickly, is to bring the Manor, and my remaining rights immediately to auction, and sell it to the highest bidder without consideration of price: it will at least pay the law expences, and part of the remaining debts.

Pray let this be done without delay, and believe me

Yours very truly, Byron.

P.S.—I presume that you proceed in the transfer from the funds to the Irish Mortgage.

1129.—To Charles Hanson.

Ravenna,
August 2d 1820.

DEAR CHARLES,—

I have received your letter. That being the case, I hereby authorize you to enter an *Appeal* immediately. Inform me when and where the further proceedings will come on.

Yours truly and affectionately,

BYRON.

1130.—To John Murray.

Ravenna,
Agosto 7°, 1820.

DEAR MURRAY,—

I have sent you *three acts* of the tragedy, and am copying the others slowly but daily. Enclosed are some verses Rose sent me two years ago and more. They are excellent description.

Pray desire Douglas K. to give you a copy of my lines to the Po in 1819: they say "they be good rhymes," and will serve to swell your next volume. Whenever you publish, publish all as you will, except the two Juans, which had better be *annexed* to a *new* edition of the two first, as they are not worth separate publication, and I won't barter about them.

Pulci is my favourite, that is, my translation: I think it the *acme* of putting one language into another.

I have sent you my say upon your recent books. *Ricciarda* I have not yet read, having lent it to the natives, who will pronounce upon it. The Italians have as yet *no tragedy*—Alfieri's are political dialogues, except *Mirra.*

Bankes *has* done *miracles* of research and enterprize—salute him.

I am yours,

B.

Pray send me by the first opportunity some of *Waite's red* tooth-powder.

1131.—To John Murray.

Ravenna,
August 12th, 1820.

DEAR MURRAY,—

Ecco, the fourth Act.

Received *powder—tincture—books.* The first welcome, second ditto—the prose at least; but no *more modern* poesy, I pray; neither Mrs. Hewoman's, nor any female or male Tadpole of Poet Wordsworth's, nor any of his ragamuffins.

Send me more *tincture* by all means, and Scott's novels—the *Monastery.*

We are on the eve of a *row* here: Italy's primed and loaded, and many a finger itching for the trigger. So write letters while you can. I can say no more in mine, for they open all.

Yours very truly, B.

P.S.—Recollect that I told you months ago what would happen; it is the same all over the *boot,* though the *heel* has been the first to kick: never mind these enigmas —they'll explain themselves.

1132.—To John Murray.

Ravenna,
August 17th 1820.

Dear Moray,—

In t'other parcel is the 5th Act. Enclosed in this are some notes—historical. Pray send me *no proofs*; it is the thing I can least bear to see. The preface shall be written and sent in a few days. Acknowledge the arrival by return of post.

Yours.

P.S.—The time for the *Dante* would be good now (did not her Majesty occupy all nonsense), as Italy is on the eve of great things.

I hear Mr. Hoby says "that it makes him weep to see her—She reminds him so much of Jane Shore."

> Mr. Hoby the Bootmaker's soft heart is sore,
> For seeing the Queen makes him think of Jane Shore;
> And, in fact, such a likeness should always be seen—
> Why should *Queens not* be *whores*? Every *Whore* is a Quean.

This is only an epigram to the *ear.* I think she will win: I am sure she ought, poor woman.

Is it true that absent peers are to be mulcted? does this include those who have not taken the oaths in the present parliament? I can't come, and I won't pay.

1133.—To the Hon Augusta Leigh.

Ravenna, August 19th 1820.

My Dearest Augusta—

I always loved you better than any earthly existence, and I always shall unless I go mad. And if I did *not* so love you—still I would not persecute or oppress any one wittingly—especially for debts, of which I know the *agony by experience*. Of Colonel Leigh's bond, I really have forgotten all particulars, except that it was *not* of *my wishing*. And I never would nor ever will be pressed into the Gang of his creditors.—I would *not take the money* if he had it. You may judge if I would dun him having it not.— —

Whatever measure I can take for his extrication will be taken. Only tell me how—for I am ignorant, and far away. *Who does* and *who can* accuse you of "interested views"? I think people must have gone into Bedlam such things appear to me so very incomprehensible. Pray explain—

yors ever

& truly

Byron

1134.—To John Murray.

August 22nd 1820.

Dear Murray,—

None of your *damned proofs* now *recollect*; print, paste, plaster, and destroy—but don't let me have any of your cursed printers' trash to pore over. For the rest, I neither know nor care.

Yours,

B.

1135.—To John Murray.

Ravenna,
August 24th 1820.

Dear Murray,—

Enclosed is an additional *note* to the play sent you the other day. The preface is sent too, but as I wrote it in a hurry (the latter part particularly), it may want some alterations: if so, let me know, and what your parlour boarders think of the matter.

Remember, I can form no opinion of the merits of this production, and will abide by your Synod's. If you should publish, publish them all about the same time; it will be at least a collection of opposites.

You should not publish the new Cantos of *Juan* separately; but let them go in quietly with the first reprint of the others, so that they may make little noise, as they are not equal to the first. The Pulci, the Dante, and the Drama, you are to publish as you like, if at all. B.

1136.—To John Murray.

Ravenna,
August 29th 1820.

Dear Murray,—

I enclose to you for Mr. Hobhouse (with liberty to read and translate, or get translated if you can—it will be *nuts* for *Rose*) *copies* of the letter of Cavalier Commendatore G. to his wife's brother at Rome, and other documents explaining this business which has put us all in hot water here. Remember that Guiccioli is *telling his own story,* true in some things, and *very false* in the details. The Pope has decreed against him; so also have his wife's relations, which is much. No man has a right to pretend blindness, after letting a girl of twenty travel with another man, and afterwards taking that man into his house. *You* want to know *Italy*: there's more than Lady Morgan can tell me in these sheets, if carefully perused.

The enclosed are authentic: I have seen the originals.

Yours ever, B.

1137.—To John Murray.

Ravenna,
August 31st, 1820.

Dear Murray,—

I *have* "*put my Soul* into the tragedy" (as you *if* it); but you know that there are damned souls as well as tragedies. Recollect that it is not a political play, though it may look like it; it is strictly historical: read the history and judge.

Ada's picture is her mother's: I am glad of it—the mother made a good daughter. Send me Gifford's opinion, and never mind the Archbishop. I can neither send you away, nor give you a hundred pistoles, nor a better taste. I send you a tragedy, and you ask for "facetious epistles;" a little like your predecessor, who advised Dr. Prideaux to "put some more humour into his Life of Mahomet."

The drawings for *Juan* are superb: the brush has beat the poetry. In the annexed proof of *Marino Faliero,* the half line—"The law, my Prince" must be stopped thus —as the Doge interrupts Bertuccio Faliero.

Bankes is a wonderful fellow; there is hardly one of my School and College cotemporaries that has not turned out more or less celebrated. Peel, Palmerstone, Bankes, Hobhouse, Tavistock, Bob Mills, Douglas Kinnaird, etc., etc., have all of them talked and been talked of. Then there is your Galley Knight, and all that—; but I believe that (except Milman perhaps) I am still the youngest of the fifteen hundred first of living poets, as W^m *worth is the oldest. Galley Knight is some Seasons my Senior: pretty Galley! *so "amiable"*!! You Goose, you—such fellows should be flung into Fleet Ditch. I would rather be a Galley Slave than a Galley Knight—so utterly do I despise the middling mountebank's mediocrity in every thing but his Income.

We are here going to fight a little, next month, if the Huns don't cross the Po, and probably if they do: I can't say more now. If anything happens, you have matter for a posthumous work, and Moore has my memoirs in MSS.; so pray be civil. Depend upon it, there will be savage work, if once they begin here. The French courage proceeds from vanity, the German from phlegm, the Turkish from fanaticism and opium, the Spanish from pride, the English from coolness, the Dutch from obstinacy, the Russian from insensibility, but the *Italian* from *anger*; so you'll see that they will spare nothing.

What you say of Lady Caroline Lamb's "Juan" at the Masquerade don't surprise me: I only wonder that she went so far as "the *Theatre*" for "*the Devils,*" having them so much more natural at home; or if they were busy, she might have borrowed the *, her Mother's —Lady Besborough to wit—the * * of the last half Century.

Yours, B.

1138.—To John Hanson.

Ravenna,
August 31st 1820.

DEAR SIR,—

I pray you to make haste with the title deeds; otherwise there will be a half year's interest lost, and the funds are falling daily. See what you do by your confounded delays. Pray, expedite, dispatch.

You have never sent me Counsel's opinion on an appeal, as promised. I am in favour of the appeal, if it shows a glimpse of ultimate success. The deeds you sent me in the winter cannot be signed for lack of English witnesses.

With my best remembrances to all your family, believe me,

Yours very truly and affectionately, BYRON.

1139.—To Thomas Moore.

Ravenna,
August 31, 1820.

D—n your *mezzo cammin*—you should say "the prime of life," a much more consolatory phrase. Besides, it is not correct. I was born in 1788, and consequently am but thirty-two. You are mistaken on another point. The "Sequin Box" never came into requisition, nor is it likely to do so. It were better that it had, for then a man is not *bound,* you know. As to reform, I did reform—what would you have? "Rebellion lay in his way, and he found it." I verily believe that nor you, nor any man of poetical temperament, can avoid a strong passion of some kind. It is the poetry of life. What should I have known or written, had I been a quiet, mercantile politician, or a lord in waiting? A man must travel, and turmoil, or there is no existence. Besides, I only meant to be a Cavalier Servente, and had no idea it would turn out a romance, in the Anglo fashion.

However, I suspect I know a thing or two of Italy— more than Lady Morgan has picked up in her posting. What do Englishmen know of Italians beyond their museums and saloons—and some hack * *, *en passant*? Now, I have lived in the heart of their houses, in parts of Italy freshest and least influenced by strangers,—have seen and become (*pars magna fui*) a portion of their hopes, and fears, and passions, and am almost inoculated into a family. This is to see men and things as they are.

You say that I called you "quiet"—I don't recollect any thing of the sort. On the contrary, you are always in scrapes.

What think you of the Queen? I hear Mr. Hoby says, "that it makes him weep to see her, she reminds him so much of Jane Shore."

> Mr. Hoby the bootmaker's heart is quite sore,
> For seeing the Queen makes him think of Jane Shore;
> And, in fact, * *

Pray excuse this ribaldry. What is your poem about? Write and tell me all about it and you.

Yours, etc.

P.S.—Did you write the lively quiz on Peter Bell? It has wit enough to be yours, and almost too much to be any body else's now going. It was in Galignani the other day or week.

1140.—To John Murray.

Ravenna,
September 7, 1820.

DEAR MURRAY,—

In correcting the proofs you must refer to the *Manuscript,* because there are in it *various readings.* Pray attend to this, and choose what Gifford thinks best. Let me know what he thinks of the whole.

You speak of Lady Noel's illness: she is not of those who die:—the amiable only do; and those whose death would *do good* live. Whenever she is pleased to return, it may be presumed that she will take her "*divining rod*" along with her; it may be of use to her at home, as well as to the "*rich man*" of the Evangelists.

Pray do not let the papers paragraph me back to England: they may say what they please—any loathsome abuse—but that. Contradict it.

My last letters will have taught you to expect an explosion here: it was primed and loaded, but they hesitated to fire the train. One of the Cities shirked from the league. I cannot write more at large for a thousand reasons. Our "*puir hill folk*" offered to strike, and to raise the first banner. But Bologna paused—and now 'tis Autumn, and the season half over. "Oh Jerusasalem, Jerusalem!" the Huns are on the Po; but if once they pass it on their march to Naples, all Italy will rise behind them: the Dogs—the Wolves—may they perish like the Host of Sennacherib! If you want to publish the *Prophecy of Dante,* you never will have a better time.

Thanks for books—but as yet no *Monastery* of Walter Scott's, the ONLY book except *Edinburgh* and *Quarterly* which I desire to see. Why do you send me so much *trash* upon Italy—such tears, etc., which I know *must be false*? Matthews is good—very good: all the rest are like Sotheby's "*Good,*" or like Sotheby himself, that old rotten Medlar of Rhyme. The Queen—how is it? prospers She?

1141.—To John Murray.

Ravenna,
Septr 8th 1820.

Dear Murray,—

You will please to publish the enclosed *note without* altering a word, and to inform the author, that I will answer personally any offence to him. He is a cursed impudent liar,—you shall not alter or omit a syllable: publish the note at the end of the play, and answer this.

Yours, B.

P.S.—You sometimes take the liberty of *omitting* what I send for publication: if you do so in this instance, I will never speak to you again as long as I breathe.

1142.—To Richard Belgrave Hoppner.

Ravenna,
Septr 10th 1820.

My dear Hoppner,—

Ecco Advocate Fossati's letter. No paper has nor will be signed. Pray *draw* on me for the Napoleons, for I have no mode of remitting them otherwise; Missiaglia would empower some one here to receive them for you, as it is not a *piazza bancale.*

I regret that you have such a bad opinion of Shiloh; you used to have a good one. Surely he has talent and honour, but is crazy against religion and morality. His tragedy is sad work; but the subject renders it so. His *Islam* had much poetry. You seem lately to have got some notion against him.

Clare writes me the most insolent letters about Allegra; see what a man gets by taking care of natural children! Were it not for the poor little child's sake, I am almost tempted to send her back to her atheistical mother, but that would be too bad; you cannot conceive the excess of her insolence, and I know not why, for I have been at great care and expense,—taking a house in the country on purpose for her. She has *two* maids and every possible attention. If Clare thinks that she shall ever interfere with the child's morals or education, she mistakes; she never shall. The girl shall be a Christian and a married woman, if possible. As to seeing her, she may see her—under proper restrictions; but she is not to throw every thing into confusion with her Bedlam behaviour. To express it delicately, I think Madame Clare is a damned bitch. What think you?

Yours ever and truly, B^N

1143.—To John Murray.

Ravenna,
Sept. 11, 1820.

Dear Murray,—

Here is another historical *note* for you. I want to be as near truth as the Drama can be. Last post I sent you a note fierce as Faliero himself, in answer to a trashy tourist, who pretends that he could have been introduced to me. Let me have a proof of it, that I may cut its lava into some shape.

What Gifford says is very consolatory (of the first act). "English, sterling *genuine English,*" is a desideratum amongst you, and I am glad that I have got so much left; though heaven knows how I retain it: I *hear* none but from my Valet, and his is *Nottinghamshire*: and I *see* none but in your new publications, and theirs is *no* language at all, but jargon. Even your "New Jerusalem" is terribly stilted and affected, with "*very, very*"—so soft and pamby.

Oh! if ever I *do* come amongst you again, I will give you such a *Baviad and Mæviad*! not as *good* as the old, but even *better merited.* There never was such a *Set* as your *ragamuffins* (I mean *not* yours only, but every body's). What with the Cockneys, and the Lakers, and the *followers* of Scott, and Moore, and Byron, you are in the very uttermost decline and degradation of literature. I can't think of it without all the remorse of a murderer. I wish that Johnson were alive again to crush them!

I have as yet only had the first and second acts, and no opinion upon the second.

1144.—To John Murray.

Ravenna,
Sept. 14, 1820.

What? not a line. Well, have it your own way.

I wish you would inform Perry, that his stupid paragraph is the cause of all my newspapers being stopped in Paris. The fools believe me in your infernal country, and have not sent on their Gazettes, so that I know nothing of your beastly trial of the Queen.

I cannot avail myself of Mr. Gifford's remarks, because I have received none, except on the first act.

Yours, B.

P.S.—Do, pray, beg the Editors of papers to say anything blackguard they please; but not to put me amongst their arrivals: they do me more mischief by such nonsense than all their abuse can do.

1145.—To John Murray.

Ravenna,
Sept. 21, 1820.

So you are at your old tricks again. This is the second packet I have received unaccompanied by a single line of good, bad, or indifferent. It is strange that you have never forwarded any further observations of Gifford's: how am I to alter or amend, if I hear no further? or does this silence mean that it is well enough as it is, or too bad to be repaired? If the last, why do you not say so at once, instead of playing pretty, since you know that soon or late you must out with the truth.

Yours, B.

P.S.—My Sister tells me that you sent to her to enquire where I was, believing in my arrival "*driving a curricle,*" etc., etc., into palace yard: do you think me a coxcomb or a madman, to be capable of such an exhibition? My Sister knew me better, and told you that *could not* be true: you might as well have thought me entering on "a pale horse," like Death in the Revelations.

1146.—To John Cam Hobhouse.

Ravenna,
September 2lst, 1820.

My dear H.,—

If I could be of any real use to the Queen, or to anybody else, I would have come long ago, but I see no advantage to her, nor to others. I have done my best to get the Pesaro Patricians to travel (which lies about tumults and ill-treatment seemed about to prevent), but I made Count Gamba here write to the Macchiavellis (the first family in Pesaro, and his relatives), and he has sent one of them agoing, who has letters from me for divers; and amongst others for *you.*

Be civil to the bearer when he arrives; he is a great man at Fano, and a witness for her Maesta!

Another thing that kept me here (besides my serventismo), was that here we all expected, and had actually got on "our bandoliers," with "an unco band of blue bonnets at our backs," for a regular rising and all that; in which I, amongst thousands, was to have a part, being urged thereto by my love of liberty in general, and of Italy in particular; and also by the good opinion which some of the confederates had of me as a coadjutor, but all of a sudden the *City of Sausages* (do you understand me?) withdrew from the league; and wanted to temper and to temporize, and so leave us in the lurch. Of course without *B*[*ologna*] the Romagnuole towns can do but little, with the Germans on the Po; and so here we are, the principals, liable to arrest every day, "some taken and some left," like the "foolish virgins" (or some other parable) in the Evangelist.

In the meantime there is a little stabbing and shooting, but in a small way; guards doubled, palace shut at ten o' nights, and the Cardinal praying to Saint Apollinari, the patron saint of the city, who should protect the city against the Austrians, if he does his duty.

I never was fool enough to think of having Brougham out till the Queen's settled; but as "Nullum tempus occurrit regi," so, nullum tempus occurrit *honori.*

In Purefoy and Roper's business, *seven* years had taken place. In Tollemache (the son's) *fifteen*; in Stackpole and Cecil's *three,* since the provocation. All depends upon the parties having met, or no. You know that I have never been near Brougham since his insults; and was ignorant of them till long after their occurrence. *Keep this in mind, as you yourself were* one of my informants, and I am sorry to say, though (from a good motive) a late one. If I come to England now, I must wait till his trial of the Queen is over before I can have him out, but if his meeting me is *guaranteed me* for the moment that's over, I will come, and do my best for her, otherwise not. He would be sure at present to make that a plea and an excuse, and I should be a fool to think of overruling it, but neither that nor four, nor five years, nor ten, nor twenty, do, nor ought to prevent me from satisfaction, whenever, and wherever we encounter.

My cartel and its reasons I have already in writing, and have had since the hour I thought of returning to England. Sure I am that you and Douglas K. will approve it, when you see them. I have no other object nor view till this can be settled.

Here at Ravenna nobody believes the evidence against the Queen; they say that for half the money they could have any testimony they please, this is the public talk.

The "Hints, &c." are good; are they? As to the friends, we can change their names unless they rhyme well, in that case they must stand. Except Scott and Jeffrey and Moore, Sir B. Burges and a few more, I know no friends who need to be left out of a good poem.

Has Murray shown you my play? Pray look at it, I want your opinion, you know I have taken it lately in such good part, that you need not mind being a little rough, if necessary. It is long enough, an' that be all.

Murray told me that Lady Noel was ill; he lied I believe. I suppose, if she returns to whence she came, she will take her "divining rod" with her; it may be of use to her at home, and to her neighbour the rich man (Dives, clothed in purple), mentioned in the play of Henry 4th, and by the evangelists.

But the lady will not die, her living does too much ill. You'll see, she'll recover and bury her betters,

Write to yours, B.

P.S. Pray make your motion; you make a great figure in Galignani, who, by the way, has withheld his messengers since the paragraphs of my arrival in England, believing them.

Fletcher is ill, and has had three pounds of blood let since yesterday, for a sore throat. In his jacket and handkerchief and foolish face he looks like Liston, or much such a figure as he did in Albania in 1809 during the autumnal rains in his jerkin and umbrella. As Justice Shallow says, "Oh the merry days that we have seen!"

1147.—To John Murray.

Ravenna,
Sept. 23, 1820.

Dear Murray,—

Get from Mr. Hobhouse, and send me a proof (with the Latin) of my *Hints from H,* etc.: it has now the "*nonum prematur in annum*" complete for its production, being written at Athens in 18*11*. I have a notion that, with some omissions of names and passages, it will do; and I could put my late observations *for* Pope among the notes, with the date of 1820, and so on. As far as versification goes, it is good; and, on looking back to what I wrote about that period, I am astonished to see how *little* I have trained on. I wrote better then than now; but that comes from my having fallen into the atrocious bad state of the times—partly. It has been kept too, *nine years*; nobody keeps their piece nine years now-a-days, except Douglas K.; he kept his nine years and then restored her to the public. If I can trim it for present publication, what with the other things you have of mine, you will have a volume or two of *variety* at least; for there will be all measures, styles, and topics, whether good or no. I am anxious to hear what Gifford thinks of the tragedy; pray let me know. I really do not know what to think myself.

If the Germans pass the Po, they will be treated to a Mass out of the Cardinal de Retz's *Breviary.* Galley Knight's a fool, and could not understand this—Frere will: it is as pretty a conceit as you would wish to see upon a Summer's day.

Nobody here believes a word of the evidence against the Queen: the very mob cry shame against their countrymen, and say, that for half the money spent upon the trial, any testimony whatever may be brought out of Italy.1 This you may rely upon as fact: I told you as much before. As to what travellers report, *what are travellers*? Now I have *lived* among the Italians—not *Florenced,* and *Homed,* and Galleried, and Conversationed it for a few months, and then home again—but been of their families, and friendships, and feuds, and loves, and councils, and correspondence, in a part of Italy least known to foreigners; and have been amongst them of all classes, from the Conte to the Contadino; and you may be sure of what I say to you.

Yours, B.

1148.—To John Cam Hobhouse.

September 25th, 1820.

DEAR H[OBHOUSE],—

I open my letter to enclose you one which contains some hints which may be useful to Queeney, and her orators, but mind and don't betray the writer *H.* or he will lose *his place.*

When you wanted me to come, you forgot that absence during the earlier part of the stages of the bill *precludes voting.* I see by the papers that more than two days' absence does. Dunque, or adunque—argal.

Yours, B.

P.S. Brougham says "*discorso*" is not Italian! Oh rare! It and "*discórrere*" are as common as c—. I suppose that fellow thinks "*conversazione*" means *conversation.*

Apropos of Italian witnesses, since I have been in Italy I have had *six* law-suits, twice as plaintiff against debtors, once about horseflesh as plaintiff, twice about men's wives as defendant, and once as defendant against shopkeepers wanting to be paid *twice* over for the same bills. I gained them all but the horse-dealer's; he diddled me. In the shopkeeper's one last Nov. the fellow declared positively in a court, that *I ordered in person the articles in company with my secretaries,* and when desired to describe me, described me as a *tall thin flaxen-haired man!!* Of course he was non-suited. This fellow was reckoned one of the *most respectable negocianti* in Venice.

If you can quote this you may, and I'll prove it if necessary.

1149.—To John Murray.

Sept[r] 28th 1820.

Mr. J. Murray,—

Can you keep a Secret? not you: you would rather keep a w—e, I believe, of the two, although a moral man and "all that, Egad," as Bayes says.

However, I request and recommend to you to keep the enclosed one, viz. to *give no copies,* to permit *no publication*—else you and I will be two. It was written nearly three years ago upon the doublefaced fellow: its argument—in consequence of a letter exposing some of his usual practices. You may *show* it to Gifford, Hobhouse, D. Kinnaird, and any two or three of your own Admiralty favourites; but don't betray *it* or me; else you are the worst of men.

Is it like? if not, it has no merit. Does he deserve it? if not, burn it. He wrote to M. (so M. says) the other day, saying on some occasion, "what a fortunate fellow you are! surely you were born with a rose in your lips, and a Nightingale singing on the bed-top." M. sent me this extract as an instance of the old Serpent's sentimental twaddle. I replied, that I believed that "he (the twaddler) was born with a Nettle in his *, and a Carrion Crow croaking on the bolster," a parody somewhat *un*delicate; but such trash puts one stupid, besides the Cant of it in a fellow who hates every body.

Is this good? tell me, and I will send you one still better of that blackguard Brougham; there is a batch of them.

1150.—To John Murray.

Ravenna,
Sept. 28, 1820.

D[R] M[Y],—

I thought that I had told you long ago, that it *never* was intended nor written with any view to the Stage. I have said so in the preface too. It is too long and too regular for your stage. The persons too few, and the *unity* too much observed. It is more like a play of Alfieri's than of your stage (I say this humbly in speaking of that great Man); but there is poetry, and it is equal to *Manfred,* though I know not what esteem is held of *Manfred.*

I have now been nearly as long *out* of England as I was *there* during the time when I saw you frequently. I came home July 14th, 1811, and left again April 25th, 1816: so that Sept[r] 28th, 1820, brings me within a very few months of the same duration of time of my stay and my absence. In course, I can know nothing of the public taste and feelings, but from what I glean from letters, etc. Both seem to be as bad as possible.

I thought *Anastasius excellent*: did I not say so? Matthews's Diary most excellent: it, and Forsyth, and parts of Hobhouse, are all we have of truth or sense upon Italy. The letter to Julia very good indeed. I do not despise Mrs. Heman; but if she knit blue stockings instead of wearing them, it would be better. *You* are taken in by that false stilted trashy style, which is a mixture of all the styles of the day, which are *all bombastic* (I don't except my *own*—no one has done more through negligence to corrupt the language); but it is neither English nor poetry. Time will show.

I am sorry Gifford has made no further remarks beyond the first act: does he think all the English equally sterling, as he thought the first? You did right to send the proofs: I was a fool; but I do really detest the sight of proofs: it is an absurdity, but comes from laziness.

You can steal the two Juans into the world quietly, tagged to the others. The play as you will—the Dante too; but the *Pulci* I am proud of: it is superb; you have no such translation. It is the best thing I ever did in my life. I wrote the play, from beginning to end, and not a *single scene without interruption,* and being obliged to break off in the middle; for I had my hands full, and my head, too, just then; so it can be no great shakes—I mean the play, and the head too, if you like.

Yours.

P.S.—Send me proofs of "*the* Hints:" get them from Hobhouse.

P.S.—Politics here still savage and uncertain: however, we are all in our "bandaliers," to join the "Highlanders if they cross the Forth," i.e. to crush the Austrians if they pass the Po. The rascals!—and that Dog Liverpool, to say their subjects were *happy*! what a liar! If ever I come back, I'll work some of these ministers.

DEAR MURRAY,—

You ask for a "*Volume of Nonsense*"
Have all of your authors exhausted their store?
I thought you had published a good deal not long since
And doubtless the Squadron are ready with more.
But on looking again, I perceive that the Species
Of "Nonsense" you want must be purely "*facetious*;"
And, as that is the case, you had best put to press
Mr. Sotheby's tragedies now in M.S.S.

Some Syrian Sally
From common-place Gally,
Or, if you prefer the bookmaking of women,
Take a spick and Span "Sketch" of your feminine *He-Man.*

Yours, B.

Why do you ask me for opinions of your ragamuffins? You see what you get by it; but recollect, I never give opinions till required.

Sept. 29th.

I open my letter to say, that on reading *more* of the 4 volumes on Italy, where the Author says "*declined* an introduction," I perceive (*horresco referens*) that it is written by a WOMAN!!! In that case you must suppress my note and answer, and all I have said about the book and the writer. I never dreamed of it till now, in my extreme wrath at that precious note. I can only say that I am sorry that a Lady should say anything of the kind. What I would have said to [one of the other sex] you know already. Her book too (as a *She* book) is not a bad one; but she evidently don't know the Italians, or rather don't like them, and forgets the *causes* of their misery and profligacy (*Matthews* and *Forsyth* are your men for truth and tact), and has gone over Italy in *company—always* a *bad* plan. You must be *alone* with people to know them well. Ask her, *who* was the "*descendant of Lady M. W. Montague,*" and by *whom*? By Algarotti?

I suspect that, in *Marino Faliero,* you and yours won't like the *politics,* which are perilous to you in these times; but recollect that it is *not* a *political* play, and that I was obliged to put into the mouths of the Characters the sentiments upon which they acted. I hate all things written like *Pizarro,* to represent France, England, and so forth: all I have done is meant to be purely Venetian, even to the very prophecy of its present state.

Your Angles in general know little of the *Italians,* who detest them for their numbers and their Genoa treachery. Besides, the English travellers have not been composed of the best Company: how could they?—out of 100,000, how many gentlemen were there, or honest men?

Mitchell's *Aristophanes* is excellent: send me the rest of it.

I think very small beer of Mr. Goliffe, and his dull book. Here and there some good things though, which might have been better.

These fools will force me to write a book about Italy myself, to give them "the loud lie." They prate about assassination: what is it but the origin of duelling—and "*a wild Justice,*" as Lord Bacon calls it? It is the fount of the modern point of honour, in what the laws can't or *won't* reach. Every man is liable to it more or less, according to circumstances or place. For instance, I am living here exposed to it daily, for I have happened to make a powerful and unprincipled man my enemy;

and I never sleep the worse for it, or ride in less solitary places, because precaution is useless, and one thinks of it as of a disease which may or may not strike. It is true that there are those here, who, if he did, would "live to think on't;" but that would not awake my bones: I should be sorry if it would, were they once at rest.

1151.—To Richard Belgrave Hoppner.

Ravenna,
8bre 1° 1820.

My dear Hoppner,—

Your letters and papers came very safely, though slowly, missing one post.

The Shiloh story is true no doubt, though Elise is but a sort of *Queen's evidence.* You remember how eager she was to return to them, and then she goes away and abuses them. Of the facts, however, there can be little doubt; it is just like them. You may be sure that I keep your counsel.

I have not remitted the 30 Napoleons (or *what* was it?), till I hear that Missiaglia has received his safely, when I shall do so by the like channel.

What you say of the Queen's affair is very just and true; but the event seems not very easy to anticipate.

I enclose an epistle from Shiloh.

Yours ever and truly, Byron.

1152.—To Douglas Kinnaird.

Ravenna,
8bre 1st, 1820.

Dear Douglas,—

I have sent H[obhouse] some letters on the Queen's affairs (one goes by this post), has he got them?

I sent Murray a tragedy (written *not* for the stage), read it if you can. It is full of republicanism, so will find no favour in Albemarle Street.

They had got up as pretty a plot here as Hotspur's, when lo a City with sixty thousand men *bilked* them, and here we all are, in great confusion, some in arrest, some for flying to the hills, and for making a guerilla fight for it, others for waiting for better times, and both sides watching each other like hunting leopards. The fact is the Government is weak, for a Government, and the constitutionals strong for such, but what will be the issue is doubtful. My *voice* was, like that of Sempronius, somewhat warlike, but the autumnal rains have damped a deal of military ardour. In the meantime both sides embody and pay bands of assassins, or *brigands* as they call them, at about ninepence a head per diem, so you may suppose that I could soon whistle a hundred or two lads to my back when I want them, Portugal and Spain are the Whiteheaded boys after all.

Everything was ready, and we were all in our bandoliers. What a pity to have missed such an opportunity, but it was all the bloody Austrians on the Po. If they do but ever get a grip of those fellows, you will hear strange things, the Huns will have enough of it, at least such as fall into the hands of the natives. You may suppose that with such matters in possibility, it would be a satisfaction to know something of my worldly affairs, and to be as decently in cash as need be, so as to take the field with fair forage as [words torn off] every sixpence is a sinew of war. When you have perpended the drama at Murray's, let me know at what you rate it.

I have not come to England, not feeling myself pious enough to decide whether the Queen fell or no.

What trash your Parliament is.

Yours, B.

8bre 10°. I wrote this letter on the first of the moon, and kept back ten days, expecting to have a letter from you or Spooney. I have written twice to Hobby; ask him whether "*Lankey* has been into the slaughter-house yet," and whether there is not "too much *Tig. Tiri* in it?" *he will* understand these questions, *you* won't, for you have not taken the "Dunce's degree." Give Murray the Po verses, and let me have some of your own prose.

1153.—To John Murray.

Ravenna,
8bre 6°, 1820.

Dear My,—

You will have now received all the acts, corrected, of the *M*[*arino*] *F*[*aliero*]. What you say of the "Bet of 100 guineas," made by some one who says that he saw me last week, reminds me of what happened in 1810. You can easily ascertain the fact, and it is an odd one.

In the latter end of 1811, I met one evening at the Alfred my old School and form-fellow, (for we were within two of each other—*he* the higher, though both very near the top of our remove,) *Peel,* the Irish Secretary. He told me that, in 1810, he met me, as he thought, in St. James's Street, but we passed without speaking. He mentioned this, and it was denied as impossible, I being then in Turkey. A day or two after, he pointed out to his brother a person on the opposite side of the way; "there," said he, "is the man whom I took for Byron:" his brother instantly answered, "why, it *is* Byron, and no one else." But this is not all: I was *seen* by somebody to *write down my name* amongst the Enquirers after the King's health, then attacked by insanity. Now, at this very period, as nearly as I could make out, I was ill of a *strong fever* at Patras, caught in the marshes near Olympia, from the *Malaria.* If I had died there, this would have been a new Ghost Story for you. You can easily make out the accuracy of this from Peel himself, who told it in detail. I suppose you will be of the opinion of Lucretius, who (denies the immortality of the Soul, but) asserts that from the "flying off of the Surfaces of bodies perpetually, these surfaces or cases, like the Coats of an onion, are sometimes seen entire when they are separated from it, so that the shapes and shadows of both the dead and absent are frequently beheld."

But if they are, are their coats and waistcoats also seen? I do not disbelieve that we may be *two* by some unconscious process, to a certain sign; but which of these two I happen at present to be, I leave you to decide. I only hope that *t'other me* behaves like a Gemman.

I wish you would get Peel asked how far I am accurate in my recollection of what he told me; for I don't like to say such things without authority.

I am not sure that I was *not spoken* with; but this also you can ascertain. I have written to you such lots that I stop.

Yours, B.

P.S.—Send me the proofs of the "*Hints from H., etc.*"

P.S.—Last year (in June, 1819), I met at Count Mosti's, at Ferrara, an Italian who asked me "if I knew Lord Byron?" I told him *no* (no one knows himself, *you* know): "then," says he, "I do; I met him at Naples the other day." I pulled out my card and asked him if that was the way he spelt his name: and he answered, *yes.* I suspect that it was a blackguard Navy Surgeon, named *Bury* or *Berry,* who attended a young travelling Madman about, named Graham, and passed himself for a Lord at the Posthouses: he was a vulgar dog—quite of the Cockpit order—and a precious representative I must have had of him, if it was even so; but I don't know. He passed himself off as a Gentleman, and squired about a Countess Zinnani (of this place), then at Venice, an ugly battered woman, of bad morals even for Italy.

1154.—To John Murray.

Ravenna,
8bre 8°, 1820.

Dear Moray,—

Foscolo's letter is exactly the thing wanted; 1st, because he is a man of Genius; and, next, because he is an Italian, and therefore the best Judge of Italics. Besides,

"He's more an antique Roman than a Dane;"

that is, he has more of the antient Greek than of the modern Italian. Though, "somewhat," as Dugald Dalgetty says, "too wild and salvage " (like "Ronald of the Mist"), 'tis a wonderful man; and my friends Hobhouse and Rose both swear by him—and they are good Judges of men and of Italian humanity.

"Here are in all *two* worthy voices gained."

Gifford says it is good "sterling genuine English," and Foscolo says that the characters are right Venetian. Shakespeare and Otway had a million of advantages over me, besides the incalculable one of being *dead* from one to two centuries, and having been both born blackguards (which ARE such attractions to the Gentle living reader): let me then preserve the only one which I could possibly have—that of having been at Venice, and entered more into the local Spirit of it. I claim no more.

I know what F. means about Calendaro's *spitting* at Bertram: *that's* national—the *objection,* I mean. The Italians and French, with those "flags of Abomination," their pocket handkerchiefs, spit there, and here, and every where else—in your face almost, and therefore *object* to it on the Stage as *too familiar*. But we who *spit* nowhere—but in a man's face when we grow savage—are not likely to feel this. Remember *Massinger,* and Kean's Sir Giles Overreach—

"Lord! *thus* I *spit* at thee and thy Counsel!"

Besides, Calendaro does *not* spit in Bertram's face: he spits *at* him, as I have seen the Mussulmans do upon the ground when they are in a rage. Again, he *does not* in *fact despise* Bertram, though he affects it—as we all do, when angry with one we think our inferior: he is angry at *not being* allowed to die in his own way (although not afraid of death); and recollect, that he suspected and hated Bertram from the first. Israel Bertuccio, on the other hand, is a cooler and more concentrated fellow: he acts upon *principle* and *impulse;* Calendaro upon *impulse* and *example.*

So there's argument for you.

The Doge *repeats*;—*true,* but it is from engrossing passion, and because he sees *different* persons, and is always obliged to recur to the *cause* uppermost in his mind. His speeches are long;—true, but I wrote for the *Closet,* and on the French and Italian model rather than yours, which I think not very highly of, for all your *old* dramatists, who are long enough too, God knows: *look* into any of them.

I wish *you,* too, to recollect one thing which is nothing to the reader. I never wrote nor copied *an entire Scene of that play,* without being obliged to *break off*—to *break* a commandment, to obey a woman's, and to forget God's. Remember the drain of this upon a man's heart and brain, to say nothing of his immortal soul. *Fact,* I assure you. The Lady always apologized for the interruption; but you know the answer a man must make when and while he can. It happened to be the only hour I had in the four and twenty for composition, or reading, and I was obliged to divide even it. Such are the defined duties of a *Cavalier' Servente* or *Cavalier' Schiavo.*

I return you F[oscolo]'s letter, because it alludes also to his private affairs. I am sorry to see such a man in straits, because I know what they are, or what they were. I never met but three men who would have held out a finger to me: one was yourself, the other Wm Bankes, and the third a Nobleman long ago dead But of these the first was the only one who offered it while I *really* wanted it; the second from good will—but I was not in need of Bankes's aid, and would not have accepted it if I had (though I love and esteem him); and the *third*—[i]

So you see that I have seen some strange things in my time. As for your own offer, it was in 1815, when I was in actual uncertainty of five pounds. I rejected it; but I have not forgotten it, although you probably have.

You are to publish when and how you please; but I thought you and Mr. Hobhouse had decided *not* to print the whole of "*Blackwood*" as being *partly* unproducible: do as ye please after consulting Hobhouse about it.

P.S.—Foscolo's *Ricciarda* was lent, with the *leaves uncut,* to some Italians now in Villeggiatura, so that I have had no opportunity of heanng their opinion, or of reading it. They seized on it as Foscolo's, and on account of the beauty of the paper and printing, directly. If I find it takes, I will reprint it *here.* The Italians think as highly of Foscolo as they can of any man, divided and miserable as they are, and with neither leisure at present to read, nor head nor heart to judge of anything but extracts from French newspapers and the Lugano Gazette.

We are all looking at one another, like wolves on their prey in pursuit, only waiting for the first faller on, to do unutterable things. They are a great world in Chaos, or Angels in Hell, which you please; but out of Chaos came Paradise, and *out* of hell—I don't know what; but the Devil went *in* there, and he was a fine fellow once, you know.

You need never favour me with any periodical publications, excepting the *Edinburgh, Quarterly,* and an occasional *Blackwood,* or now and then a *Monthly Review*; for the rest I do not feel curiosity enough to look beyond their covers.

To be sure I took in the British Roberts finely; he fell precisely into the glaring trap laid for him: it was inconceivable how he could be so absurd as to think us serious with him.

Recollect, that if you put my name to *Don Juan* in these canting days, any lawyer might oppose my Guardian right of my daughter in Chancery, on the plea of its containing the *parody*; such are the perils of a foolish jest. I was not aware of this at the time, but you will find it correct, I believe; and you may be sure that the Noels would not let it slip. Now I prefer my child to a poem at any time, and so should you, as having half a dozen. Let me know your notions.

If you turn over the earlier pages of the H[untingdon] peerage story, you will see how common a name *Ada* was in the early Plantagenet days. I found it in my own pedigree in the reign of John and Henry, and gave it to my daughter. It was also the name of Charlemagne's sister. It is in an early chapter of Genesis, as the name of the wife of Lameth: and I suppose Ada is the feminine of *Adam*. It is short, ancient, vocalic, and had been in my family; for which reason I gave it to my daughter.

1155.—To John Murray.

Ravenna,
8bre 12°, 1820.

D[R] MURRAY,—

By land and Sea Carriage a considerable quantity of books have arrived; and I am obliged and grateful. But *Medio de fonte leporum surgit amari aliquid,* etc., etc.; which, being interpreted, means,

> I'm thankful for your books, dear Murray;
> But why not send Scott's Monastery?

the only book in four *living* volumes I would give a baiocco to see—abating the rest by the same author, and an occasional *Edinburgh* and *Quarterly,* as brief Chroniclers of the times. Instead of this, here are Johnny Keats's *p—ss a bed* poetry, and three novels by God knows whom, except that there is Peg Holford's name to one of them—a Spinster whom I thought we had sent back to her spinning. Crayon is very good; Hogg's Tales rough, but RACY, and welcome.

Lord Huntingdon's blackguard portrait may serve for a sign to his "Ashby de la Zouche" Alehouse: is it to such a drunken, half-pay looking raff that the Chivalrous Moira is to yield a portion of his titles? into what a puddle has stagnated the noble blood of the Hastings'? And the bog-trotting barrister's advertisement of himself and causes!! Upon my word, the house and the courts have made a pair of precious acquisitions? I have seen worse peers than this fellow, but then they were *made, not begotten* (these Lords are opposites to *the*

Lord in all respects); but, however stupid, however idle and profligate, all the peers by inheritance had something of the gentleman look about them: only the lawyers and the bankers "promoted into *Silver* fish" looked like ragamuffins till this new foundling came amongst them.

Books of *travels* are expensive, and I don't want them, having travelled already; besides, they lie. Thank the Author of *the Profligate,* a comedy, for his (or her) present. Pray send me *no more* poetry but what is rare and decidedly good. There is such a trash of Keats and the like upon my tables, that I am ashamed to look at them. I say nothing against your parsons, your Smedleys and your Crolys: it is all very fine; but pray dispense me from the pleasure, as also from Mrs. Hemans. Instead of poetry if you will favour me with a few Soda powders, I shall be delighted; but all prose (bating travels and *novels* NOT by Scott) is welcome, especially Scott's *tales of my Landlord,* and so on. In the notes to *Marino Faliero,* it may be as well to say that "*Benintende*" was not really of *the ten,* but merely *Grand Chancellor,* a separate office (although important): it was an arbitrary alteration of mine. The Doges too were all *buried* in *St. Marks before* Faliero: it is singular that when his immediate predecessor, *Andrea Dandolo,* died, the ten made a law that *all* the *future doges* should be *buried with their families, in their own churches,—one would think by a kind of presentiment.* So that all that is said of his *Ancestral Doges,* as buried at Saint John's and Paul's, is altered from the fact, *they being in Saint Mark's. Make a Note* of this, and put *Editor* as the subscription to it.

As I make such pretensions to accuracy, I should not like to be *twitted* even with such trifles on that score. Of the play they may say what they please, but not so of my costume and dram, pers., they having been real existences.

I omitted Foscolo in my list of living *Venetian worthies, in the Notes,* considering him as an *Italian* in general, and not a mere provincial like the rest; and as an Italian I have spoken of him in the preface to Canto 4th of *Childe Harold.*

The French translation of us!!! *Oime! Oime!*—and the German; but I don't understand the latter nor his long dissertation at the end about the Fausts. Excuse haste. Of politics it is not safe to speak, but nothing is decided as yet.

I should recommend your *not* publishing the *prose*: it is *too late* for the letter to Roberts, and that to Blackwood is too egoistical; and Hobhouse don't like it—except the part about *Pope,* which is truth and very good.

I am in a very fierce humour at not having Scott's *Monastery.* You are *too liberal* in *quantity,* and somewhat careless of the quality, of your missives. All the *Quarterlies* (4 in number) I had had before from you, and *two* of the *Edinburghs*; but no matter; we shall have new ones by and bye. No more Keats, I entreat: —flay him alive; if some of you don't, I must skin him myself: there is no bearing the drivelling idiotism of the Mankin.

I don't feel inclined to care further about *Don Juan.* What do you think a very pretty Italian lady said to me the other day? She had read it in the French, and paid me some compliments, with due DRAWBACKS, upon it. I answered that what she said was true, but that I suspected it would live longer than *Childe Harold.* "*Ah but* (said She) *I would rather have the fame of Childe Harold for* THREE YEARS *than an* IMMORTALITY *of Don Juan!*" The truth is that *it is* TOO TRUE, and the women hate every thing which strips off the tinsel of *Sentiment*; and they are right, as it would rob them of their weapons. I never knew a woman who did not hate *De Grammont's memoirs* for the same reason. Even Lady Oxford used to abuse them.

Thorwaldsen is in Poland, I believe: the bust is at Rome still, as it has been *paid* for these 4 years. It should have been sent, but I have no remedy *till* he returns.

Rose's work I never received: it was seized at Venice. Such is the liberality of the Huns, with their two hundred thousand men, that they dare not let such a volume as his circulate.

1156.—To John Hanson.

Ravenna,
8bre 12° 1820.

SIR,—

I can enter into no appeal without Counsel's opinion: this was promised and has *not* been sent. I would still much rather sell the Manor, at any price, than enter into a new and hopeless litigation.

Your delay (which seems a purposed and unwarrantable one) in completing the Irish Mortgage surprizes and distresses me; you will finish by causing me to lose many thousand pounds. You may delay as you please, but the mortgage *must* be completed; for I would rather sell out at any loss than trust to the infamous bubble of the British funds, into which (had I been upon the spot) I could never have entered.

It is also surprizing that you have never sent in your account to Mr. Kinnaird: if it is not sent, how can we ever come to any final settlement?

In expectation of an answer on these points,

I remain, yours very truly, BYRON.

1157.—To Richard Belgrave Hoppner.

Ravenna,
8bre 13th 1820.

My dear Hoppner,—

By the boat of a certain Bonaldo, bound for Venice, I forward to you certain Novels of Mrs. Opie and others, for Mrs. Hoppner and you as you desired. Amongst the rest there is a *German* translation of *Manfred,* with a plaguy long dissertation at the end of it; it would be out of all measure and conscience to ask you to translate the whole; but, if you could give me a short sketch of it, I should thank you, or if you would make somebody do the whole into *Italian,* it would do as well; and I would willingly pay some poor Italian German Scholar for his trouble. My own papers are at last come from Galignani. With many thanks for yours,

I am, yours very truly, Byron.

P.S.—I remit by *Missiaglia* 30 Napoleons, is that the sum?

1158.—To John Murray.

Ravenna,
8bre 16°, 1820.

Dear Moray,—

The Abbot has just arrived: many thanks; as also for the *Monastery—when you send it!!!*

The Abbot will have a more than ordinary interest for me; for an ancestor of mine by the mother's side, Sir J. Gordon of Gight, the handsomest of his day, died on a Scaffold at Aberdeen for his loyalty to Mary, of whom he was an imputed paramour as well as her relation. His fate was much commented on in the Chronicles of the times. If I mistake not, he had something to do with her escape from Loch Leven, or with her captivity there. But this you will know better than I.

I recollect Loch Leven as it were but yesterday: I saw it in my way to England in 1798, being then ten years of age. My Mother (who was as haughty as Lucifer with her descent from the Stuarts, and her right line, from the *old Gordons, not* the *Seyton Gordons,* as she disdainfully termed the Ducal branch,) told me the Story, always reminding me how superior *her* Gordons were to the Southron Byrons, notwithstanding our Norman, and always direct masculine descent, which has never lapsed into a female, as my mother's Gordons had done in her own person.

I have written to you so often lately, that the brevity of this will be welcome.

Yours ever and truly, BYRON.

1159.—To John Murray.

Ravenna,
8bre 17°, 1820.

D[R] M[Y].,—

Enclosed is the dedication of *Marino Faliero* to *Goethe.* Query? is his title *Baron* or not? I think yes. Let me know your opinion, and so forth.

Yours, B.

P.S.—Let me know what Mr. Hobhouse and you have decided about the two *prose* letters and their publication. I enclose you an Italian abstract of the German translator of *Manfred's* appendix, in which you will perceive quoted what Goethe says of the *whole body* of English poetry (and *not* of one in particular). On this the dedication is founded, as you will perceive, though I had thought of it before, for I look upon him as a Great Man.

FOR *MARINO FALIERO.*

DEDICATION TO BARON GOETHE, ETC., ETC., ETC.

SIR,—

In the Appendix to an English work lately translated into German and published at Leipsic, a judgment of yours upon English poetry is quoted as follows: "That in English poetry, great genius, universal power, a feeling of profundity, with sufficient tenderness and force, are to be found; but that *altogether these do not constitute poets,*" etc., etc.

I regret to see a great man falling into a great mistake. This opinion of yours only proves that the "*Dictionary of Ten Thousand living English Authors*" has not been translated into German. You will have read, in your friend Schlegel's version, the dialogue in Macbeth—

"There are *ten thousand*!
Macbeth. Geese, villain?
Answer. *Authors,* sir."

Now, of these "ten thousand authors," there are actually nineteen hundred and eighty-seven poets, all alive at this moment, whatever their works may be, as their booksellers well know; and amongst these there are several who possess a far greater reputation than mine, although considerably less than yours. It is owing to this neglect on the part of your German translators that you are not aware of the works of William Wordsworth, who has a baronet in London who draws him frontispieces and leads him about to dinners and to the play; and a Lord in the country, who gave him a place in the Excise—and a cover at his table. You do not know perhaps that this Gentleman is the greatest of all poets past—present and to come—besides which he has written an "*Opus Magnum*" in prose—during the late election for Westmoreland. His principal publication is entitled "*Peter Bell*" which he had withheld from the public for "*one and twenty years*"—to the irreparable loss of all those who died in the interim, and will have no opportunity of reading it before the resurrection. There is also another named Southey, who is more than a poet, being actually poet Laureate,—a post which corresponds with what we call in Italy *Poeta Cessareo,* and which you call in German—I know not what; but as you have a "*Caesar*"—probably you have a name for it. In England there is no *Caesar* —only the Poet.

I mention these poets by way of sample to enlighten you. They form but two bricks of our Babel, (Windsor bricks, by the way,) but may serve for a specimen of the building. It is, moreover, asserted that "the predominant character of the whole body of the present English poetry is a *disgust* and *contempt* for life." But I rather suspect that by one single work of *prose, you* yourself, have excited a greater contempt for life than all the English volumes of poesy that ever were written. Madame de Stael says, that "Werther has occasioned more suicides than the most beautiful woman;" and I really believe that he has put more individuals out of this world than Napoleon himself, except in the way of his profession. Perhaps, Illustrious Sir, the acrimonious judgment passed by a celebrated northern journal upon you in particular, and the Germans in general, has rather indisposed you towards English poetry as well as criticism. But you must not regard our critics, who are at bottom good-natured fellows, considering their two professions—taking up the law in court, and laying it down out of it. No one can more lament their hasty and unfair judgment, in your particular, than I do; and I so expressed myself to your friend Schlegel, in 1816, at Coppet.

In behalf of my "ten thousand" living brethren, and of myself, I have thus far taken notice of an opinion expressed with regard to "English poetry" in general, and which merited notice, because it was YOURS.

My principal object in addressing you was to testify my sincere respect and admiration of a man, who, for half a century, has led the literature of a great nation, and will go down to posterity as the first literary Character of his Age.

You have been fortunate, Sir, not only in the writings which have illustrated your name, but in the name itself, as being sufficiently musical for the articulation of posterity. In this you have the advantage of some of your countrymen, whose names would perhaps be immortal also—if any body could pronounce them.

It may, perhaps, be supposed, by this apparent tone of levity, that I am wanting in intentional respect towards you; but this will be a mistake: I am always flippant in prose. Considering you, as I really and warmly do, in common with all your own, and with most other nations, to be by far the first literary Character which has existed in Europe since the death of Voltaire, I felt, and feel, desirous to inscribe to you the following work,—*not* as being either a tragedy or a *poem,* (for I cannot pronounce upon its pretensions to be either one or the other, or both, or neither,) but as a mark of esteem and admiration from a foreigner to the man who has been hailed in Germany "THE GREAT GOETHE."

I have the honour to be,
With the truest respect,
Your most obedient and
Very humble servant, BYRON.

Ravenna, 8bre 14°, 1820.

P.S.—I perceive that in Germany, as well as in Italy, there is a great struggle about what they call "*Classical*" and "*Romantic*"—terms which were not subjects of classification in England, at least when I left it four or five years ago. Some of the English Scribblers, it is true, abused Pope and Swift, but the reason was that they themselves did not know how to write either prose or verse; but nobody thought them worth making a sect of. Perhaps there may be something of the kind sprung up lately, but I have not heard much about it, and it would be such bad taste that I shall be very sorry to believe it.

1160.—To Thomas Moore.

Ravenna,
October 17, 1820.

You owe me two letters—pay them. I want, to know what you are about. The summer is over, and you will be back to Paris. Apropos of Paris, it was not Sophia *Gail,* but Sophia *Gay*—the English word *Gay*—who was my correspondent. Can you tell who *she* is, as you did of the defunct * *?

Have you gone on with your poem? I have received the French of mine. Only think of being *traduced* into a foreign language in such an abominable travesty! It is useless to rail, but one can't help it.

Have you got my Memoir copied? I have begun a continuation. Shall I send it you, as far as it is gone?

I can't say any thing to you about Italy, for the Government here look upon me with a suspicious eye, as I am well informed. Pretty fellows!—as if I, a solitary stranger, could do any mischief. It is because I am fond of rifle and pistol shooting,

I believe; for they took the alarm at the quantity of cartridges I consumed, —the wiseacres!

You don't deserve a long letter—nor a letter at all—for your silence. You have got a new Bourbon, it seems, whom they have christened *Dieu-donné*;—perhaps the honour of the present may be disputed. Did you write the good lines on —, the Laker? * * * * *

The Queen has made a pretty theme for the journals. Was there ever such evidence published? Why it is worse than *Little's Poems* or *Don Juan.* If you don't write soon, I will "make you a speech."

Yours, etc.

1161.—To John Cam Hobhouse.

Ravenna,
8bre 17th, 1820.

I hope that you have safely received my two late letters, which contained *two* letters from H[oppne]r relative to the Queen's concern. D[ougla]s K[innair]d has written to me, but he lets that legal Spooney go on as he pleases, so that the funds will fall and fall, and who knows what thousands of pounds may be lost by his dawdling? Do pray stir him up with a long pole, and make him a speech, sharp as those you produce in Parliament. Recollect that distance makes me helpless.

Have you seen Murray? and read my "Tig. and Tiri?" Have you "gone again into the slaughterhouse, Lankey?"

Murray hath projects of publication, about the *purse* too, regarding which I will abide by *your opinion,* which was against publishing the *Blackwood,* &c. I will rest with y^r^ decision in that matter, whatever it be.

Foscolo thinks the tragedy very good Venetian, and Gifford says it is sterling English.

Now is a good time for the Prophecy of Dante; events have acted as an advertisement thereto—egad I think I am as good a vates (prophet, videlicet) as Fitzgerald of the Morning Post.

On politics I shall say nothing, the post being somewhat suspect.

I see that you are still "campaining at the King of Bohemy." Your last speech is at great length in Galignani, and so you were "called to order"; but I think you had the best of it.

You have done your part very well in parliament to my mind; it was just the place for you, keep it up, and go on.

If ever I come home, I will make a speech too, though I doubt my extempore talents in that line; and then *our* house is not animating like the hounds of the Commons when in full cry. 'Tis but cold hunting at best in the Lords.

I never could command my own attention to either side of their oratory, but either went away to a ball, or to a beef-steak at Bellamy's, and as there is no answering without listening, nor listening without patience, I doubt whether I should ever make a debater.

I think I spoke four times in all there; and I did not find my facility increase with practice.

D[ougla]s K[innair]d did not mention you in his letters, which are always filled with radical politics, all which I have in the newspapers. I wish he was in parliament again, which I suppose he wishes too.

We have sad sirocco weather here at present, and no very bright political horizon. But on that I shall say nothing, because I *know* that they have spies upon me, because I sometimes shoot with a rifle! The exquisite reason! you will laugh, and think of Pope and the clerks of the Post Office, but in fact I assure you, they are in such a state of suspicion as to dread everything and everybody; and though I have been a year here, and they know why I came hence, yet they don't think a woman a sufficing reason for so long a residence.

As for the scoundrel Austrians, they are bullying Lombardy as usual. It would be pleasant to see those Huns get their paiks, and it is not off the cards that they may.

Yours ever, B.

They sent an order from Rome to disarm my servants. The best of it is that they were *not armed*!

1162.—To John Murray.

Ravenna,
8bre 25°, 1820.

D[R] MORAY,—

Pray forward the enclosed to Lady Byron: it is on business. In thanking you for the *Abbot,* I made four grand mistakes. Sir John Gordon was not of Gight, but of Bogagicht, and a Son of Huntley's. He suffered, *not* for his loyalty, but in an insurrection. He had *nothing* to do with Loch Leven, having been dead some time at the period of the Queen's confinement. And 4[thly] I am not sure that he was the

Queen's paramour or no; for Robertson does not allude to this, though *Walter Scott does,* in the list she gives of her admirers (as unfortunate) at the close of *the Abbot.*

I must have made all these mistakes in recollecting my Mother's account of the matter, although she was more accurate than I am, being precise upon points of genealogy, like all the Aristocratical Scotch. She had a long list of ancestors, like Sir Lucius O'Trigger's, most of whom are to be found in the old Scotch Chronicles, Spalding, etc., in arms and doing mischief. I remember well passing Loch Leven, as well as the Queen's Ferry: we were on our way to England in 1798.

Why do the papers call *Hobhouse young*? he is a year and a half older than I am; and I was thirty-two last January.

Of Italy I can say nothing by the post: we are in instant expectation of the Barbarians passing the Po; and then there will be a war of fury and extermination.

Pray write sometimes; the communications will not long be open.

Yours,

B.

P.S.—Send me the *Monastery* and some Soda powders. You had better not publish Blackwood and the Roberts *prose,* except what regards *Pope*;—you have let the time slip by.

1163.—To Douglas Kinnaird.

Ravenna,
8bre 26th, 1820.

Dear Douglas,—

By last post I consigned to Mr. Murray a letter on business for the Lady Byron. In this I recommended strongly to her consideration (and to that of her trustees) the speedy removal of the settled property from the funds.

My motives are the almost immediate explosion which must take place in Italy in the impending event of the passage of the Po by the barbarians, now in great force on that river—and the further fall of the English funds in consequence; as your Tory scoundrels will, right or wrong, take part in any foreign war.

I wish you to write to her in aid of my representation; for God's sake, take advantage of any rise to sell out, otherwise it will ere long be too ,late. I know better than any of you what is brewing in Italy. Do not let the fortunes of my family be totally sacrificed at home, whatever I may be. Recollect that a month—a week—a day—may render all this abortive, and press upon this implacable woman and her trustees, as well as upon that dog Hanson, the necessity of selling out immediately.

If I did not abhor your Tory country to a degree of detestation, this would have been remedied. I would last year have gone among you, and settled my own business at least, but I prefer anything almost, to making one of such a people as your present government has made of the present English.

I prefer almost anything else to living amongst you English, but it is still my duty to represent as far as I can what ought to be done by my trustees in my absence.

Yrs. truly and affectly., BYRON.

P.S. I have read lately several speeches of Hobhouse in taverns, his eloquence is better than his company. Tell him that if *Bergami* goes to England, the Courier of the innocent Queen will beat him for *Westminster.*

To give you a hint of the doings *here.* Since I began this letter, the news have arrived from Forli (the next and nearest city) that last night the liberals blew up, by means of a mine, the house of a "*Brigand*" (so they call here the Satellites of the tyrants during comedy time or opera time), but the master *was out,* and so escaped. People were arrested [words torn off] released them, and shot a blackguard, or one of the Carabineers. They have also intimated gently to his Eminence of Forli, that if he continues to arm *assassins* (here they war in private in this way, there are bands in every town at so much a head, for those who like such expenses), they will throw him out of his palace windows, which are rather lofty. If these things don't prelude "sword and gun fighting," you can judge for yourself.

Get me out of your funds; write in your best manner to the Mathematician—your letters of business are *models,* your other letters somewhat brief and hasty— and persuade that excellent female to allow me to be an "Irish Absentee" before the three per cents are at no per cent. If she don't, I will come over, be a radical, and take possession of the Kirkby Estate before Lady Noel is in Hell—no long time if people went there alive, but she will live for ever to plague her betters.

You should set up a Radical newspaper and call it "the *Bergami,*" it would beat Mr. Street's now-a-days.

1164.—To John Murray.

Ravenna,
9bre 4°, 1820.

I have received from Mr. Galignani the enclosed letters, duplicates and receipts, which will explain themselves. As the poems are your property by purchase, right, and justice, *all matters of publication,* etc., etc., *are for you to decide upon.* I know not how far my compliance with Mr. G.'s request might be legal, and I doubt that it would not be honest. In case you choose to arrange with him, I enclose the permits to *you,* and in so doing I wash my hands of the business altogether. I sign them merely to enable you to exert the power you justly possess more properly. I will have nothing to do with it further, except, in my answer to Mr. Galignani, to state that the letters, etc., etc., are sent to you, and the causes thereof.

If you can check those foreign Pirates, do; if not, put the permissive papers in the fire: *I* can have no view nor object whatever, but to secure to you your property.

Yours, BYRON.

P.S.—There will be shortly "*the Devil to pay*" *here*; and, as there is no saying that I may not form an *Item in his bill,* I shall not now write at greater length: *you* have *not answered* my late letters; and you have acted foolishly, as you will find out some day.

P.S.—I have read part of the *Quarterly* just arrived: Mr. Bowles shall be answered; he is not *quite* correct in his statement about *E*[*nglish*] *B*[*ards*] *and S*[*cotch*] *R*[*eviewers*]. They support Pope, I see, in the *Quarterly.* Let them continue to do so: it is a Sin, and a Shame, and a *damnation* to think that *Pope!!* should require it —but he does. Those miserable mountebanks of the day, the poets, disgrace themselves and deny God, in running down Pope, the most *faultless* of Poets, and almost of men.

The *Edinburgh* praises Jack Keats or Ketch, or whatever his names are: why, his is the * of Poetry—something like the pleasure an Italian fiddler extracted out of being suspended daily by a Street Walker in Drury Lane. This went on for some weeks: at last the Girl went to get a pint of Gin—met another, chatted too long, and Cornelli was *hanged outright before she returned.* Such like is the trash they praise, and such will be the end of the * * poesy of this miserable Self-polluter of the human Mind.

W. Scott's *Monastery* just arrived: many thanks for that Grand Desideratum of the last Six Months.

P.S.—You have cut up old Edgeworth, it seems, amongst you. You are right: he was a bore. I met the whole batch—Mr., Mrs., and Miss—at a blue breakfast of Lady Davy's in Blue Square; and he proved but bad, in taste and tact and decent breeding. He began by saying that *Parr* (Dr. Parr) had attacked him, and that he (the father of Miss E.) had *cut him up* in his answer. Now, Parr would have annihilated him; and if he had not, why tell *us* (a long story) *who* wanted to breakfast? I saw them different times in different parties, and I thought him a very tiresome coarse old Irish half-and-half Gentleman, and her a pleasant reserved old woman— * * * * * * * * * * * * *

Have you gotten *The Hints* yet?

I know Henry Matthews: he is the image, to the very voice, of his brother Charles, only darker: his *laugh* his in particular. The first time I ever met him was in Scrope Davies's rooms after his brother's death, and I nearly dropped, thinking that it was his Ghost. I have also dined with him in his rooms at King's College. Hobhouse once purposed a similar memoir; but I am afraid that the letters of Charles's correspondence with me (which are at Whitton with my other papers) would hardly do for the public: for our lives were not over strict, and our letters somewhat lax upon most subjects.

His Superiority over all his cotemporaries was quite indisputable and acknowledged: none of us ever thought of being *at all near* Matthews; and yet there were some high men of his standing—Bankes, Bob Milnes, Hobhouse, Bailey, and many others—without numbering the *mere Academical* men, of whom we hear little out of the University, and whom he beat *hollow* on *their own* Ground.

His gaining the Downing Fellowship was the completest thing of the kind ever known. He carried off both declamation prizes: in short, he did whatever he chose. He was three or four years my Senior, but I lived a good deal with him latterly, and with his friends. He wrote to me the very day of his death (I believe), or at least a day before, if not the very day. He meant to have stood for the University Membership. He was a very odd and humourous fellow besides, and spared nobody: for instance, walking out in Newstead Garden, he stopped at Boatswain's monument inscribed "Here lies Boatswain, a Dog," etc., and then observing a *blank* marble tablet on the other side, "So (says he) there is room for another friend, and I propose that the Inscription be 'Here lies H—bh—se, a Pig,'" etc. You may as well not let *this* transpire to the worthy member, lest he regard neither his dead friend nor his living one, with his wonted Suavity.

Rose's *lines* must be at his own option: *I* can have no objection to their publication. Pray salute him from me. Mr. Keats, whose poetry you enquire after, appears to me what I have already said: such writing is a sort of mental * * * *—* * * * * * * * his *Imagination.* I don't mean he is *indecent,* but viciously soliciting his own ideas into a state, which is neither poetry nor any thing else but a Bedlam vision produced by raw pork and opium. Barry Cornwall would write well, if he would let himself. Croly is superior to many, but seems to think himself inferior to Nobody.

Last week I sent you a correspondence with Galignani, and some documents on your property. You have now, I think, an opportunity of *checking,* or at least *limiting,* those *French re-publications.* You may let all your authors publish what they please *against me* or *mine*; a publisher is not, and cannot be, responsible for all the works that issue from his printer's.

The "White Lady of Avenel" is not quite so good as a *real well-authenticated* ("Donna bianca") *White Lady* of *Colalto,* or spectre in the Marca Trivigiana, who has been repeatedly seen: there is a man (a huntsman) now alive who saw her also.

Hoppner could tell you all about her, and so can Rose perhaps. I myself have *no doubt* of the fact, historical and spectral. She always appeared on particular occasions, before the deaths of the family, etc., etc. I heard M[e] Benzoni say, that she knew a Gentleman who had seen her cross his room at Colalto Castle. Hoppner saw and spoke with the Huntsman who met her at the Chase, and never *hunted* afterwards. She was a Girl attendant, who, one day dressing the hair of a Countess Colalto, was seen by her mistress to smile upon her husband in the Glass. The Countess had her shut up in the wall at the Castle, like Constance de Beverley. Ever after, she haunted them and all the Colaltos. She is described as very beautiful and fair. It is well authenticated.

Yours, B.

1168.—To John Cam Hobhouse.

R[avenn]a,
November 9th, 1820.

My dear H[obhouse],—

I admit the force of your facetiousness, which it will go hard but I pay off some day or other; as Scrope used to say, "I have things in store." Indolent I am to be sure, and yet I can back a horse and fire a carbine, like Major Sturgeon, "without winking or blinking," and I can go without my dinner without scolding, or eat it without finding fault with the cooking or quality; and I could slumber as in Turkey, when some of my friends were loudly execrating their bed and its tenantry. Yours is now a more active life, I admit; you write pamphlets against Canning, and make speeches, and "greatly *daring dine*" at the Crown and Anchor. And this *is* being active and useful, and justifies your reproach of my slumbers. We will divide the parts between us of "*player* and poet," as you have taken up the former one with great success. Now "I have the best of that," I think, as I used to say to you in the wilderness. And then *you* counsel me to keep out of a *scrape. You!* Why, have your prudence and activity kept you out of one? I think not; you will find some day that your radicals will embarrass you sufficiently. But, in the meantime, you are certainly making a figure in point of *talent,* that is a fact, and so you would in any other line, because you *happen to have great talent,* more, *I* think, than you yourself or others have yet given you credit for; and you are besides sure to train on, because you have strong powers of application; but the *line* itself is not the true one, and was not your own choice, but the result of circumstances, united to a little natural impatience for having waited for an opening. Egad, I talk like an angel!

Oh, you must know that I sent H[oppner]'s letter without asking him, so say nothing about that; I thought it might serve the *Queen* in her cause, and you in her behalf, and sent it, trusting to your discretion; pray do not compromise him, nor anybody else. "*Young man,*" quotha! he is six and thirty, that is, two years older than you, and three years and three months more than me. I see the papers call *you* "young," I am glad of it, but though I am your junior, I have thought myself *eldern* this many a day.

I hope that you will turn out those Tory scoundrels.

I do not quarrel with my "*old cronies,*" nor my "old cronies" with me, I hope, and as for the ballad, *you* have *balladed* me fifty times, and are welcome to fifty more; recollect at *Brighton,* at Newstead, and just before leaving England, and *since.*

Yours ever and truly, BN.

1169.—To John Murray.

Ravenna,
9bre 18°, 1820.

DEAR MORAY,—

The death of Waite is a shock to the—teeth, as well as to the feelings of all who knew him. Good God, he and *Blake* both gone! I left them both in the most robust health, and little thought of the national loss in so short a time as five years. They were both as much superior to Wellington in rational greatness, as he who preserves the hair and the teeth is preferable to the "bloody blustering booby" who gains a name by breaking heads and knocking out grinders. Who succeeds *him*? where is tooth powder? *mild* and yet efficacious—where is *tincture*? where are cleansing *roots* and *brushes* now to be obtained? Pray obtain what information you can upon these "*Tusc*ulan questions:" my jaws ache to think on't. Poor fellows! I anticipated seeing both again; and yet they are gone to that place where both teeth and hair last longer than they do in this life. I have seen a thousand graves opened, and always perceived, that, whatever was gone, the *teeth and hair* remained of those who had died with them. Is not this odd? they go the very first things in *youth,* and yet last the longest in the dust, if people will but *die* to preserve them! It is a queer life, and a queer death, that of mortals.

I knew that Waite had married, but little thought that the other decease was so soon to overtake him. Then he was such a delight, such a Coxcomb, such a Jewel of a Man! There is a taylor at Bologna so like him, and also at the top of his profession. Do not neglect this commission: *who* or *what* can replace him? what says the public?

I remand you the preface. *Don't forget* that the Italian extract from the Chronicle must *be translated.* With regard to what you say of retouching the *Juans* and the *Hints,* it is all very well; but I can't *furbish.* I am like the tyger (in poesy), if I miss my first Spring, I go growling back to my Jungle. There is no second. I can't correct; I can't, and I won't. Nobody ever succeeds in it, great or small. Tasso remade the whole of his Jerusalem; but who ever reads that version? All the world goes to the first. Pope *added* to *the "Rape of the Lock,"* but did not reduce it. You must take my things as they happen to be: if they are not likely to suit, reduce their *estimate* then accordingly. I would rather give them away than hack and hew them. I don't say that you are not right: I merely assert that I cannot better them. I must either "make a spoon, or spoil a horn." And there's an end.

The parcel of the *second* of June, with the late *Edgeworth* and so forth, has *never* arrived: parcels of a later date have, of which I have given you my opinions in late letters. I remit you what I think a Catholic curiosity—the Pope's brief, authenticating the body of Saint Francis of Assisi, a town on the road to Rome.

Yours ever, B.

P.S.—Of the praises of that little dirty blackguard Keates in the *Edinburgh,* I shall observe as Johnson did when Sheridan the actor got a *pension:* "What! has *he* got a pension? Then it is time that I should give up *mine*!" Nobody could be prouder of the praises of the *Edinburgh* than I was, or more alive to their censure, as I showed in *E*[*nglish*] *B*[*ards*] *and S*[*cotch*] *R*[*eviewers*]. At present *all the men* they have ever praised are degraded by that insane article. Why don't they review and praise "Solomon's Guide to Health"? it is better sense and as much poetry as Johnny Keates.

Bowles must be *bowled* down: 'tis a sad match at Cricket, if that fellow can get any Notches at Pope's expence. If he once gets into "*Lord's* ground," (to continue the pun, because it is foolish,) I think I could beat him in one Innings. You did not know, perhaps, that I was once *(not metaphorically,* but *really*) a good Cricketer, particularly in *batting,* and I played in the Harrow match against the Etonians in 1805, gaining more notches (as one of our chosen Eleven) than any, except Ld Ipswich and Brookman, on our side.

1170.—To the Hon. Augusta Leigh.

Ravenna. 9b^{re} 18th 1820

My dearest Augusta—

You will I hope have received a discreetly long letter from me—not long ago,—Murray has just written that *Waite*—is dead—poor fellow—he and Blake—both deceased—what is to become of our hair & teeth.—The hair is less to be minded—any body can cut hair—though not so well—but the mouth is a still more serious concern.— —

Has he no Successor ?—pray tell me the next best—for what am I to do for brushes & powder?— —And then the *Children*—only think—what will become of their jaws? Such men ought to be immortal—& not your stupid heroes—orators & poets.— —

I am really so sorry—that I can't think of anything else just now.—Besides I liked him with all his Coxcombry.— —

Let me know what we are all to do,—& to whom we can have recourse without damage for our cleaning—scaling & powder.—

How do you get on with your affairs ?—and how does every body get on.— —

How is all your rabbit-warren of a family? I gave you an account of mine by last letter.—The Child Allegra is well—but the Monkey has got a cough—and the tame Crow has lately suffered from the head ache.— —Fletcher has been bled for a Stitch—& looks flourishing again—Pray write—excuse this short scrawl—

yours ever B

P. S.

Recollect about Waite's Successor—why he was only married the other day—& now I don't wonder so much that the poor man died of it.— —

1171.—To John Murray.

Ravenna,
9bre 19, 1820.

What you said of the late Charles Skinner Matthews has set me to my recollections; but I have not been able to turn up any thing which would do for the purposed Memoir of his brother,—even if he had previously done enough during his life to sanction the introduction of anecdotes so merely personal. He was, however, a very extraordinary man, and would have been a great one. No one ever succeeded in a more surpassing degree than he did as far as he went. He was indolent, too; but whenever he stripped, he overthrew all antagonists. His conquests will be found registered at Cambridge, particularly his *Downing* one, which was hotly and highly contested, and yet easily *won.* Hobhouse was his most intimate friend, and can tell you more of him than any man. William Bankes also a great deal. I myself recollect more of his oddities than of his academical qualities, for we lived most together at a very idle period of *my* life. When I went up to Trinity, in 1805, at the age of seventeen and a half, I was miserable and untoward to a degree. I was wretched at leaving Harrow, to which I had become attached during the two last years of my stay there; wretched at going to Cambridge instead of Oxford (there were no rooms vacant at Christchurch); wretched from some private domestic circumstances of different kinds, and consequently about as unsocial as a wolf taken from the troop. So that, although I knew Matthews, and met him often *then* at Bankes's, (who was my collegiate pastor, and master, and patron,) and at Rhode's, Milnes's, Price's, Dick's, Macnamara's, Farrell's, Gally Knight's, and others of that *set* of contemporaries, yet I was neither intimate with him nor with any one else, except my old schoolfellow Edward Long (with whom I used to pass the day in riding and swimming), and William Bankes, who was good-naturedly tolerant of my ferocities.

It was not till 1807, after I had been upwards of a year away from Cambridge, to which I had returned again to *reside* for my degree, that I became one of Matthews's familiars, by means of Hobhouse, who, after hating me for two years, because I wore a *white hat,* and a *grey* coat, and rode a *grey* horse (as he says himself), took me into his good graces because I had written some poetry. I had always lived a good deal, and got drunk occasionally, in their company—but now we became really friends in a morning. Matthews, however, was not at this period resident in College. I met *him* chiefly in London, and at uncertain periods at Cambridge. Hobhouse, in the mean time, did great things: he founded the Cambridge "Whig Club" (which he seems to have forgotten), and the "Amicable Society," which was dissolved in consequence of the members constantly quarrelling, and made himself very popular with "us youth," and no less formidable to all tutors, professors, and heads of Colleges. William Bankes was gone; while he stayed, he ruled the roast—or rather the *roasting*— and was father of all mischiefs.

Matthews and I, meeting in London, and elsewhere, became great cronies. He was not good tempered—nor am I—but with a little tact his temper was manageable, and I thought him so superior a man, that I was willing to sacrifice something to his humours, which were often, at the same time, amusing and provoking. What became of his *papers* (and he certainly had many), at the time of his death, was never known. I mention this by the way, fearing to skip it over, and *as* he *wrote* remarkably well, both in Latin and English. We went down to Newstead together, where I had got a famous cellar, and *Monks'* dresses from a masquerade warehouse. We were a company of some seven or eight, with an occasional neighbour or so for visiters, and used to sit up late in our friars' dresses, drinking burgundy, claret, champagne, and what not, out of the *skull-cup,* and all sorts of glasses, and buffooning all round the house, in our conventual garments. Matthews always denominated me "the Abbot," and never called me by any other name in his good humours, to the day of his death. The harmony of these our symposia was somewhat interrupted, a few days after our assembling, by Matthews's threatening to throw Hobhouse out of a *window,* in consequence of I know not what commerce of jokes ending in this epigram. Hobhouse came to me and said, that "his respect and regard for me as host would not permit him to call out any of my guests, and that he should go to town next morning." He did. It was in vain that I represented to him that the window was not high, and that the turf under it was particularly soft. Away he went.

Dear Moray,—

There have arrived the preface, the translation—the first sixteen pages, also from page *sixty-five* to *ninety-six;* but *no intermediate sheets* from y^{e} *sixteenth* to *sixty-fifth* page. I apprize you of this, in case any such should have been sent.

I hope that the printer will perfectly understand *where* to insert some three or four additional lines, which Mr. Gifford has had the goodness to copy out in his own hand.

The translation is extremely well done, and I beg to present my thanks and respects to Mr. Cohen for his time and trouble. The old Chronicle Style is far better done than I could have done it: some of the old words are past the understanding even of the present Italians. Perhaps if Foscolo was to cast a glance over it, he could rectify such, or confirm them.

Your *two volume won't* do: the *first* is very well, but the second must be *anonymous,* and the *first with* the *name,* which would make a confusion or an *identity,* both of which ought to be avoided. You had better put the Doge, Dante, etc., into *one* volume, and bring out the other *soon* afterwards, but not on the same day.

The *Hints,* Hobhouse says, will require a good deal of slashing, to suit the times, which will be a work of time, for I don't feel at all laborious just now. Whatever effect they are to have would perhaps be greater in a separate form, and *they* also must have my name to them. Now, if you publish them in the same volume with "*Don Juan,*" they identify *Don Juan* as mine, which I don't think worth a Chancery Suit about my daughter's guardianship; as in your present code a facetious poem is sufficient to take away a man's rights over his family.

I regret to hear that the Queen has been so treated on the second reading of her bill.

Of the state of things here it would be difficult and not very prudent to speak at large, the Huns opening all letters: I wonder if they can read them when they have opened them? if so, they may see, in my most legible hand, that I think them damned scoundrels and barbarians, their emperor a fool, and themselves more fools than he; all which they may send to Vienna, for anything I care. They have got themselves masters of the Papal police, and are bullying away; but some day or other they will pay for it all. It may not be very soon, because these unhappy Italians have no union nor consistency among themselves; but I suppose Providence will get tired of them at last, and show that God is not an Austrian.

Ever yours truly, B.

P.S.—I enclosed a letter to you for Lady B. on business some time ago: did you receive and forward it?

Adopt Mr. Gifford's alterations in the proofs.

1174.—To John Hanson.

Ravenna,
9bre 30° 1820.

Dear Sir,—

I have received your letter with Counsel's opinion upon the Appeal. You had better then enter the Appeal immediately not to lose further time.

Mr. Kinnaird acted by my directions about Col. Leigh's bond.

Let me hope that the Blessington Mortgage will proceed without further delays.

You have my full directions to proceed in making Mr. Claughton fulfil his payments.

I do not know whether it will be best to send a Courier to Ravenna with the deeds, or to send them by the post. *Consult weight* and security, and adopt the mode which will be most speedy.

The *Scotch deeds directions* I do not understand, notwithstanding all the pencil marks; but I will try to sign them correctly.

My "rough rebukes," as you call them, have been excited by the not very smooth delays, which have intervened. What can a man say at such a distance to you gentlemen of the law? You best know how far they are deserved.

I shall be very glad to hear any good news, and, with respects and remembrances to Charles and all your family,

I am, yours very truly and faithfully, Byron.

1175.—To the Hon. Augusta Leigh.

[Fragment]

Hobhouse cares about as much for the Queen as he does for S^{t}. Paul's. One ought to be glad however of anything which makes either of them go to Church. I am also delighted to see *you* grown so *moral*. It is edifying. Pray write, and believe me ever dearest A,

Yours

1176.—To Thomas Moore.

Ravenna,
Dec. 9, 1820.

Besides this letter, you will receive *three* packets, containing, in all, 18 more sheets of Memoranda, which, I fear, will cost you more in postage than they will ever produce by being printed in the next century. Instead of waiting so long, if you could make any thing of them *now* in the way of *reversion,* (that is, after *my* death,) I should be very glad,—as, with all due regard to your progeny, I prefer you to your grandchildren. Would not Longman or Murray advance you a certain sum *now,* pledging themselves *not* to have them published till after *my* decease, think you?—and what say you?

Over these latter sheets I would leave you a discretionary power; because they contain, perhaps, a thing or two which is too sincere for the public. If I consent to your disposing of their reversion *now,* where would be the harm? Tastes may change. I would, in your case, make my essay to dispose of them, *not* publish, now; and if *you* (as is most likely) survive me, add what you please from your own knowledge; and, *above all, contradict* any thing, if I have *mis*-stated; for my first object is the truth, even at my own expense.

I have some knowledge of your countryman Muley Moloch, the lecturer. He wrote to me several letters upon Christianity, to convert me; and, if I had not been a Christian already, I should probably have been now, in consequence. I thought there was something of wild talent in him, mixed with a due leaven of absurdity,—as there must be in all talent, let loose upon the world, without a martingale.

The ministers seem still to persecute the Queen * * *; but they *won't* go out, the sons of b—es. Damn Reform—I want a place—what say you? You must applaud the honesty of the declaration, whatever you may think of the intention.

I have quantities of paper in England, original and translated—tragedy, etc., etc., and am now copying out a fifth canto of *Don Juan,* 149 stanzas. So that there will be near *three thin* Albemarle, or *two thick* volumes of all sorts of my Muses. I mean to plunge thick, too, into the contest upon Pope, and to lay about me like a dragon till I make manure of Bowles for the top of Parnassus.

These rogues are right—*we do* laugh at *t'others*—eh?—don't we? You shall see—you shall see what things I'll say, an' it pleases Providence to leave us leisure. But in these parts they are all going to war; and there is to be liberty, and a row, and a constitution—when they can get them. But I won't talk politics—it is low. Let us talk of the Queen, and her bath, and her bottle—that's the only *motley* nowadays.

If there are any acquaintances of mine, salute them. The priests here are trying to persecute me,—but no matter.

Yours, etc.

1177.—To Thomas Moore.

Ravenna,
Dec. 9, 1820.

I open my letter to tell you a fact, which will show the state of this country better than I can. The commandant of the troops is *now* lying *dead* in my house. He was shot at a little past eight o'clock, about two hundred paces from my door. I was putting on my great-coat to visit Madame la Contessa G. when I heard the shot. On coming into the hall, I found all my servants on the balcony, exclaiming that a man was murdered. I immediately ran down, calling on Tita (the bravest of them) to follow me. The rest wanted to hinder us from going, as it is the custom for every body here, it seems, to run away from "the stricken deer."

However, down we ran, and found him lying on his back, almost, if not quite, dead, with five wounds; one in the heart, two in the stomach, one in the finger, and the other in the arm. Some soldiers cocked their guns, and wanted to hinder me from passing. However, we passed, and I found Diego, the adjutant, crying over him like a child—a surgeon, who said nothing of his profession—a priest, sobbing a frightened prayer—and the commandant, all this time, on his back, on the hard, cold pavement, without light or assistance, or any thing around him but confusion and dismay.

As nobody could, or would, do any thing but howl and pray, and as no one would stir a finger to move him, for fear of consequences, I lost my patience—made my servant and a couple of the mob take up the body—sent off two soldiers to the guard—despatched Diego to the Cardinal with the news, and had the commandant carried upstairs into my own quarter. But it was too late, he was gone—not at all disfigured—bled inwardly—not above an ounce or two came out.

I had him partly stripped—made the surgeon examine him, and examined him myself. He had been shot by cut balls or slugs. I felt one of the slugs, which had gone through him, all but the skin. Everybody conjectures why he was killed, but no one knows how. The gun was found close by him—an old gun, half filed down.

He only said, *O Dio!* and *Gesu!* two or three times, and appeared to have suffered very little. Poor fellow! he was a brave officer, but had made himself much disliked by the people. I knew him personally, and had met with him often at conversazioni and elsewhere. My house is full of soldiers, dragoons, doctors, priests, and all kinds of persons,—though I have now cleared it, and clapt sentinels at the doors. To-morrow the body is to be moved. The town is in the greatest confusion, as you may suppose.

You are to know that, if I had not had the body moved, they would have left him there till morning in the street, for fear of consequences. I would not choose to let even a dog die in such a manner, without succour:—and, as for consequences, I care for none in a duty.

Yours, etc.

P.S.—The lieutenant on duty by the body is smoking his pipe with great composure.—A queer people this.

1178.—To John Murray.

Ravenna,
D^ecr^ 9th 1820.

Dear Murray,—

I intended to have written to you at some length by this post, but as the Military Commandant is now lying dead in my house, on Fletcher's bed, I have other things to think of.

He was shot at 8 o'Clock this evening about two hundred paces from our door. I was putting on my great Coat to pay a visit to the Countess G., when I heard a shot, and on going into the hall, found all my servants on the balcony exclaiming that "a Man was murdered." As it is the custom here to let people fight it through, they wanted to hinder me from going out; but I ran down into the Street: Tita, the bravest of them, followed me; and we made our way to the Commandant, who was lying on his back, with five wounds, of which three in the body—one in the heart. There were about him Diego, his Adjutant, crying like a Child; a priest howling; a Surgeon who dared not touch him j two or three confused and frightened Soldiers; one or two of the boldest of the mob; and the Street dark as pitch, with the people flying in all directions. As Diego could only cry and wring his hands, and the Priest could only pray, and nobody seemed able or willing to do anything except exclaim, shake and stare, I made my Servant and one of the mob take up the body; sent off Diego crying to the Cardinal, the Soldiers for the Guard; and had the Commandant conveyed up Stairs to my own quarters. But he was quite gone. I made the Surgeon examine him, and examined him myself. He had bled inwardly, and very little external blood was apparent. One of the Slugs had gone quite through—all but the Skin: I felt it myself. Two more shots in the body, one in a finger, and another in the arm. His face not at all disfigured: he seems asleep, but is growing livid. The Assassin has not been taken; but the gun was found—a gun filed down to half the barrel.

He said nothing but *O Dio!* and *O Gesu* two or three times.

The house was filled at last with Soldiers, officers, police, and military; but they are clearing away—all but the Sentinels, and the body is to be removed tomorrow. It seems that, if I had not had him taken into my house, he might have lain in the Streets till morning; as here nobody meddles with such things, for fear of the consequences—either of public suspicion, or private revenge on the part of the

Slayers. They may do as they please: I shall never be deterred from a duty of humanity by all the assassins of Italy, and that is a wide word.

He was a brave officer, but an unpopular man. The whole town is in confusion.

You may judge better of things here by this detail, than by anything which I could add on the Subject: communicate this letter to Hobhouse and Douglas K[d], and believe me

Yours ever truly, B.

P.S.—The poor Man's wife is not yet aware of his death: they are to break it to her in the morning.

The Lieutenant, who is watching the body, is smoaking with the greatest *Sangfroid*: a strange people.

1179.—To John Murray.

R[a] 10[bre] 10[o] 1820.

D[R] M.,—

I wrote to you by last post. Acknowledge that and this letter, which you are requested to forward immediately.

Yours truly, B.

P.S.—I have finished fifth Canto of *D. J.*; 143 Stanzas. So prepare.

1180.—To John Murray.

Ravenna,
10[bre] 14[o] 1820.

DEAR MORAY,—

As it is a month since I have had any packets of proofs, I suppose some must have miscarried. Today I had a letter from *Rogers.*

The fifth Canto of *D. J.* is now under copy: it consists of 151 Stanzas. I want to know what the devil you mean to do?

By last post I wrote to you, detailing the murder of the Commandant here. I picked him up shot in the Street at 8 in the Evening; and perceiving that his adjutant and the Soldiers about him had lost their heads completely with rage and alarm, I carried him to my house, where he lay a corpse till next day, when they removed

1184.—To John Murray.

R[a] 10[bre] 28° 1820.

D[R] M.,—

I have had no communication from you of any kind since the second reading of the Queen's bill. I write merely to apprize you that, by this Post, I have transmitted to Mr. Douglas Kinnaird the fifth Canto of *Don Juan;* and you will apply (if so disposed) to him for it. It consists of 155 Octave Stanzas, with a few notes.

I wrote to you several times, and told you of the various events, assassinations, etc., which have occurred here. War is certain. If you write, write soon.

Yours, B.

P.S.—Did you receive two letters, etc., from Galignani to me, which I enclosed to you long ago? I suppose your answer must have been intercepted, as they were of importance to you, and you would naturally have acknowledged their arrival.

CHAPTER XXI. EXTRACTS FROM A DIARY, JANUARY 4–FEBRUARY 27, 1821

Ravenna, January 4, 1821.

"A sudden thought strikes me." Let me begin a Journal once more. The last I kept was in Switzerland, in record of a tour made in the Bernese Alps, which I made to send to my sister in 1816, and I suppose that she has it still, for she wrote to me that she was pleased with it. Another, and longer, I kept in 1813–1814, which I gave to Thomas Moore in the same year.

This morning I gat me up late, as usual—weather bad—bad as England—worse. The snow of last week melting to the sirocco of to-day, so that there were two damned things at once. Could not even get to ride on horseback in the forest. Stayed at home all the morning —looked at the fire—wondered when the post would come. Post came at the Ave Maria, instead of half-past one o'clock, as it ought. Galignani's *Messengers,* six in number—a letter from Faenza, but none from England. Very sulky in consequence (for there ought to have been letters), and ate in consequence a copious dinner; for when I am vexed, it makes me swallow quicker—but drank very little.

I was out of spirits—read the papers—thought what *fame* was, on reading, in a case of murder, that "Mr. Wych, grocer, at Tunbridge, sold some bacon, flour, cheese, and, it is believed, some plums, to some gipsy woman accused. He had on his counter (I quote faith-" fully) a *book,* the Life of *Pamela,* which he was *tearing* for *waste* paper, etc., etc. In the cheese was found, etc., "and a *leaf* of *Pamela wrapt round the bacon.*" What would Richardson, the vainest and luckiest of *living* authors *(i.e.* while alive)—he who, with Aaron Hill, used to prophesy and chuckle over the presumed fall of Fielding (the *prose* Homer of human nature) and of Pope (the most beautiful of poets)—what would he have said, could he have traced his pages from their place on the French prince's toilets (see Boswell's Johnson) to the grocer's counter and the gipsy-murderess's bacon!!!

What would he have said? What can any body say, save what Solomon said long before us? After all, it is but passing from one counter to another, from the bookseller's to the other tradesman's—grocer or pastry-cook. For my part, I have met with most poetry upon trunks; so that I am apt to consider the trunk-maker as the sexton of authorship. Wrote five letters in about half an hour, short and savage, to all my rascally correspondents. Carriage came. Heard the news of three murders at Faenza and Forli—a carabinier, a smuggler, and an attorney—all last night. The two first in a quarrel, the latter by premeditation.

Three weeks ago—almost a month—the 7th it was— I picked up the commandant, mortally wounded, out of the street; he died in my house; assassins unknown, but presumed political. His brethren wrote from Rome last night to thank me for having assisted him in his last moments. Poor fellow! it was a pity; he was a good soldier, but imprudent. It was eight in the evening when they killed him. We heard the shot; my servants and I ran out, and found him expiring, with five wounds, two whereof mortal—by slugs they seemed. I examined him, but did not go to the dissection next morning.

Carriage at 8 or so—went to visit La Contessa G.—found her playing on the piano-forte—talked till ten, when the Count, her father, and the no less Count, her brother, came in from the theatre. Play, they said, Alfieri's *Fileppo*—well received.

Two days ago the King of Naples passed through Bologna on his way to congress. My servant Luigi brought the news. I had sent him to Bologna for a lamp. How will it end? Time will show.

Came home at eleven, or rather before. If the road and weather are comfortable, mean to ride to-morrow. High time—almost a week at this work—snow, sirocco, one day—frost and snow the other—sad climate for Italy. But the two seasons, last and present, are extraordinary. Read a Life of Leonardo da Vinci by Rossi—ruminated—wrote this much, and will go to bed.

January 5, 1821.

Rose late—dull and drooping—the weather dripping and dense. Snow on the ground, and sirocco above in the sky, like yesterday. Roads up to the horse's belly, so that riding (at least for pleasure) is not very feasible. Added a postscript to my letter to Murray. Read the conclusion, for the fiftieth time (I have read all W. Scott's novels at least fifty times), of the third series of *Tales of my Landlord*—grand work—Scotch Fielding, as well as great English poet—wonderful man! I long to get drunk with him.

Dined *versus* six o' the clock. Forgot that there was a plum-pudding, (I have added, lately, *eating* to my "family of vices,") and had dined before I knew it. Drank half a bottle of some sort of spirits—probably spirits of wine; for what they call brandy, rum, etc., etc., here is nothing but spirits of wine, coloured accordingly. Did *not* eat two apples, which were placed by way of dessert. Fed the two cats, the hawk, and the tame (but *not tamed*) crow. Read Mitford's *History of Greece*—Xenophon's *Retreat of the Ten Thousand.* Up to this present moment writing, 6 minutes before eight o' the clock—French hours, not Italian.

Hear the carriage—order pistols and great coat, as usual—necessary articles. Weather cold—carriage open, and inhabitants somewhat savage—rather treacherous and highly inflamed by politics. Fine fellows, though,—good materials for a nation. Out of chaos God made a world, and out of high passions comes a people.

Clock strikes—going out to make love. Somewhat perilous, but not disagreeable. Memorandum—a new screen put up to-day. It is rather antique, but will do with a little repair.

Thaw continues—hopeful that riding may be practicable to-morrow. Sent the papers to All[i].—grand events coming.

11 o' the clock and nine minutes. Visited La Contessa G[uiccioli] *nata* G[hisleri] G[amba]. Found her beginning my letter of answer to the thanks of Alessio del Pinto of Rome for assisting his brother the late Commandant in his last moments, as I had begged her to pen my reply for the purer Italian, I being an ultramontane, little skilled in the set phrase of Tuscany. Cut short the letter—finish it another day. Talked of Italy, patriotism, Alfieri, Madame Albany, and other branches of learning. Also Sallust's *Conspiracy of Catiline,* and the *War of Jugurtha.* At 9 came in her brother, Il Conte Pietro—at 10, her father, Conte Ruggiero.

Talked of various modes of warfare—of the Hungarian and Highland modes of broad-sword exercise, in both whereof I was once a moderate "master of fence." Settled that the R. will break out on the 7th or 8th of March, in which appointment I should trust, had it not been settled that it was to have broken out in October, 1820. But those Bolognese shirked the Romagnuoles.

"It is all one to Ranger." One must not be particular, but take rebellion when it lies in the way. Come home—read the *Ten Thousand* again, and will go to bed.

Mem.—Ordered Fletcher (at four o'clock this afternoon) to copy out seven or eight apophthegms of Bacon, in which I have detected such blunders as a schoolboy might detect rather than commit. Such are the sages! What must they be, when such as I can stumble on their mistakes or misstatements? I will go to bed, for I find that I grow cynical.

January 6, 1821.

Mist—thaw—slop—rain. No stirring out on horseback. Read Spence's *Anecdotes.* Pope a fine fellow—always thought him so. Corrected blunders in *nine* apophthegms of Bacon—all historical—and read Mitford's *Greece.* Wrote an epigram. Turned to a passage in Guinguené—ditto in Lord Holland's *Lope de Vega.* Wrote a note on *Don Juan.*

At eight went out to visit. Heard a little music—like music. Talked with Count Pietro G. of the Italian comedian Vestris, who is now at Rome—have seen him often act in Venice—a good actor—very. Somewhat of a mannerist; but excellent in broad comedy, as well as in the sentimental pathetic. He has made me frequently laugh and cry, neither of which is now a very easy matter —at least, for a player to produce in me.

Thought of the state of women under the ancient Greeks—convenient enough. Present state a remnant of the barbarism of the chivalric and feudal ages—artificial and unnatural. They ought to mind home—and be well fed and clothed—but not mixed in society. Well educated, too, in religion—but to read neither poetry nor politics—nothing but books of piety and cookery. Music—drawing—dancing—also a little gardening and ploughing now and then. I have seen them mending the roads in Epirus with good success. Why not, as well as haymaking and milking?

Came home, and read Mitford again, and played with my mastiff—gave him his supper. Made another reading to the epigram, but the turn the same. To-night at the theatre, there being a prince on his throne in the last scene of the comedy,—the audience laughed, and asked him for a *Constitution.* This shows the state of the public mind here, as well as the assassinations. It won't do. There must be an universal republic,—and there ought to be.

The crow is lame of a leg—wonder how it happened—some fool trod upon his toe, I suppose. The falcon pretty brisk—the cats large and noisy—the monkeys I have not looked to since the cold weather, as they suffer by being brought up. Horses must be gay—get a ride as soon as weather serves. Deuced muggy still—an Italian winter is a sad thing, but all the other seasons are charming.

What is the reason that I have been, all my lifetime, more or less *ennuyé*? and that, if any thing, I am rather less so now than I was at twenty, as far as my recollection serves? I do not know how to answer this, but presume that it is constitutional,—as well as the waking in low spirits, which I have invariably done for many years. Temperance and exercise, which I have practised at times, and for a long time together vigorously and violently, made little or no difference. Violent passions did;—when under their immediate influence—it is odd, but—I was in agitated, but *not* in depressed, spirits.

A dose of salts has the effect of a temporary inebriation, like light champagne, upon me. But wine and spirits make me sullen and savage to ferocity—silent, however, and retiring, and not quarrelsome, if not spoken to. Swimming also raises my spirits,—but in general they are low, and get daily lower. That is *hopeless*; for I do not think I am so much *ennuyé* as I was at nineteen. The proof is, that then I must game, or drink, or be in motion of some kind, or I was miserable. At present, I can mope in quietness; and like being alone better than any company—except the lady's whom I serve. But I feel a something, which makes me think that, if I ever reach near to old age, like Swift, "I shall die at top" first. Only I do not dread idiotism or madness so much as he did. On the contrary, I think some quieter stages of both must be preferable to much of what men think the possession of their senses.

January 7, 1821, Sunday.

Still rain—mist—snow—drizzle—and all the incalculable combinations of a climate where heat and cold struggle for mastery. Read Spence, and turned over Roscoe, to find a passage I have not found. Read the fourth vol. of W. Scott's second series of *Tales of my Landlord.* Dined. Read the *Lugano Gazette.* Read—I forget what. At eight went to conversazione. Found there the Countess Geltrude, Betti V. and her husband, and others. Pretty black-eyed woman that—*only* nineteen —same age as Teresa, who is prettier, though.

The Count Pietro G[amba] took me aside to say that the Patriots have had notice from Forli (twenty miles off) that to-night the government and its party mean to strike a stroke—that the Cardinal here has had orders to make several arrests immediately, and that, in consequence, the Liberals are arming, and have posted patroles in the streets, to sound the alarm and give notice to fight for it.

He asked me "what should be done?" I answered, "Fight for it, rather than be taken in detail;" and offered, if any of them are in immediate apprehension of arrest, to receive them in my house (which is defensible), and to defend them, with my servants and themselves (we have arms and ammunition), as long as we can,—or to try to get them away under cloud of night. On going home, I offered him the pistols which I had about me—but he refused, but said he would come off to me in case of accidents.

It wants half an hour of midnight, and rains;—as Gibbet says, "a fine night for their enterprise—dark as hell, and blows like the devil." If the row don't happen *now,* it must soon. I thought that their system of shooting people would soon produce a re-action—and now it seems coming. I will do what I can in the way of combat, though a little out of exercise. The cause is a good one.

Turned over and over half a score of books for the passage in question, and can't find it. Expect to hear the drum and the musquetry momently (for they swear to resist, and are right,)—but I hear nothing, as yet, save the plash of the rain and the gusts of the wind at intervals. Don't like to go to bed, because I hate to be waked, and would rather sit up for the row, if there is to be one.

Mended the fire—have got the arms—and a book or two, which I shall turn over. I know little of their numbers, but think the Carbonari strong enough to beat the troops, even here. With twenty men this house might be defended for twenty-four hours against any force to be brought against it, *now* in this place, for the same time; and, in such a time, the country would have notice, and would rise,—if ever they *will* rise, of which there is some doubt. In the mean time, I may as well read as do any thing else, being alone.

January 8, 1821, Monday.

Rose, and found Count P. G. in my apartments. Sent away the servant. Told me that, according to the best information, the Government had not issued orders for the arrests apprehended; that the attack in Forli had not taken place (as expected) by the *Sanfedisti*—the opponents of the *Carbonari* or Liberals—and that, as yet, they are still in apprehension only. Asked me for some arms of a better sort, which I gave him. Settled that, in case of a row, the Liberals were to assemble *here* (with me), and that he had given the word to Vincenzo G. and others of the *Chiefs* for that purpose. He himself and father are going to the chase in the forest; but V. G. is to come to me, and an express to be sent off to him, P. G., if any thing occurs. Concerted operations. They are to seize—but no matter.

I advised them to attack in detail, and in different parties, in different *places* (though at the *same* time), so as to divide the attention of the troops, who, though few, yet being disciplined, would beat any body of people (not trained) in a regular fight—unless dispersed in small parties, and distracted with different assaults. Offered to let them assemble here if they choose. It is a strongish post—narrow street, commanded from within—and tenable walls.

Dined. Tried on a new coat. Letter to Murray, with corrections of Bacon's *Apophthegms* and an epigram—the *latter not* for publication. At eight went to Teresa, Countess G. At nine and a half came in II Conte P. and Count P. G. Talked of a certain proclamation lately issued. Count R. G. had been with * * (the * *), to sound him about the arrests. He, * *, is a *trimmer,* and deals, at present, his cards with both hands. If he don't mind, they'll be full. * * pretends (*I* doubt him—*they* don't,—we shall see) that there is no such order, and seems staggered by the immense exertions of the Neapolitans, and the fierce spirit of the Liberals here. The truth is, that * * cares for little but his place (which is a good one), and wishes to play pretty with both parties. He has changed his mind thirty times these last three moons, to my knowledge, for he corresponds with me. But he is not a bloody fellow—only an avaricious one.

It seems that, just at this moment (as Lydia Languish says), "there will be no elopement after all." I wish that I had known as much last night—or, rather, this morning—I should have gone to bed two hours earlier. And yet I ought not to complain; for, though it is a sirocco, and heavy rain, I have not *yawned* for these two days.

Came home—read *History of Greece*—before dinner had read Walter Scott's *Rob Roy.* Wrote address to the letter in answer to Alessio del Pinto, who has thanked me for helping his brother (the late Commandant, murdered here last month) in his last moments. Have told him I only did a duty of humanity—as is true. The brother lives at Rome.

Mended the fire with some *sgobole* (a Romagnuole word), and gave the falcon some water. Drank some Seltzer-water. Mem.—received to-day a print, or etching, of the story of Ugolino, by an Italian painter—different, of course, from Sir Joshua Reynolds's, and I think (as far as recollection goes) *no worse,* for Reynolds's is not good in history. Tore a button in my new coat.

I wonder what figure these Italians will make in a regular row. I sometimes think that, like the Irishman's gun (somebody had sold him a crooked one), they will only do for "shooting round a corner;" at least, this sort of shooting has been the late tenor of their exploits. And yet there are materials in this people, and a noble energy, if well directed. But who is to direct them? No matter. Out of such times heroes spring. Difficulties are the hotbeds of high spirits, and Freedom the mother of the few virtues incident to human nature.

Tuesday, January 9, 1821.

Rose—the day fine. Ordered the horses; but Lega (my *secretary,* an Italianism for steward or chief servant) coming to tell me that the painter had finished the work in fresco for the room he has been employed on lately, I went to see it before I set out. The painter has not copied badly the prints from Titian, etc., considering all things.

Dined. Read Johnson's *Vanity of Human Wishes,* —all the examples and mode of giving them sublime, as well as the latter part, with the exception of an occasional couplet. I do not so much admire the opening. I remember an observation of Sharpe's, (the *Conversationist,* as he was called in London, and a very clever man,) that the first line of this poem was superfluous, and that Pope (the best of poets, *I* think,) would have begun at once, only changing the punctuation—

"Survey mankind from China to Peru."

The former line, "Let observation," etc., is certainly heavy and useless. But 'tis a grand poem—and *so true*!—true as the 10th of Juvenal himself. The lapse of ages *changes* all things—time—language—the earth—the bounds of the sea—the stars of the sky, and every thing "about, around, and underneath" man, *except man himself,* who has always been, and always will be, an unlucky rascal. The infinite variety of lives conduct but to death, and the infinity of wishes lead but to disappointment.1 All the discoveries which have yet been made have multiplied little but existence. An extirpated disease is succeeded by some new pestilence; and a discovered world has brought little to the old one, except the p— first and freedom afterwards—the *latter* a fine thing, particularly as they gave it to Europe in exchange for slavery. But it is doubtful whether "the Sovereigns" would not think the *first* the best present of the two to their subjects.

At eight went out—heard some news. They say the King of Naples has declared by couriers from Florence, to the *Powers* (as they call now those wretches with crowns), that his Constitution was compulsive, etc., etc., and that the Austrian barbarians are placed again on *war* pay, and will march. Let them—"they come like sacrifices in their trim," the hounds of hell! Let it still be a hope to see their bones piled like those of the human dogs at Morat, in Switzerland, which I have seen.

Heard some music. At nine the usual visitors—news, *war,* or rumours of war. Consulted with P. G., etc., etc. They mean to *insurrect* here, and are to honour me with a call thereupon. I shall not fall back; though I don't think them in force or heart sufficient to make much of it. But, *onward!*—it is now the time to act, and what signifies *self,* if a single spark of that which would be worthy of the past can be bequeathed unquenchedly to the future? It is not one man, nor a million, but the *spirit* of liberty which must be spread. The waves which dash upon the shore are, one by one, broken, but yet the *ocean* conquers, nevertheless. It overwhelms the Armada, it wears the rock, and, if the *Neptunians* are to be believed, it has not only destroyed, but made a world. In like manner, whatever the sacrifice of individuals, the great cause will gather strength, sweep down what is rugged, and fertilise (for *sea-weed* is *manure*) what is cultivable. And so, the mere selfish calculation ought never to be made on such occasions; and, at present, it shall not be computed by me. I was never a good arithmetician of chances, and shall not commence now.

January 10, 1821.

Day fine—rained only in the morning. Looked over accounts. Read Campbell's *Poets*—marked errors of Tom (the author) for correction. Dined—went out—music—Tyrolese air, with variations. Sustained the cause of the original simple air against the variations of the Italian school.

Politics somewhat tempestuous, and cloudier daily. To-morrow being foreign post-day, probably something more will be known.

Came home—read. Corrected Tom Campbell's slips of the pen. A good work, though—style affected—but his defence of Pope is glorious. To be sure, it is his *own cause* too,—but no matter, it is very good, and does him great credit.

Midnight.

I have been turning over different *Lives* of the Poets. I rarely read their works, unless an occasional flight over the classical ones, Pope, Dryden, Johnson, Gray, and those who approach them nearest (I leave the *rant* of the rest to the *cant* of the day), and—I had made several reflections, but I feel sleepy, and may as well go to bed.

January 11, 1821.

Read the letters. Corrected the tragedy and the *Hints from Horace.* Dined, and got into better spirits. Went out—returned—finished letters, five in number. Read *Poets,* and an anecdote in Spence.

All[i] writes to me that the Pope, and Duke of Tuscany, and King of Sardinia, have also been called to Congress; but the Pope will only deal there by proxy. So the interests of millions are in the hands of about twenty coxcombs, at a place called Leibach!

I should almost regret that my own affairs went well, when those of .nations are in peril. If the interests of mankind could be essentially bettered (particularly of these oppressed Italians), I should not so much mind my own "sma peculiar." God grant us all better times, or more philosophy!

In reading, I have just chanced upon an expression of Tom Campbell's;—speaking of Collins, he says that "no reader cares any more about the *characteristic manners* of his Eclogues than about the authenticity of the tale of Troy." 'Tis false—we *do* care about "the authenticity of the tale of Troy." I have stood upon that plain *daily,* for more than a month in 1810; and if any thing diminished my pleasure, it was that the blackguard Bryant had impugned its veracity. It is true I read *Homer Travestied* (the first twelve books), because Hobhouse and others bored me with their learned localities, and I love quizzing. But I still venerated the grand original as the truth of *history* (in the material *facts*) and of *place.* Otherwise, it would have given me no delight. Who will persuade me, when I reclined upon a mighty tomb, that it did not contain a hero?—its very magnitude proved this. Men do not labour over the ignoble and petty dead—and why should not the *dead* be *Homer's* dead? The secret of Tom Campbell's defence of *inaccuracy* in costume and description is, that his *Gertrude,* etc., has no more locality in common with Pennsylvania than with Penmanmaur. It is notoriously full of grossly false scenery, as all Americans declare, though they praise parts of the poem. It is thus that self-love for ever creeps out, like a snake, to sting anything which happens, even accidentally, to stumble upon it.

January 12, 1821.

The weather still so humid and impracticable, that London, in its most oppressive fogs, were a summer-bower to this mist and sirocco, which has now lasted (but with one day's interval), chequered with snow or heavy rain only, since the 30th of December, 1820. It is so far lucky that I have a literary turn;—but it is very tiresome not to be able to stir out, in comfort, on any horse but Pegasus, for so many days. The roads are even worse than the weather, by the long splashing, and the heavy soil, and the growth of the waters.

Read the Poets—English, that is to say—out of Campbell's edition. There is a good deal of taffeta in some of Tom's prefatory phrases, but his work is good as a whole. I like him best, though, in his own poetry.

Murray writes that they want to act the Tragedy of *Marino Faliero*—more fools they, it was written for the closet. I have protested against this piece of usurpation, (which, it seems, is legal for managers over any printed work, against the author's will) and I hope they will not attempt it. Why don't they bring out some of the numberless aspirants for theatrical celebrity, now encumbering their shelves, instead of lugging me out of the library? I have written a fierce protest against any such attempt; but I still would hope that it will not be necessary, and that they will see, at once, that it is not intended for the stage. It is too regular—the time, twenty-four hours— the change of place not frequent—nothing *melo*-dramatic—no surprises, no starts, nor trap-doors, nor opportunities "for tossing their heads and kicking their heels"—and no *love*—the grand ingredient of a modern play.

I have found out the seal cut on Murray's letter. It is meant for Walter Scott—or *Sir* Walter—he is the first poet knighted since Sir Richard Blackmore. But it does not do him justice. Scott's—particularly when he recites —is a very intelligent countenance, and this seal says nothing.

Scott is certainly the most wonderful writer of the day. His novels are a new literature in themselves, and his poetry as good as any—if not better (only on an erroneous system)—and only ceased to be so popular, because the vulgar learned were tired of hearing "Aristides called the Just," and Scott the Best, and ostracised him.

I like him, too, for his manliness of character, for the extreme pleasantness of his conversation, and his goodnature towards myself, personally. May he prosper!—for he deserves it. I know no reading to which I fall with such alacrity as a work of W. Scott's. I shall give the seal, with his bust on it, to Madame la Comtesse G. this evening, who will be curious to have the effigies of a man so celebrated.

How strange are my thoughts!—The reading of the song of Milton, "Sabrina fair" has brought back upon me—I know not how or why—the happiest, perhaps, days of my life (always excepting, here and there, a Harrow holiday in the two latter summers of my stay there) when living at Cambridge with Edward Noel Long, afterwards of the Guards,—who, after having served honourably in the expedition to Copenhagen (of which two or three thousand scoundrels yet survive in plight and pay), was drowned early in 1809, on his passage to Lisbon with his regiment in the *St. George* transport, which was run foul of in the night by another transport. We were rival swimmers—fond of riding—reading—and of conviviality. We had been at Harrow together; but—*there,* at least—his was a less boisterous spirit than mine. I was always cricketing—rebelling—fighting—*row*ing (from *row,* not *boat*-rowing, a different practice), and in all manner of mischiefs; while he was more sedate and polished. At Cambridge—both of Trinity—my spirit rather softened, or his roughened, for we became very great friends. The description of Sabrina's seat reminds me of our rival feats in *diving.* Though Cam's is not a very translucent wave, it was fourteen feet deep, where we used to dive for, and pick up—having thrown them in on purpose—plates, eggs, and even shillings. I remember, in particular, there was the stump of a tree (at least ten or twelve feet deep) in the bed of the river, in a spot where we bathed most commonly, round which I used to cling, and "wonder how the devil I came there."

Our evenings we passed in music (he was musical, and played on more than one instrument, flute and violoncello), in which I was audience; and I think that our chief beverage was soda-water. In the day we rode, bathed, and lounged, reading occasionally. I remember our buying, with vast alacrity, Moore's new quarto (in 1806), and reading it together in the evenings.

We only passed the summer together;—Long had gone into the Guards during the year I passed in Notts, away from college. *His* friendship, and a violent, though *pure,* love and passion—which held me at the same period—were the then romance of the most romantic period of my life.

* * * * *

I remember that, in the spring of 1809, Hobhouse laughed at my being distressed at Long's death, and amused himself with making epigrams upon his name, which was susceptible of a pun—*Long, short,* etc. But three years after, he had ample leisure to repent it, when our mutual friend, and his, Hobhouse's, particular friend, Charles Matthews, was drowned also, and he himself was as much affected by a similar calamity. But *I* did not pay him back in puns and epigrams, for I valued Matthews too much myself to do so; and, even if I had not, I should have respected his griefs.

Long's father wrote to me to write his son's epitaph. I promised—but I had not the heart to complete it. He was such a good amiable being as rarely remains long in this world; with talent and accomplishments, too, to make him the more regretted. Yet, although a cheerful companion, he had strange melancholy thoughts sometimes. I remember once that we were going to his uncle's, I think—I went to accompany him to the door merely, in some Upper or Lower Grosvenor or Brook Street, I forget which, but it was in a street leading out of some square,—he told me that, the night before, he "had taken up a pistol—not knowing or examining whether it was loaded or no—and had snapped it at his head, leaving it to chance whether it might not be charged." The letter, too, which he wrote me on leaving college to join the Guards, was as melancholy in its tenour as it could well be on such an occasion. But he showed nothing of this in his deportment, being mild and gentle;—and yet with much turn for the ludicrous in his disposition. We were both much attached to Harrow, and sometimes made excursions there together from London to revive our schoolboy recollections.

Midnight.

Read the Italian translation by Guido Sorelli of the German Grillparzer—a devil of a name, to be sure, for posterity; but they *must* learn to pronounce it. With all the allowance for a *translation,* and above all, an *Italian* translation (they are the very worst of translators, except from the Classics—Annibale Caro, for instance—and *there,* the bastardy of their language helps them, as, by way of *looking legitimate,* they ape their father's tongue); —but with every allowance for such a disadvantage, the tragedy of *Sappho* is superb and sublime! There is no denying it. The man has done a great thing in writing that play. And *who is he*? I know him not; but *ages will.* 'Tis a high intellect.

I must premise, however, that I have read *nothing* of Adolph Milliner's (the author of *Guilt*), and much less of Goethe, and Schiller, and Wieland, than I could wish. I only know them through the medium of English, French, and Italian translations. Of the *real* language I know absolutely nothing,—except oaths learned from postillions and officers in a squabble! I can *swear* in German potently, when I like —"Sacrament—*Verfluchter—Hundsfott*"—and so forth; but I have little less of their energetic conversation.

I like, however, their women, (I was once *so desperately* in love with a German woman, Constance,) and all that I have read, translated, of their writings, and all that I have seen on the Rhine of their country and people—all, except the Austrians, whom I abhor, loathe, and—I cannot find words for my hate of them, and should be sorry to find deeds correspondent to my hate; for I abhor cruelty more than I abhor the Austrians—except on an impulse, and then I am savage—but not deliberately so.

Grillparzer is grand—antique—*not so simple* as the ancients, but very simple for a modern—too Madame de Stael*ish*, now and then—but altogether a great and goodly writer.

January 13, 1821, Saturday.

Sketched the outline and Drams. Pers. of an intended tragedy of Sardanapalus, which I have for some time meditated. Took the names from Diodorus Siculus, (I know the history of Sardanapalus, and have known it since I was twelve years old,) and read over a passage in the ninth vol. octavo, of Mitford's *Greece,* where he rather vindicates the memory of this last of the Assyrians.

Dined—news come—the *Powers* mean to war with the peoples. The intelligence seems positive—let it be so—they will be beaten in the end. The king-times are fast finishing. There will be blood shed like water, and tears like mist; but the peoples will conquer in the end. I shall not live to see it, but I foresee it.

I carried Teresa the Italian translation of Grillparzer's *Sappho,* which she promises to read. She quarrelled with me, because I said that love was *not the loftiest* theme for true tragedy; and, having the advantage of her native language, and natural female eloquence, she overcame my fewer arguments. I believe she was right. I must put more love into *Sardanapalus* than I intended. I speak, of course, *if* the times will allow me leisure. That *if* will hardly be a peace-maker.

January 14, 1821.

Turned over Seneca's tragedies. Wrote the opening lines of the intended tragedy of *Sardanapalus.* Rode out some miles into the forest. Misty and rainy. Returned—dined—wrote some more of my tragedy.

Read Diodorus Siculus—turned over Seneca, and some other books. Wrote some more of the tragedy. Took a glass of grog. After having ridden hard in rainy weather, and scribbled, and scribbled again, the spirits (at least mine) need a little exhilaration, and I don't like laudanum now as I used to do. So I have mixed a glass of strong waters and single waters, which I shall now proceed to empty. Therefore and thereunto I conclude this day's diary.

The effect of all wines and spirits upon me is, however, strange. It *settles,* but it makes me gloomy—gloomy at the very moment of their effect, and not gay hardly ever. But it composes for a time, though sullenly.

January 15, 1821.

Weather fine. Received visit. Rode out into the forest—fired pistols. Returned home—dined—dipped into a volume of Mitford's *Greece*—wrote part of a scene of *Sardanapalus.* Went out—heard some music—heard some politics. More ministers from the other Italian powers gone to Congress. War seems certain—in that case, it will be a savage one. Talked over various important matters with one of the initiated. At ten and half returned home.

I have just thought of something odd. In the year 1814, Moore ("the poet," *par excellence,* and he deserves it) and I were going together, in the same carriage, to dine with Earl Grey, the *Capo Politico* of the remaining Whigs. Murray, the magnificent (the illustrious publisher of that name), had just sent me a Java gazette —I know not why, or wherefore. Pulling it out, by way of curiosity, we found it to contain a dispute (the said Java gazette) on Moore's merits and mine. I think, if I had been there, that I could have saved them the trouble of disputing on the subject. But, there is *fame* for you at six and twenty! Alexander had conquered India at the same age; but I doubt if he was disputed about, or his conquests compared with those of Indian Bacchus, at Java.

It was a great fame to be named with Moore; greater to be compared with him; greatest—-*pleasure,* at least— to be *with* him; and, surely, an odd coincidence, that we should be dining together while they were quarrelling about us beyond the equinoctial line. Well, the same evening, I met Lawrence the painter, and heard one of Lord Grey's daughters (a fine, tall, spirit-looking girl, with much of the *patrician thoroughbred look* of her father, which I dote upon) play on the harp, so modestly and ingenuously, that she *looked music.* Well, I would rather have had my talk with Lawrence (who talked delightfully) and heard the girl, than have had all the fame of Moore and me put together.

The only pleasure of fame is that it paves the way to pleasure; and the more intellectual our pleasure, the better for the pleasure and for us too. It was, however, agreeable to have heard our fame before dinner, and a girl's harp after.

January 16, 1821.

Read—rode—fired pistols—returned—dined—wrote—visited—heard music—talked nonsense—and went home.

Wrote part of a Tragedy—advanced in Act 1st with "all deliberate speed." Bought a blanket. The weather is still muggy as a London May—mist, mizzle, the air replete with Scotticisms, which, though fine in the descriptions of Ossian, are somewhat tiresome in real, prosaic perspective. Politics still mysterious.

January 17, 1821.

Rode i' the forest—fired pistols—dined. Arrived a packet of books from England and Lombardy—English, Italian, French and Latin. Read till eight—went out.

January 18, 1821.

To-day, the post arriving late, did not ride. Read letters—only two gazettes instead of twelve now due. Made Lega write to that negligent Galignani, and added a postscript. Dined.

At eight proposed to go out. Lega came in with a letter about a bill *unpaid* at Venice, which I thought paid months ago. I flew into a paroxysm of rage, which almost made me faint. I have not been well ever since. I deserve it for being such a fool—but it *was* provoking—a set of scoundrels! It is, however, but five and twenty pounds.

January 19, 1821.

Rode. Winter's wind somewhat more unkind than ingratitude, though Shakspeare says otherwise. At least, I am so much more accustomed to meet with ingratitude than the north wind, that I thought the latter the sharper of the two. I had met with both in the course of the twenty-four hours, so could judge.

Thought of a plan of education for my daughter Allegra, who ought to begin soon with her studies. Wrote a letter—afterwards a postsrcipt. Rather in low spirits—certainly hippish—liver touched—will take a dose of salts.

I have been reading the Life, by himself and daughter, of Mr. R. L. Edgeworth, the father of *the* Miss Edgeworth. it is altogether a great name. In 1813, I recollected to have met them in the fashionable world of London (of which I then formed an item, a fraction, the segment of a circle, the unit of a million, the nothing of something) in the assemblies of the hour, and at a breakfast of Sir Humphry and Lady Davy's, to which I was invited for the nonce. I had been the lion of 1812: Miss Edgeworth and Madame de Stael, with "the Cossack," towards the end of 1813, were the exhibitions of the succeeding year.

I thought Edgeworth a fine old fellow, of a clarety, elderly, red complexion, but active, brisk, and endless. He was seventy, but did not look fifty—no, nor forty-eight even. I had seen poor Fitzpatrick not very long before—a man of pleasure, wit, eloquence, all things. He tottered—but still talked like a gentleman, though feebly. Edgeworth bounced about, and talked loud and long; but he seemed neither weakly nor decrepit, and hardly old.

He began by telling "that he had given Dr. Parr a dressing, who had taken him for an Irish bogtrotter," etc., etc. Now I, who know Dr. Parr, and who know (*not* by experience—for I never should have presumed so far as to contend with him—but by hearing him *with* others, and pothers) that it is not so easy a matter to "dress him," thought Mr. Edgeworth an assertor of what was not true. He could not have stood before Parr for an instant. For the rest, he seemed intelligent, vehement, vivacious, and full of life. He bids fair for a hundred years.

He was not much admired in London, and I remember a "ryghte merrie" and conceited jest which was rife among the gallants of the day,—viz. a paper had been presented for the *recall of Mrs. Siddons to the stage,* (she having lately taken leave, to the loss of ages,—for nothing ever was, or can be, like her,) to which all men had been called to subscribe. Whereupon Thomas Moore, of profane and poetical memory, did propose that a similar paper should be *sub*scribed and *circum*scribed "for the recall of Mr. Edgeworth to Ireland."

The fact was—every body cared more about *her.* She was a nice little unassuming "Jeanie Deans-looking body," as we Scotch say—and, if not handsome, certainly not ill-looking. Her conversation was as quiet as herself. One would never have guessed she could write *her name*; whereas her father talked, *not* as if he could write nothing else, but as if nothing else was worth writing.

As for Mrs. Edgeworth, I forget—except that I think she was the youngest of the party. Altogether, they were an excellent cage of the kind; and succeeded for two months, till the landing of Madame de Stael.

To turn from them to their works, I admire them; but they excite no feeling, and they leave no love—except for some Irish steward or postillion. However, the impression of intellect and prudence is profound—and may be useful.

January 21, 1821.

Rode—fired pistols. Read from Grimm's *Correspondence.* Dined—went out—heard music—returned— wrote a letter to the Lord Chamberlain to request him to prevent the theatres from representing the Doge, which the Italian papers say that they are going to act. This is pretty work—what! without asking my consent, and even in opposition to it!

January 21, 1821.

Fine, clear, frosty day—that is to say, an Italian frost, for their winters hardly get beyond snow; for which reason nobody knows how to skate (or skait)—a Dutch and English accomplishment. Rode out, as usual, and fired pistols. Good shooting —broke four common, and rather small, bottles, in four shots, at fourteen paces, with a common pair of pistols and indifferent powder. Almost as good *wafering* or shooting—considering the difference of powder and pistol,—as when, in 1809, 1810, 1811, 1812, 1813, 1814, it was my luck to split walking-sticks, wafers, half-crowns, shillings, and even the *eye* of a walking-stick, at twelve paces, with a single bullet—and all by *eye* and calculation; for my hand is not steady, and apt to change with the very weather. To the prowess which I here note, Joe Manton and others can bear testimony; for the former taught, and the latter has seen me do, these feats.

Dined—visited—came home—read. Remarked on an anecdote in Grimm's *Correspondence,* which says that "Regnard et la plûpart des poëtes comiques étaient gens bilieux et mélancoliques; et que M. de Voltaire, qui est très gai, n'a

Francesca of Rimini, in five acts; and I am not sure that I would not try Tiberius. I think that I could extract a something, of *my* tragic, at least, out of the gloomy sequestration and old age of the tyrant—and even out of his sojourn at Caprea—by softening the *details,* and exhibiting the despair which must have led to those very vicious pleasures. For none but a powerful and gloomy mind overthrown would have had recourse to such solitary horrors,—being also, at the same time, *old,* and the master of the world.

Memoranda.

What is Poetry?—The feeling of a Former world and Future.

Thought Second.

Why, at the very height of desire and human pleasure,—worldly, social, amorous, ambitious, or even avaricious,—does there mingle a certain sense of doubt and sorrow—a fear of what is to come—a doubt of what *is*—a retrospect to the past, leading to a prognostication of the future? (The best of Prophets of the future is the Past.) Why is this, or these?—I know not, except that on a pinnacle we are most susceptible of giddiness, and that we never fear falling except from a precipice—the higher, the more awful, and the more sublime; and, therefore, I am not sure that Fear is not a pleasurable sensation; at least, *Hope* is; and *what Hope* is there without a deep leaven of Fear? and what sensation is so delightful as Hope? and, if it were not for Hope, where would the Future be?—in hell. It is useless to say *where* the Present is, for most of us know; and as for the Past, *what* predominates in memory?—*Hope baffled.* Ergo, in all human affairs, it is Hope—Hope—Hope. I allow sixteen minutes, though I never counted them, to any given or supposed possession. From whatever place we commence,! we know where it all must end. And yet, what good is there in knowing it? It does not make men better or wiser. During the greatest horrors of the greatest plagues, (Athens and Florence, for example—see Thucydides and Machiavelli,) men were more cruel and profligate than ever. It is all a mystery. I feel most things, but I know nothing, except

— — — — — — — —

— — — — — — — —

— — — — — — — —[iii]

Thought for a Speech of Lucifer, in the Tragedy of Cain:—

> Were *Death* an *evil,* would *I* let thee *live*?
> Fool! live as I live—as thy father lives,
> And thy son's sons shall live for evermore.

Past Midnight. One o' the clock.

I have been reading Frederick Schlegel (brother to the other of the name) till now, and I can make out nothing. He evidently shows a great power of words, but there is nothing to be taken hold of. He is like Hazlitt, in English, who *talks pimples*—a red and white corruption rising up (in little imitation of mountains upon maps), but containing nothing, and discharging nothing, except their own humours.

I dislike him the worse, (that is, Schlegel,) because he always seems upon the verge of meaning; and, lo, he goes down like sunset, or melts like a rainbow, leaving a rather rich confusion,—to which, however, the above comparisons do too much honour.

Continuing to read Mr. Frederick Schlegel. He is not such a fool as I took him for, that is to say, when he speaks of the North. But still he speaks of things *all over the world* with a kind of authority that a philosopher would disdain, and a man of common sense, feeling, and knowledge of his own ignorance, would be ashamed of. The man is evidently wanting to make an impression, like his brother,—or like George in the Vicar of Wakefield, who found out that all the good things had been said already on the right side, and therefore "dressed up some paradoxes" upon the wrong side—ingenious, but false, as he himself says—to which " the learned world "said nothing, nothing at all, sir." The "learned world," however, *has* said something to the brothers Schlegel.

It is high time to think of something else. What they say of the antiquities of the North is best.

January 29, 1821.

Yesterday, the woman of ninety-five years of age was with me. She said her eldest son (if now alive) would have been seventy. She is thin—short, but active—hears, and sees, and talks incessantly. Several teeth left—all in the lower jaw, and single front teeth. She is very deeply wrinkled, and has a sort of scattered grey beard over her chin, at least as long as my mustachios. Her head, in fact, resembles the drawing in crayons of Pope the poet's mother, which is in some editions of his works.

I forgot to ask her if she remembered Alberoni (legate here), but will ask her next time. Gave her a louis—ordered her a new suit of clothes, and put her upon a weekly pension. Till now, she had worked at gathering wood and pine-nuts in the forest—pretty work at ninety-five years old! She had a dozen children, of whom some are alive. Her name is Maria Montanari.

Met a company of the sect (a kind of Liberal Club) called the *Americani* in the forest, all armed, and singing, with all their might, in Romagnuole—"*Sem* tutti soldat' per la liberta" ("we are all soldiers for liberty"). They cheered me as I passed—I returned their salute, and rode on. This may show the spirit of Italy at present.

My to-day's journal consists of what I omitted yesterday. To-day was much as usual. Have rather a better opinion of the writings of the Schlegels than I had four-and-twenty hours ago; and will amend it still further, if possible.

They say that the Piedmontese have at length arisen—*ça ira!*

Read Schlegel. Of Dante he says, "that at no time has the greatest and most national of all Italian poets ever been much the favourite of his countrymen." 'Tis false! There have been more editors and commentators (and imitators, ultimately) of Dante than of all their poets put together. *Not* a favourite! Why, they talk Dante —write Dante—and think and dream Dante at this moment (1821) to an excess, which would be ridiculous, but that he deserves it.

In the same style this German talks of gondolas on the Arno—a precious fellow to dare to speak of Italy!

He says also that Dante's chief defect is a want, in a word, of gentle feelings. Of gentle feelings!—and Francesca of Rimini—and the father's feelings in Ugolino— and Beatrice—and "La Pia!" Why, there is gentleness in Dante beyond all gentleness, when he is tender. It is true that, treating of the Christian Hades, or Hell, there is not much scope or site for gentleness—but who *but* Dante could have introduced any "gentleness" at all into *Hell*? Is there any in Milton's? No—and Dante's Heaven is all love, and glory and majesty.

One o'clock.

I have found out, however, where the German is right —it is about the *Vicar of Wakefield.* "Of all romances in miniature (and, perhaps, this is the best shape in which Romance can appear) the *Vicar of Wakefield* is, I think, the most exquisite." He *thinks*!—he might be sure. But it is very well for a Schlegel. I feel sleepy, and may as well get me to bed. To-morrow there will be fine weather.

"Trust on, and think to-morrow will repay."

January 30, 1821.

The Count P. G. this evening (by commission from the Ci.) transmitted to me the new *words* for the next six months. * * * and * * *. The new sacred word is * * * —the reply * * *—the rejoinder * * *. The former word (now changed) was * * * —there is also * * *—* * *.[iv] Things seem fast coming to a crisis—*ça ira!*

We talked over various matters of moment and movement. These I omit;—if they come to any thing, they will speak for themselves. After these, we spoke of Kosciusko. Count R. G. told me that he has seen the Polish officers in the Italian war burst into tears on hearing his name.

Something must be up in Piedmont—all the letters and papers are stopped. Nobody knows anything, and the Germans are concentrating near Mantua. Of the decision of Leybach nothing is known. This state of things cannot last long. The ferment in men's minds at present cannot be conceived without seeing it.

January 31, 1821.

For several days I have not written any thing except a few answers to letters. In momentary expectation of an explosion of some kind, it is not easy to settle down to the desk for the higher kinds of composition. I *could* do it, to be sure, for, last summer, I wrote my drama in the very bustle of Madame la Contessa G.'s divorce, and all its process of accompaniments. At the same time, I also had the news of the loss of an important lawsuit in England. But these were only private and personal business; the present is of a different nature.

I suppose it is this, but have some suspicion that it may be laziness, which prevents me from writing; especially as Rochefoucalt says that "laziness often masters them all"—speaking of the *passions.* If this were true, it could hardly be said that "idleness is the "root of all evil," since this is supposed to spring from the passions only: *ergo,* that which masters all the passions (laziness, to wit) would in so much be a good. Who knows?

Midnight.

I have been reading Grimm's *Correspondence.* He repeats frequently, in speaking of a poet, or a man of genius in any department, even in music, (Grétry, for instance,) that he must have *une ame qui se tourmente, un esprit violent.* How far this may be true, I know not; but if it were, I should be a poet "*per excellenza*;" for I have always had *une ame,* which not only tormented itself but every body else in contact with it; and an *esprit violent,* which has almost left me without any *esprit* at all. As to defining what a poet *should* be, it is not worth while, for what are *they* worth? what have they done?

Grimm, however, is an excellent critic and literary historian. His *Correspondence* forms the annals of the literary part of that age of France, with much of her politics, and still more of her "way of life." He is as valuable, and far more entertaining than Muratori or Tiraboschi—I had almost said, than Ginguené—but there we should pause. However, 't is a great man in its line.

Monsieur St. Lambert has,

> "Et lorsqu'à ses regards la lumière est ravie,
> Il n'a plus, en mourant, à perdre que la vie."

This is, word for word, Thomson's

> "And dying, all we can resign is breath,"

without the smallest acknowledgment from the Lorrainer of a poet. M. St. Lambert is dead as a man, and (for any thing I know to the contrary) damned, as a poet, by this time. However, his *Seasons* have good things, and, it may be, some of his own.

February 2, 1821.

I have been considering what can be the reason why I always wake, at a certain hour in the morning, and always in very bad spirits—I may say, in actual despair and despondency, in all respects—even of that which pleased me over night. In about an hour or two, this goes off, and I compose either to sleep again, or, at least, to quiet. In England, five years ago, I had the same kind of hypochondria, but accompanied with so violent a thirst that I have drank as many as fifteen bottles of soda-water in one night, after going to bed, and been still thirsty—calculating, however, some lost from the bursting out and effervescence and overflowing of the soda-water, in drawing the corks, or striking off the necks of the bottles from mere thirsty impatience. At present, I have *not* the thirst; but the depression of spirits is no less violent.

I read in Edgeworth's *Memoirs* of something similar (except that his thirst expended itself on *small beer*) in the case of Sir F. B. Delaval;—but then he was, at least, twenty years older. What is it?—liver? In England, Le Man (the apothecary) cured me of the thirst in three days, and it had lasted as many years. I suppose that it is all hypochondria.

What I feel most growing upon me are laziness, and a disrelish more powerful than indifference. If I rouse, it is into fury. I presume that I shall end (if not earlier by accident, or some such termination), like Swift—"dying at top." I confess I do not contemplate this with so much horror as he apparently did for some years before it happened. But Swift had hardly *begun life* at the very period (thirty-three) when I feel quite an *old sort* of feel.

Oh! there is an organ playing in the street—a waltz, too! I must leave off to listen. They are playing a waltz which I have heard ten thousand times at the balls in London, between 1812 and 1815. Music is a strange thing.

February 5, 1821.

At last, "the kiln's in a low." The Germans are ordered to march, and Italy is, for the ten thousandth time to become a field of battle. Last night the news came.

This afternoon—Count P. G. came to me to consult upon divers matters. We rode out together. They have sent off to the C. for orders. To-morrow the decision ought to arrive, and then something will be done. Returned—dined—read—went out—talked over matters. Made a purchase of some arms for the new enrolled Americani, who are all on tiptoe to march. Gave order for some *harness* and portmanteaus necessary for the horses.

Read some of Bowles's dispute about Pope, with all the replies and rejoinders. Perceive that my name has been lugged into the controversy, but have not time to state what I know of the subject. On some "piping day of peace " it is probable that I may resume it.

February 9, 1821.

Before dinner wrote a little; also, before I rode out, Count P. G. called upon me, to let me know the result of the meeting of the Ci. at F. and at B. * * returned late last night. Every thing was combined under the idea that the Barbarians would pass the Po on the 15th inst. Instead of this, from some previous information or otherwise, they have hastened their march and actually passed two days ago; so that all that can be done at present in Romagna is, to stand on the alert and wait for the advance of the Neapolitans. Every thing was ready, and the Neapolitans had sent on their own instructions and intentions, all calculated for the *tenth* and *eleventh,* on which days a general rising was to take place, under the supposition that the Barbarians could not advance before the 15th.

As it is, they have but fifty or sixty thousand troops, a number with which they might as well attempt to conquer the world as secure Italy in its present state. The artillery marches *last,* and alone, and there is an idea of an attempt to cut part of them off. All this will much depend upon the first steps of the Neapolitans. *Here,* the public spirit is excellent, provided it be kept up. This will be seen by the event.

It is probable that Italy will be delivered from the Barbarians if the Neapolitans will but stand firm, and are united among themselves. *Here* they appear so.

February 10, 1821.

Day passed as usual—nothing new. Barbarians still in march—not well equipped, and, of course, not well received on their route. There is some talk of a commotion at Paris. Rode out between four and six—finished my letter to Murray on Bowles's pamphlets—added postscript. Passed the evening as usual—out till eleven—and subsequently at home.

February 11, 1821.

Wrote—had a copy taken of an extract from Petrarch's Letters, with reference to the conspiracy of the Doge, Marino Faliero, containing the poet's opinion of the matter. Heard a heavy firing of cannon towards Comacchio—the Barbarians rejoicing for their principal pig's birthday, which is to-morrow—or Saint day—I forget which. Received a ticket for the first ball to-morrow. Shall not go to the first, but intend going to the second, as also to the Veglioni.

February 13, 1821.

To-day read a little in Louis B.'s *Hollande,* but have written nothing since the completion of the letter on the Pope controversy. Politics are quite misty for the present. The Barbarians still upon their march. It is not easy to divine what the Italians will now do.

Was elected yesterday *Socio* of the Carnival Ball Society. This is the fifth carnival that I have passed. In the four former, I racketed a good deal. In the present, I have been as sober as Lady Grace herself.

Log-book continued.

February 27, 1821.

I have been a day without continuing the log, because I could not find a blank book. At length I recollected this.

Rode, etc.—wrote down an additional stanza for the 5th canto of *D*[*on*] *J*[*uan*] which I had composed in bed this morning. Visited *l'Amica.* We are invited, on the night of the Veglione (next Dominica) with the Marchesa Clelia Cavalli and the Countess Spinelli Rasponi. I promised to go. Last night there was a row at the ball, of which I am a *socio.* The Vice-legate had the imprudent insolence to introduce *three* of his servants in masque—*without tickets,* too! and in spite of remonstrances. The consequence was, that the young men of the ball took it up, and were near throwing the Vice-legate out of the window. His servants, seeing the scene, withdrew, and he after them. His reverence Monsignore ought to know, that these are not times for the predominance of priests over decorum. Two minutes more, two steps further, and the whole city would have been in arms, and the government driven out of it.

Such is the spirit of the day, and these fellows appear not to perceive it. As far as the simple fact went, the young men were right, servants being prohibited always at these festivals.

Yesterday wrote two notes on the "Bowles and Pope" controversy, and sent them off to Murray by the post. The old woman whom I relieved in the forest (she is ninety-four years of age) brought me two bunches of violets. *Nam vita gaudet mortua floribus.* I was much pleased with the present. An English woman would have presented a pair of worsted stockings, at least, in the month of February. Both excellent things; but the former are more elegant. The present, at this season, reminds one of Gray's stanza, omitted from his elegy:—

> "Here scatter'd oft, the *earliest* of the year,
> By hands unseen, are showers of violets found;
> The red-breast loves to build and warble here,
> And little footsteps lightly print the ground."

As fine a stanza as any in his elegy. I wonder that he could have the heart to omit it.

Last night I suffered horribly—from an indigestion, I believe. I *never* sup—that is, never at home. But, last night, I was prevailed upon by the Countess Gamba's persuasion, and the strenuous example of her brother, to swallow, at supper, a quantity of boiled cockles, and to dilute them, *not* reluctantly, with some Imola wine. When I came home, apprehensive of the consequences, I swallowed three or four glasses of spirits, which men (the venders) call brandy, rum, or hollands, but which gods would entitle spirits of wine, coloured or sugared. All was pretty well till I got to bed, when I became somewhat swollen, and considerably vertiginous. I got out, and mixing some soda-powders, drank them off. This brought on temporary relief. I returned to bed} but grew sick and sorry once and again. Took more soda-water. At last I fell into a dreary sleep. Woke, and was ill all day, till I had galloped a few miles. Query—was it the cockles, or what I took to correct them, that caused the commotion? I think both. I remarked in my illness the complete inertion, inaction, and destruction of my chief mental faculties. I tried to rouse them, and yet could not—and this is the *Soul*!!! I should believe that it was married to the body, if they did not sympathise so much with each other. If the one rose, when the other fell, it would be a sign that they longed for the natural state of divorce. But as it is, they seem to draw together like post-horses.

Let us hope the best—it is the grand possession.

CHAPTER XXII. JANUARY–OCTOBER, 1821

1185.—To Thomas Moore.

Ravenna,
January 2, 1821.

Your entering into my project for the *Memoir,* is pleasant to me. But I doubt (contrary to me my dear Mad[e] Mac F * *, whom I always loved, and always shall —not only because I really *did* feel attached to her *personally,* but because she and about a dozen others of that sex were all who stuck by me in the grand conflict of 1815)—but I doubt, I say, whether the *Memoir* could appear in my lifetime;—and, indeed, I had rather it did not; for a man always *looks dead* after his Life has appeared, and I should certes not survive the appearance of mine. The first part I cannot consent to alter, even although Madame de S[tael]'s opinion of B. C. and my remarks upon Lady C.'s beauty (which is surely great, and I suppose that I have said so—at least, I ought) should go down to our grandchildren in unsophisticated nakedness.

As to Madame de S[tael], I am by no means bound to be her beadsman—she was always more civil to me in person than during my absence. Our dear defunct friend, Monk Lewis, who was too great a bore ever to lie, assured me upon his tiresome word of honour, that at Florence, the said Madame de S[tael] was open-*mouthed* against me; and when asked, in *Switzerland, why* she had changed her opinion, replied, with laudable sincerity, that I had named her in a sonnet with Voltaire, Rousseau, etc. and that she could not help it through decency. Now, I have not forgotten this, but I have been generous,—as mine acquaintance, the late Captain Whitby, of the navy, used to say to his seamen (when "married to the gunner's daughter")—"two dozen and let you off easy." The "two dozen" were with the cat-o'-nine tails;—the "let you off easy" was rather his own opinion than that of the patient. My acquaintance with these terms and practices arises from my having been much conversant with ships of war and naval heroes in the year of my voyages in the Mediterranean. Whitby was in the gallant action off Lissa in 1811. He was brave, but a disciplinarian. When he left his frigate, he left a *parrot,* which was taught by the crew the following sounds—(it must be remarked that Captain Whitby was the image of Fawcett1 the actor, in voice, face, and figure, and that he squinted).

The Parrot *loquitur.*

"Whitby! Whitby! funny eye! funny eye! two dozen, and let you off easy. Oh you —!"

Now, if Madame de B. has a parrot, it had better be taught a French parody of the same sounds.

With regard to our purposed Journal, I will call it what you please, but it should be a newspaper, to make it *pay.* We can call it "The Harp," if you like—or any thing.

I feel exactly as you do about our "art," but it comes over me in a kind of rage every now and then, like * * * *, and then, if I don't write to empty my mind, I go mad. As to that regular, uninterrupted love of writing, which you describe in your friend, I do not understand it. I feel it as a torture, which I must get rid of, but never as a pleasure. On the contrary, I think composition a great pain.

I wish you to think seriously of the Journal scheme—for I am as serious as one can be, in this world, about any thing. As to matters here, they are high and mighty—but not for paper. It is much about the state of things betwixt Cain and Abel. There is, in fact, no law or government at all; and it is wonderful how well things go on without them. Excepting a few occasional murders, (every body killing whomsoever he pleases, and being killed, in turn, by a friend, or relative, of the defunct,) there is as quiet a society and as merry a Carnival as can be met with in a tour through Europe. There is nothing like habit in these things.

I shall remain here till May or June, and, unless "honour comes unlooked for," we may perhaps meet, in France or England, within the year.

Yours, etc.

Of course, I cannot explain to you existing circumstances, as they open all letters.

Will you set me right about your curst *Champs Elysées*?—are they "*és*" or "*ées*" for the adjective? I know nothing of French, being all Italian. Though I can read and understand French, I never attempt to speak it; for I hate it. From the second part of the Memoirs cut what you please.

1186.—To John Murray.

Ravenna,
J^{y} 4th, 1821.

D^{R} M^{Y},—

I write to you in considerable surprise, that, since the first days of November, I have never had a line from you. It is so incomprehensible, that I can only account for it by supposing some accident. I have written to you at least ten letters, to none of which I have had a word of answer: one of them was on your own affairs—a proposal of Galignani, relative to your publications, which I referred to you (as was proper), for your own decision.

Last week I sent (addressed to Mr. D. Kinnaird) two packets containing the 5th Canto of *D.J.* I wish to know what you mean to do? anything or nothing.

Of the State of this country I can only say, that, besides the assassination of the Commandant of the 7th (of which I gave you an account, as I took him up, and he died in my house) that there have been *six* murders committed within twenty miles —three last night.

Yours very truly, B.

P.S.—Have you gotten *the Hints,* that I may alter parts and portions?

I just see, by the papers of Galignani, that there is a new tragedy of great expectation, by Barry Cornwall: of what I have read of his works I liked the *Dramatic Sketches,* but thought his *Sicilian Story* and *Marcian Colonna,* in rhyme, quite spoilt by I know not what affectation of Wordsworth, and Hunt, and Moore, and Myself, all mixed up into a kind of Chaos. I think him very likely to produce a good tragedy, if he keep to a natural style, and not play tricks to form Harlequinades for an audience. As he (B. C. is not his *true* name) was a school-fellow of mine, I take more than common interest in his success, and shall be glad to hear of it speedily. If I had been aware that he was in that line, I should have spoken of him in the preface to *M*[*arino*] *F*[*aliero*]: he will do a World's wonder if he produce a great tragedy. I am, however, persuaded, that this is not to be done by following the old dramatists, who are full of gross faults, pardoned only for the beauty of their language; but by writing naturally and *regularly,* and producing *regular* tragedies, like the *Greeks*; but not in *imitation,*—merely the outline of their conduct, adapted to our own times and circumstances, and of course *no* chorus.

You will laugh, and say, "why don't *you* do so?" I have, you see, tried a Sketch in *Marino Faliero;* but many people think my talent "*essentially undramatic,*" and I am not at all clear that they are not right. If *Marino Faliero* don't fall, in the perusal, I shall, perhaps, try again (but not for the Stage); and, as I think that *love* is not the principal passion for tragedy (and yet most of ours turn upon it), you will not find me a popular writer. Unless it is Love, *furious, criminal,* and *hapless,* it ought not to make a tragic subject: when it is melting and maudlin, it *does,* but it ought not to do; it is then for the Gallery and second price boxes.

If you want to have a notion of what I am trying, take up a *translation* of any of the *Greek* tragedians. If I said the original, it would be an impudent presumption of mine; but the translations are so inferior to the originals, that I think I may risk it. Then judge of the "simplicity of plot, etc.," and do not judge me by your mad old dramatists, which is like drinking Usquebaugh and then proving a fountain: yet after all, I suppose that you do not mean that spirits is a nobler element than a clear spring bubbling in the sun; and this I take to be the difference between the Greeks and those turbid mountebanks—always excepting B. Jonson, who was a Scholar and a Classic. Or, take up a translation of Alfieri, and try the interest, etc., of these my new attempts in the old line, by *him* in *English.* And then tell me fairly your opinion. But don't measure me by YOUR OWN *old* or *new* tailor's yards. Nothing so easy as intricate confusion of plot, and rant. Mrs. Centlivre, in comedy, has *ten times the bustle of Congreve*; but are they to be compared? and yet she drove Congreve from the theatre.

1187.—To John Murray.

Ravenna,
January 6th 1821.

On the "Braziers' Address to be presented in *Armour* by the Company, etc., etc.," as stated in the Newspapers:—

It seems that the Braziers propose soon to pass
An Address and to bear it themselves *all* in *brass*;
A Superfluous Pageant, for by the Lord Harry!
They'll *find,* where they're going, much *more* than they carry.

Or,

The Braziers it seems are determined to pass
An Address and present it themselves All in brass,

A superfluous {pageant / trouble,} for by the Lord Harry!

They'll find, where they're going, much more than they carry.

Ra Jy 8th 1821.

ILLUSTRIOUS SIR,—

I enclose you a long note for the 5th Canto of *Don Juan*; you will find where it should be placed on referring to the MS., which I sent to Mr. Kinnaird. I had subscribed the authorities—Arrian, Plutarch, Hume, etc.—for the *corrections* of Bacon, but, thinking it pedantic to do so, have since erased them.

I have had no letter from you since *one* dated the 3rd of Novr You are a pretty fellow, but I will be even with you some day.

Yours, etc., etc.,
BYRON.

P.S.—The enclosed *epigram* is *not* for publication, recollect.

1188.—To John Murray.

Ra Jy 11th 1821.

Dr My.,—

Put this:—"I am obliged for this excellent translation of the old Chronicle to Mr. Cohen, to whom the reader will find himself indebted for a version which I could not myself (though after so many years intercourse with Italians) have given by any means so purely and so faithfully."

I have looked over *The Hints* (of which, by the way, you have not sent the whole), and see little to alter; I do not see yet any *name* which would be offended, at least of my friends. As an advertisement, a short preface, say, as follows: (Let me have the rest though first.)

"However little this poem may resemble the annexed Latin, it has been submitted to one of the great rules of Horace, having been kept in the desk for more than *nine* years. It was composed at Athens in the Spring of 1811, and received some additions after the author's return to England in the same year."

I protest, and desire you to *protest* stoutly and *publicly* (if it be necessary), against any attempt to bring the tragedy on *any* stage. It was written solely for the reader. It is too regular, and too simple, and of too remote an interest, for the Stage. I will not be exposed to the insolences of an audience, without a remonstrance. As thus,—

"The Author, having heard that, notwithstanding his request and remonstrance, it is the intention of one of the London Managers to attempt the introduction of the tragedy of M.F. upon the Stage, does hereby protest publicly that such a proceeding is as totally against his wishes, as it will prove against the interests of the theatre. That Composition was intended for the Closet only, as the reader will readily perceive. By no kind of adaptation can it be made fit for the present English Stage. If the Courtesy of the Manager is not sufficient to withhold him from exercising his power over a published drama, which the Law has not sufficiently protected from such usurpation"[v]

1189.—To Lady Byron.

Ra. January 11th 1821.

I have just heard from Mr. Kinnaird that (through the jugglery of Hanson) Mr. Bland (with the advice of Counsel) has refused to consent to the Irish loan on mortgage, to Lord Blessington. As you of course did not do this intentionally, I shall not upbraid you or yours, though the connection has proved so unfortunate a one for us all, to the ruin of my fame, of my peace, and the hampering of my fortune. I suppose that the trustees will not object to an English Security—if it can be found-though the terms may necessarily be less advantageous. I had, God knows, unpleasant things enough to contend with just now, without this addition. I presume that you were aware that the Rochdale Cause also was lost last Summer. However it is appealed upon, but with no great hopes on my part. The State of things *here*, you will have seen, if you have received my two letters of last month. But the grand consolation is that all things must end, whether they mend or no.

yrs. ever B

P.S. I wrote to thank you for your consent about the futurities of Augusta's family.— —

I had set my heart upon getting out of those infernal funds, which are all false, and thought that the difficulties were at length over. Yours has been a bitter connection to me in every sense, it would have been better for me never to have been born than to have ever seen you. This sounds harsh, but is it not true? and recollect that I do not mean that you were my *intentional* evil Genius but an Instrument for my destruction—and you yourself have suffered too (poor thing) in the agency, as the lightning perishes in the instant with the Oak which it strikes.

1190.—To John Murray.

R^a^ J^y^ 11th 1821.

DEAR MURRAY,—

I have read with attention the enclosed, of which you have not sent me, however, the *whole* (which *pray* send), and have made the few corrections I shall make—in what I have seen at least. I will omit nothing and alter little: the fact is (as I perceive), that I wrote a great deal better in 1811, than I have ever done since. I care not a sixpence whether the work is popular or not—*that* is *your* concern; and, as I neither name price, nor care about terms, it can concern you little either, so that it pays its expence of printing. I leave all those matters to your magnanimity (which is something like Lady Byron's), which will decide for itself. You have about—I know not what quantity of my stuff on hand just now (a 5th Canto of *Don Juan* also by this time), and must cut according to your cloth.

Is not one of the Seals meant for my Cranium? and the other—who or what is he?

Yours ever truly, BYRON.

P.S.—What have you decided about Galignani? I think you might at least have acknowledged my letter, which would have been civil; also a letter on the late murders here: also, pray do not omit to protest and impede (as far as possible) any

Stage-playing with the tragedy. I hope that the Histrions will see their own interest too well to attempt it See my other letter.

P.S.—You say, speaking of acting, "let me know your pleasure in this." I reply that there is no pleasure in it; the play is *not for acting*: Kemble or Kean could *read* it, but where are they? Do not let me be sacrificed in such a manner: depend upon it, it is some party-work to run down you and your favourite horse. I know something of Harris and Elliston personally; and, if they are not Critics enough to see that it would not do, I think them Gentlemen enough to desist at my request. Why don't they bring out some of the thousands of meritorious and neglected men, who cumber their shelves, instead of dragging me out of the library?

Will you excuse the severe postage, with which my late letters will have taxed you?

"I had taken such strong resolutions against anything of that kind, from seeing how much every body that *did* write for the Stage, was obliged to subject themselves to the players and the town."—Spence's *Anecdotes,* page 22.

1191.—To John Murray.

Ravenna,
January 19, 1821.

DEAR MORAY,—

Yours of ye 29th Ult^{mo} hath arrived. I must really and seriously request that you will beg of Messrs. Harris or Elliston to let the *Doge* alone: it is *not* an acting play; it will not serve *their* purpose; it will destroy *yours* (the Sale); and it will distress me. It is not courteous, it is hardly even gentlemanly, to persist in this appropriation of a man's writings to their Mountebanks.

I have already sent you by last post a short protest to the Public (against this proceeding); in *case* that *they* persist, which I trust that they will not, you must then publish it in the Newspapers. I shall not let them off with that only, if they go on; but make a longer appeal on that subject, and state what I think the injustice of their mode of behaviour. It is hard that I should have all the buffoons in Britain to deal with—*pirates* who *will* publish, and *players* who *will* act—when there are thousands of worthy and able men who can get neither bookseller nor manager for love nor money.

You never answered me a word about *Galignani:* if *you* mean to use the two *documents, do*; if *not, burn* them. I do not choose to leave them in any one's possession: suppose some one found them without the letters, what would they *think*? why, that *I* had been doing the *opposite* of what I *have done,* to wit, referred the whole thing to *you*—an act of civility at least, which required saying, "I have received your letter." I thought that you might have some hold upon those publications by this means: to *me* it can be no interest one way or the other.

The *third* canto of *Don Juan is dull,* but you must really put up with it: if the two first and the two following are tolerable, what do you expect? particularly as I neither dispute with you on it as a matter of criticism, or a matter of business.

Besides, what am I to understand? you and D[s] Kinnaird, and others, write to me, that *the two first* published Cantos are among the *best* that I ever wrote, and are reckoned so: Mrs. Leigh writes that they are thought "*execrable*" (bitter word *that* for an author—Eh, Murray!) as a *composition* even, and that she had heard so much against them that she would *never read them,* and never has. Be that as it may, I can't alter. That is not my forte. If you publish the three new ones without ostentation, they may perhaps succeed.

Pray publish the Dante and the *Pulci* (the *Prophecy of Dante,* I mean): I look upon the Pulci as my grand performance. The remainder of *The Hints,* where be they? Now bring them all out about the same time, otherwise "the *variety*" you wot of will be less obvious.

I am in bad humour: some obstructions in business with the damned trustees, who object to an advantageous loan which I was to furnish to a Nobleman on Mortgage, because his property is in *Ireland,* have shown me how a man is treated in his absence. Oh, if I *do* come back, I will make some of those, who little dream of it, *spin*— or they or I shall go down.

The news here is, that Col. Brown (the Witness-buyer) has been stabbed at Milan, but *not* mortally. I wonder that anybody should dirty their daggers in him. They should have beaten him with Sandbags—an old Spanish fashion.

I sent you a line or two on the Braziers' Company last week, *not* for publication.

Yours ever, B.

The lines were even worthy

> Of —dsworth, the great Metaquizzical poet,
> A man of great merit amongst those who know it,
> Of whose works, as I told Moore last autumn at **Mestri*
> I owe all I know to my passion for *Pastry.*

**Mestri* and *Fusina* are the ferry trajects to Venice: I believe, however, that it was at Fusina that Moore and I embarked in 1819, when Thomas came to Venice, like Coleridge's Spring "slowly up this way."

Omit the dedication to Goethe.

So, you have had a book dedicated to you? I am glad of it, and shall be very happy to see the volume.

I am in a peck of troubles about a tragedy of mine, which is fit only for the (* * * *) closet, and which it seems that the managers, assuming a *right* over published poetry, are determined to enact, whether I will or no, with their own alterations by Mr. Dibdin, I presume. I have written to Murray, to the Lord Chamberlain, and to others, to interfere and preserve me from such an exhibition. I want neither the impertinence of their hisses, nor the insolence of their applause. I write only for the *reader,* and care for nothing but the *silent* approbation of those who close one's book with good humour and quiet contentment.

Now, if you would also write to our friend Perry, to beg of him to mediate with Harris and Elliston to *forbear* this intent, you will greatly oblige me. The play is quite unfit for the stage, as a single glance will show them, and, I hope, *has* shown them; and, if it were ever so fit, I will never have any thing to do willingly with the theatres.

Yours ever, in haste, etc.

1195.—To John Murray.

Ravenna,
J^y 27, 1821.

Dear Moray,—

I *have* mentioned Mr. Cohen in a letter to you list week, from which the passage should be extracted aid prefixed to his translation. You will also have received two or three letters upon the subject of the *Manager*: in one I enclosed an epistle for the Lord Chamberlain (in case of the worst), and I even prohibited the *publication* of the Tragedy, limiting it to a few copies for my private friends. But this would be useless, after going so far; so you *may publish* as we intended—only, (if the Managers attempt to act), pray present my letter to the Ld Chamberlain, and publish my appeal in the paper, adding that it has all along been against my wishes that it should be represented.

I differ from you about the *Dante*, which I think should be published *with* the tragedy. But do as you please: you must be the best judge of your own craft. I agree with you about the *title.* The play may be good or bad, but I flatter myself that it is original as a picture of *that* kind of passion, which to my mind is so natural, that I am convinced that I should have done precisely what the Doge did on those provocations.

I am glad of Foscolo's approbation.

I wish you would send me the remainder of *The Hints*—you only sent about half of them. As to the other volume, you should publish them about:he same period, or else *what* becomes of the "*variety*" which you talk so much of?

Excuse haste. I believe I mentioned to you that— I forget what it was; but no matter.

Thanks for your compliments of the year: I hope that it will be pleasanter than the last. I speak with reference to *England* only, as far as regards myself, *where* I had every kind of disappointment—lost an important lawsuit—and the trustees of that evil Genius of a woman, L[y] Byron (who was born for my desolation), refusing to allow of an advantageous loan to be made from my property to Lord Blessington, etc., etc., by way of closing the four seasons. These, and a hundred other such things, made a year of bitter business for me in England: luckily, things were a little pleasanter for me *here,* else I should have taken the liberty of Hannibal's ring.

Pray thank Gifford for all his goodnesses: the winter is as cold *here* as Parry's polarities. I must now take a canter in the forest; my horses are waiting.

Yours ever and truly, B.

P.S.—It is exceedingly strange that you have never acknowledged the receipt of *Galignani's letters,* which I enclosed to you three months ago: what the devil does that mean?

1196.—To Richard Belgrave Hoppner.

Ravenna,
January 28th 1821.

My dear Hoppner,—

I have not heard from you for a long time, and now I must trouble you—as usual. Messrs. Siri and Wilhalm have given up business. They had three cases of mine. I desired them to consign these cases to Missiaglia. There were 4 Telescopes, a case of Watches and a tin case of English gunpowder, containing about five pounds of the same, which I have had for *five years.* Messrs. Siri and Wilhalm *own* to all three, and the telescopes and watches they have consigned to M., of the others (though they mention it in a letter of last week) they *now* say nothing—and M. pretends that it is not to be found.

Will you make enquiry? It is of importance to me, because I can find no other such in these countries, and can be of none to the Government because it is so small a quantity. If it has in fact been seized by these fellows, I will present a slight memorial to the Governor of Venice; which (though it may not get me back my three or four pounds of powder) will at least tell him some truths upon things in general, as I shall use pretty strong terms in expressing myself.

I shall feel very much obliged by your making this enquiry.

Of course upon other topics I can say nothing at present, except that your Dutch friends will have their hands full one of these days probably.

Pray let me know how you are.

I am, yours very truly, BYRON.

My best respects to Madame Hoppner. Could not you and I contrive to meet somewhere this spring? I should be *solus.*

P.S.—I sent you all the romances and light reading which Murray has furnished—except the *Monastery,* which you told me that you had already seen. I wish the things which were at Siri and W.'s to *remain* with Missiaglia, and not to be *sent* here, at least for the present. Pray do what you can about the p—r; it is hard those rascals should seize the poor little miserable canister, after the many I shot in relieving their wretched population at Venice. I did not trouble you with the things, because I thought that they would bore you. I never got the *translation* of the German *translation,* but it don't signify as you said it was not worth while. They are printing some things of mine in England, and if any parcel comes from London addressed to me at Venice, pray take any work of mine out you like—and keep it, as well as any other books you choose.

They are always addressed to Missiaglia.

1197.—To John Murray.

Ravenna,
Febr[y] 2, 1821.

D[R] MORAY,—

Your letter of excuses has arrived. I receive the letter, but do not admit the excuses, except in courtesy; as when a man treads on your toes and begs your pardon, the pardon is granted, but the joint aches, especially if there be a corn upon it. However, I shall scold you presently.

In the last speech of *The Doge,* there occurs (I think, from memory) the phrase

"And Thou who makest and unmakest Suns;"

Change this to

"And Thou who kindlest and who quenchest Suns;"

that is to say, if the verse runs equally well, and Mr. Gifford thinks the expression improved. Pray have the bounty to attend to this. You are grown quite a minister of State: mind if some of these days you are not thrown out. God will not be always a Tory, though Johnson says the first Whig was the Devil.

You have learnt one secret from Mr. Galignani's (somewhat tardily acknowledged) correspondence. This is, that an *English* Author may dispose of his exclusive copyright in *France*—a fact of some consequence (in *time of peace*), in the case of a popular writer. Now I will tell you what *you* shall do, and take no advantage of you, though you were scurvy enough never to acknowledge my letter for three months. Offer Galignani the *refusal* of the copyright in France; if he refuses, appoint any bookseller in France you please, and I will sign any assignment you please, and it shall never cost you a Sou on *my* account.

Recollect that *I* will have nothing to do with it, except as far as it may secure the copyright to yourself. I will have no bargain but with English publishers, and I desire no interest out of that country.

Now, that's fair and open, and a little handsomer than your *dodging* silence, to see what would come of it. You are an excellent fellow, *mio Caro* Moray, but there is still a little leaven of Fleet-street about you now and then—a crumb of the old loaf. You have no right to act suspiciously with me, for I have given you no reasons. I shall always be frank with you; as, for instance, whenever you talk with the votaries of Apollo arithmetically, it should be in guineas, not pounds—to poets as well as physicians, and bidders at Auctions.

I shall say no more at this present, save that I am,

Yours very truly, BYRON.

P.S.—If you venture, as you say, to Ravenna this year, through guns, which (like the Irishman's), "shoot round a corner," I will exercise the rites of hospitality while you live, and bury you handsomely (though not in holy ground), if you get "shot or slashed in a creagh or splore," which are rather frequent here of late among the native parties. But perhaps your visit may be anticipated; for Lady Medea's trustees and my Attorneo do so thwart all business of mine, in despite of Mr. K^d and myself, that I may probably come to your country; in which case write to her Ladyship the duplicate of the epistle the King of France wrote to Prince John. She and her Scoundrels shall find it so.

1198.—To John Murray.

R^a F^y 12th 1821.

D^R S^R,—

You are requested to take particular care that the enclosed note is printed with the drama. Foscolo or Hobhouse will correct the Italian; but do not *you* delay: every one of your cursed proofs is a two months' delay, which you only employ to gain time, because you think it a bad speculation.

Yours,

BYRON.

P.S.—If the thing fails in the publication, you are not *pinned* even to your own terms: merely print and publish *what* I desire you, and if you don't succeed, I will abate whatever you please. I care nothing about that; but I wish what I desire to be printed, to be so.

I have never had the remaining sheet of the *Hints from H*[*orace*].

In the letter on Bowles, after the words "the long walls of Palestrina and Malamocco," add "*i Murazzi,*" which is their Venetian title.

Mr. M. is requested to acknowledge receipt of this by return of post.

1199.—To Elizabeth, Duchess of Devonshire.

Ravenna,
February 15, 1821.

MADAM,—

I am about to request a favor of your Grace without the smallest personal pretensions to obtain it. It is not however for myself, and yet I err—for surely what we solicit for our friends is, or ought to be, nearest to ourselves. If I fail in this application, my intrusion will be its own reward; if I succeed, your Grace's reward will consist in having done a good action, and mine in your pardon for my presumption. My reason for appealing to you is this—your Grace has been long in Rome, and could not be long any where without the influence and the inclination to do good.

Among the list of exiles on account of the late suspicions—and the intrigues of the Austrian Government (the most infamous in history) there are many of my acquaintances in Romagna and some of my friends; of these more particularly are the two Counts Gamba (father and son) of a noble and respected family in this city. In common with thirty or more of all ranks they have been hurried from their home without process—without hearing—without accusation. The father is universally respected and like, his family is numerous and mostly young—and these are now left without protection: the son is a very fine young man, with very little of the vices of his age or climate; he has I believe the honor of an acquaintance with your Grace—having been presented by Madame Martinetti. He is but one and twenty and lately returned from his studies at Rome. Could your Grace, or would you—ask the repeal of both, or at least of *one* of these from those in power in the holy City? They are not aware of my solicitation in their behalfs—but I will take it upon me to say that they shall neither dishonour your goodness nor my request. If only one can be obtained—let it be the father on account of his family. I can assure your Grace and the very pious Government in question that there can be no danger in this act of—*clemency* shall I call it? It would be but justice with us—but here! let them call it what they will....I cannot express the obligation which I should *feel* —I say *feel* only—because I do not see how I could repay it to your Grace—I have not the slightest claim upon you, unless perhaps through the memory of our late friend, Lady Melbourne—I say friend only—for my relationship with her family has not been fortunate for them, nor for me. If therefore you should be disposed to grant my request I shall set it down to your tenderness for her who is gone, and who was to me the best and kindest of friends. The persons for whom I solicit will (in case of success) neither be in ignorance of their protectress, nor indisposed to acknowledge their sense of her kindness by a strict observance of such conduct as may justify her interference. If my acquaintance with your Grace's character were even slighter than it through the medium of some of our English friends, I had only to turn to the letters of Gibbon (now on my table) for a full testimony to its high and amiable qualities.

I have the honor to be, with great respect,

Your Grace's most obedient very humble Servant, BYRON.

P.S.—Pray excuse my scrawl which perhaps you may be enabled to decypher from a long acquaintance with the handwriting of Lady Bessborough. I omitted to mention that the measures taken here have been as *blind* as impolitic—this I happen to *know*. Out of the list in Ravenna—there are at least *ten* not only innocent, but even opposite in principles to the liberals. It has been the work of some blundering Austrian spy or angry priest to gratify his private hatreds. Once more your pardon.

1200.—To John Murray.

Ravenna,
February 16, 1821.

DEAR MORAY,—

In the month of March will arrive from Barcelona Signor Curioni, engaged for the Opera. He is an acquaintance of mine, and a gentlemanly young man, high in his profession. I must request your personal kindness and patronage in his favour. Pray introduce him to such of the theatrical people, Editors of Papers, and others, as may be useful to him in his profession, publicly and privately.

He is accompanied by the Signora Arpalice Taruscelli, a Venetian lady of great beauty and celebrity, and a particular friend of mine: your natural gallantry will I am sure induce you to pay her proper attention. Tell Israeli that, as he is fond of *literary* anecdotes, she can tell him some of your acquaintance abroad. I presume that he speaks Italian. Do not neglect this request, but do them and me this favour in their behalf. I shall write to some others to aid you in assisting them with your countenance.

I agree to your request of leaving in abeyance the terms for the three *D. J.s,* till you can ascertain the effect of publication. If I refuse to alter, you have a claim to so much courtesy in return. I had let you off your proposal about the price of the Cantos, last year (the 3rd and 4th always to reckon as *one* only), and I do not call upon you to renew it. You have therefore no occasion to fight so shy of such subjects, as I am not, conscious of having given you occasion.

The 5th is so far from being the last of *D. J.,* that it is hardly the beginning. I meant to take him the tour of Europe, with a proper mixture of siege, battle, and adventure, and to make him finish as *Anacharsis Cloots* in the French revolution. To how many cantos this may extend, I know not, nor whether (even if I live) I shall complete it; but this was my notion: I meant to have made him a *Cavalier Servente* in Italy, and a cause for a divorce in England, and a Sentimental "Werther-faced man" in Germany, so as to show the different ridicules of the society in each of those countries, and to have displayed him gradually *gâté* and *blasé* as he grew older, as is natural. But I had not quite fixed whether to make him end in Hell, or in an unhappy marriage, not knowing which would be the severest. The Spanish tradition says Hell: but it is probably only an Allegory of the other state. You are now in possession of my notions on the subject.

You say *The Doge* will not be popular: did I ever write for *popularity*? I defy you to show a work of mine (except a tale or two) of a popular style or complexion. It appears to me that there is room for a different style of the drama; neither a servile following of the old drama, which is a grossly erroneous one, nor yet *too French,* like those who succeeded the older writers. It appears to me, that good English, and a severer approach to the rules, might combine something not dishonorable to our literature. I have also attempted to make a play without love. And there are neither rings, nor mistakes, nor starts, nor outrageous ranting villains, nor melodrame, in it. All this will prevent it's popularity, but does not persuade me that it is *therefore* faulty. Whatever faults it has will arise from deficiency in the conduct, rather than in the conception, which is simple and severe.

So *you epigrammatize* upon *my epigram*? I will *pay you* for *that,* mind if I don't, some day. I never let any one off in the long run (*who first begins*): remember *Sam,* and see if I don't do you as good a turn. You unnatural publisher 1 what! quiz your own authors! You are a paper Cannibal.

In the letter on Bowles (which I sent by Tuesday's post) after the words "*attempts had been made*" (alluding to the republication of *English Bards*), add the words "*in Ireland*;" for I believe that Cawthorn did not begin his attempts till after I had left England the second time. Pray attend to this. Let me know what you and your Squad think of the letter on Bowles.

I did not think the second *Seal* so bad: surely it is far better than the Saracen's head with which you have sealed your *last letter*; the larger, in *profile,* was surely much better than that.

So Foscolo says he will get you a *seal cut* better in Italy: he means a *throat*—that is the only thing they do dexterously. The Arts—all but Canova's, and Morghen's, and *Ovid's* (I don't *mean poetry*),—are as low as need be: look at the Seal which I gave to Wm Bankes, and own it. How came George Bankes to quote *English Bards* in the House of Commons? All the World keep flinging that poem in my face.

Belzoni *is* a grand traveller, and his English is very prettily broken.

As for News, the Barbarians are marching on Naples, and if they lose a single battle, all Italy will be up. It will be like the Spanish war, if they have any bottom.

Letters opened!—to be sure they are, and that's the reason why I always put in my opinion of the German Austrian Scoundrels: there is not an Italian who loathes them more than I do; and whatever I could do to scour Italy and the earth of their infamous oppression, would be done *con amore.*

Yours, ever and truly, B.

Recollect that the *Hints* must be printed with the *Latin,* otherwise there is no sense.

1201.—To John Murray.

Ravenna,
February 21, 1821.

DEAR SIR,—

In the 44th page, vol. 1st, of Turner's travels (which you lately sent me), it is stated that "Lord Byron, when he expressed such confidence of it's practicability, seems to have forgotten that Leander swam both ways, with and *against* the tide; whereas *he* (Ld B.) only performed the easiest part of the task by swimming *with* it from Europe to Asia." I certainly could not have forgotten, what is known to every Schoolboy, that Leander crossed in the Night and returned towards the morning. My object was, to ascertain that the Hellespont could be crossed *at all* by swimming, and in this Mr. Ekenhead and myself both succeeded, the one in an hour and ten minutes, and the other in one hour and five minutes. The *tide* was *not* in our favour: on the contrary, the great difficulty was to bear up against the current, which, so far from helping us to the Asiatic side, set us down right towards the Archipelago. Neither Mr. Ekenhead, myself, nor, I will venture to add, any person on board the frigate, from Captain (now Admiral) Bathurst downwards, had any notion of a difference of the current on the Asiatic side, of which Mr. Turner speaks. I never heard of it till this moment, or I would have taken the other course. Lieutenant Ekenhead's sole motive, and mine also, for setting out from the European side was, that the little Cape above Sestos was a more prominent starting place, and the frigate, which lay below, close under the Asiatic castle, formed a better point of view for us to swim towards; and, in fact, we landed immediately below it.

Mr. Turner says, "Whatever is thrown into the Stream on this part of the European bank *must* arrive at the Asiatic shore." This is so far from being the case, that it *must* arrive in the Archipelago, if left to the Current, although a strong wind in the Asiatic direction might have such an effect occasionally.

Mr. Turner attempted the passage from the Asiatic side, and failed. "After five and twenty minutes, in which he did not advance a hundred yards, he gave it up from complete exhaustion." This is very possible, and might have occurred to him just as readily on the European side. He should have set out a couple of miles higher, and could then have come out below the European castle. I particularly stated, and Mr. Hobhouse has done so also, that we were obliged to make the real passage of one mile extend to between *three* and *four,* owing to the force of the stream. I can assure Mr. Turner, that his Success would have given me great pleasure, as it would have added one more instance to the proofs of the practicability. It is not quite fair in him to infer, that because *he* failed, Leander could not succeed. There are still four instances on record: a Neapolitan, a young Jew, Mr. Ekenhead, and myself; the two last done in the presence of hundreds of *English* Witnesses.

With regard to the difference of the *current,* I perceived none: it is favourable to the Swimmer on neither side, but may be stemmed by plunging into the Sea, a considerable way above the opposite point of the coast which the Swimmer wishes to make, but still bearing up against it: it is strong, but if you *calculate* well, you may reach land. My own experience and that of others bids me pronounce the passage of Leander perfectly practicable: any young man, in good health and tolerable skill in swimming, might succeed in it from *either* side. I was three hours in swimming across the Tagus, which is much more hazardous, being two hours longer than the passage of the Hellespont. Of what may be done in swimming, I will mention one more instance. In 1818, the Chevalier Mengaldo (a Gentleman of Bassano), a good Swimmer, wished to swim with my friend Mr. Alexander Scott and myself. As he seemed particularly anxious on the subject, we indulged him. We all three started from the Island of the Lido and swam to Venice. At the entrance of the Grand Canal, Scott and I were a good way ahead, and we saw no more of our foreign friend, which, however, was of no consequence, as there was a

Gondola to hold his cloathes and pick him up. Scott swum on till past the Rialto, where he got out, less from fatigue than from *chill,* having been *four hours* in the water, without rest or stay, except what is to be obtained by floating on one's back —this being the *condition* of our performance. I continued my course on to Santa Chiara, comprizing the whole of the Grand Canal (besides the distance from the Lido), and got out where the Laguna once more opens to Fusina. I had been in the water, by my watch, without help or rest, and never touching ground or boat, *four hours* and *twenty minutes.* To this Match, and during the greater part of it's performance, Mr. Hoppner, the Consul General, was witness; and it is well known to many others. Mr. Turner can easily verify the fact, if he thinks it worth while, by referring to Mr. Hoppner. The distance we could not *accurately* ascertain; it was of course considerable.

I crossed the *Hellespont* in *one* hour and ten minutes only. I am now ten years older in time, and twenty in constitution, than I was when I passed the Dardanelles; and yet two years ago I was capable of swimming four hours and twenty minutes; and I am sure that I could have continued two hours longer, though I had on a pair of trowsers, an accoutrement which by no means assists the performance. My two companions were also *four* hours in the water. Mengaldo might be about thirty years of age; Scott about six and twenty.

With this experience in swimming at different periods of life, not only upon the spot, but elsewhere, of various persons, what is there to make me doubt that Leander's exploit was perfectly practicable? If three individuals did more than the passage of the Hellespont, why should he have done less? But Mr. Turner failed, and, naturally seeking a plausible reason for his failure, lays the blame on the *Asiatic* side of the Strait. To me the cause is evident. He tried to swim *directly* across, instead of going higher up to take the vantage. He might as well have tried to *fly* over Mount Athos.

That a young Greek of the heroic times, in love, and with his limbs in full vigour, might have *succeeded* in such an attempt is neither wonderful nor doubtful. Whether he *attempted* it or *not* is another question, because he might have had a small *boat* to save him the trouble.

I am yours very truly, BYRON.

P.S.—Mr. Turner says that the swimming from Europe to Asia was "the *easiest* part of the task." I doubt whether Leander found it so, as it was the return: however, he had several hours between the intervals. The argument of Mr. T., "that higher up or lower down, the strait widens so considerably that he would save little labour by his starting," is only good for indifferent swimmers: a man of any practice or skill will always consider the distance less than the strength of the stream. If Ekenhead and myself had thought of crossing at the *narrowest point,* instead of going up to the Cape above it, we should have been swept down to Tenedos. The Strait is, however, not extremely wide, even where it broadens above and below the forts. As the frigate was stationed some time in the Dardanelles waiting for the firman, I bathed often in the strait subsequently to our traject, and generally on the Asiatic side, without perceiving the greater Strength of the opposing Stream by which the diplomatic traveller palliates his own failure. An amusement in the small bay which opens immediately below the Asiatic fort was to *dive* for the LAND tortoises, which we flung in on purpose, as they amphibiously crawled along the bottom. *This* does not argue any vaster violence of current than on the European shore. With regard to the modest insinuation that we chose the European side as "easier," I appeal to Mr. Hobhouse and Admiral Bathurst if it be true or no? (poor Ekenhead being since dead): had we been aware of any such difference of Current as is asserted, we would at least have proved it, and were not likely to have given it up in the twenty five minutes of Mr. T.'s own experiment. The secret of all this is, that Mr. Turner failed, and that we succeeded; and he is consequently disappointed, and seems not unwilling to overshadow whatever little merit there might be in our Success. Why did he not try the European side? If he had succeeded there, after failing on the Asiatic, his plea would have been more graceful and gracious. Mr. T. may find what fault he pleases with my poetry, or my politics; but I recommend him to leave aquatic reflections, till he is able to swim "five and twenty minutes" without being "*exhausted,*" though I believe he is the first modern Tory who ever swam "*against* the Stream" for half the time.

1202.—To Thomas Moore.

Ravenna,
February 22, 1821.

As I wish the soul of the late Antoine Galignani to rest in peace, (you will have read his death, published by himself, in his own newspaper,) you are requested particularly to inform his children and heirs, that of their "*Literary Gazette,*" to which I subscribed more than *two* months ago, I have only received one *number,* notwithstanding I have written to them repeatedly. If they have no regard for me, a subscriber, they ought to have some for their deceased parent, who is undoubtedly no better off in his present residence for this total want of attention. If not, let me have my francs. They were paid by Missiaglia, the Venetian bookseller. You may also hint to them that when a gentleman writes a letter, it is usual to send an answer. If not, I shall make them "a speech," which will comprise an eulogy on the deceased.

We are here full of war, and within two days of the seat of it, expecting intelligence momently. We shall now see if our Italian friends are good for any thing but "shooting round a corner," like the Irishman's gun. Excuse haste,—I write with my spurs putting on. My horses are at the door, and an Italian Count waiting to accompany me in my ride.

Yours, etc.

P.S.—Pray, amongst my letters, did you get one detailing the death of the commandant here? He was killed near my door, and died in my house.

BOWLES AND CAMPBELL.
To the air of "*How now, Madame Flirt,*" in the *Beggars' Opera.*

BOWLES. Why, how now, saucy Tom,
If you thus must ramble,
I will publish some
Remarks on Mr. Campbell.

Answer.

CAMPBELL. Why, how now, Billy Bowles?
Sure the priest is maudlin!
(*To the public*) How can you, damn your souls!
Listen to his twaddling?

1203.—To Douglas Kinnaird.

Ravenna,
Fy. 22nd, 1821.

DEAR DOUGLAS,—

Read the enclosed letter to Murray, put a wafer in it, and either present or forward it, as you please.

On reading your letter again, I do not know (if the landed interest be so low) whether we should not rather sell out and *purchase,* rather than lend on mortgage, what think you? if a bargain offered. My mother's estate of Gight was sold to the former Lord Aberdeen many years ago, before I was born, I believe; I have always preferred my mother's family for its *roy*alty, and if I could buy it back, I would consent, even at a reduction of income. It is in Scotland. What think you of this or some such? Write to

Yrs. ever, BYRON.

1204.—To John Murray.

Ravenna,
February 26th 1821.

DEAR MORAY,—

Over the *second Note,* viz. the one on Lady M. Montague, I leave you a complete discretionary power of *omission altogether,* or curtailment, as you please, since it may be scarcely chaste enough for the Canting prudery of the day. The *first* note on a different subject you had better append to the letter.

Let me know what your Utican Senate say, and acknowledge all the packets.

Yours ever, BYRON.

Write to *Moore,* and ask him for my lines to *him* beginning with

"My Boat is at the shore:"

they have been published incorrectly: *you* may publish them. I have written *twice* to Thorwalsen without any answer!! Tell *Hobhouse* so; he was *paid* four years ago: you must address some English at Rome upon the subject—I know none there myself.

On the 2nd January 1821.

Upon this day I married and full sore
Repent that marriage, but my father's more.

Or

Upon this day I married, and deplore
That Marriage deeply, but my father's more.

On the same day to
MEDEA.

This day of all our days has done
The most for me and you:
'Tis just *six* years since We were *One*
And *five* since we were two.

1205.—To John Murray.

Ravenna,
March 1st 1821.

DEAR MORAY,—

After the Stanza, near the close of Canto 5th, which ends with

"Has quite the contrary effect on Vice,"

Insert the following:—

Thus in the East they are extremely strict
And *Wedlock* and a *Padlock* mean the same,
Excepting only when the former's picked
It ne'er can be replaced in proper frame,
Spoilt, as a pipe of Claret is when pricked—
But then their own Polygamy's to blame:
Why don't they knead two virtuous souls for life,
Into that moral Centaur, Man and Wife?

I have received the remainder of the *Hints without* the *Latin,* and *without the Note* upon *Pope* from the Letter to the *E*[*dinburgh*] *B*[*lackwood's*] *M*[*agazine*]. Instead of this you send the *lines* on *Jeffrey,* though you know so positively that they were to be omitted, that I *left the direction, that they should be cancelled, appended to my power of Attorney* to you previously to my leaving England, and in case of my demise before the publication of the *Hints.* Of course they must be omitted, and I feel vexed that they were sent.

Has the whole English text been sent regularly continued from the part broken off in the first proofs? And, pray request Mr. Hobhouse to adjust the *Latin* to the English: the imitation is so close, that I am unwilling to deprive it of its principal merit—its closeness. I look upon it and my Pulci as by far the best things of my doing: *you* will not think so, and get frightened for fear I should charge accordingly; but I know that they will *not* be popular, so don't be afraid—publish them together.

The enclosed letter will make you laugh. Pray answer it for me and *secretly,* not to mortify him.

Tell Mr. Balfour that I never wrote for a *prize* in my life, and that the very thought of it would make me write worse than the very worst Scribbler. As for the twenty pounds he wants to gain, you may *send* them to him for me, and *deduct* them in reckoning with Mr. Kinnaird. *Deduct also your own bill for books and powders, etc., etc.,* which must be considerable.

Give my love to Sir W. Scott, and tell him to write more novels: pray send out *Waverley* and the *Guy M.,* and the *Antiquary.* It is five years since I have had a copy. I have read all the others forty times.

Have you received all my packets, on Pope, letters, etc., etc., etc.? I write in great haste.

Yours ever, B.

P.S.—I have had a letter from Hodgson, who, it seems, has also taken up Pope, and adds "the liberties I have taken with *your* poetry in this pamphlet are no more than I might have ventured in those delightful days, etc.:" that may very well be; but if he has said any thing that I don't like, I'll Archbishop of Grenada him. I am in a polemical humour.

1206.—To John Murray.

March 2, 1821.

D[R] MURRAY,—

This was the beginning of a letter which I meant for Perry, but stopt short, hoping you would be able to prevent the theatres. Of course you need not send it; but it explains to you my feelings on the subject. You say that "there is nothing to fear, let them do what they please;" that is to say, that you would see me damned with great tranquillity. You are a fine fellow.

Ravenna,
January 22, 1821.

DEAR SIR,—

I have received a strange piece of news, which cannot be more disagreeable to your Public than it is to me. Letters and the Gazettes do me the honour to say that it is the intention of some of the London Managers to bring forward on their Stage the poem of *Marino Faliero, etc.,* which was never intended for such an exhibition, and I trust will never undergo it. It is certainly unfit for it. I have never written but for the solitary *reader,* and require no experiments for applause beyond his silent approbation. Since such an attempt to drag me forth as a Gladiator in the Theatrical Arena is a violation of all the courtesies of Literature: I trust that the impartial part of the Press will step between me and this pollution. I say pollution, because every violation of a *right* is such, and I claim my right as an author to prevent what I have written from being turned into a Stage-play. I have too much respect for the Public to permit this of my own free will. Had I sought their favour, it would have been by a Pantomime.

I have said that I write only for the reader. Beyond this I cannot consent to any publication, or to the abuse of any publication of mine to the purposes of Histrionism. The applauses of an audience would give me no pleasure; their disapprobation might, however, give me pain. The wager is therefore not equal. You may, perhaps, say, "how can this be? if their disapprobation gives pain, their praise might afford pleasure?" By no means. The kick of an Ass or the Sting of a Wasp may be painful to those who would find nothing agreeable in the Braying of the one or in the Buzzing of the other.

This may not seem a courteous comparison, but I have no other ready; and it occurs naturally.

1207.—To John Murray.

R^{a} March 9th 1821.

ILLUSTRIOUS MORAY,—

You are requested with the "advice of friends" to continue to patch the enclosed "*Addenda*" into my letter to you on the Subject of Bill Bowles's Pope, etc. I think that it may be inoculated into the body of the letter with a little care. Consult, and engraft it.

I enclose you the proposition of a Mr. Fearman, one of your brethren: there is a civil gentleman for you.

Yours truly, B.

1208.—To Douglas Kinnaird.

Ravenna,
March 9th, 1821.

DEAR DOUGLAS,—

You ask me why I don't go to Paris. Ask the trustees. But independent of that consideration, though I read and comprehend French with far more ease and pleasure than Italian (which is a heavy language to read in *prose*), yet my foreign speech is Italian, and my way of life very little adapted to the eternal French vivaciousness, and gregarious loquacity. As to the impression which you say that I should make; at *three* and *twenty* it might perhaps have fascinated me, at three and thirty it is indifferent. It is also incomprehensible to me, how it can be as Moore and you both say, for surely my habits of thought and writing must cut a queer figure in a prose translation, which is the only medium through which they know them. Besides, I am in some measure familiarized and domesticated in Italy, where I put my daughter the other day in a convent for education.

You say nothing of Canto 5th, whence I infer that it has not your imperial approbation. Never mind. Tell Hobhouse that I wrote to him a fortnight ago.

Of politics I *could* say a good deal, and must therefore be silent, for all letters are opened now, and though I care not about myself, I might perhaps compromise others. They *missed* here only by five days. Understand you?

I have had a civil proposal from a Mr. Fearman, bookseller, 170 New Bond Street, to treat for the "Don Juan." Pray give him a *civil* answer for me, and say, "*supposing* that I were the author of that poem, Mr. Murray would have naturally the refusal." F. wrote under the idea that I had not treated with Murray.

It is not my intention to come to England at present. Perhaps I may take a run over after the *coronation,* because I have a little affair to settle which has been on my mind some time. But in case of settling it, and surviving the settlement, I should wish to return to Italy. Till Lady N. goes home how could the *fee* suffice?

Yours ever, B.

Mr. Murray has requested to publish the *Juan,* before he settles, and I have acceded to this. He must also publish the Italian translation from the Morgante, and the Hints from Horace. Have you seen my letter on Bowles' Pope?

1209.—To John Murray.

Rª Mº 12º 1821.

D^{R} M^{Y},—

Insert, where they may seem apt, the inclosed *addenda* to the *Letter on Bowles,* etc.: they will come into the body of the letter, if you consult any of your Utica where to place them. If there is too much, or too harsh, or not intelligible, etc., let me know, and I will alter or omit the portion pointed out.

Yours, B.

P.S.—Please to acknowledge all *packets* containing matters of print by return of post: letters of mere *convenance* may wait your bibliopolar pleasure and leisure.

1210.—To John Murray.

Ravenna,
Marzo, 1821.

DEAR MORAY,—

In my packet of the 12th Instant, in the last sheet (*not* the *half* sheet), last page, *omit* the sentence which (defining, or attempting to define, what and who are gentlemanly) begins,"I should say at least in life, that most military men have it, and few naval; that several men of rank have it, and few lawyers," etc., etc. I say, omit the whole of that Sentence, because, like the "Cosmogony, or Creation of the World," in the *Vicar of Wakefield,* it is not much to the purpose.

In the Sentence above, too, almost at the top of the same page, after the words "that there ever was, or can be, an Aristocracy of poets," add and insert these words—"I do not mean that they should write in the Style of "the Song by a person of Quality, or *parle Euphuism*; but there is a *Nobility* of thought and expression to be found no less in Shakespeare, Pope, and Burns, than in Dante, Alfieri, etc., etc.," and so on. Or, if you please, perhaps you had better omit the whole of the latter digression on the *vulgar* poets, and insert only as far as the end of the Sentence upon Pope's Homer, where I prefer it to Cowper's, and quote Dr. Clarke in favour of its accuracy.

Upon all these points, take an opinion—take the Sense (or nonsense) of your learned visitants, and act thereby. I am very tractable—in PROSE.

Whether I have made out the case for Pope, I know not; but I am very sure that I have been zealous in the attempt. If it comes to the proofs, we shall beat the Blackguards. I will show more *imagery* in twenty lines of Pope than in any equal length of quotation in English poesy, and that in places where they least expect it: for instance, in his lines on *Sporus,*—now, do just *read* them over—the subject is of no consequence (whether it be Satire or Epic)—we are talking of *poetry* and *imagery* from *Nature and Art.* Now, mark the images separately and arithmetically:—

1. The thing of *Silk.*
2. *Curd* of *Ass's* milk.
3. The *Butterfly.*
4. The *Wheel.*
5. Bug with gilded wings.
6. *Painted* Child of dirt.
7. Whose *Buzz.*
8. Well-bred *Spaniels.*
9. *Shallow streams run dimpling.*
10. *Florid impotence.*
11. *Prompter. Puppet squeaks.*
12. *The Ear of Eve.*
13. *Familiar toad.*
14. *Half-frothy half-venom, spits* himself abroad.
15. *Fop* at the *toilet.*
16. *Flatterer* at the *board.*
17. *Amphibious thing.*
18. Now *trips a Lady.*
19. Now *struts a Lord.*
20. A *Cherub's face.*
21. A *reptile* all the rest.
22. The *Rabbins.*
23. Pride that *licks the dust.*

"Beauty that shocks you, parts that none will trust,
Wit that can creep, and *Pride* that *licks* the *dust.*"

I sent you by last *postis* a large packet, which will *not* do for publication (I suspect), being, as the Apprentices say, "damned *low*." I put off also for a week or two sending the Italian Scrawl which will form a Note to it. The reason is that, letters being opened, I wish to "bide a wee."

Well, have you published the Tragedy? and does the Letter take? Is it true, what Shelley writes me, that poor John Keats died at Rome of the *Quarterly Review*? I am very sorry for it, though I think he took the wrong line as a poet, and was spoilt by Cockneyfying, and Suburbing, and versifying Tooke's Pantheon and Lempriere's Dictionary. I know, by experience, that a savage review is Hemlock to a sucking author; and the one on me (which produced the *English Bards, etc.*) knocked me down—but I got up again. Instead of bursting a bloodvessel, I drank three bottles of Claret, and began an answer, finding that there was nothing in the Article for which I could lawfully knock Jeffrey on the head, in an honourable way. However, I would not be the person who wrote the homicidal article, for all the honour and glory in the World, though I by no means approve of that School of Scribbling which it treats upon.

You see the Italians have made a sad business of it. All owing to treachery and disunion amongst themselves. It has given me great vexation. The Execrations heaped upon the Neapolitans by the other Italians are quite in unison with those of the rest of Europe.

Mrs. Leigh writes that Lady *No—ill* is getting *well* again. See what it is to have luck in this world.

I hear that Rogers is not pleased with being called "venerable"—a pretty fellow: if I had thought that he would have been so absurd, I should have spoken of him as defunct—as he really is. Why, betwixt the years he really lived, and those he has been dead, Rogers has lived upon the Earth nearly seventy three years and upwards, as I have proved in a postscript of my letter, by this post, to Mr. Kinnaird.

Let me hear from you, and send me some Soda-powders for the Summer dilution. Write soon.

Yours ever and truly, B.

P.S.—Your latest packet of books is on its way here, but not arrived. *Kenilworth* excellent. Thanks for the pocket-books, of whilk I have made presents to those ladies who like cuts, and landscapes, and all that. I have got an Italian book or two which I should like to send you if I had an opportunity.

I am not at present in the very highest health. Spring probably; so I have lowered my diet and taken to Epsom Salts.

As you say my *prose* is good, why don't you treat with *Moore* for the reversion of the Memoirs?—*conditionally, recollect*; not to be published before decease. *He* has the permission to dispose of them, and I advised him to do so.

1215.—To John Cam Hobhouse.

Ravenna,
April 26th, 1821.

Dear Hobhouse,—

You know by this time, with all Europe, the precious treachery and desertion of the Neapolitans. I was taken in, like many others by their demonstrations, and have probably been more ashamed of them than they are of themselves.

I can write nothing by the post, but if ever we meet, I will tell you a thing or two, of no great importance perhaps, but which will serve you to laugh at. I can't laugh yet, the thing is a little too serious; if the scoundrels had only compromised themselves, it would matter little; but they were busy everywhere, and all for this! The rest of the Italians execrate them as you will do, and all honest men of all nations.

Poland and Ireland were Sparta and Spartac*us* compared to these villains. But there is no room to be sufficiently bilious, nor bile enough to spit upon them.

I have had a letter from the Dougal. And one from you some weeks ago. I can give you no news in return that would interest you, and indeed what can interest one after such a business?

I hear "Rogers cuts *you*" because I called him "venerable." The next time I will state his age, without the respectable epithet annexed to it, which in fact he does not deserve. However he is seventy-three, and I can prove it by the register. We see by the papers that you dine, and return thanks as usual. Fletcher says that "he supposes you have got Bergami's place by this time"; his literal words I assure you, and not a clinch of mine.

With regard to your objections to my chastising that scoundrel Brougham, it will be time enough to answer them (and Douglas's also) if ever we meet again, which is not very certain. When you take away an honourable motive for returning to England, why should I return? To be abused and belied, and to live like a beggar with an income which in any other country would suffice for all the decencies of a gentleman.

Pray write when it suits you. I did not write because there was nothing to say that could be said without being pried into in this country of tyrants and spies, and foreign barbarians let loose upon it again.

From Murray I have had no news to signify, except some literary intelligence about myself and other scribblers. I know nothing of the fortunes of my publications, and can wait.

I hope that you and yours prosper.

Ever yours most affectionately, Bn.

1220.—To Richard Belgrave Hoppner.

Ravenna,
May 11, 1821.

If I had but known your notion about Switzerland before, I should have adopted it at once. As it is, I shall let the child remain in her convent, where she seems healthy and happy, for the present; but I shall feel much obliged if you will *enquire,* when you are in the cantons, about the usual and better modes of education there for females, and let me know the result of your opinions. It is some consolation that both Mr. and Mrs. Shelley have written to approve entirely my placing the child with the nuns for the present. I can refer to my whole conduct, as having neither spared care, kindness, nor expense, since the child was sent to me. The people may say what they please, I must content myself with not deserving (in this instance) that they should speak ill.

The place is a *country* town in a good air, where there is a large establishment for education, and many children, some of considerable rank, placed in it. As a *country* town, it is less liable to objections of every kind. It has always appeared to me, that the moral defect in Italy does *not* proceed from a *conventual* education,—because, to my certain knowledge, they come out of their convents innocent even to *ignorance* of moral evil,—but to the state of society into which they are directly plunged on coming out of it. It is like educating an infant on a mountain-top, and then taking him to the sea and throwing him into it and desiring him to swim. The evil, however, though still too general, is partly wearing away, as the women are more permitted to marry from attachment: this is, I believe, the case also in France. And after all, what is the higher society of England? According to my own experience, and to all that I have seen and heard (and I have lived there in the very highest and what is called the *best*), no way of life can be more corrupt. In Italy, however, it is, or rather *was,* more *systematised*; but *now,* they themselves are ashamed of *regular* Serventism. In England, the only homage which they pay to virtue is hypocrisy. I speak of course of the *tone* of high life;—the middle ranks may be very virtuous.

I have not got any copy (nor have yet had) of the letter on Bowles; of course I should be delighted to send it to you. How is Mrs. H.? well again, I hope. Let me know when you set out. I regret that I cannot meet you in the Bernese Alps this summer, as I once hoped and intended. With my best respects to madam,

I am ever, etc.

P.S.—I gave to a musician*er* a letter for you some time ago—has he presented himself? Perhaps you could introduce him to the Ingrams and other dilettanti. He is simple and unassuming—two strange things in his profession—and he fiddles like Orpheus himself or Amphion: 't is a pity that he can't make Venice dance away from the brutal tyrant who tramples upon it.

1221.—To Francis Hodgson.

Ravenna,
May 12, 1821.

DEAR HODGSON,—

At length your two poems have been sent. I have read them over (with the notes) with great pleasure. I receive your compliments kindly and your censures temperately, which I suppose is all that can be expected among poets. Your poem is, however, excellent, and if not popular only proves that there is a *fortune* in *fame* as in every thing else in this world. Much, too, depends upon a publisher, and much upon luck; and the number of writers is such, that as the mind of a reader can only contain a certain quantum of poetry and poet's glories, he is sometimes saturated, and allows many good dishes to go away untouched (as happens at great dinners), and this not from fastidiousness but fulness.

You will have seen from my pamphlet on Bowles that our opinions are not very different. Indeed, my modesty would naturally *look* at least bashfully on being termed the "first of living minstrels" (by a brother of the art) if both our estimates of "living minstrels" in general did not leaven the praise to a sober compliment. It is something like the priority in a retreat. There is but one of your tests which is not infallible: Translation. There are three or four *French* translations, and several German and Italian which I have seen. Moore wrote to me from Paris months ago that "the French had caught the contagion of Byronism to the highest pitch" and has written since to say that nothing was ever like their "entusymusy" (you remember Braham) on the subject, even through the "slaver of a prose translation:" these are his words. The Paris translation is also very inferior to the Geneva one, which is very fair, although in prose also, so you see that your test of "translateable or not" is not so sound as could be wished. It is no pleasure, however, you may suppose, to be criticised through such a translation, or indeed through any. I give up *Beppo,* though you know that it is no more than an imitation of Pulci and of a style common and esteemed in Italy. I have just published a drama, which is at least good English, I presume, for Gifford lays great stress on the purity of its diction.

I have been latterly employed a good deal more on politics than on anything else, for the Neapolitan treachery and desertion have spoilt all our hopes here, as well as our preparations. The whole country was ready. Of course I should not have sate still with my hands in my breeches' pockets. In fact they were full; that is to say, the hands. I cannot explain further now, for obvious reasons, as all letters of all people are opened. Some day or other we may have a talk over that and other matters. In the mean time there did not want a great deal of my having to finish like Lara.

Are you doing nothing? I have scribbled a good deal in the early part of last year, most of which scrawls will now be published, and part is, I believe, actually printed. Do you mean to sit still about Pope? If you do, it will be the first time. I have got such a headache from a cold and swelled face, that I must take a gallop into the forest and jumble it into torpor. My horses are waiting. So good-bye to you.

Yours ever,

BYRON.

Two hours after the Ave Maria, the Italian date of twilight.

DEAR HODGSON,—

I have taken my canter, and am better of my headache. I have also dined, and turned over your notes. In answer to your note of page 901 I must remark from *Aristotle* and *Rymer,* that the *hero* of tragedy and (I add *meo periculo*) a tragic poem must *be guilty,* to excite "*terror and pity*" the end of tragic poetry. But hear not *me,* but my betters. "The pity which the poet is to labour for is *for* the criminal. The terror is likewise in the punishment of the said criminal, who, if he be represented too great an offender, will *not be pitied*; if altogether *innocent* his punishment will be unjust." In the Greek Tragedy innocence is unhappy often, and the offender escapes. I must also ask you is *Achilles* a *good* character? or is even Æneas anything but a successful runaway? It is for Turnus men feel and not for the Trojan. Who is the hero of *Paradise Lost*? Why Satan,—and Macbeth, and Richard, and Othello, Pierre, and Lothario, and Zanga? If you talk so, I shall "cut you up like a gourd," as the Mamelukes say. But never mind, go on with it.

1222.—To John Murray.

Ravenna,
May 14th 1821.

DEAR MURRAY,—

A Milan paper states that the play has been represented and universally condemned. As remonstrance has been vain, complaint would be useless. I presume, however, for your own sake (if not for mine), that you and my other friends will have at least published my different protests against its being brought upon the stage at all; and have shown that Elliston (in spite of the writer) *forced* it upon the theatre. It would be nonsense to say that this has not vexed me a good deal; but I am not dejected, and I shall not take the usual resource of blaming the public (which was in the right), or my friends for not preventing—what they could not help, nor I neither—a *forced* representation by a Speculating Manager. It is a pity that you did not show them its *unfitness* for ye stage before the play was *published,* and exact a promise from the managers not to act it. In case of their refusal, we would not have published it at all. But this is too late.

Yours,

B.

P.S.—I enclose Mr. Bowles's letters: thank him in my name for their candour and kindness. Also a letter for Hodgson, which pray forward. The Milan paper states that "*I brought forward the play!!!*" This is pleasanter still. But don't let yourself be worried about it; and if (as is likely) the folly of Elliston checks the sale, I am ready to make any deduction, or the entire cancel of your agreement.

You will of course *not* publish my defence of Gilchrist, as, after Bowles's good humour upon the subject, it would be too savage.

Let me hear from you the particulars; for, as yet, I have only the simple fact.

If you knew *what* I have had to go through here, on account of the failure of these rascally Neapolitans, you would be amused. But it is now apparently over. They seemed disposed to throw the whole project and plans of these parts upon me chiefly.

1223.—To Thomas Moore.

May 14, 1821.

If any part of the letter to Bowles has (unintentionally, as far as I remember the contents) vexed you, you are fully avenged; for I see by an Italian paper that, notwithstanding all my remonstrances through all my friends (and yourself among the rest), the managers persisted in attempting the tragedy, and that it has been "unanimously hissed!!" This is the consolatory phrase of the Milan paper, (which detests me cordially, and abuses me, on all occasions, as a Liberal,) with the addition, that *I* "brought the play out" of my own good will.

All this is vexatious enough, and seems a sort of dramatic Calvinism—predestined damnation, without a sinner's own fault. I took all the pains poor mortal could to prevent this inevitable catastrophe—partly by appeals of all kinds, up to the Lord Chamberlain, and partly to the fellows themselves. But, as remonstrance was vain, complaint is useless. I do not understand it —for Murray's letter of the 24th, and all his preceding ones, gave me the strongest hopes that there would be no representation. As yet, I know nothing but the fact, which I presume to be true, as the date is Paris, and the 30th. They must have been in a *hell* of a hurry for this damnation, since I did not even know that it was published; and, without its being first published, the histrions could not have got hold of it. Any one might have seen, at a glance, that it was utterly impracticable for the stage; and this little accident will by no means enhance its merit in the closet.

Well, patience is a virtue, and, I suppose, practice will make it perfect. Since last year (spring, that is) I have lost a lawsuit, of great importance, on Rochdale collieries—have occasioned a divorce—have had my poesy disparaged by Murray and the critics—my fortune refused to be placed on an advantageous settlement (in

Ireland) by the trustees;—my life threatened last month (they put about a paper here to excite an attempt at my assassination, on account of politics, and a notion which the priests disseminated that I was in a league against the Germans,)—and, finally, my mother-in-law recovered last fortnight, and my play was damned last week! These are like "the eight-and-twenty misfortunes of Harlequin." But they must be borne. If I give in, it shall be after keeping up a spirit at least. I should not have cared so much about it, if our southern neighbours had not bungled us all out of freedom for these five hundred years to come.

Did you know John Keats? They say that he was killed by a review of him in the *Quarterly*—if he be dead, which I really don't know. I don't understand that *yielding* sensitiveness. What I feel (as at this present) is an immense rage for eight-and-forty hours, and then, as usual—unless this time it should last longer. I must get on horseback to quiet me.

Yours, etc.

Francis I. wrote, after the battle of Pavia, "All is lost except our honour." A hissed author may reverse it—"*Nothing* is lost, except our honour." But the horses are waiting, and the paper full. I wrote last week to you.

1224.—To Richard Belgrave Hoppner.

Ravenna,
May 17th 1821.

My dear Hoppner,—

You will have seen a paragraph in the Italian papers stating that "Ld B. had exposed his t[ragedy] of *M*[*arino*] *F*[*aliero*] etc., and that it was universally hissed." You will have also seen in *Galignani* (what is confirmed by my letters from London), that this is *twice* false; for, in the first place, *I opposed* the representation at all, and in the *next,* it was *not* hissed, but is continued to be acted, in spite of Author, publisher, and the Lord Chancellor's injunction.

Now I wish *you* to obtain a statement of this short and simple truth in the Venetian and Milan papers, as a contradiction to their former lie. I say *you,* because your consular dignity will obtain this justice, which out of their hatred to *me* (as a *liberal*) they would not concede to an unofficial Individual.

Will you take this trouble? I think two words from you to those in power will do it, because I require nothing but the statement of what we both know to be the fact, and that a *fact* in no way political. Am I presuming too much upon your good nature?

I suppose that I have no other resource, and to whom can an Englishman apply, in a case of ignorant insult like this (where no *personal* redress is to be had), but to the person resident most nearly connected with his own government?

I wrote to you last week, and am now, in all haste,

Yours ever and most truly, BYRON.

P.S.—Humble reverences to Madame. Pray favour me with a line in answer. If the play had been condemned, the injunction would be *superfluous* against the continuance of the representation.

1225.—To John Murray.

Ravenna,
May 19th 1821.

DEAR MURRAY,—

Enclosed is a letter of Valpy's, which it is for you to answer. I have nothing further to do with the mode of publication By the papers of Thursday, and two letters from Mr. Kd, I perceive that the Italian Gazette had lied most *Italic*ally, and that the drama had *not* been hissed, and that my friends *had* interfered to prevent the representation. So it seems they continue to act it, in spite of us all. For this we must "trouble them at *'Size*:" let it by all means be brought to a plea: I am determined to try the right, and will *meet* the expences. The reason of the Lombard lie was that the Austrians—who keep up an Inquisition throughout Italy, and a *list* of *names* of all who think or speak of any thing but in favour of their despotism—have for five years past abused me in every form in the Gazette of Milan, etc. I wrote to you a week ago upon the subject.

Now, I should be glad to know what compensation Mr. Elliston could make me, not only for dragging my writings on the stage in *five* days, but for being the cause that I was kept for *four* days (from Sunday to Thursday morning, the only post days) in the *belief* that the *tragedy* had been acted and "unanimously hissed:" and this with the addition that "*I* had brought it upon the stage," and consequently that none of my friends had attended to my request to the contrary. Suppose that I had burst a blood vessel, like John Keats, or blown [out] my brains in a fit of rage,—neither of which would have been unlikely a few years ago. At present I am, luckily, calmer than I used to be, and yet I would not pass those four days over again for—I know not what.

I wrote to you to keep up your spirits, for reproach is useless always, and irritating; but my feelings were very much hurt, to be dragged like a Gladiator to the fate of a Gladiator by that "*Retiarius*," Mr. Elliston. As to his defence and offers of compensation, what is all this to the purpose? It is like Louis the 14th, who insisted upon buying at any price Algernon Sydney's horse, and, on refusal, on taking it by force, Sydney shot his horse. I could not shoot my tragedy, but I would have flung it into the fire rather than have had it represented.

I have now written nearly *three* acts of another (intending to complete it in five), and am more anxious than ever to be preserved from such a breach of all literary courtesy and gentlemanly consideration.

If we succeed, well: if not, previous to any future publication, we will request a *promise* not to be acted, which I would even pay for (as money is their object), or I will not publish—which, however, you will probably not much regret.

The Chancellor has behaved nobly. You have also conducted yourself in the most satisfactory manner; and I have no fault to find with any body but the Stage-players and their proprietor. I was always so civil to Elliston personally, that he ought to have been the last to attempt to injure me.

There is a most rattling thunder-storm pelting away at this present writing; so that I write neither by day, nor by candle, nor torch light, but by *lightning*-light: the flashes are as brilliant as the most Gaseous glow of the Gas-light company. My chimney-board has just been thrown down by a gust of wind: I thought that it was the "bold Thunder" and "brisk Lightning" in person—*three* of us would be too many. There it goes—*flash* again! but,

> I tax not you, ye elements, with unkindness;
> I never gave ye *franks,* nor *called* upon you;

as I have done by and upon Mr. Elliston.

Why do not you write? You should have at least sent me a line of particulars: I know nothing yet but by Galignani and the honourable Douglas.

Hobhouse has been paying back Mr. Canning's assault. He was right; for Canning had been, like Addison, trying to "*cuff down new-fledged merit.*" Hobhouse has in him "something dangerous" if not let alone.

Well, and how does our Pope Controversy go on, and the pamphlet? It is impossible to write any news: the Austrian scoundrels rummage all letters.

Yours, B.

P.S.—I could have sent you a good deal of Gossip and some *real* information, were it not that all letters pass through the Barbarians' inspection, and I have no wish to inform *them* of any thing but my utter abhorrence of them and theirs. They have only conquered by treachery, however.

Send me some Soda-powders, some of "Acton's Com-rubbers," and W. Scott's romances. And do pray write: when there is anything to interest, you are always silent.

1226.—To Madame Guiccioli.

[EXTRACT]

Ecco la verità di ciò che io vi dissi pocbi giorni fa, come vengo sacrificato in tutte le maniere senza sapere il *perché* e il *come.* La tragedia di cui si parla non è (e non era mai) nè scritta nè adatta al teatro; ma non è però romantico il disegno, è piuttosto regolare—regolarissimo per l'unità del tempo, e mancando poco a quella del sito. Voi sapete bene se io aveva intenzione di farla rappresentare, poichè era scritta al vostro fianco e nei momenti per certo più *tragici* per me come *uomo* che come *autore,*—perchè *voi* eravate in affanno ed in pericolo. Intanto sento dalla vostra Gazetta che sia nata una cabala, un partito, e senza ch' io vi abbia presa la minima parte. Si dice che *l'autore ne fece la lettura!!!*—quì forse? a Ravenna?—ed a chi? forse a Fletcher!!! quel illustre litterato, etc., etc.[vi]

1227.—To Thomas Moore.

Ravenna,
May 20, 1821.

Since I wrote to you last week I have received English letters and papers, by which I perceive that what I took for an Italian *truth* is, after all, a French lie of the *Gazette de France.* It contains two ultra-falsehoods in as many lines. In the first place, Lord B. did *not* bring forward his play, but opposed the same; and, secondly, it was *not* condemned, but is continued to be acted, in despite of publisher, author, Lord Chancellor, and (for aught I know to the contrary) of audience, up to the first of May, at least—the latest date of my letters. You will oblige me, then, by causing Mr. Gazette of France to contradict himself, which, I suppose, he is used to. I never answer a foreign *criticism*; but this is a mere matter of *fact,* and not of *opinions.* I presume that you have English and French interest enough to do this for me—though, to be sure, as it is nothing but the *truth* which we wish to state, the insertion may be more difficult.

As I have written to you often lately at some length, I won't bore you further now, than by begging you to comply with my request; and I presume the *esprit du corps* (is it "*du*" or "*de*"? for this is more than I know) will sufficiently urge you, as one of "*ours,*" to set this affair in its real aspect. Believe me always yours ever and most affectionately, BYRON.

1228.—To John Cam Hobhouse.

Ravenna,
May 20th, 1821.

My dear Hobhouse,—

Galignani gave with great accuracy your defence, and offence; for "this defence offensive comes by cause"—against Mr. Canning, which is as pretty a piece of invective as one would wish to read on a summer's day. You served him right, because he had attempted, like Addison, "to cuff down new-fledged merit." Besides, to talk of "a demagogue's dimensions" to a gentleman of the middle stature was downright "scurrilous."

But you have not spared him, like the boatswain in boarding the French vessel (don't you remember Bathurst's story?) "No, no, you —, *you* fired first." It is a piece of eloquence, and the style much more *easy* than your usual prose (in *writing* that is), and I begin to think that your real strength lies in vituperation.

How did he look under it? He has not attempted any rejoinder, but I suppose that you will be both at it for the remainder of your lives. It must have had a great effect. I am glad that you quoted Pope too; that's always right, though you might have left out the further quotation from Sir Car Scrope, a vulgar lampooner of the most licentious gang of Charles the Second's reign.

You will be well acquainted with the row about the ryghte merry and conceitede tragedy of your humble servant. But you do not know that for *four* days I believed it damned, owing to a paragraph from an Italian French paper, which added that *I had brought* it on the stage! The next post set me at ease on that point, by papers and letters explaining the whole thing, but making me wonder that either the town or the Chancellor permitted the buffoons to go on acting it. I bore the belief with philosophy, as my letter to Murray, written during the interval, will show. But this very circumstance is an additional one against the managers, for what can compensate for such days to a man who had so anxiously avoided the exhibition?

Ten years ago I should have gone crazy; at present I have lived on as usual. I will have the question brought to a pleading, however, just to see how the right really stands.

It is thus far of import to all writers for the future.

Douglas has written, but neither you nor Moray nor anybody else. I cannot write news because the letters are all opened. However, I suppose you know what is no news, that the Neapolitans were bought and sold.

The *Spy* is *here* (in Ravenna) who carried the letters between Frimont and Carrascosa, and complains publicly of being but ill-paid for his pains. Perhaps he may be *better* paid of he don't take care. It is a savage sort of neighbourhood.

Our Greek acquaintance are making a fight for it, which must be a dilemma for the Allies, who can neither take their part (as liberals) nor help longing for a leg and a wing, and bit of the heart of Turkey.

Will you tell Douglas that as he had agreed (and I also) upon *that* price with M[urray], that of course I abide by it; but he should recollect that I have been entirely guided by *himself* (Douglas) and you in your opinions of what I ought to ask or receive. From my absence and ignorance how things stand in literature in England, it is impossible for me to know how to act otherwise. I do not even know how the Bowles pamphlet has sold, nor the drama, nor anything else.

Lady Noel is dangerously *well* again, I hear, Mrs. Leigh's news, who never sends anything agreeable, of herself or anybody else.

Yrs. ever, B.

Fletcher's respects, and *expects* that you and Canning will *fight,* but *hopes not.*

1229.—To Richard Belgrave Hoppner.

Ravenna,
May 25,1821.

I am very much pleased with what you say of Switzerland, and will ponder upon it. I would rather she married there than here for that matter. For fortune, I shall make all that I can spare (if I live and she is correct in her conduct); and if I die before she is settled, I have left her by will five thousand pounds, which is a fair provision *out* of England for a natural child. I shall increase it all I can, if circumstances permit me; but, of course (like all other human things), this is very uncertain.

You will oblige me very much by interfering to have the FACTS of the play-acting stated, as these scoundrels appear to be organising a system of abuse against me, because I am in their "*list.*" I care nothing for *their criticism,* but the matter of fact. I have written *four* acts of another tragedy, so you see they *can't* bully me.

You know, I suppose, that they actually keep a *list* of all individuals in Italy who dislike them—it must be numerous. Their suspicions and actual alarms, about my conduct and presumed intentions in the late row, were truly ludicrous—though, not to bore you, I touched upon them lightly. They believed, and still believe here, or affect to believe it, that the whole plan and project of rising was settled by me, and the *means* furnished, etc., etc. All this was more fomented by the barbarian agents, who are numerous here (one of them was stabbed yesterday, by the way, but not dangerously):—and although when the Commandant was shot here before my door in December, I took him into my house, where he had every assistance, till he died on Fletcher's bed; and although not one of them dared to receive him into their houses but myself, they leaving him to perish in the night in the streets, they put up a paper about three months ago, denouncing me as the Chief of the Liberals, and stirring up persons to assassinate me. But this shall never silence nor bully my opinions. All this came from the German Barbarians.

1230.—To John Murray.

R^{a} May 25th 1821.

Mr. Moray,—

Since I wrote the enclosed a week ago, and for some weeks before, I have not had a line from you. Now I should be glad to know upon what principle of common or *un*common feeling, you leave me without any information but what I derive from garbled gazettes in English, and abusive ones in Italian (the Germans hating me as a *Coal-heaver*), while all this kick up has been going on about the play? You SHABBY fellow!!! Were it not for two letters from Douglas Kinnaird, I should have been as ignorant as you are negligent.

I send you an Elegy as follows:—

> Behold the blessings of a lucky lot!
> My play *is damned,* and Lady Noel *not.*

So, I hear Bowles has been abusing Hobhouse: if that's the case, he has broken the truce, like Morillo's successor, and I will cut him out, as Cochrane did the Esmeralda.

Since I wrote the enclosed packet, I have completed (but not copied out) four acts of a new tragedy. When I have finished the fifth, I will copy it out. It is on the subject of *Sardanapalus,* the last king of the Assyrians. The words *Queen* and *pavilion* occur, but it is not an allusion to his Britannic Majesty, as you may tremulously (for the admiralty custom) imagine. This you will one day see (if I finish it), as I have made Sardanapalus *brave,* (though voluptuous, as history represents him,) and also as *amiable* as my poor powers could render him. So that it could neither be truth nor satire on any living monarch. I have strictly preserved all the unities hitherto, and mean to continue them in the fifth, if possible; but *not for the Stage.* Yours, in haste and hatred, you scrubby correspondent! B.

1231.—To John Murray.

Ravenna,
May 28th 1821.

Dear Moray,—

Since my last of the 26th or 25th, I have dashed off my fifth act of the tragedy called *Sardanapalus.* But now comes the copying over, which may prove heavy work—heavy to the writer as to the reader. I have written to you at least 6 times *sans* answer, which proves you to be a—bookseller. I pray you to send me a copy of Mr. "*Wrangham's*" reformation of "*Langhorne's Plutarch:*" I have the Greek, which is somewhat small of print, and the Italian, which is too heavy in style, and as false as a Neapolitan patriot proclamation. I pray you also to send me a life, published some years ago, of the *Magician Apollonius* of T[yana], etc., etc. It is in English, and I think edited or written by what "Martin Marprelate" calls "*a bouncing priest.*" I shall trouble you no further with this sheet than ye postage.

Yours, etc., B.

P.S.—Since I wrote this, I determined to inclose it (as a half sheet) to Mr. K., who will have the goodness to forward it. Besides, it saves sealing wax.

1232.—To John Murray.

R^a May 30th 1821.

DEAR MORAY,—

You say you have written often: I have only received yours of the eleventh, which is very short. By this post, in *five* packets, I send you the tragedy of *Sardanapalus,* which is written in a rough hand: perhaps Mrs. Leigh can help you to decypher it. You will please to acknowledge it by *return* of post. You will remark that the *Unities* are all *strictly* observed. The Scene passes in the same *Hall* always. The time, a *Summer's night,* about nine hours, or less, though it begins before Sunset and ends after Sunrise. In the third act, when Sardanapalus calls for a *mirror* to look at himself in his *armour,* recollect to quote the Latin passage from *Juvenal* upon *Otho* (a similar character, who did the same thing): Gifford will help you to it. The trait is perhaps too familiar, but it is historical (of *Otho,* at least,) and natural in an effeminate character.

Preface, etc., etc., will be sent when I know of the arrival. For the historical account, I refer you to Diodorus Siculus, from which you must have the *chapters* of the Story translated, as an explanation and a *note* to the drama.

You write so seldom and so shortly, that you can hardly expect from me more than I receive.

Yours truly, etc.

P.S.—Remember me to Gifford, and say that I doubt that this MSS. will puzzle him to decypher it. The Characters are quite different from any I have hitherto attempted to delineate.

You must have it *copied out* directly, as you best can, and *printed off* in *proofs* (more than one), as I have retained no copy in my hands.

With regard to the publication, I can only protest as heretofore against its being acted, it being expressly written *not* for the theatre.

1233.—To Richard Belgrave Hoppner.

Ravenna,
May 31, 1821.

I enclose you another letter, which will only confirm what I have said to you.

About Allegra—I will take some decisive step in the course of the year; at present, she is so happy where she is, that perhaps she had better have her *alphabet* imparted in her convent.

What you say of the *Dante* is the first I have heard of it—all seeming to be merged in the *row* about the tragedy. Continue it!—Alas! what could Dante himself *now* prophesy about Italy? I am glad you like it, however, but doubt that you will be singular in your opinion. My *new* tragedy is completed.

The B[enzoni] is *right,*—I ought to have mentioned her *humour* and *amiability,* but I thought at her *sixty,* beauty would be most agreeable or least likely. However, it shall be rectified in a new edition; and if any of the parties have either looks or qualities which they wish to be noticed, let me have a minute of them. I have no private nor personal dislike to *Venice,* rather the contrary: but I merely speak of what is the subject of all remarks and all writers upon her present state. Let me hear from you before you start.

Believe me ever, etc.

P.S.—Did you receive two letters of Douglas Kinnaird's in an endorse from me? Remember me to Mengaldo, Seranzo, and all who care that I should remember them. The letter alluded to in the enclosed, "to the *Cardinal,*" was in answer to some *queries* of the government, about a poor devil of a Neapolitan, arrested at Sinigaglia on suspicion, who came to beg of me here; being without breeches, and consequently without pockets for halfpence, I relieved and forwarded him to his country, and they arrested him at Pesaro on suspicion, and have since interrogated me (civilly and politely, however,) about him. I sent them the poor man's petition, and such information as I had about him, which I trust will get him out again, that is to say, if they give him a fair hearing.

I *am* content with the article. Pray, did you receive, some posts ago, Moore's lines which I enclosed to you, written at Paris?

1234.—To Thomas Moore.

Ravenna,
June 4, 1821.

You have not written lately, as is the usual custom with literary gentlemen, to console their friends with their observations in cases of magnitude. I do not know whether I sent you my "Elegy on the *recovery* of Lady Noel:"—

> Behold the blessings of a lucky lot—
> My play is damn'd, and Lady Noel *not.*

The papers (and perhaps your letters) will have put you in possession of Muster Elliston's dramatic behaviour. It is to be presumed that the play was *fitted* for the stage by Mr. Dibdin, who is the tailor upon such occasions, and will have taken measure with his usual accuracy. I hear that it is still continued to be performed—a piece of obstinacy for which it is some consolation to think that the discourteous histrio will be out of pocket.

You will be surprised to hear that I have finished another tragedy in *five* acts, observing all the unities strictly. It is called *Sardanapalus,* and was sent by last post to England. It is *not for* the stage, any more than the other was intended for it —and I shall take better care *this* time that they don't get hold on't. I have also sent, two months ago, a further letter on Bowles, etc.; but he seems to be so taken up with my "respect" (as he calls it) towards him in the former case, that I am not sure that it will be published, being somewhat too full of "pastime and prodigality." I learn from some private letters of Bowles's, that *you* were "the gentleman in asterisks." Who would have dreamed it? you see what mischief that clergyman has done by printing notes without names. How the deuce was I to suppose that the first four asterisks meant "Campbell" and *not* "*Pope*" and that the blank signature meant Thomas Moore? You see what comes of being familiar with parsons. His answers have not yet reached *me,* but I understand from Hobhouse, that *he* (H.) is attacked in them. If that be the case, Bowles has broken the truce, (which he himself proclaimed, by the way,) and I must have at him again.

Did you receive my letters with the two or three concluding sheets of Memoranda?

There are no news here to interest much. A German spy (*boasting* himself such) was stabbed last week, but *not* mortally. The moment I heard that he went about bullying and boasting, it was easy for me, or any one else, to foretell what would occur to him, which I did, and it came to pass in two days after. He has got off, however, for a slight incision.

A row the other night, about a lady of the place, between her various lovers, occasioned a midnight discharge of pistols, but nobody wounded. Great scandal, however—planted by her lover—*to be* thrashed by her husband, for inconstancy to her regular *Servente,* who is coming home post about it, and she herself retired in confusion into the country, although it is the acme of the opera season. All the women furious against her (she herself having been censorious) for being *found out.* She is a pretty woman—a Countess Rasponi—a fine old Visigoth name, or Ostrogoth.

The Greeks! what think you? They are my old acquaintances—but what to think I know not. Let us hope howsomever.

Yours, B.

1235.—To Giovanni Battista Missiaglia.

June 12, 1821.

Dear Sir,—

Tell Count V. Benzone (with my respects to him and to his Mother) that I have received his books—and that I shall *write to thank him* in a few days.

Murray sends me books of travels—I do not know why; for I have travelled enough myself to know that such books are *full of lies.*

If you come here you will find me very glad to see you, and very ready to dispute with you.

Yours ever, Byron.

1236.—To John Murray.

Ravenna,
June 14th 1821.

Dear Murray,—

I *have* resumed my "majestic march" (as Gifford is pleased to call it) in *Sardanapalus,* which by the favour of Providence and the Post Office should be arrived by this time, if not interrupted. It was sent on the 2nd June, 12 days ago.

Let me know, because I had but that one copy.

Can your printers make out the MS.? I suppose long acquaintance with my scrawl may help them; if not, ask Mrs. Leigh, or Hobhouse, or D. K.: they know my writing.

The whole five acts were sent in one cover, ensured to England, paying forty five scudi *here* for the insurance.

I received some of your parcels: the *Doge* is longer than I expected: pray, why did you print the face of M[argarita] C[ogni] by way of frontispiece? It has almost caused a row between the Countess G. and myself. And pray, why did you add the note about the Kelso woman's *Sketches*? Did I not request you to omit it, the instant I was aware that the *writer* was a *female*?

The whole volume looks very respectable, and sufficiently dear in price, but you do not tell me whether it succeeds: your first letter (before the performance) said that it was succeeding far beyond all anticipation; but this was before the piracy of Elliston, which (for anything I know, as I have had no news—your letter with papers not coming) may have affected the circulation.

I have read Bowles's answer: I could easily reply, but it would lead to a long discussion, in the course of which I should perhaps lose my temper, which I would rather not do with so civil and forbearing an antagonist. I suppose he will mistake being *silent* for *silenced.*

I wish to know when you publish the remaining things in MS.? I do not mean the *prose,* but the verse.

I am truly sorry to hear of your domestic loss; but (as I know by experience), all attempts at condolence in such cases are merely varieties of solemn impertinence. There is nothing in this world but *Time.*

Yours ever and truly, B.

P.S.—You have never answered me about *Holmes,* the Miniature painter: can he come or no? I want him to paint the miniatures of my daughter and two other persons.

In the 1st pamphlet it is printed "*a* Mr. J. S.": it should be "Mr. J. S.," and not "*a,*" which is contemptuous; it is a printer's error and was not thus written.

1237.—To Thomas Moore.

Ravenna,
June 22, 1821.

Your dwarf of a letter came yesterday. That is right;—keep to your *magnum opus* —magnoperate away. Now, if we were but together a little to combine our *Journal of Trevoux*! But it is useless to sigh, and yet very natural,—for I think you and I draw better together, in the social line, than any two other living authors.

I forgot to ask you, if you had seen your own panegyric in the correspondence of Mrs. Waterhouse and Colonel Berkeley? To be sure *their* moral is not quite exact; but *your passion* is fully effective; and all poetry of the *Asiatic* kind—I mean

Asiatic, as the Romans called "Asiatic oratory," and not because the scenery is Oriental—must be tried by that test only. I am not quite sure that I shall allow the Miss Byrons (legitimate or illegitimate) to read *Lalla Rookh*—in the first place, on account of this said *passion*; and, in the second, that they may'nt discover that there was a better poet than papa.

You say nothing of politics—but, alas! what can be said?

> The world is a bundle of hay,
>   Mankind are the asses who pull,
> Each tugs it a different way,—
>   And the greatest of all is John Bull!

How do you call your new project? I have sent Murray a new tragedy, ycleped *Sardanapalus,* writ according to Aristotle—all, save the chorus—I could not reconcile me to that. I have begun another, and am in the second act;—so you see I saunter on as usual.

Bowles's answers have reached me; but I can't go on disputing for ever,—particularly in a polite manner. I suppose he will take being *silent* for *silenced.* He has been so civil that I can't find it in my liver to be facetious with him,—else I had a savage joke or two at his service.

* * * * *

I can't send you the little journal, because it is in boards, and I can't trust it per post. Don't suppose it is any thing particular; but it will show the *intentions* of the natives at that time—and one or two other things, chiefly personal, like the former one.

So, Longman don't *bite.*—It was my wish to have made that work of use. Could you not raise a sum upon it (however small), reserving the power of redeeming it, on repayment?

Are you in Paris, or a villaging? If you are *in* the city, you will never resist the Anglo-invasion you speak of. I do not see an Englishman in half a year, and, when I do, I turn my horse's head the other way. The fact, which you will find in the last note to the Doge, has given me a good excuse for quite dropping the least connection with travellers.

I do not recollect the speech you speak of, but suspect it is not the Doge's, but one of Israel Bertuccio to Calendaro. I hope you think that Elliston behaved shamefully—it is my only consolation. I made the Milanese fellows contradict their lie, which they did with the grace of people used to it.

Yours, etc., B.

1238.—To the Hon. Augusta Leigh.

Ravenna. June 22nd. 1821.

My Dearest A.—

What was I to write about? I live in a different world. You know from others that I was in tolerable plight, and all that. However write I will since you desire it. I have put my daughter in a convent for the present to begin her accomplishments by reading, to which she had a learned aversion, but the arrangement is merely temporary till I can settle some plan for her; if I return to England, it is likely that she will accompany me—if not—I sometimes think of Switzerland, & sometimes of the Italian Conventional education; I shall hear both sides (for I have Swiss Friends—through Mr. Hoppner the Consul General, he is connected by marriage with that country) and choose what seems most rational. My menagerie—(which you enquire after) has had some vacancies by the elopement of one cat, the decease of two monkies and a crow, by indigestion—but it is still a flourishing and somewhat obstreperous establishment.

You may suppose that I was sufficiently provoked about Elliston's behaviour, the more so as the foreign Journals, the Austrian ones at least (who detest me for my politics) had misrepresented the whole thing. The moment I knew the real facts from England, I made these Italical Gentry contradict themselves and tell the truth—the former they are used to—the latter was a sad trial to them, but they did it, however, by dint of Mr. Hoppner's and my own remonstrances.

Tell Murray that I enclosed him a month ago (on the 2d.) another play, which I presume that he has received (as I ensured it at the post Office) *you* must help him to decypher it, for I sent the only copy, and you can better make out my *griffonnage*; tell him it must be printed (aye and published too) immediately, and copied out, for I do not choose to have only that *one* copy.

Will you for the hundredth time apply to Lady B. about the *funds*, they are now *high*, and I could sell out to a great advantage. Don't forget this, that cursed connection crosses at every turn my fortunes, my feelings and my fame. I had no wish to nourish my detestation of her and her family, but they pursue, like an Evil Genius. I send you an Elegy upon Lady Noel's *recovery*—(made too[vii]

the parish register—I will reserve my tears for the demise of Lady Noel, but the old — will live forever because she is so amiable and useful.

Yours ever & [*illegible*] B

P.S.—Let me know about Holmes.—Oh La!—is he as great a mountebank as ever?

1239.—To John Murray.

Ravenna,
June 29th 1821.

DEAR MURRAY,—

From the last parcel of books, the two first volumes of Butler's *Catholics* are missing. As the book is "*from* the author," in thanking him for me, mention this circumstance. Waldegrave and Walpole are not arrived; Scott's novels all safe.

By the time you receive this letter, the Coronation will be over, and you will be able to think of business. Long before this you ought to have received the MSS. of *Sardanapalus.* It was sent on the 2d Inst. By the way, you must permit me to choose my *own* seasons of publication. All that you have a right to on such occasions is the mere matter of barter: if you think you are likely to lose by such or such a time of printing, you will have full allowance made for it, on statement. It is now two years nearly that MSS. of mine have been in your hands *in statu quo.* Whatever I may have thought (and, not being on the spot, nor having any exact means of ascertaining the thermometer of success or failure, I have had no *determinate* opinion upon the subject), I have allowed you to go on in your own way, and acquiesced in all your arrangements hitherto.

I pray you to forward the proofs of *Sardanapalus* as soon as you can, and let me know if it be deemed press-and print-worthy. I am quite ignorant how far *the Doge* did or did not succeed: your first letters seemed to say yes—your last say nothing. My own immediate friends are naturally partial: one review (Blackwood's) speaks highly of it, another pamphlet calls it "a failure." It is proper that you should apprize me of this, because I am in the *third* act of a *third* drama; and if I have nothing to expect but coldness from the public and hesitation from yourself, it were better to break off in time. I had proposed to myself to go on, as far as my Mind would carry me, and I have thought of plenty of subjects. But *if* I am trying an impracticable experiment, it is better to say so at once.

So Canning and Burdett have been quarrelling: if I mistake not, the last time of their single combats, each was shot in the thigh by his Antagonist; and their Correspondence might be headed thus, by any wicked wag:—

Brave Champions! go on with the farce!
  Reversing the spot where you bled;
Last time both were shot in the *;
  Now (damn you) get knocked on the *head*!

I have not heard from you for some weeks; but I can easily excuse the silence from it's occasion.

Believe me, yours ever and truly, B.

P.S.—Do you or do you not mean to print the MSS. Cantos—Pulci, etc.?

P.S. 2ᵈ—To save you the bore of writing yourself, when you are "not i' the vein," make one of your Clerks send me a few lines to apprize me of arrivals, etc., of MSS., and matters of business. I shan't take it ill; and I know that a bookseller in large business must have his time too over-occupied to answer every body himself.

P.S. 3ᵈ—I have just read "John Bull's letter:" it is diabolically *well* written, and full of fun and ferocity. I must forgive the dog, whoever he is. I suspect three people: one is *Hobhouse,* the other Mr. Peacock (a very clever fellow), and lastly Israeli; there are parts very like Israeli, and he has a present grudge with Bowles and Southey, etc. There is something too of the author of the *Sketch-book* in the Style. Find him out.

The packet or letter addressed under covʳ to Mr. H. has never arrived, and never will. You should address directly to *me here,* and by the post.

1240.—To Thomas Moore.

Ravenna,
July 5, 1821.

How could you suppose that I ever would allow any thing that *could* be said on your account to weigh with *me*? I only regret that Bowles had not *said* that you were the writer of that note, until afterwards, when out he comes with it, in a private letter to Murray, which Murray sends to me. D—n the controversy!

"D—n Twizzle,
D—n the bell,
And d—n the fool who rung it—Well!
From all such plagues I'll quickly be delivered."

I have had a friend of your Mr. Irving's—a very pretty lad—a Mr. Coolidge, of Boston—only somewhat too full of poesy and "entusymusy." I was very civil to him during his few hours' stay, and talked with him much of Irving, whose writings are my delight But I suspect that he did not take quite so much to me, from his having expected to meet a misanthropical gentleman, in wolfskin breeches, and answering in fierce monosyllables, instead of a man of this world. I can never get people to understand that poetry is the expression of *excited passion,* and that there is no such thing as a life of passion any more than a continuous earthquake, or an eternal fever. Besides, who would ever *shave* themselves in such a state?

I have had a curious letter to-day from a girl in England (I never saw her), who says she is given over of a decline, but could not go out of the world without thanking me for the delight which my poesy for several years, etc., etc., etc. It is signed simply N. N. A. and has not a word of "cant" or preachment in it upon *any*

You are very niggardly in your letters.

Yours truly, B.

P.S.—In the first soliloquy of Salemenes, read

"at once his *Chorus* and his Council;"

"Chorus" being in the higher dramatic sense, meaning his accompaniment, and not a mere *musical* train.

1246.—To John Murray.

R[a] July 22[d] 1821.

Dear Murray,—

By this post is expedited a parcel of notes, addressed to J. Barrow, Esq[re], etc. Also, by y[e] former post, the returned proofs of *S[ardanapalus]* and the MSS. of the *Two Foscaris.* Acknowledge these.

The printer has done wonders; he has read what I cannot—my own handwriting.

I *oppose* the "delay till Winter:" I am particularly anxious to print while the *Winter theatres* are *closed*, to gain time, in case they try their former piece of politeness. Any *loss* shall be considered in our contract, whether occasioned by the season or other causes; but print away, and publish.

I think they must own that I have more styles than one. "Sardanapalus" is, however, almost a comic character: but, for that matter, so is Richard the thrid. Mind the Unities, which are my great object of research. I am glad that Gifford likes it: as for "the Million," you see I have carefully consulted anything but that taste of the day for extravagant coups de théâtre. Any probable loss, as I said before, will be allowed for in our accompts. The reviews (except one or two—Blackwood's, for instance) are cold enough; but never mind those fellows: I shall send them to the right about, if I take it into my head. Perhaps that in the Monthly is written by Hodgson, as a reward for having paid his debts, and travelled all night to beg his mother-in-law (by his own desire) to let him marry her daughter; though I had never seen her in my life, it succeeded. But such are mankind, and I have always found the English *better* in some things than any other nation. You stare, but it's true as to *gratitude*,—perhaps, because they are prouder, and proud people hate obligations.

The tyranny of the government here is breaking out: they have exiled about a thousand people of the best families all over the Roman States. As many of my friends are amongst them, I think of moving too, but not till I have had your answers. Continue *your address* to me *here*, as usual, and quickly. What you will *not* be sorry to hear is, that the *poor* of the place, hearing that I meant to go, got together a petition to the Cardinal to request that *he* would request me to *remain.* I only heard of it a day or two ago, and it is no dishonour to them nor to me; but it will have displeased the higher powers, who look upon me as a Chief of the Coalheavers. They arrested a servant of mine for a Street quarrel with an Officer (they drew upon one another knives and pistols); but as *the Officer* was out of uniform, and in the *wrong* besides, on my protesting stoutly, he was released. I was not present at the affray, which happened by night near my stables. My man (an Italian), a very stout and not over patient personage, would have taken a fatal revenge afterwards, if I had not prevented him. As it was, he drew his stiletto, and, but for passengers, would have carbonadoed the Captain, who (I understand) made but a poor figure in the quarrel, except by beginning it. He applied to me, and I offered him any satisfaction, either by turning away the man, or otherwise, because he had drawn a knife. He answered that a reproof would be sufficient. I reproved him; and yet, after this, the shabby dog complained to the *Government,*—after being quite satisfied, as he said. *This* roused me, and I gave them a remonstrance which had some effect. If he had not enough, he should have called me *out*; but that is not the Italian line of conduct: the Captain has been reprimanded, the servant released, and the business at present rests there.

Write and let me know of the arrivals.

Yours, B.

P.S.—You will of course publish the two tragedies of *Sardanapalus* and the *Foscaris* together. You can afterwards collect them with *Manfred,* and *The Doge* into the works. Inclosed is an additional note.

1247.—To Richard Belgrave Hoppner.

Ravenna,
July 23, 1821.

This country being in a state of proscription, and all my friends exiled or arrested —the whole family of Gamba obliged to go to Florence for the present—the father and son for politics—(and the Guiccioli, because menaced with a *convent,* as her father is *not* here,) I have determined to remove to Switzerland, and they also. Indeed, my life here is not supposed to be particularly safe—but that has been the case for this twelvemonth past, and is therefore not the primary consideration.

I have written by this post to Mr. Hentsch, junior, the banker of Geneva, to provide (if possible) a house for me, and another for Gamba's family, (the father, son, and daughter,) on the *Jura* side of the lake of Geneva, furnished, and with stabling (for *me* at least) for eight horses. I shall bring Allegra with me. Could you assist me or Hentsch in his researches? The Gambas are at Florence, but have authorised me to

Is there no chance of your return to England, and of *our* Journal? I would have published the two plays in it—two or three scenes per number—and indeed *all* of mine in it. If you went to England, I would do so still.

1251.—To John Murray.

Rª August 4th 1821.

DEAR SIR,—

I return the proofs of the 2d pamphlet. I leave it to your choice and Mr. Gifford's, to publish it or not, with such omissions as he likes. You must, however, omit the whole of the observations against the *Suburban School*: they are meant against Keats, and I cannot war with the dead—particularly those already killed by Criticism. Recollect to omit all that portion in *any case.*

Lately I have sent you several packets, which require answer: you take a gentlemanly interval to answer them.

Yours, etc., BYRON.

P.S.—They write from Paris that Schlegel is making a fierce book against ME: what can I have done to the literary Col-captain of late Madame? *I*, who am neither of his country nor his horde? Does this Hundsfott's intention appal *you*? if it does, say so. It don't *me*; for, if he is insolent, I will go to Paris and thank him. There is a distinction between *native* Criticism, because it belongs to the Nation to judge and pronounce on natives; but what have *I* to do with Germany or Germans, neither my subjects nor my language having anything in common with that Country? He took a dislike to me, because I refused to flatter him in Switzerland, though Madame de Broglie begged me to do so, "because he is so fond of it. *Voilà les hommes!*"

1252.—To John Murray.

Ravenna,
August 7th 1821.

DEAR SIR,—

I send you a thing which I scratched off lately, a mere buffoonery, to quiz *The Blues,* in two literary eclogues. If published, it must be *anonymously*: but it is too short for a separate publication; and *you* have no miscellany, that I know of, for the reception of such things. You may send me a proof, if you think it worth the trouble; but don't let *my* name out for the present, or I shall have all the old women in London about my ears, since it sneers at the solace of their antient Spinsterstry.

Acknowledge this, and the various packets lately sent.

Yours, B[N]

1253.—To John Murray.

Ravenna,
August 7th 1821.

Dear Sir,—

By last post I forwarded a packet to you: as usual, you are avised by this post.

I should be loth to hurt Mr. Bowles's feelings by publishing the second pamphlet; and, as he has shown considerable regard for mine, we had better suppress it altogether: at any rate I would not publish it without letting him see it first, and omitting all such matter as might be *personally* offensive to him. Also all the part about the Suburb School must be omitted, as it referred to poor Keats now slain by the *Quarterly Review.*

If I do not err, I mentioned to you that I had heard from Paris, that Schlegel announces a meditated abuse of me in a criticism. The disloyalty of such a proceeding towards a foreigner, who has uniformly spoken so well of Me de Stael in his writings, and who, moreover, has nothing to do with continental literature or Schlegel's country and countrymen, is such, that I feel a strong inclination to bring the matter to a *personal* arbitrament, provided it can be done without being ridiculous or unfair. His intention, however, must be first fully ascertained, before I can proceed; and I have written for some information on the subject to Mr. Moore. The Man was also my personal acquaintance; and though I refused to flatter him grossly (as Me de B. requested me to do), yet I uniformly treated him with respect —with much more, indeed, than any one else: for his peculiarities are such, that they, one and all, laughed at him; and especially the Abbe Chevalier di Breme, who did nothing but make me laugh at him so much behind his back, that nothing but the politeness, on which I pique myself in society, could have prevented me from doing so to his face. He is just such a character as William the testy in Irving's *New York.* But I must have him out for all that, since his proceeding (supposing it to be true), is ungentlemanly in all its bearings—at least in my opinion; but perhaps my partiality misleads me.

It appears to me that there is a distinction between *native* and *foreign* criticism in the case of living authors, or at least should be; I don't speak of *Journalists* (who are the same all over the world), but where a man, with his name at length, sits down to an elaborate attempt to defame a foreigner of his acquaintance, without provocation and without legitimate object: for what can I import to the Germans?

What effect can I have upon their literature? Do you think me in the wrong? if so, say so.

Yours ever, B.

P.S.—I mentioned in my former letters, that it was my intention to have the two plays published *immediately.*

Acknowledge the various packets.

I am extremely angry with *you,* I beg leave to add, for several reasons too long for present explanation. Mr. D. K. is in possession of some of them.

I have just been turning over the homicide review of J. Keats. It is harsh certainly and contemptuous, but not more so than what I recollect of the *Edinburgh R.* of "*the Hours of Idleness*" in 1808. The Reviewer allows him "a degree of talent which deserves to be put in the right way," " rays of fancy," "gleams of Genius," and "powers of language." It is harder on L. Hunt than upon Keats, and professes fairly to review only *one* book of his poem. Altogether, though very provoking, it was hardly so bitter as to kill, unless there was a morbid feeling previously in his system.

1254.—To John Murray.

Ravenna,
August 10, 1821.

Dear Sir,—

Your conduct to Mr. Moore is certainly very handsome; and I would not say so if I could help it, for you are not at present by any means in my good graces.

With regard to additions, etc., there is a Journal which I kept in 1814 which you may ask him for; also a Journal which you must get from Mrs. Leigh, of my journey in the Alps, which contains all the germs of *Manfred.* I have also kept a small Diary here for a few months last winter, which I would send you, and any continuation. You would easy find access to all my papers and letters, and do *not neglect this* (in case of accidents) on account of the mass of confusion in which they are; for out of that chaos of papers you will find some curious ones of mine and others, if not lost or destroyed. If circumstances, however (which is almost impossible), made me ever consent to a publication in my lifetime, you would in that case, I suppose, make Moore some advance, in proportion to the likelihood or non-likelihood of success. You are both sure to survive me, however.

You must also have from Mr. Moore the correspondence between me and Lady B., to whom I offered the sight of all which regards herself in these papers. This is important. He has *her* letter, and a copy of my answer. I would rather Moore edited me than another.

I sent you Valpy's letter to decide for yourself, and Stockdale's to amuse you. *I* am always loyal with you, as I was in Galignani's affair, and *you* with me—now and then.

I return you Moore's letter, which is very creditable to him, and you, and me.

Yours ever, B.

1255.—To Douglas Kinnaird.

Ravenna,
August 10th, 1821.

My dear Douglas,—

Murray has behaved very handsomely to Moore about the memoirs or memoranda, as you may know by this time.

I wrote to you lately; pray let me have my *fee,* and let me know what you think to ax Murray for the MSS. His good conduct to Moore has almost reconciled me to him again.

My respects to Hobhouse and all friends.

Yours, in haste, and ever truly, B.

1256.—To John Murray.

R[a] August 13th 1821.

Dear Sir,—

I think it as well to remind you that, in "the *Hints*," all the part, which regards Jeffrey and the *E.R.,* must be *omitted.* Your late mistake about the Kelso-woman induces me to remind you of this, which I appended to your power of Attorney six years ago, viz., to *omit* all that could touch upon Jeffrey in that publication, which was written a year before our reconciliation in 1812.

Have you got the Bust? I expect with anxiety the proofs of *The Two Foscaris.*

Yours, B.

P.S.—Acknowledge the various packets.

1257.—To John Murray.

R^a^. August 16th 1821.

DEAR SIR,—

I regret that Holmes can't or won't come: it is rather shabby, as I was always very civil and punctual with him; but he is but one rascal more—one meets with none else amongst the English.

You may do what you will with my answer to Stockdale, of whom I know nothing, but answered his letter civilly: you may open it, and burn it or not, as you please. It contains nothing of consequence to any-body. How should I, or, at least, *was* I then to know that he was a rogue? I am not aware of the histories of London and its inhabitants.

Your more recent parcels are not yet arrived, but are probably on their way. I sprained my knee the other day in swimming, and it hurts me still considerably. I wait the proofs of the MSS. with proper impatience. So you have published, or mean to publish, the new *Juans*? an't you afraid of the Constitutional Assassination of Bridge street? when first I saw the name of *Murray,* I thought it had been yours; but was solaced by seeing that your Synonime is an Attorneo, and that you are not one of that atrocious crew.

I am in a great discomfort about the probable war, and with my damned trustees not getting me out of the funds. If the funds break, it is my intention to go upon the highway: all the other English professions are at present so ungentlemanly by the conduct of those who follow them, that open robbery is the only fair resource left to a man of any principles; it is even honest, in comparison, by being undisguised.

I wrote to you by last post, to say that you had done the handsome thing by Moore and the Memoranda. You are very good as times go, and would probably be still better but for the "March of events" (as Napoleon called it), which won't permit any body to be better than they should be.

Love to Gifford. Believe me,

Yours ever and truly, B.

P.S.—I restore Smith's letter, *whom* thank for his good opinion. Is the Bust by Thorwaldsen arrived?

1258.—To John Murray.

R^a^. August 23^d^ 1821.

DEAR SIR,—

Enclosed are the two acts corrected. With regard to the charges about the Shipwreck,—I think that I told both you and Mr. Hobhouse, years ago, that [there] was not a *single circumstance* of it *not* taken from *fact*; not, indeed, from any *single* shipwreck, but all from *actual* facts of different wrecks. Almost all *Don Juan* is *real* life, either my own, or from people I knew. By the way, much of the description of the *furniture,* in Canto 3[d], is taken from *Tully's Tripoli* (pray *note this*), and the rest from my own observation. Remember, I never meant to conceal this at all, and have only not stated it, because *Don Juan* had no preface nor name to it. If you think it worth while to make this statement, do so, in your own way. *I* laugh at such charges, convinced that no writer ever borrowed less, or made his materials more his own. Much is coincidence: for instance, Lady Morgan (in a really *excellent* book, I assure you, on Italy) calls Venice an *Ocean Rome*; I have the very same expression in *Foscari,* and yet *you* know that the play was written months ago, and sent to England. The *Italy* I received only on the 16th in[st].

Your friend, like the public, is not aware, that my dramatic simplicity is *studiously* Greek, and must continue so: *no* reform ever succeeded at first. I admire the old English dramatists; but this is quite another field, and has nothing to do with theirs. I want to make a *regular* English drama, no matter whether for the Stage or not, which is not my object,—but a *mental theatre.*

Yours ever, B.

Is the bust arrived?

P.S.—Can't accept your courteous offer.

For Orford and for Waldegrave
You give much more than me *you gave;*
Which is not fairly to behave,
My Murray!

Because if a live dog, 'tis said,
Be worth a Lion fairly sped,
A *live lord* must be worth *two* dead,
My Murray!

And if, as the opinion goes,
Verse hath a better sale than prose—
Certes, I should have more than those,
My Murray!

But now this sheet is nearly crammed,
So, if *you will, I* shan't be shammed,
And if you *won't,—you* may be damned,
My Murray!

1262.—To J. Mawman.[viii]

R[a] A[o] 31st 1821.

L[d] Byron presents his Compliments to Mr. Mawman and would be particularly glad to see that Gentleman if he can make it convenient to call at half past *two* tomorrow afternoon.

B. takes the liberty of sending his Carnage and horses in case Mr. M. would like to make the round of the remarkable buildings of Ravenna.

1263.—To Thomas Moore.

Ravenna,
September 3, 1821.

By Mr. Mawman (a paymaster in the corps, in which you and I are privates) I yesterday expedited to your address, under cover one, two paper books, containing the *Giaour*-nal, and a thing or two. It won't *all* do—even for the posthumous public —but extracts from it may. It is a brief and faithful chronicle of a month or so— parts of it not very discreet, but sufficiently sincere. Mr. Mawman saith that he will, in person or per friend, have it delivered to you in your Elysian fields.

If you have got the new *Juans,* recollect that there are some very gross printer's blunders, particularly in the fifth canto,—such as "praise" for "pair"—"precarious" for "precocious"—"Adriatic" for "Asiatic"—"case" for "chase"—besides gifts of additional words and syllables, which make but a cacophonous rhythmus. Put the pen through the said, as I would mine through Murray's ears, if I were alongside him. As it is, I have sent him a rattling letter, as abusive as possible. Though he is publisher to the "Board of *Longitude,*" he is in no danger of discovering it.

I am packing for Pisa—but direct your letters *here,* till further notice.

Yours ever, etc.

1264.—To John Murray.

Sept[r]. 4th 1821.

Dear Sir,—

Enclosed are some notes, etc. You will also have the goodness to hold yourself in readiness to publish the long delayed letter to *Blackwood's,* etc.; but previously let me have a proof of it, as I mean it for a separate publication. The enclosed note you will annex to the *Foscaris*; also the dedication.

Yours, B.

1265.—To John Murray.

R^a September 4th 1821.

Dear Sir,—

By Saturday's post, I sent you a fierce and furibond letter upon the subject of the printer's blunders in *Don Juan.* I must solicit your attention to the topic, though my wrath hath subsided into sullenness.

Yesterday I received Mr. Mawman, a friend of yours, and because he is a friend of *yours*; and that's more than I would do in an *English* case, except for those whom I honour. I was as civil as I could be among packages, even to the very chairs and tables; for I am going to *Pisa* in a few weeks, and have sent and am sending off my chattels. It regretted me that, my books and every thing being packed, I could not send you a few things I meant for you; but they were all sealed and baggaged, so as to have made it a Month's work to get at them again. I gave him an envelope, with the Italian Scrap in it,1 alluded to in my Gilchrist defence. Hobhouse will make it out for you, and it will make you laugh, and him too, the *spelling* particularly. The "*Mericani,*" of whom they call me the "Capo" (or Chief), mean "Americans," which is the name given in *Romagna* to a part of the Carbonari; that is to say, to the *popular* part, the *troops* of the Carbonari. They were originally a society of hunters in the forest, who took that name of Americans, but at present comprize some thousands, etc.; but I shan't let you further into the secret, which may be participated with the postmasters. Why they thought me their Chief, I know not: their Chiefs are like "Legion, being Many." However, it is a post of more honour than profit, for, now that they are persecuted, it is fit that I should aid them; and so I have done, as far as my means will permit. They will rise again some day, for these fools of the Government are blundering: they actually seem to know *nothing*; for they have arrested and banished many of their *own* party, and let others escape who are not their friends.

What thinkst thou of Greece?

Address to me *here* as usual, till you hear further from me.

By Mawman I have sent a journal to Moore; but it won't do for the public,—at least a great deal of it won't;—*parts* may.

I read over the *Juans,* which are excellent. Your Synod was quite wrong; and so you will find by and bye. I regret that I do not go on with it, for I had all the plan for several cantos, and different countries and climes. You say nothing of the *note* I enclosed to you, which will explain why I agreed to discontinue it (at Madame G.'s request); but you are so grand, and sublime, and occupied, that one would think, instead of publishing for "the Board of *Longitude*," that you were trying to discover it.

Let me hear that Gifford is *better.* He can't be spared either by you or me.

Enclosed is a note, which I will thank you *not* to forget to acknowledge and to publish.

Yours, B.

1266.—To Douglas Kinnaird.

Ravenna,
September 4th, 1821.

My dear Douglas,—

I intend to dedicate the "two Foscari's" to Walter Scott, "Sardanapalus" to Goethe, and "Faliero" to you. The two first I have sent to Murray; your own I enclose to *you,* that you may see it first, and accept it or not. If content, send it to Murray.

You are a good German Scholar, I am not even a bad one, but would feel greatly obliged if you would write two lines to the "Grosser Mann" at my request to tell him my intent, and ask his leave. See the inscription at Murray's; it goes by this post.

Yrs. ever, B.

1267.—To John Murray.

Dear Sir,—

Will you have the goodness to forward the enclosed to Mr. Gilchrist, whose address I do not exactly know? *If* that Gentleman would like to see my *second* letter to *you,* on the attack upon himself, you can forward him a copy of the proof.

Yours ever, B.

1268.—To John Murray.

Septr. 9th 1821.

Dear Sir,—

Please to forward the enclosed also to Mr. Gilchrist. I cut my finger, in diving yesterday, against a sharp shell, and can hardly write. Last week, I sent a long note (in English) to the play: let me have a *proof of it*; but, as I am in haste, you can publish the play with the *whole of it, except the part referring* to Southey, to which I wish to add something; and we will then append the whole to a re-print. All the part, down to where it begins on that rascal, will do for publication without my reviewing it—that is to say, if your printer will take pains, and not be careless, as about the new *Juans,*

Let me hear that Mr. Gifford is better, and your family well.

Yours, B.

1269.—To John Murray.

Ravenna,
Sept^{r}, 10th 1821.

Dear Sir,—

By this post I send you three packets containing *Cain, a Mystery* (i.e. a tragedy on a sacred subject) in three acts. I think that it contains some poetry, being in the style of "*Manfred.*" Send me a proof of the whole by return of *post.* If *there is time,* publish it with the other *two*: if not, print it separately, and as soon as you can.

Of the dedications (sent lately), I wish to transfer that to Sir Walter Scott to *this* drama of *Cain,* reserving that of the "*Foscaris*" for another, for a particular reason, of which more by and bye. Write.

Yours, B.

1270.—To John Murray.

Ravenna,
September 12th 1821.

Dear Sir,—

By Tuesday's post, I forwarded, in three packets, the drama of "*Cain,*" in three acts, of which I request the acknowledgement when arrived. To the last speech of *Eve,* in the last act (*i.e.* where she curses Cain), add these three lines to the concluding one—

colony of English all over the cantons of Geneva, etc., I immediately gave up the thought, and persuaded the Gambas to do the same.

By the last post I sent you "The Irish Avatar,"—what think you? The last line—"a name never spoke but with curses or jeers"—must run either "a name only uttered with curses or jeers," or, "a wretch never named but with curses or jeers." Be*case* as *how,* "spoke" is not grammar, except in the House of Commons; and I doubt whether we can say "a name *spoken,*" for *mentioned.* I have some doubts, too, about "repay,"—"and for murder repay with a shout and a smile." Should it not be, "and for murder repay him with shouts and a smile," or "*reward* him with shouts and a smile?"

So, pray put your poetical pen through the MS. and take the least bad of the emendations. Also, if there be any further breaking of Priscian's head, will you apply a plaster? I wrote in the greatest hurry and fury, and sent it to you the day after; so, doubtless, there will be some awful constructions, and a rather lawless conscription of rhythmus.

With respect to what Anna Seward calls "the liberty of transcript,"—when complaining of Miss Matilda Muggleton, the accomplished daughter of a choral vicar of Worcester Cathedral, who had abused the said "liberty of transcript," by inserting in the *Malvern Mercury* Miss Seward's "Elegy on the South Pole," as her *own* production, with her *own* signature, two years after having taken a copy, by permission of the authoress—with regard, I say, to the "liberty of transcript," I by no means oppose an occasional copy to the benevolent few, provided it does not degenerate into such licentiousness of Verb and Noun as may tend to "disparage my parts of speech" by the carelessness of the transcribblers.

I do not think that there is much danger of the "King's Press being abused" upon the occasion, if the publishers of journals have any regard for their remaining liberty of person. It is as pretty a piece of invective as ever put publisher in the way to "Botany." Therefore, if *they* meddle with it, it is at *their* peril. As for myself, I will answer any jontleman—though I by no means recognise a "right of search" into an unpublished production and unavowed poem. The same applies to things published *sans* consent. I hope you like, at least the concluding lines of the *Pome*?

What are you doing, and where are you? in England? Nail Murray—nail him to his own counter, till he shells out the thirteens. Since I wrote to you, I have sent him another tragedy—*Cain* by name—making three in MS. now in his hands, or in the printers. It is in the *Manfred* metaphysical style, and full of some Titanic declamation;—Lucifer being one of the *dram, pers.,* who takes Cain a voyage among the stars, and afterwards to "Hades," where he shows him the phantoms of a former world, and its inhabitants. I have gone upon the notion of Cuvier, that the world has been destroyed three or four times, and was inhabited by mammoths, behemoths, and what not; but *not* by man till the Mosaic period, as, indeed, is proved by the strata of bones found;—those of all unknown animals, and known, being dug out, but none of mankind. I have, therefore, supposed Cain to be shown, in the *rational* Preadamites, beings endowed with a higher intelligence than man, but totally unlike him in form, and with much greater strength of mind and person. You may suppose the small talk which takes place between him and Lucifer upon these matters is not quite canonical.

The consequence is, that Cain comes back and kills Abel in a fit of dissatisfaction, partly with the politics of Paradise, which had driven them all out of it, and partly because (as it is written in Genesis) Abel's sacrifice was the more acceptable to the Deity. I trust that the Rhapsody has arrived—it is in three acts, and entitled "*A Mystery,*" according to the former Christian custom, and in honour of what it probably will remain to the reader.

Yours, etc.

1275.—To Thomas Moore.

September 20, 1821.

After the stanza on Grattan, concluding with "His soul o'er the freedom implored and denied," will it please you to cause insert the following "Addenda," which I dreamed of during to-day's Siesta:—

Ever glorious Grattan! etc., etc., etc.

I will tell you what to do. Get me twenty copies of the whole carefully and privately printed off, as *your* lines were on the Naples affair. Send me *six,* and distribute the rest according to your own pleasure.

I am in a fine vein, "so full of pastime and prodigality!"—So here's to your health, in a glass of grog. Pray write, that I may know by return of post—address to me at Pisa. The Gods give you joy!

Where are you? in Paris? Let us hear. You will take care that there be no printer's name, nor author's, as in the Naples stanza, at least for the present.

1276.—To John Murray.

R^{a}. Septr. 20th 1821.

DEAR MURRAY,—

You need not send "*The Blues,*" which is a mere buffoonery, never meant for publication.

The papers to which I allude, in case of Survivorship, are collections of letters, etc., since I was sixteen years old, contained in the trunks in the care of Mr. Hobhouse. This collection is at least doubled by those I have now here; all received since my last Ostracism. To these I should wish the Editor to have access, *not* for the purpose of *abusing confidences,* nor of *hurting* the feelings of correspondents living, or the memories of the dead; but there are things which would do neither, that I have left unnoticed or unexplained, and which (like all such things) Time only can permit to be noticed or explained, though some are to my credit. The task will, of course, require delicacy; but that will not be wanting, if Moore and Hobhouse survive me, and, I may add, yourself; and that you may all three do so, is, I assure you, my very sincere wish. I am not sure that long life is desirable for one of my temper and constitutional depression of Spirits, which of course I suppress in society; but which breaks out when alone, and in my writings, in spite of myself. It has been deepened, perhaps, by some long past events (I do not allude to my marriage, etc.—on the contrary, *that* raised them by the persecution giving a fillip to my Spirits); but I call it constitutional, as I have reason to think it. You know, or you do *not* know, that my maternal Grandfather (a very clever man, and amiable, I am told) was strongly suspected of Suicide (he was found drowned in the Avon at Bath), and that another very near relative of the same branch took poison, and was merely saved by antidotes. For the first of these events there was no apparent cause, as he was rich, respected, and of considerable intellectual resources, hardly forty years of age, and not at all addicted to any unhinging vice. It was, however, but a strong suspicion, owing to the manner of his death and to his melancholy temper. The *second had* a cause, but it does not become me to touch upon it; it happened when I was far too young to be aware of it, and I never heard of it till after the death of that relative, many years afterwards. I think, then, that I may call this dejection *constitutional.* I had always been told that in *temper* I more resembled my maternal Grandfather than any of *my father's* family—that is, in the gloomier part of his temper, for he was what you call a good natured man, and I am not.

The Journal here I sent by Mawman to Moore the other day; but as it is a mere diary, only *parts* of it would ever do for publication. The other Journal, of the tour in 1816, I should think Augusta might let you have a copy of; but her nerves have been in such a state since 1815, that there is no knowing. Lady Byron's people, and L^y Caroline Lamb's people, and a parcel of that set, got about her and frightened her with all sorts of hints and menaces, so that she has never since been able to write to *me* a *clear common letter,* and is so full of mysteries and miseries, that I can only sympathize, without always understanding her. All my loves, too, make a point of calling upon her, which puts her into a flutter (no difficult matter); and, the year before last I think, Lady F. W. W. marched in upon her, and Lady O., a few years ago, spoke to her at a party; and these and such like calamities have made her afraid of her shadow. It is a very odd fancy that they all take to her: it was only six months ago, that I had some difficulty in preventing the Countess G. from invading her with an Italian letter. I should like to have seen Augusta's face, with an Etruscan Epistle, and all its Meridional style of *issimas,* and other superlatives, before her.

I am much mortified that Gifford don't take to my new dramas: to be sure, they are as opposite to the English drama as one thing can be to another; but I have a notion that, if understood, they will in time find favour (though *not* on the stage) with the reader. The Simplicity of plot is intentional, and the avoidance of *rant* also, as also the compression of the Speeches in the more severe situations. What I seek to show in *The Fosearis* is the *suppressed* passion, rather than the rant of the present day. For that matter—

"Nay, if thou'lt mouth,
I'll rant as well as thou"—

would not be difficult, as I think I have shown in my younger productions—*not dramatic* ones, to be sure. But, as I said before, I am mortified that Gifford don't like them; but I see no remedy, our notions on the subject being so different. How is he? well, I hope: let me know. I regret his demur the more that he has been always my grand patron, and I know no praise which would compensate me in my own mind for his censure. I do not mind *reviews,* as I can work them at their own weapons.

Yours ever and truly, B.

P.S.—By the way, on our next settlement (which will take place with Mr. Kinnaird), you will please to deduct the various sums for *books,* packages *received* and *sent,* the *bust,* tooth-powder, etc., etc., expended by you on my account.

Hobhouse, in his preface to "*Rimini,*" will probably be better able to explain my dramatic system, than I could do, as he is well acquainted with the whole thing. It is more upon the Alfieri School than the English.

I hope that we shall not have Mr. Rogers here: there is a mean minuteness in his mind and tittle-tattle that I dislike, ever since I *found him out* (which was but slowly); besides he is not a good man: why don't he go to bed? What does he do travelling?

The Journal of 1814 I dare say Moore will give, or a copy.

Has *Cain* (the dramatic third attempt), arrived yet? Let me know.

Address to me at *Pisa,* whither I am going. The reason is, that all my Italian friends here have been exiled, and are met there for the present; and I go to join them, as agreed upon, for the Winter.

1277.—To John Murray.

Ravenna,
September 24th 1821.

Dear Murray,—

I have been thinking over our late correspondence, and wish to propose to you the following articles for our future:—

1stly That you shall write to me of yourself, of the health, wealth, and welfare of all friends; but of *me* (*quoad me*) little or nothing.

2dly That you shall send me Soda powders, tooth-powder, tooth-brushes, or any such anti-odontalgic or chemical articles, as heretofore, *ad libitum,* upon being re-imbursed for the same.

3dly That you shall *not* send me any modern, or (as they are called) *new,* publications in *English whatsoever,* save and excepting any writing, prose or verse, of (or reasonably presumed to be of) Walter Scott, Crabbe, Moore, Campbell, Rogers, Gifford, Joanna Baillie, *Irving* (the American), Hogg, Wilson (*Isle of Palms* Man), or *any* especial *single* work of fancy which is thought to be of considerable merit; *Voyages* and *travels,* provided that they are *neither in Greece, Spain, Asia Minor, Albania, nor Italy,* will be welcome: having travelled the countries mentioned, I know that what is said of them can convey nothing further which I desire to know about them. No other English works whatsoever.

4thly That you send me *no periodical works* whatsoever—*no Edinburgh, Quarterly, Monthly,* nor any Review, Magazine, Newspaper, English or foreign, of any description.

5thly That you send me no opinions whatsoever, either *good, bad,* or *indifferent,* of yourself, or your friends, or others, concerning any work, or works, of mine, past, present, or to come.

6thly That au negotiations in matters of business between you and me pass through the medium of the Honble Douglas Kinnaird, my friend and trustee, or Mr. Hobhouse, as *Alter Ego,* and tantamount to myself during my absence, or presence.

Some of these propositions may at first seem strange, but they are founded. The quantity of trash I have received as books is incalculable, and neither amused nor instructed. Reviews and Magazines are at the best but ephemeral and superficial reading: *who thinks* of the *grand article* of *last year* in any *given review*? in the next place, if they regard *myself,* they tend to increase *Egotism*; if favourable, I do not deny that the praise *elates,* and if unfavourable, that the abuse *irritates*—the latter may conduct me to inflict a species of Satire, which would neither do good to you nor to your friends: *they* may smile *now,* and so may *you;* but if I took you all in hand, it would not be difficult to cut you up like gourds. I did as much by as powerful people at nineteen years old, and I know little as yet, in three and thirty, which should prevent me from making all your ribs Gridirons for your hearts, if such were my propensity. But it is *not.* Therefore let me hear none of your provocations. If any thing occurs so very *gross* as to require my notice, I shall hear of it from my personal friends. For the rest, I merely request to be left in ignorance.

The same applies to opinions, *good, bad,* or *indifferent,* of persons in conversation or correspondence: these do not *interrupt,* but they *soil* the *current* of my *Mind.* I am sensitive enough, but *not* till I am *touched*; and *here* I am beyond the touch of the short arms of literary England, except the few feelers of the Polypus that crawl over the Channel in the way of Extract.

All these precautions *in* England would be useless: the libeller or the flatterer would there reach me in spite of all; but in Italy we know little of literary England, and think less, except what reaches us through some garbled and brief extract in some miserable Gazette. For *two years* (excepting two or three articles cut out and sent to *you,* by the post) I never read a newspaper which was not forced upon me by some accident, and know, upon the whole, as little of England as you all do of Italy, and God knows *that* is little enough, with all your travels, etc., etc., etc. The English travellers *know Italy* as *you* know Guernsey: how much is *that*?

If any thing occurs so violently gross or personal as to require notice, Mr. D[s] Kinnaird will let me *know*; but of *praise* I desire to hear *nothing.*

You will say, "to what tends all this?" I will answer THAT;—to keep my mind *free and unbiassed* by all paltry and personal irritabilities of praise or censure;—to let my Genius take its natural direction, while my feelings are like the dead, who know nothing and feel nothing of all or aught that is said or done in their regard.

If you can observe these conditions, you will spare yourself and others some pain: let me not be worked upon to rise up; for if I do, it will not be for a little: if you can *not* observe these conditions, we shall cease to be correspondents, but *not friends*; for I shall always be

Yours ever and truly, BYRON.

P.S.—I have taken these resolutions not from any irritation against *you* or *yours,* but simply upon reflection that all reading, either praise or censure, of myself has done me harm. When I was in Switzerland and Greece, I was out of the way of hearing either, and *how I wrote there!* In Italy I am out of the way of it too; but latterly, partly through my fault, and partly through your kindness in wishing to send me the *newest* and most periodical publications, I have had a crowd of reviews, etc., thrust upon me, which have bored me with their jargon, of one kind or another, and taken off my attention from greater objects. You have also sent me a parcel of trash of poetry, for no reason that I can conceive, unless to provoke me to write a new *English Bards.* Now *this* I wish to avoid; for if ever I *do,* it will be a strong production; and I desire peace, as long as the fools will keep their nonsense out of my way.

1283.—To Thomas Moore.

September—no—October 1, 1821.

I have written to you lately, both in prose and verse, at great length, to Paris and London. I presume that Mrs. Moore, or whoever is your Paris deputy, will forward my packets to you in London.

I am setting off for Pisa, if a slight incipient intermittent fever do not prevent me. I fear it is not strong enough to give Murray much chance of realising his thirteens again. I hardly should regret it, I think, provided you raised your price upon him—as what Lady Holderness (my sister's grandmother, a Dutchwoman) used to call Augusta, her *Residee Legatoo*—so as to provide for us all: *my* bones with a splendid and *larmoyante* edition, and you with double what is extractable during my lifetime.

I have a strong presentiment that (bating some out of the way accident) you will survive me. The difference of eight years, or whatever it is, between our ages, is nothing. I do not feel (nor am, indeed, anxious to feel) the principle of life in me tend to longevity. My father and mother died, the one at thirty-five or six, and the other at forty-five; and Dr. Rush, or somebody else, says that nobody lives long, without having *one parent,* at least, an old stager.

I *should,* to be sure, like to see out my eternal mother-in-law, not so much for her heritage, but from my natural antipathy. But the indulgence of this natural desire is too much to expect from the Providence who presides over old women. I bore you with all this about lives, because it has been put in my way by a calculation of insurances which Murray has sent me. I *really think* you should have more, if I evaporate within a reasonable time.

I wonder if my *Cain* has got safe to England. I have written since about sixty stanzas of a poem, in octave stanzas, (in the Pulci style, which the fools in England think was invented by Whistlecraft—it is as old as the hills in Italy,) called *The Vision of Judgment,* by Quevedo Redivivus, with this motto—

> "A Daniel come to *judgment,* yea, a Daniel:
> I thank thee, Jew, for teaching me that word."

In this it is my intent to put the said George's Apotheosis in a Whig point of view, not forgetting the Poet Laureate for his preface and his other demerits.

I am just got to the pass where Saint Peter, hearing that the royal defunct had opposed Catholic Emancipation, rises up, and, interrupting Satan's oration, declares *he* will change places with Cerberus sooner than let him into heaven, while *he* has the keys thereof.

I must go and ride, though rather feverish and chilly. It is the ague season; but the agues do me rather good than harm. The feel after the *fit* is as if one had got rid of one's body for good and all.

The gods go with you!—Address to Pisa.

Ever yours.

P.S.—Since I came back, I feel better, though I stayed out too late for this malaria season, under the thin crescent of a very young moon, and got off my horse to walk in an avenue with a Signora for an hour. I thought of you and

> "When at eve thou rovest
> By the star thou lovest."

But it was not in a romantic mood, as I should have been once; and yet it was a *new* woman, (that is, new to me,) and, of course, expected to be made love to. But I merely made a few common-place speeches. I feel, as your poor friend Curran said, before his death, "a mountain of lead upon my heart," which I believe to be constitutional, and that nothing will remove it but the same remedy.

1284.—To John Murray.

Octr. 4th 1821.

DEAR MURRAY,—

I send you in 8 sheets, and 106 stanzas (octave), a poem entitled a *Vision of Judgement,* etc., by Quevedo Redivivus, of which you will address the proof to me at *Pisa,* and an answer by return of post. Pray, let the Printer be as careful as he can to decypher it, which may be not so easy.

It may happen that you will be afraid to publish it: in that case, find me a publisher, assuring him that, if he gets into a scrape, I will give up *my name* or person. I do not approve of your mode of not putting publisher's names on title pages (which was unheard of, till *you* gave yourself that *air*): an author's case is different, and from time immemorial have published anonymously.

I wait to hear the arrival of various packets.

Yours, B.

Address to *Pisa.*

1285.—To the Hon. Augusta Leigh.

Octr. 5th 1821.—

MY DEAREST AUGUSTA/

"Burton's Anatomy of Melancholy."

1288.—To John Cam Hobhouse.

[FRAGMENT.]

P.S. I have just received a very inconsistent epistle from our friend Douglas K. Now all I ask is that he will not write contradictions of *himself* every two months.

Could you without trouble rummage out from my papers the first (or half) act of tragedy that I began in 1815, called "*Werner*." Make Murray cut out "the German's tale" in Lee's Canterbury tales (the subject of the drama), and send me both by the post. They will come in a letter, like the proofs.

I am determined to make a struggle for the more regular drama, without encouragement; for Murray and his synod do nothing but throw cold water on what I have done hitherto. But they may be damned for aught that I mind them.

On the 11th inst. I sent a "Manfred" sort of thing called "Cain." Has he shown it to you?

Of course I write for the reader, and not for the stage, so no need of "Mr. Upton."

I have also sent him letter (enclosed to Ds. K.) requesting him to send me no more reviews either of *praise* or censure, nor opinions of any sort from him, or his friends. The fact is, that they irritate and take off one's attention, which may be better employed than in listening to either libels or flattery. I have begged this of him, under pains and penalties of another "English Bards &c." My bile would easily make chyle of him and his in such a production, if they don't let me alone; or at least keep me in ignorance, of their prate. Let them chatter or scribble, so that I neither hear, nor see them; which is not likely here, unless they send on purpose.

1289.—To John Cam Hobhouse.

October 12th, 1821.

MY DEAR HOBHOUSE,—

I had written already to ask "Mr. Nisby what he thought of the Grand Vizier," and of the Greeks, our old acquaintances.

I think you have given Bowles his gruel with your parody on Savage, which is certainly much better than *his* parody on the *legitimate* Savage (I once saw somewhere a parallel between us), and must have put him into a fine tantrum. As for "*Argument*" "I never dispute your talents in making a Goose pye, Mrs. Primrose, so pray leave argument to me."

As to the printers' errors,—Oons! what do you think of "*Adriatic* side of the Bosphorus,"—of "*praise*" for "*pair*"—"*precarious*" for "*precocious*," and "*case*" for "*chase*." Mr. Murray has received a trimmer, I promise you, not without cause. Our friend Douglas has also been seducing me into mercantile contradictions, lstly by writing letter after letter to convince me that M. never offered me *enough* for the past MSS., and then when I had refused what was really an *inadequate* offer, turning round upon me and desiring me to accept it! Now, as Croaker says, "plague take it, there must be a right and a wrong," and which is it? [Why] Douglas contradicted himself so suddenly I don't know. However, since that I have sent two more Poeshies to A[lbemarle] Street, "*Cain*" a tragedy in three acts, "A Vision of Judgment" by way of reversing rogue Southey's, in my finest, ferocious, Caravaggio style, and a *third* entitled "the Irish Avatar," upon the late Irishisms of the Blarney people in Dublin. All which I pray you to look at. I am mistaken if the *two* letters are not after your own radical heart.

Your infamous government will drive all honest men into the necessity of reversing it. I see nothing left for it but a republic *now*; an opinion which I have held aloof as long as it would let me. *Come* it must. *They* do not see this, but all this driving will do it, it may not be in ten or twenty years, but it is inevitable, and I am sorry for it.

When we read of the *beginnings* of revolutions in a *few* pages, it seems as if they had happened in *five* minutes; whereas *years* have always been, and must be their prologues; it took from eighty-eight to ninety-three, to decide the French one; and the English are a tardy people. I am so persuaded that an English one is inevitable, that I am moving Heaven and Earth (that is to say Douglas Kinnaird, and Medea's trustee) to get me out of the funds. I would give all I have to see the country *fairly free,* but till I know that *giving,* or rather *losing* it, *would free* it, you will excuse my natural anxiety for my temporal affairs.

Still I can't approve of the ways of the radicals; they seem such very low imitations of the Jacobins. I do not allude to you, and Burdett, but to the Major, and to Hunt of Bristol, and little Waddington, &c, &c.

If I came home (which I never shall) I should take a *decided* part in politics, with pen and person; and (if I could revive my English) in the house; but am not yet quite sure *what* part, except that it would *not* be in favour of these abominable tyrants.

I certainly lean towards a republic. All history and experience is in its favour, even the French; for they butchered thousands of citizens at first, yet *more* were killed in any one of the great battles, than ever perished by a democratical proscription.

infamy, and patronage of their master rogues and slave renegadoes, if they do once rouse me up,

"They had better gall the devil, Salisbury."

I have that for two or three of them, which they had better not move me to put in motion;—and yet, after all, what a fool I am to disquiet myself about such fellows! It was all very well ten or twelve years ago, when I was a "curled darling," and *minded* such things. At present, I *rate* them at their true value; but, from natural temper and bile, am not able to keep quiet.

Let me hear from you on your return from Ireland, which ought to be ashamed to see you, after her Brunswick blarney. I am of Longman's opinion, that you should allow your friends to liquidate the Bermuda claim. Why should you throw away the two thousand *pounds* (of the *non*-guinea Murray) upon that cursed piece of treacherous inveiglement? I think you carry the matter a little too far and scrupulously. When we see patriots begging publicly, and know that Grattan received a fortune from his country, I really do not see why a man, in no whit inferior to any or all of them, should shrink from accepting that assistance from his private friends which every tradesman receives from his connections upon much less occasions. For, after all, it was not *your debt*—it was a piece of swindling *against* you. As to * * * *, and the "what noble creatures! etc., etc.," it is all very fine and very well, but, till you can persuade me that there is *no credit,* and no *self-applause* to be obtained by being of use to a celebrated man, I must retain the same opinion of the human spe*cies,* which I do of our friend Mr. Spe*cie.*

Yours ever, etc., BYRON.

1295.—To John Murray.

8bre 30th 1821.

DEAR MORAY,—

You say the errors were in the MSS. of *D. J.*—but the *omitted* stanza, which I sent you in an after letter, and the omitted notes? please to replace them.

Yours, B.

I am just setting off for Pisa.
Favour the enclosed to Mr. Moore.
Address to Pisa.

CHAPTER XXXIII. "MY DICTIONARY," MAY, 1821; DETACHED THOUGHTS, OCTOBER 15, 1821–MAY 18, 1822

Ravenna, May 1st 1821.

Amongst various journals, memoranda, diaries, etc., which I have kept in the course of my living, I began one about three months ago, and carried it on till I had filled one paper-book (thinnish), and two sheets or so of another. I then left off, partly because I thought we should have some business here, and I had furbished up my arms, and got my apparatus ready for taking a turn with the Patriots, having my drawers full of their proclamations, oaths, and resolutions, and my lower rooms of their hidden weapons of most calibres; and partly because I had filled my paper book. But the Neapolitans have betrayed themselves and all the World, and those who would have given their blood for Italy can now only give her their tears.

Some day or other, if dust holds together, I have been enough in the Secret (at least in this part of the country) to cast perhaps some little light upon the atrocious treachery which has replunged Italy into Barbarism. At present I have neither the time nor the temper. However, the *real* Italians are *not* to blame—merely the scoundrels at the *Heel of the Boot,* which the *Hun* now wears, and will trample them to ashes with for their Servility.

I have risked myself with the others *here,* and how far I may or may not be compromised is a problem at this moment: some of them like "Craigengelt" would "tell all and more than all to save themselves;" but, come what may, the cause was a glorious one, though it reads at present as if the Greeks had run away from Xerxes.

Happy the few who have only to reproach themselves with believing that these rascals were less *rascaille* than they proved. *Here* in Romagna the efforts were necessarily limited to preparations and good intentions, until the Germans were fairly engaged in *equal* warfare, as we are upon their very frontiers without a single fort, or hill, nearer than San Marino. Whether "Hell will be paved with" those "good intentions," I know not; but there will probably be good store of Neapolitans to walk upon the pavement, whatever may be it's composition. Slabs of lava from their mountain, with the bodies of their own damned Souls for cement, would be the fittest causeway for Satan's *Corso.*

But what shall I write? another Journal? I think not. Anything that comes uppermost—and call it "my Dictionary."

My Dictionary.

Augustus.—I have often been puzzled with his character. Was he a great Man? Assuredly. But not one of *my* great men. I have always looked upon Sylla as the greatest Character in History, for laying down his power at the moment when it was

> "too great to keep or to resign,"

and thus despising them all. As to the retention of his power by Augustus, the thing was already settled. If he had given it up, the Commonwealth was gone, the republic was long past all resuscitation. Had Brutus and Cassius gained the battle of Philippi, it would not have restored the republic—its days ended with the Gracchi, the rest was a mere struggle of parties. You might as well cure a Consumption, restore a broken egg, as revive a state so long a prey to every uppermost Soldier as Rome had long been.

As for a despotism, if Augustus could have been sure that all his Successors would have been like himself (I mean *not* as *Octavius,* but Augustus), or Napoleon would have insured the world that *none* of his Successors would have been like himself, the antient or modern World might have gone on like the Empire of China—in a state of lethargic prosperity.

Suppose, for instance, that, instead of Tiberius and Caligula, Augustus had been immediately succeeded by Nerva, Trajan, the Antonines, or even by Titus and his father, what a difference in our estimate of himself? So far from gaining by the *contrast,* I think that one half of our dislike arises from his having been heired by Tiberius, and one half of Julius Cæsar's fame from his having had his empire consolidated by Augustus.

Suppose that there had been *no Octavius,* and Tiberius had "jumped the life" between, and at once succeeded Julius? And yet it is difficult to say whether hereditary right, or popular choice, produce the worse Sovereigns. The Roman Consuls make a goodly show, but then they only reigned for a year, and were under a sort of personal obligation to distinguish themselves. It is still more difficult to say which form of Government is the *worst* —all are so bad. As for democracy, it is the worst of the whole; for what is (*in fact*) democracy? an Aristocracy of Blackguards.

Aberdeen—Old and New, or the Auldtoun and Newtoun.

For several years of my earliest childhood I was in that City, but have never revisited it since I was ten years old. I was sent at five years old, or earlier, to a School kept by a Mr. *Bowers,* who was called "*Bodsy* Bowers" by reason of his dapperness. It was a School for both sexes. I learned little there, except to repeat by rote the first lesson of Monosyllables—"God made man, let us love him"—by hearing it often repeated, without acquiring a letter. Whenever proof was made of my progress at home, I repeated these words with the most rapid fluency; but on turning over a new leaf, I continued to repeat them, so that the narrow boundaries of my first year's accomplishments were detected, my ears boxed (which they did not deserve, seeing that it was by *ear* only that I had acquired my letters), and my intellects consigned to a new preceptor. He was a very decent, clever, little Clergyman, named Ross, afterwards Minister of one of the Kirks (*East* I think). Under *him* I made an astonishing progress, and I recollect to this day his mild manners and good-natured pains-taking.

The moment I could read, my grand passion was *history*; and why, I know not, but I was particularly taken with the battle near the Lake Regillus in the Roman History, put into my hands the first.

Four years ago, when standing on the heights of Tusculum, and looking down upon the little round Lake, that was once Regillus, and which dots the immense expanse below, I remembered my young enthusiasm and my old instructor.

Afterwards I had a very serious, samrnine, but kind young man, named Paterson, for a Tutor: he was the son of my Shoemaker, but a good Scholar, as is common with the Scotch. He was a rigid Presbyterian also. With him I began Latin in Ruddiman's Grammar, and continued till I went to the "Grammar School" (*Scotice* "Schule"—*Aberdonice* "Squeel"), where I threaded all the Classes to the *fourth,* when I was re-called to England (where I had been hatched) by the demise of my Uncle.

I acquired this handwriting, which I can hardly read myself, under the fair copies of Mr. Duncan of the same city. I don't think that he would plume himself upon my progress. However, I wrote much better then than I have ever done since. Haste and agitation of one kind or another have quite spoilt as pretty a scrawl as ever scratched over a frank.

The Grammar School might consist of a hundred and fifty of all ages under age. It was divided into five classes, taught by four masters, the Chief teaching the fifth and fourth himself, as in England the fifth, sixth forms, and Monitors are heard by the Head Masters.

DETACHED THOUGHTS.

Octr 15th 1821.

I have been thinking over the other day on the various comparisons, good or evil, which I have seen published of myself in different journals English and foreign. This was suggested to me by accidentally turning over a foreign one lately; for I have made it a rule latterly never to *search* for anything of the kind, but not to avoid the perusal if presented by Chance.

To begin then—I have seen myself compared personally or poetically, in English, French, *German* (*as* interpreted to me), Italian, and Portuguese, within these nine years, to Rousseau—Göethe—Young—Aretino—Timon of Athens—"An Alabaster Vase lighted up within"—Satan—Shakespeare—Buonaparte—Tiberius—Aeschylus—Sophocles—Euripides—Harlequin—The Clown—Sternhold and Hopkins—to the Phantasmagoria—to Henry the 8th—to Chenies—to Mirabeau—to young R. Dallas (the Schoolboy)—to Michael Angelo—to Raphael—to a *petit maître*—to Diogenes—to Childe Harold—to Lara—to the Count in Beppo—to Milton—to Pope—to Dryden—to Burns—to Savage—to Chatterton—to "oft have I heard of thee my Lord Biron" in Shakespeare—to Churchill the poet—to Kean the Actor—to Alfieri, etc., etc., etc. The likeness to Alfieri was asserted very seriously by an Italian, who had known him in his younger days: it of course related merely to our apparent personal dispositions. He did not assert it to *me* (for we were not then good friends), but in society.

The Object of so many contradictory comparisons must probably be like something different from them all; but what *that* is, is more than *I* know, or any body else.

My Mother, before I was twenty, would have it that I was like Rousseau, and Madame de Staël used to say so too in 1813, and the *Edinh Review* has something of the sort in its critique on the 4th Canto of *Che Had*. I can't see any point of resemblance: he wrote prose, I verse: he was of the people, I of the Aristocracy: he was a philosopher, I am none: he published his first work at forty, I mine at eighteen: his first essay brought him universal applause, mine the contrary: he married his housekeeper, I could not keep house with my wife: he thought all the world in a plot against *him,* my little world seems to think *me* in a plot against it, if I may judge by their abuse in print and coterie: he liked Botany, I like flowers, and herbs, and trees, but know nothing of their pedigrees: he wrote Music, I limit my knowledge of it to what I catch by *Ear*—I never could learn any thing by *study,* not even a language, it was all by rote and ear and memory: he had a bad memory, I *had* at least an excellent one (ask Hodgson the poet, a good judge, for he has an astonishing one): he wrote with hesitation and care, I with rapidity and rarely with pains: *he* could never ride nor swim "nor was cunning of fence," *I* am an excellent swimmer, a decent though not at all a dashing rider (having staved in a rib at eighteen in the course of scampering), and was sufficient of fence—particularly of the Highland broadsword; not a bad boxer when I could keep my temper, which was difficult, but which I strove to do ever since I knocked down Mr. Purling and put his knee-pan out (with the gloves on) in Angelo's and Jackson's rooms in 1806 during the sparring; and I was besides a very fair cricketer—one of the Harrow Eleven when we play[ed] against Eton in 1805. Besides, Rousseau's way of life, his country, his manners, his whole character, were so very different, that I am at a loss to conceive how such a comparison could have arisen, as it has done three several times, and all in rather a remarkable manner. I forgot to say, that *he* was also short-sighted, and that hitherto my eyes have been the contrary to such a degree, that, in the largest theatre of Bologna, I distinguished and read some busts and inscriptions painted near the stage, from a box so distant, and so *darkly* lighted, that none of the company (composed of young and very bright-eyed people—some of them in the same box) could make out a letter, and thought it was a trick, though I had never been in that theatre before.

Altogether, I think myself justified in thinking the comparison not well founded. I don't say this out of pique, for Rousseau was a great man, and the thing if true were flattering enough; but I have no idea of being pleased with a chimera.

1.

When I met old Courtenay, the Orator, at Rogers the poet's in 1811–1812, I was much taken with the portly remains of his fine figure, and the still acute quickness of his conversation. It was *he* who silenced Flood in the English House by a crushing reply to a hasty debût of the rival of Grattan in Ireland. I asked Courtenay (for I like to trace motives), if he had not some personal provocation; for the acrimony of his answer seemed to me (as I had read it) to involve it. Courtenay said "he had —that when in Ireland (being an Irishman) at the *bar* of the Irish house of Commons that Flood had made a personal and unfair attack upon *himself,* who, not being a member of that house, could not defend himself; and that some years afterwards, the opportunity of retort offering in the English Parliament, he could not resist it." He certainly repaid F. with interest, for Flood never made any figure, and only a speech or two afterwards in the E. H. of Commons. I must except, however, his speech on Reform in 1790, which "Fox called the best he ever heard upon that Subject."

2.

When Fox was asked what he thought the best speech he had ever heard, he replied "Sheridan's on the Impeachment of Hastings in the house of Commons" (*not* that in Westminster Hall). When asked what he thought of his *own* speech on the breaking out of the War? he replied "that was a damned good speech too."—From Ld Holland.

3.

When Sheridan made his famous speech already alluded to, Fox advised him to speak it over again in Westminster Hall on the trial, as nothing better *could* be made of the subject; but Sheridan made his new speech as different as possible, and, according to the best Judges, very inferior to the former, notwithstanding the laboured panegyric of Burke upon his *Colleague.*—L^{d} H.

4.

Burke spoilt his own speaking afterwards by an imitation of Sheridan's in Westminster Hall: this Speech he called always "the grand desideratum, which was neither poetry nor eloquence, but something *better* than both."

his distant signals of distance and distress. All the time he went on talking without intermission, for he was a man of many words.

Poor fellow, he died, a martyr to his new riches, of a second visit to Jamaica—

> "I'll give the lands of Deloraine
> Dark Musgrave were alive again"
>
> *that is*
>
> I would give many a Sugar Cane
> Monk Lewis were alive again!

18.

Lewis said to me, "Why do you talk *Venetian*" (such as I could talk, not very fine to be sure) "to the Venetians? and not the usual Italian?" I answered, partly from habit, and partly to be understood, if possible. "It may be so," said Lewis, "but it sounds to me like talking with a *brogue* to an *Irishman.*"

19.

Baillie (commonly called Long Baillie, a very clever man, but odd), complained in riding to our friend Scrope B. Davies, "that he had a *stitch* in his side." "I don't wonder at it" (said Scrope) "for you ride *like* a *tailor.*" Whoever had seen B. on horseback, with his very tall figure on a small nag, would not deny the justice of the repartee.

20.

In 1808, Scrope and myself being at Supper at Steevens's (I think Hobhouse was there too) after the Opera, young Goulburne (of the Blues and of the Blueviad) came in full of the praises of his horse, Grimaldi, who had just won a race at Newmarket. "Did he win easy?" said Scrope. "Sir," replied Goulburne, "he did not even condescend to *puff* at coming in." "No" (said Scrope) "and so *you puff for* him."

21.

Captain Wallace, a notorious character of that day, and *then* intimate with most of the more dissipated young men of the day, asked me one night at the Gaming table, where I thought *his Soul* would be found after death? I answered him, "In *Silver Hell*" (a cant name for a second rate Gambling house).

22.

When the Honble J. W. Ward quitted the Whigs, he facetiously demanded, at Sir James Macintosh's table, in the presence of Mad[e] de Staël, Malthus, and a large and goodly company of all parties and countries, "what it would take to *re-whig him,* as he thought of turning again." "Before you can be *re-whigged*" (said I), "I am afraid you must be *re- Warded.*" This pun has been attributed to others: they are welcome to it; but it was mine notwithstanding, as a numerous company and Ward himself doth know. I believe Luttrel versified it afterwards to put into the *M. Chronicle*—at least the late Lady Melbourne told me so. Ward took it good-humouredly at the time.

23.

When Sheridan was on his death-bed, Rogers aided him with purse and person: this was particularly kind in Rogers, who always spoke ill of Sheridan (to me at least); but indeed he does that of every-body to any body. Rogers is the reverse of the line

"The *best good man* with the *worst Matured* Muse,"

being

"The *worst* good man with the *best* natured Muse."

His Muse being all Sentiment and Sago and Sugar, while he himself is a venomous talker. I say "*worst good* man" because he is (perhaps) a *good* man—at least he does good now and then, as well he may, to purchase himself a shilling's worth of Salvation for his Slanders. They are so *little* too—small talk, and old Womanny; and he is malignant too, and envious, and—he be damned!

24.

Curran! Curran's the Man who struck me most. Such Imagination! There never was any thing like it, that ever I saw or heard of. His *published* life, his published speeches, give you *no* idea of the Man—none at all. He was a *Machine* of Imagination, as some one said that Piron was an "Epigrammatic Machine."

I did not see a great deal of Curran—only in 1813; but I met him at home (for he used to call on me), and in society, at Mac'Intosh's, Holland House, etc., etc., etc., and he was wonderful, even to me, who had seen many remarkable men of the time.

25.

A young American, named Coolidge, called on me not many months ago: he was intelligent, very handsome, and not more than twenty years old according to appearances. A little romantic, but that sits well upon youth, and mighty fond of poesy as may be suspected from his approaching me in my cavern. He brought me a message from an old Servant of my family (Joe Murray), and told me that *he* (Mr. Coolidge) had obtained a copy of my bust from Thorwal[d]sen at Rome, to send to America. I confess I was more flattered by this young enthusiasm of a solitary trans-atlantic traveller, than if they had decreed me a Statue in the Paris Pantheon (I have seen Emperors and demagogues cast down from their pedestals even in my own time, and Grattan's name razed from the Street called after him in Dublin) I say that I was more nattered by it, because it was *single, un-political,* and was without motive or ostentation—the pure and warm feeling of a boy for the poet he admired. It must have been expensive though. *I* would not pay the price of a Thorwaldsen bust for any human head and shoulders, except Napoleon's, or my children's, or some "*absurd Womankind's*" as Monkbarns calls them, or my Sister's. If asked, *why* then I sate for my own—answer, that it was at the request particular of J. C. Hobhouse, Esq[re], and for no one else. A *picture* is a different matter—every body sits for their picture; but a bust looks like putting up pretensions to permanency, and smacks something of a hankering for *public* fame rather than private remembrance.

26.

One of the cleverest men I ever knew in Conversation was Scrope Beardmore Davies. Hobhouse is also very good in that line, though it is of less consequence to a man who has other ways of showing his talents than in company. Scrope was always ready, and often witty: Hobhouse as witty, but not always so ready, being more diffident.

27.

A drunken man ran against Hobhouse in the Street. A companion of the Drunkard, not much less so, cried out to Hobhouse, "*An't* you ashamed to run against a drunken man? couldn't you see that he was *drunk*?" "Damn him" (answered Hobhouse) "isn't *he* ashamed to run against *me*? couldn't he see that *I* was *sober*?"

28.

When Brummell1 was obliged (by that affair of poor Meyler, who thence acquired the name of "Dick the Dandy-killer"—it was about money and debt and all that) to retire to France, he knew no French; and having obtained a Grammar for the purposes of Study, our friend Scrope Davies was asked what progress Brummell had made in French, to which he responded, "that B. had been stopped like Buonaparte in Russia by the *Elements.*" I have put this pun into "Beppo," which is "a fair exchange and no robbery;" for Scrope made his fortune at several dinners (as he owned himself), by repeating occasionally as his own some of the buffooneries with which I had encountered him in the Morning.

29.

I liked the Dandies; they were always very civil to *me,* though in general they disliked literary people, and persecuted and mystified Me de Staël, Lewis, Horace Twiss, and the like, damnably. They persuaded Me de Stael that Alvanley had a hundred thousand a year, etc., etc., till she praised him to his *face* for his *beauty*! and made a set at him for Albertine (*Libertine,* as Brummell baptized her, though the poor Girl was and is as correct as maid or wife can be, and very amiable withal), and a hundred fooleries besides.

The truth is, that, though I gave up the business early, I had a tinge of Dandyism in my minority, and probably retained enough of it, to conciliate the great ones; at four and twenty. I had gamed, and drank, and taken my degrees in most dissipations; and having no pedantry, and not being overbearing, we ran quietly together. I knew them all more or less, and they made me a Member of Watier's (a superb Club at that time), being, I take it, the only literary man (except *two others,* both men of the world, M. and S.) in it.

Our Masquerade was a grand one; so was the Dandy Ball, too, at the Argyle, but *that* (the latter) was given by the four Chiefs, B., M., A., and P., if I err not.

30.

I was a Member of the Alfred too, being elected while in Greece. It was pleasant—a little too sober and literary, and bored with Sotheby and Sir Francis D'Ivernois! but one met Peel, and Ward, and Valentia, and many other pleasant or known people; and was upon the whole a decent resource on a rainy day, in a dearth of parties, or parliament, or an empty season.

31.

I belonged, or belong, to the following Clubs or Societies:—to the Alfred, to the Cocoa tree, to Watier's, to the Union, to Racket's (at Brighton), to the Pugilistic, to the Owls or "Fly by Night," to the *Cambridge* Whig Club, to the Harrow Club, Cambridge, and to one or two private Clubs, to the Hampden political Club, and to the Italian Carbonari, etc., etc., etc., "though last *not least.*" I got into all these, and never stood for any other—at least to my own knowledge. I declined being proposed to several others; though pressed to stand Candidate.

32.

If the papers lie not (which they generally do), Demetrius Zograffo of Athens is at the head of the Athenian part of the present Greek Insurrection. He was my Servant in 1809, 1810, 1811, 1812, at different intervals in those years (for I left him in Greece when I went to Constantinople), and accompanied me to England in 1811. He returned to Greece, Spring 1812. He was a clever, but not *apparently* an enterprizing, man; but Circumstances make men. His two sons (*then* infants) were named Miltiades and Alcibiades. May the Omen be happy!

33.

I have a notion that Gamblers are as happy as most people, being always *excited.* Women, wine, fame, the table, even Ambition, *sate* now and then; but every turn of the card, and cast of the dice, keeps the Gamester alive: besides one can Game ten times longer than one can do any thing else.

I was very fond of it when young, that is to say, of "Hazard;" for I hate all *Card* Games, even Faro. When Macco (or whatever they spell it) was introduced, I gave up the whole thing; for I loved and missed the *rattle* and *dash* of the box and dice, and the glorious uncertainty, not only of good luck or bad luck, but of *any luck at all,* as one had sometimes to throw *often* to decide at all.

I have thrown as many as fourteen mains running, and carried off all the cash upon the table occasionally; but I had no coolness or judgement or calculation. It was the *delight* of the thing that pleased me. Upon the whole, I left off in time without being much a winner or loser. Since one and twenty years of age, I played but little, and then never above a hundred or two, or three.

34.

As far as Fame goes (that is to say *living* Fame) I have had my share—perhaps, indeed, *certainly* more than my *deserts.* Some odd instances have occurred to my own experience of the wild and strange places, to which a name may penetrate, and where it may impress. Two years ago (almost three, being in August or July 1819), I received at Ravenna a letter in *English* verse from |*Drontheim* in Norway, written by a Norwegian, and full of the usual compliments, etc., etc. It is still somewhere amongst my papers. In the same month, I received an invitation into *Holstein* from a Mr. Jacobsen (I think), of Hamburgh; also (by the same medium), a translation of Medora's song in the "Corsair" by a Westphalian Baroness (not "Thunderton-tronck "), with some original verses of hers (very pretty and Klopstock-ish), and a prose translation annexed to them, on the subject of my wife. As they concerned *her* more than me, I sent them to her together with Mr. J.'s letter. It was odd enough to receive an invitation to pass the *summer* in *Holstein,* while in *Italy,* from people I never knew. The letter was addressed to Venice. Mr. J. talked to me of the "wild roses growing in the Holstein summer:" why then did the Cimbri and Teutones emigrate?

What a strange thing is life and man? Were I to present myself at the door of the house, where my daughter now is, the door would be shut in my face, unless (as is not impossible) I knocked down the porter; and if I had gone in that year (and perhaps now) to Drontheim (the furthest town in Norway), or into Holstein, I should have been received with open arms into the mansions of Strangers and foreigners, attached to me by no tie but that of mind and rumour.

As far as *Fame* goes, I have had my share: it has indeed been leavened by other human contingencies, and this in a greater degree than has occurred to most literary men of a *decent* rank in life; but on the whole I take it that such equipoise is the condition of humanity.

I doubt sometimes whether, after all, a quiet and unagitated life would have suited me: yet I sometimes long for it. My earliest dreams (as most boys' dreams are) were martial; but a little later they were all for *love* and retirement, till the hopeless attachment to M. C. began, and continued (though sedulously concealed) *very* early in my teens; and so upwards for a time. *This* threw me out again "alone on a wide, wide sea."

In the year 1804, I recollect meeting my Sister at General Harcourt's in Portland Place. I was then *one* thing, and *as* she had always till then found me. When we met again in 1805 (she told me since), that my temper and disposition were so completely altered, that I was hardly to be recognized. I was not then sensible of the change, but I can believe it, and account for it.

35.

A private play being got up at Cambridge, a Mr. *Tulk,* greatly to the inconvenience of Actors and audience, declined his part on a sudden, so that it was necessary to make an apology to the Company. In doing this, Hobhouse (indignant like all the rest at this inopportune caprice of the Seceder) stated to the audience "that in consequence of *a* Mr. Tulk having unexpectedly thrown up his part, they must request their indulgence, etc., etc." Next day, the furious Tulk demanded of Hobhouse, "did you, Sir, or did you not use *that* expression?" "Sir," (said Hobhouse) "I *did* or *did not use* that expression." "Perhaps" (said Scrope Davies, who was present), "you object to the *indefinite article,* and prefer being entitled *the Mr. Tulk*?" *The* Tulk eyed Scrope indignantly; but aware, probably, that the said Scrope, besides being a profane Jester, had the misfortune to be a very good shot, and had already fought two or three duels, he retired without further objections to either article, except a conditional menace—*if* he should ascertain that an intention, etc., etc., etc.

36.

I have been called in as Mediator or Second at least twenty times in violent quarrels, and have always contrived to settle the business without compromising the honour of the parties, or leading them to mortal consequences; and this too sometimes in very difficult and delicate circumstances, and having to deal with very hot and haughty Spirits—Irishmen, Gamesters, Guardsmen, Captains and Cornets of horse, and the like. This was of course in my youth, when I lived in hot-headed company. I have had to carry challenges from Gentlemen to Noblemen, from Captains to Captains, from lawyers to Counsellors, and once from a Clergyman to an officer in the Life-guards. It may seem strange, but I found the latter by far the most difficult

> "...to compose
> The bloody duel without blows."

The business being about a woman. I must add too that I never saw a *woman* behave so ill, like a coldblooded heartless whore as she was; but very handsome for all that. A certain Susan C. was she called. I never saw her but once, and that was to induce her but to say two words (which in no degree compromised herself), and which would have had the effect of saving a priest or a Lieutenant of Cavalry. She would *not* say them, and neither N. or myself (the Son of Sir E. N., and a friend to one of the parties) could prevail upon her to say them, though both of us used to deal in some sort with Womankind. At last I managed to quiet the combatants without her talisman, and, I believe, to her great disappointment. She was the d—st b—h that I ever saw, and I have seen a great many. Though my Clergyman was sure to lose either his life or his living, he was as warlike as the

knew no more Swedish than the Inhabitants. But in two days, by dint of dictionary, he talked with them fluently and freely, so that they were astonished, and every body else, at his acquisition of another tongue in forty eight hours. I had this anecdote first from M[e] Albrizzi, and afterwards confirmed by *himself*— and he is not a boaster.

55.

I sometimes wish that I had studied languages with more attention: those which I know, even the classical (Greek and Latin, in the usual proportion of a sixth form boy), and a smattering of modem Greek, the Armenian and Arabic Alphabets, a few Turkish and Albanian phrases, oaths, or requests, Italian tolerably, Spanish less than tolerably, French to read with ease but speak with difficulty—or rather not at all—all have been acquired by ear or eye, and never by anything like Study. Like "Edie Ochiltree," "I never dowed to bide a hard turn o' wark in my life."

To be sure, I set in zealously for the Armenian and Arabic, but I fell in love with some absurd womankind both times, before I had overcome the Characters; and at Malta and Venice left the profitable Orientalists for—for—(no matter what), notwithstanding that my master, the Padre Pasquale Aucher (for whom, by the way, I compiled the major part of two Armenian and English Grammars), assured me "that the terrestrial Paradise had been certainly in *Armenia.*" I went seeking it—God knows where—did I find it? Umph! Now and then, for a minute or two.

56.

Of Actors, Cooke was the most natural, Kemble the most supernatural, Kean a medium between the two, but Mrs. Siddons worth them all put together, of those whom I remember to have seen in England.

57.

I have seen Sheridan weep two or three times: it may be that he was maudlin; but this only renders it more impressive, for who would see—

> "From Marlborough's eyes the teats of dotage flow,
> And Swift expire a driveller and a show?"

Once I saw him cry at Robins's, the Auctioneer's, after a splendid dinner full of great names and high Spirits. I had the honour of sitting next to Sheridan. The occasion of his tears was some observation or other upon the subject of the sturdiness of the Whigs in resisting Office, and keeping to their principles. Sheridan turned round—"Sir, it is easy for my Lord G., or Earl G., or Marquis B., or L[d] H., with thousands upon thousands a year—some of it either *presently* derived or *inherited* in Sinecures or acquisitions from the public money—to boast of their patriotism, and keep aloof from temptation; but they do not know from what temptations those have kept aloof, who had equal pride—at least equal talents, and not unequal passions, and nevertheless knew not in the course of their lives what it was to have a shilling of their own." And in saying this he wept.

58.

I have more than once heard Sheridan say, that he never "had a shilling of his own:" to be sure, he contrived to extract a good many of other people's.

In 1815, I had occasion to visit my Lawyer in Chancery Lane: he was with Sheridan. After mutual greetings, etc., Sheridan retired first. Before recurring to my own business, I could not help enquiring *that* of S. "Oh" (replied the Attorneo), "the usual thing—to stave off an action from his Wine-Merchant, my Client." "Well" (said I) "and what do you mean to do?" "Nothing at all for the present," said he: "would you have us proceed against old Sherry? What would be the use of it?" And here he began laughing, and going over Sheridan's good gifts of Conversation. Now, from personal experience, I can vouch that my Attorneo is by no means the tenderest of men, or particularly accessible to any kind of impression out of the Statute or record. And yet Sheridan, in half an hour, had found the way to soften and seduce him in such a manner, that I almost think he would have thrown his Client (an honest man with all the laws and some justice on his side) out of the window, had he come in at the moment. Such was Sheridan! He could soften an Attorney! There has been nothing like it since the days of Orpheus.

59.

When the Bailiffs (for I have seen most kinds of life) came upon me in 1815, to seize my chattels (being a peer of parliament my person was beyond him), being curious (as is my habit), I first asked him "what Extents elsewhere he had for Government?" upon which he showed me one upon *one house only* for *seventy thousand pounds*! Next I asked him, if he had nothing for Sheridan? "Oh, Sheridan," said he: "aye, I have this" (pulling out a pocket-book, etc.). "But, my L., I have been in Mr. Sheridan's house a twelve-month at a time: a civil gentleman—knows how to deal with *us,* etc., etc., etc." Our own business was then discussed, which was none of the easiest for me at that time. But the Man was civil, and, (what I valued more), communicative. I had met many of his brethren years before in affairs of my friends (commoners, that is), but this was the first (or second) on my own account. A civil Man, feed accordingly: probably he anticipated as much.

60.

No man would live his life over again, is an old and true saying, which all can resolve for themselves. At the same time, there are probably *moments* in most men's lives, which they would live over the rest of life to *regain*? Else, why do we live at all? Because Hope recurs to Memory, both false; but—but—but—but—and this *but* drags on till—What? I do not know, and who does? "He that died o' Wednesday." By the way, there is a poor devil to be shot tomorrow here (Ravenna) for murder. He hath eaten half a Turkey for his dinner, besides fruit and pudding;

and he refuses to confess? Shall I go to see him exhale? No. And why? Because it is to take place at *Nine.* Now, could I *save* him, or a fly even from the same catastrophe, I would out-match years; but as I cannot, I will not get up earlier to see another man shot, than I would to run the same risk in person. Besides, I have seen more men than one die that death (and other deaths) before to-day.

It is not cruelty which actuates mankind, but excitement, on such occasions; at least, I suppose so. It is detestable to *take* life in that way, unless it be to preserve two lives.

61.

Old Edgeworth, the fourth or fifth Mrs. Edgeworth, and *the* Miss Edgeworth were in London, 1813. Miss Edgeworth liked, Mrs. Edgeworth not disliked, old Edgeworth a bore—the worst of bores—a boisterous Bore. I met them in society once at a breakfast of Sir H. D.'s. Old Edgeworth came in late, boasting that he had given "Dr. Parr a dressing the night before" (no such easy matter by the way). I thought *her* pleasant. They all abused Anna Seward's memory.

62.

When on the road, they heard of *her* brother's, and *his* Son's, death. What was to be done? Their *London* Apparel was all ordered and made! So they sunk his death for the six weeks of their Sojourn, and went into mourning on their way back to Ireland. *Fact!*

63.

While the Colony were in London, there was a book, with a Subscription for the "recall of Mrs. Siddons to the Stage," going about for signatures. Moore moved for a similar subscription for the "recall of *Mr. Edgeworth to Ireland*!"

64.

Sir Humphrey Davy told me, that the Scene of the French Valet and Irish postboy in "Ennui" was taken from *his* verbal description to the Edgeworths in Edgeworthtown of a similar fact on the road occurring to himself. So much the better—being *life.*

65.

When I was fifteen years of age, it happened that in a Cavern in Derbyshire I had to cross in a boat (in which two people only could lie down) a stream which flows under a rock, with the rock so close upon the water, as to admit the boat only to be pushed on by a ferry-man (a sort of Charon), who wades at the stern stooping all the time. The Companion of my transit was M. A. C., with whom I had been long in love, and never told it, though *she* had discovered it without. I recollect my sensations, but cannot describe them—and it is as well.

We were a party—a Mr. W., two Miss W.'s, Mr. and Mrs. Cl—ke, Miss M., and *my* M. A. C. Alas I why do I say *My*? Our Union would have healed feuds, in which blood had been shed by our fathers; it would have joined lands, broad and rich; it would have joined at least *one* heart, and two persons not ill-matched in years (she is two years my elder); and—and—and—what has been the result? *She* has married a man older than herself, been wretched, and separated. I have married, and am separated: and yet *We* are *not* united.

66.

One of my notions, different from those of my co-temporaries, is, that the present is not a high age of English Poetry: there are *more* poets (soi-disant) than ever there were, and proportionally *less* poetry.

This *thesis* I have maintained for some years, but, strange to say, it meeteth not with favour from my brethren of the Shell. Even Moore shakes his head, and firmly believes that it is the grand Era of British Poesy.

67.

When I belonged to the D. L. Committee, and was one of the S. C. of Management, the number of plays upon the shelves were about *five* hundred. Conceiving that amongst these there must be *some* of merit, in person and by proxy I caused an investigation. I do not think that, of those which I saw, there was one which could be conscientiously tolerated. There never were such things as most of them.

Mathurin was very kindly recommended to me by Walter Scott, to whom I had recourse; firstly, in the hope that he would do something for us himself; and secondly, in my despair, that he would point out to us any young (or old) writer of promise. Mathurin sent his Bertram, and a letter *without* his address, so that at first I could give him no answer. When I at last hit upon his residence, I sent him a favourable answer, and something more substantial. His play succeeded, but I was at that time absent from England.

I tried Coleridge, too; but he had nothing feasible in hand at the time. Mr. Sotheby obligingly offered *all* his tragedies, and I pledged myself; and, notwithstanding many squabbles with my Committe[e]d Brethren, did get "Ivan" accepted, read, and the parts distributed. But lo! in the very heart of the matter, upon some *tepidness* on the part of Kean, or warmth on that of the Authour, Sotheby withdrew his play.

Sir J. B. Burgess did also present four tragedies and a farce, and I moved Green-room and S. Committee; but they would not.

Then the Scenes I had to go through! The authours, and the authoresses, the Milliners, the wild Irishmen, the people from Brighton, from Black wall, from Chatham, from Cheltenham, from Dublin, from Dundee, who came in upon me! To all of whom it was proper to give a civil answer, and a hearing, and a reading. Mrs.

Glover's father, an Irish dancing-Master of Sixty years, called upon me to request to play "*Archer,*" drest in silk stockings on a frosty morning, to show his legs (which were certainly good and Irish for his age, and had been still better). Miss Emma Somebody, with a play entitled the "Bandit of Bohemia," or some such title or production. Mr. O'Higgins, then resident at Richmond, with an Irish tragedy, in which the unities could not fail to be observed, for the protagonist was chained by the leg to a pillar during the chief part of the performance. He was a wild man, of a salvage appearance; and the difficulty of *not* laughing at him was only to be got over by reflecting upon the probable consequences of such cachinnation.

As I am really a civil and polite person, and *do* hate giving pain, when it can be avoided, I sent them up to Douglas Kinnaird, who is a man of business, and sufficiently ready with a negative, and left them to settle with him. And, as at the beginning of next year, I went abroad, I have since been little aware of the progress of the theatres.

68.

Players are said to be an impracticable people. They are so. But I managed to steer clear of any disputes with them, and, excepting one debate with the Elder Byrne about Miss Smith's Pas de (Something—I forget the technicals), I do not remember any litigation of my own. I used to protect Miss Smith, because she was like Lady Jane Harley in the face; and likenesses go a great way with me. Indeed, in general, I left such things to my more bustling colleagues, who used to reprove me seriously for not being able to take such things in hand without buffooning with the Histrions, and throwing things into confusion by treating light matters with levity.

69.

Then the Committee!—then the Sub-Committee! We were but few, and never agreed! There was Peter Moore who contradicted Kinnaird, and Kinnaird who contradicted everybody: then our two managers, Rae and Dibdin, and our Secretary, Ward! And yet we were all very zealous and in earnest to do good, and so forth. Hobhouse furnished us with prologues to our revived Old English plays, but was not pleased with me for complimenting him as "the *Upton*" of our theatre (Mr. Upton is or was the poet who writes the songs for Astley's), and almost gave up prologuizing in consequence.

70.

In the Pantomime of 1815–16, there was a Representation of the Masquerade of 1814, given by "us Youth" of Wander's Club to Wellington and Co. Douglas Kinnaird, and one or two others with myself, put on Masques, and went *on* the Stage amongst the "οἱ πολλοί," to see the effect of a theatre from the Stage. It is very grand. Douglas danced among the figuranti, too; and they were puzzled to find out who we were, as being more than their number. It was odd enough that D.

K. and I should have been both at the *real* Masquerade, and afterwards in the Mimic one of the same on the stage of D. L. Theatre.

71.

When I was a youth, I was reckoned a good actor. Besides "Harrow Speeches" (in which I shone) I enacted "Penruddock" in the "Wheel of Fortune," and "Tristram Fickle" in Allingham's farce of "the Weathercock," for three nights (the duration of our compact), in some private theatricals at Southwell in 1806, with great applause. The occasional prologue for our volunteer play was also of my composition. The other performers were young ladies and gentlemen of the neighbourhood; and the whole went off with great effect upon our good-natured audience.

72.

When I first went up to College, it was a new and a heavy hearted scene for me. Firstly, I so much disliked leaving Harrow, that, though it was time (I being seventeen), it broke my very rest for the last quarter with counting the days that remained. I always *hated* Harrow till the last year and half, but then I liked it. Secondly, I wished to go to Oxford and not to Cambridge. Thirdly, I was so completely alone in this new world, that it half broke my Spirits. My companions were not unsocial, but the contrary—lively, hospitable, of rank, and fortune, and gay far beyond my gaiety. I mingled with, and dined and supped, etc., with them; but, I know not how, it was one of the deadliest and heaviest feelings of my life to feel that I was no longer a boy. From that moment I began to grow old in my own esteem; and in my esteem age is not estimable. I took my gradations in the vices with great promptitude, but they were not to my taste; for my early passions, though violent in the extreme, were concentrated, and hated division or spreading abroad. I could have left or lost the world with or for that which I loved; but, though my temperament was naturally burning, I could not share in the common place libertinism of the place and time without disgust. And yet this very disgust, and my heart thrown back upon itself, threw me into excesses perhaps more fatal than those from which I shrunk, as fixing upon me (at a time) the passions, which, spread amongst many, would have hurt only myself.

73.

People have wondered at the Melancholy which runs through my writings. Others have wondered at my personal gaiety; but I recollect once, after an hour, in which I had been sincerely and particularly gay, and rather brilliant, in company, my wife replying to me when I said (upon her remarking my high spirits) "and yet, Bell, I have been called and mis-called Melancholy—you must have seen how falsely, frequently." "No, B.," (she answered) "it is not so: at *heart* you are the most melancholy of mankind, and often when apparently gayest."

80.

My passions were developed very early—so early, that few would believe me, if I were to state the period, and the facts which accompanied it. Perhaps this was one of the reasons which caused the anticipated melancholy of my thoughts—having anticipated life.

My earlier poems are the thoughts of one at least ten years older than the age at which they were written: I don't mean for their solidity, but their Experience. The two first Cantos of C[e] H[d] were completed at twenty two, and they are written as if by a man older than I shall probably ever be.

82.

Upon Parnassus, going to the fountain of Delphi (Castri), in 1809, I saw a flight of twelve Eagles (Hobhouse says they are Vultures—at least in conversation), and I seized the Omen. On the day before, I composed the lines to Parnassus (in Childe Harold), and, on beholding the birds, had a hope that Apollo had accepted my homage. I have at least had the name and fame of a Poet during the poetical period of life (from twenty to thirty): whether it will last is another matter; but I *have been* a votary of the Deity and the place, and am grateful for what he has done in my behalf, leaving the future in his hands as I left the past.

83.

Like Sylla, I have always believed that all things depend upon Fortune, and nothing upon ourselves. I am not aware of any one thought or action worthy of being called good to myself or others, which is not to be attributed to the Good Goddess, Fortune!

84.

Two or three years ago, I thought of going to one of the Americas, English or Spanish. But the accounts sent from England, in consequence of my enquiries, discouraged me. After all, I believe most countries, properly balanced, are equal to *a Stranger* (by no means to the *native,* though). I remembered General Ludlow's domal inscription:—

"Omne solum forti patria"—

And sate down free in a country of Slavery for many centuries. But there is *no* freedom, even for *Masters,* in the midst of slaves: it makes my blood boil to see the thing. I sometimes wish that I was the Owner of Africa, to do at once, what Wilberforce will do in time, viz.—sweep Slavery from her desarts, and look on upon the first dance of their Freedom.

As to *political* slavery—so general—it is man's own fault; if they *will* be slaves, let them! Yet it is but "a word and a blow." See how England formerly, France, Spain, Portugal, America, Switzerland, freed themselves! There is no one instance of a *long* contest, in which *men* did not triumph over Systems. If Tyranny misses her *first* spring, she is cowardly as the tiger, and retires to be hunted.

85.

An Italian (the younger Count Ruota), writing from Ravenna to his friend at Rome in 1820, says of me, by way of compliment, "that in society no one would take me for an Englishman, though he believes that I *am* English at bottom—my manners were so different." This he meant as a grand eulogy, and I accept it as such. The letter was shown to me this year by the Correspondent, Count P. G., or by his Sister.

86.

I have been a reviewer. In "the Monthly Review" I wrote some articles, which were inserted. This was in the latter part of 1811. In 1807, in a Magazine called "Monthly Literary Recreations," I reviewed Wordsworth's trash of that time. Excepting these, I cannot accuse myself of anonymous Criticism (that I recollect), though I have been *offered* more than one review in our principal Journals.

87.

Till I was eighteen years old (odd as it may seem), I had never read a review. But, while at Harrow, my general information was so great on modern topics, as to induce a suspicion that I could only collect so much information from *reviews,* because I was never *seen* reading, but always idle and in mischief, or at play. The truth is that I read eating, read in bed, read when no one else reads; and had read all sorts of reading since I was five years old, and yet never *met* with a review, which is the only reason that I know of why I should not have read them. But it is true; for I remember when Hunter and Curzon, in 1804, told me this opinion at Harrow, I made them laugh by my ludicrous astonishment in asking them, "*what is* a review?" To be sure, they were then less common. In three years more, I was better acquainted with that same, but the first I ever read was in 1806–7.

88.

At School, I was (as I have said) remarked for the extent and readiness of my *general* information; but in all other respects idle; capable of great sudden exertions (such as thirty or forty Greek Hexameters—of course with such prosody as it pleased God), but of few continuous drudgeries. My qualities were much more oratorical and martial, than poetical; and Dr. D., my grand patron (our head-master), had a great notion that I should turn out an Orator, from my fluency, my turbulence, my voice, my copiousness of declamation, and my action. I remember that my first declamation astonished him into some unwonted (for he was economical of such), and sudden compliments, before the declaimers at our first rehearsal. My first Harrow verses (that is, English as exercises), a translation of a chorus from the Prometheus of Aeschylus, were received by him but cooly: no one had the least notion that I should subside into poesy.

more noted, especially in all that could reduce them to the rest, or raise the rest to them." In 1816, this was.

106.

In fact (I suppose that), if the follies of fools were all set down like those of the wise, the wise (who seem at present only a better sort of fools), would appear almost intelligent.

107.

I have met George Colman occasionally, and thought him extremely pleasant and convivial. Sheridan's humour, or rather wit, was always saturnine, and sometimes savage: he never laughed (at least that *I* saw, and I watched him), but Colman did. I have got very drunk with them both; but, if I had to *choose,* and could not have both at a time, I should say, "let me begin the evening with Sheridan, and finish it with Colman." Sheridan for dinner—Colman for Supper. Sheridan for Claret or port; but Colman for every thing, from the Madeira and Champaigne at dinner—the Claret with a *layer* of *port* between the Glasses—up to the Punch of the Night, and down to the Grog or Gin and water of day-break. All these I have threaded with both the same. Sheridan was a Grenadier Company of Life-Guards, but Colman a whole regiment—of *light Infantry,* to be sure, but still a *regiment.*

108.

Aldbiades is said to have been "successful in all his battles;" but *what* battles? Name them! If you mention Caesar, or Annibal, or Napoleon, you at once rush upon Pharsalia, Munda, Alesia, Cannae, Thrasimene, Trebia, Lodi, Marengo, Jena, Austerlitz, Friedland, Wagram, Moskwa; but it is less easy to pitch upon the victories of Alcibiades, though they may be named too—though not so readily as the Leuctra and Mantinea of Epaminondas, the Marathon of Miltiades, the Salamis of Themistocles, and the Thermopylae of Leonidas.

Yet upon the whole it may be doubted, whether there be a name of Antiquity, which comes down with such a general charm as that of *Alcibiades. Why?* I cannot answer: who can?

109.

The vanity of Victories is considerable. Of all who fell at Waterloo or Trafalgar, ask any man in company to *name you ten off hand*: they will stick at Nelson; the other will survive himself. *Nelson was* a hero: the other is a mere Corporal, dividing with Prussians and Spaniards the luck, which he never deserved. He even —but I hate the fool, and will be silent.

110.

The Miscreant Wellington is the Cub of Fortune, but she will never lick him into shape: if he lives, he will be beaten—that's certain. Victory was never before wasted upon such an unprofitable soil, as this dunghill of Tyranny, whence nothing springs but Viper's eggs.

111.

I remember seeing Blucher in the London Assemblies, and never saw anything of his age less venerable. With the voice and manners of a recruiting Sergeant, he pretended to the honours of a hero; just as if a stone could be worshipped, because a Man had stumbled over it.

112.

There is nothing left for Mankind but a Republic, and I think that there are hopes of such. The two Americas (South and North) have it; Spain and Portugal approach it; all thirst for it. Oh Washington!

113.

Pisa, Novr 5th 1821.

"There is a strange coincidence sometimes in the little things of this world, Sancho," says Sterne in a letter (if I mistake not); and so I have often found it.

Page 128, article 91, of this collection of scattered things, I had alluded to my friend Lord Clare in terms such as my feelings suggested. About a week or two afterwards, I met him on the road between Imola and Bologna, after not having met for seven or eight years. He was abroad in 1814, and came home just as I set out in 1816.

This meeting annihilated for a moment all the years between the present time and the days of *Harrow*. It was a new and inexplicable feeling, like rising from the grave, to me. Clare, too, was much agitated—*more* in appearance than even myself; for I could feel his heart beat to his fingers' ends, unless, indeed, it was the pulse of my own which made me think so. He told me that I should find a note from him, left at Bologna. I did. We were obliged to part for our different journeys —he for Rome, I for Pisa; but with the promise to meet again in Spring. We were but five minutes together, and in the public road; but I hardly recollect an hour of my existence which could be weighed against them. He had heard that I was coming on, and had left his letter for me at B., because the people with whom he was travelling could not wait longer.

Of all I have ever known, he has always been the least altered in every thing from the excellent qualities and kind affections which attached me to him so strongly at School. I should hardly have thought it possible for Society (or the World as it is called), to leave a being with so little of the leaven of bad passions. I do not speak from personal experience only, but from all I have ever heard of him from others during absence and distance.

a suspension of the action, which may either close there without impropriety, or be continued in a way that I have in view. I wish the first part to be published before the second, because, if it don't succeed, it is better to stop there than to go on in a fruitless experiment.

I desire you to acknowledge the arrival of this packet by return of post, if you can conveniently, with a proof.

Your obedient ser[t], B.

P.S.—My wish is to have it published at the same time, and, if possible, in the same volume, with the others; because, whatever the merits or demerits of these pieces may be, it will perhaps be allowed that each is of a different kind, and in a different style; so that, including the prose and the *D*[*on*] *J*[*uans*], etc., I have at least sent you *variety* during the last year or two.

The present packet consists of 12 sheets, which will make more than *fifty* printed pages additional to the Volume. I suppose that there is not enough in the four plays (or poems) to make *two* volumes, but they will form *one* large one.

Two words to say that you have received the packet will be enough.

1300.—To John Murray.

Sir,—

I only received by this day's post the enclosed, which you addressed by mistake to Ravenna. I presume that the *three plays* are to be published together; because, if not, I will not permit their *separate* publication. I repeat this, because a passage in your letter makes it doubtful. I sent you a fourth by last post (a lyrical drama on a scriptural subject—"the Deluge"), which I could wish to be published at the same time, and (if possible and in time) in the same volume. I return you the notes (not of "the Doge," as you say by mistake), but of the new poems. Most of the packets have, I believe, arrived in safety. I wrote to M[r] K[d] to accept your proposal for the *three* plays and three cantos of *D*[*on*] *J*[*uan*], distinctly giving to understand that the *other poems* did *not* enter into that agreement.

I am your obed[t] serv[t], B.

P.S.—What is the reason that I see *Cain* and the *Foscaris* announced, and not *Sardanapalus*?

1301.—To Thomas Moore.

Pisa,
November 16, 1821.

There is here Mr. Taaffe, an Irish genius, with whom we are acquainted. He hath written a really *excellent* Commentary on Dante, full of new and true information, and much ingenuity. But his verse is such as it hath pleased God to endue him withal. Nevertheless, he is so firmly persuaded of its equal excellence, that he won't divorce the Commentary from the traduction, as I ventured delicately to hint, —not having the fear of Ireland before my eyes, and upon the presumption of having shotten very well in his presence (with common pistols too, not with my Manton's) the day before.

But he is eager to publish all, and must be gratified, though the Reviewers will make him suffer more tortures than there are in his original. Indeed, the *Notes* are well worth publication; but he insists upon the translation for company, so that they will come out together, like Lady C * * t chaperoning Miss * *. I read a letter of yours to him yesterday, and he begs me to write to you about his Poeshie. He is really a good fellow, apparently, and I dare say that his verse is very good Irish.

Now, what shall we do for him? He says that he will risk part of the expense with the publisher. He will never rest till he is published and abused—for he has a high opinion of himself—and I see nothing left but to gratify him, so as to have him abused as little as possible; for I think it would kill him. You must write, then, to Jeffrey to beg him *not* to review him, and I will do the same to Gifford, through Murray. Perhaps they might notice the Comment without touching the text. But I doubt the dogs—the text is too tempting.

* * * * *

I have to thank you again, as I believe I did before, for your opinion of *Cain,* etc.

You are right to allow — to settle the claim; but I do not see why you should repay him out of your *legacy*—at least, not yet. If you *feel* about it (as you are ticklish on such points), pay him the interest now, and the principal when you are strong in cash; or pay him by instalments; or pay him as I do my creditors— that is, *not* till they make me.

I address this to you at Paris, as you desire. Reply soon, and believe me ever, etc.

P.S.—What I wrote to you about low spirits is, however, very true. At present, owing to the climate, etc. (I can walk down into my garden, and pluck my own oranges,—and, by the way, have got a diarrhoea in consequence of indulging in this meridian luxury of proprietorship,) my spirits are much better. You seem to think that I could not have written the *Vision,* etc., under the influence of low spirits; but I think there you err. A man's poetry is a distinct faculty, or soul, and has no more to do with the every-day individual than the Inspiration with the Pythoness when removed from her tripod.

1302.—To Lady Byron.

(To the care of the Hon. Mrs. Leigh, London.)

Pisa,
November 17, 1821.

I have to acknowledge the receipt of "Ada's hair," which is very soft and pretty, and nearly as dark already as mine was at twelve years old, if I may judge from what I recollect of some in Augusta's possession, taken at that age. But it don't curl, —perhaps from its being let grow.

I also thank you for the inscription of the date and name, and I will tell you why;—I believe that they are the only two or three words of your hand-writing in my possession. For your letters I returned; and except the two words, or rather the one word, "Household," written twice in an old account book, I have no other. I burnt your last note, for two reasons:—firstly, it was written in a style not very agreeable; and, secondly, I wished to take your word without documents, which are the worldly resources of suspicious people.

I suppose that this note will reach you somewhere about Ada's birthday—the 10th of December, I believe. She will then be six, so that in about twelve more I shall have some chance of meeting her;—perhaps sooner, if I am obliged to go to England by business or otherwise. Recollect, however, one thing, either in distance or nearness;—every day which keeps us asunder should, after so long a period, rather soften our mutual feelings, which must always have one rallying-point as long as our child exists, which I presume we both hope will be long after either of her parents.

The time which has elapsed since the separation has been considerably more than the whole brief period of our union, and the not much longer one of our prior acquaintance. We both made a bitter mistake; but now it is over, and irrevocably so. For, at thirty-three on my part, and a few years less on yours, though it is no very extended period of life, still it is one when the habits and thought are generally so formed as to admit of no modification; and as we could not agree when younger, we should with difficulty do so now.

I say all this, because I own to you, that, notwithstanding every thing, I considered our re-union as not impossible for more than a year after the separation;— but then I gave up the hope entirely and for ever. But this very impossibility of re-union seems to me at least a reason why, on all the few points of discussion which can arise between us, we should preserve the courtesies of life, and as much of its kindness as people who are never to meet may preserve perhaps more easily than nearer connections. For my own part, I am violent, but not malignant; for only fresh provocations can awaken my resentments. To you, who are colder and more concentrated, I would just hint, that you may sometimes mistake the depth of a cold anger for dignity, and a worse feeling for duty. I assure you that I bear you *now* (whatever I may have done) no resentment whatever. Remember, that *if you have injured me* in aught, this forgiveness is something; and that, if I have *injured you,* it is something more still, if it be true, as the moralists say, that the most offending are the least forgiving.

Whether the offence has been solely on my side, or reciprocal, or on yours chiefly, I have ceased to reflect upon any but two things,—viz. that you are the mother of my child, and that we shall never meet again. I think if you also consider the two corresponding points with reference to myself, it will be better for all three.

Yours ever, NOEL BYRON.

1303.—To Douglas Kinnaird.

Pisa,
November 20, 1821.

MY DEAR KINNAIRD,—

I ought to have answered your letter long ago, but I am but just subsiding into my new residence, after all the bore and bustle of changing. The traveller can "take his ease in his inn," but those who are settled in a place, and must move with bag and baggage, are (as I suppose you know by experience) necessarily more tardy in their arrangements.

I have a very good spacious house, upon the Arno, and have nothing to complain of, except that it is less quiet than my house in Ravenna.—And so you are at Rome?—I am glad you have got rid of the gout;—the tumour, if not of podagrous origin, will subside of itself.

At Bologna I met with Rogers, and we crossed the Apennines together—probably you have got him at Rome by this time. I took him to visit our old friend the sexton, at the Certosa, (where you and I met with Bianchetti), who looked at him very *hard,* and seemed well disposed to keep him back in his skull-room. The said sexton, by the way, brought out his two daughters, to renew our acquaintance; one of them is very pretty, and the other sufficiently so. He talked pathetically of the venality of the age, in which young virgins could not be espoused without a *dower*: so that, if you are disposed to portion them in your way to Milan, you have an opportunity of exercising your benevolence.

P.S. What Sir Henry Halford or you say of Lady Noel is all very fine, but she is immortal, that you may depend on; an ill-tempered woman turned of seventy never dies, though they may be buried sometimes. Besides, my luck does not run in that family.

1307.—To John Murray.

Pisa,
December 4, 1821.

Dear Sir,—

By extracts in the English papers,—in your holy Ally, Galignani's *Messenger,*—I perceive that "the two greatest examples of human vanity in the "present age" are, firstly, "the ex-Emperor Napoleon," and secondly, "his Lordship, etc., the noble poet," meaning your humble servant, "poor guiltless I."

Poor Napoleon! he little dreamed to what "vile comparisons" the turn of the Wheel would reduce him! I cannot help thinking, however, that had our learned brother of the newspaper office seen my very moderate answer to the very scurrile epistle of my radical patron, John Hobhouse, M.P., he would have thought the thermometer of my "Vanity" reduced to a very decent temperature. By the way you do not happen to know whether Mrs. Fry had commenced her reform of the prisoners at the time when Mr. Hobhouse was in Newgate? there are some of his phrases, and much of his style (in that same letter), which led me to suspect that either she had not, or that he had profited less than the others by her instructions. Last week I sent back the deed of Mr. Moore signed and witnessed. It was inclosed to Mr. Kinnaird with a request to forward it to you. I have also transmitted to him my opinions upon your proposition, etc., etc., but addressed them to himself.

I have got here into a famous old feudal palazzo, on the Arno, large enough for a garrison, with dungeons below and cells in the walls, and so full of *Ghosts,* that the learned Fletcher (my valet) has begged leave to change his room, and then refused to occupy his *new* room, because there were more ghosts there than in the other. It is quite true that there are most extraordinary noises (as in all old buildings), which have terrified the servants so as to incommode me extremely. There is one place where people were evidently *walled up*; for there is but one possible passage, *broken* through the wall, and then meant to be closed again upon the inmate. The house belonged to the Lanfranchi family, (the same mentioned by Ugolino in his dream, as his persecutor with Sismondi,) and has had a fierce owner or two in its time. The staircase, etc., is said to have been built by Michel Agnolo. It is not yet cold enough for a fire. What a climate!

I am, however, bothered about these spectres, (as they say the last occupants were, too,) of whom I have as yet seen nothing, nor, indeed, heard (*myself*); but all the other ears have been regaled by all kinds of supernatural sounds. The first night I thought I heard an odd noise, but it has not been repeated. I have now been here more than a month.

Yours, BYRON.

P.S. Pray send me two or three dozen of "*Acton's corn-rubbers*" in a parcel by the post—*packed dry* and well—if you can.

I have received safely the parcel containing the Seal—the *E. Review*—and some pamphlets, etc. The others are I presume upon their way.

Are there not designs from *Faust*? Send me some, and a translation of it,—if such there is. Also of Goethe's life if such there be; if not—the original German.

1308.—To John Sheppard.

Pisa,
December 8, 1821.

SIR,—

I have received your letter. I need not say, that the extract which it contains has affected me, because it would imply a want of all feeling to have read it with indifference. Though I am not quite *sure* that it was intended by the writer for *me,* yet the date, the place where it was written, with some other circumstances that you mention, render the allusion probable. But for whomever it was meant, I have read it with all the pleasure which can arise from so melancholy a topic. I say *pleasure* —because your brief and simple picture of the life and demeanour of the excellent person whom I trust you will again meet, cannot be contemplated without the admiration due to her virtues, and her pure and unpretending piety. Her last moments were particularly striking; and I do not know that, in the course of reading the story of mankind, and still less in my observations upon the existing portion, I ever met with any thing so unostentatiously beautiful. Indisputably, the firm believers in the Gospel have a great advantage over all others,—for this simple reason, that, if true, they will have their reward hereafter; and if there be no hereafter, they can be but with the infidel in his eternal sleep, having had the assistance of an exalted hope, through life, without subsequent disappointment, since (at the worst for them) "out of nothing, nothing can arise," not even sorrow. But a man's creed does not depend upon *himself*: *who* can say, I *will* believe this, that, or the other? and least of all, that which he least can comprehend. I have, however, observed, that those who have begun life with extreme faith, have in the end greatly narrowed it, as Chillingworth, Clarke (who ended as an Arian), Bayle, and Gibbon (once a Catholic), and some others; while, on the other hand, nothing is more common than for the early sceptic to end in a firm belief, like Maupertuis, and Henry Kirke White.

But my business is to acknowledge your letter, and not to make a dissertation. I am obliged to you for your good wishes, and more than obliged by the extract from the papers of the beloved object whose qualities you have so well described in a few words. I can assure you that all the fame which ever cheated humanity into higher notions of its own importance would never weigh in my mind against the pure and pious interest which a virtuous being may be pleased to take in my welfare. In this point of view, I would not exchange the prayer of the deceased in my behalf for the united glory of Homer, Cæsar, and Napoleon, could such be accumulated upon a living head. Do me at least the justice to suppose, that

"Video meliora proboque,"

however the "deteriora sequor" may have been applied to my conduct.

I have the honour to be

Your obliged and obedient servant, BYRON.

P.S.—I do not know that I am addressing a clergyman; but I presume that you will not be affronted by the mistake (if it is one) on the address of this letter. One who has so well explained, and deeply felt, the doctrines of religion, will excuse the error which led me to believe him its minister.

1309.—To John Murray.

Pisa,
December 10, 1821.

DEAR SIR,—

This day and this hour, (one, on the clock,) my daughter is six years old. I wonder when I shall see her again, or if ever I shall see her at all.

I have remarked a curious coincidence, which almost looks like a fatality.

My *mother,* my *wife,* my *daughter,* my *half-sister,* my *sister's mother,* my natural daughter (as far at least as *I* am concerned), and *myself,* are all *only children.*

My father, by his first marriage with Lady Conyers (an only child), had only my sister; and by his second marriage with another only child, an only child again. Lady Byron, as you know, was one also, and so is my daughter, etc.

Is not this rather odd—such a complication of only children? By the way, send me my daughter Ada's miniature. I have only the print, which gives little or no idea of her complexion.

I heard the other day from an English voyager, that her temper is said to be extremely violent. Is it so? It is not unlikely considering her parentage. My temper is what it is—as you may perhaps divine,—and my Lady's was a nice little sullen nucleus of concentrated Savageness to mould my daughter upon,—to say nothing of her two Grandmothers, both of whom, to my knowledge, were as pretty specimens of female Spirit as you might wish to see on a Summer's day.

I have answered your letters, etc., either to you in person, or through M[r] D. K[d]

The broken Seal and *Edinburgh R[eview]*, etc., arrived safely. The others are I presume upon their way.

Yours, etc., N. B.

1310.—To Thomas Moore.

Pisa,
December 12, 1821.

What you say about Galignani's two biographies is very amusing: and, if I were not lazy, I would certainly do what you desire. But I doubt my present stock of facetiousness—that is, of good *serious* humour, so as not to let the cat out of the bag. I wish *you* would undertake it. I will forgive and *indulge* you (like a Pope) beforehand, for any thing ludicrous, that might keep those fools in their own dear belief that a man is a *loup garou.*

I suppose I told you that the *Giaour* story had actually some foundation on facts; or, if I did not, you will one day find it in a letter of Lord Sligo's, written to me *after* the publication of the poem. I should not like marvels to rest upon any account of my own, and shall say nothing about it. However, the *real* incident is still remote enough from the poetical one, being just such as, happening to a man of any imagination, might suggest such a composition. The worst of any *real* adventures is that they involve living people—else Mrs. —'s, —'s, etc., are as "German to the matter" as Mr. Maturin could desire for his novels. * * *

The consummation you mentioned for poor Taaffe was near taking place yesterday. Riding pretty sharply after Mr. Medwin and myself in turning the corner of a lane between Pisa and the hills, he was spilt,—and, besides losing some claret on the spot, bruised himself a good deal, but is in no danger. He was bled, and keeps his room. As I was ahead of him some hundred yards, I did not see the accident; but my servant, who was behind, did, and says the *horse* did not fall—the usual excuse of floored equestrians. As Taaffe piques himself upon his horsemanship, and his horse is really a pretty horse enough, I long for his personal narrative,—as I never yet met the man who would *fairly claim a tumble* as his own property.

Could not you send me a printed copy of the "Irish Avatar?"—I do not know what has become of Rogers since we parted at Florence.

Don't let the Angles keep you from writing. Sam told me that you were somewhat dissipated in Paris, which I can easily believe. Let me hear from you at your best leisure.

Ever and truly, etc.

P.S.—December 13.

I enclose you some lines written not long ago, which you may do what you like with, as they are very harmless. Only, if copied, or printed, or set, I could wish it more correctly than in the usual way, in which one's "nothings are monstered," as Coriolanus says.

You must really get Taaffe published—he never will rest till he is so. He is just gone with his broken head to Lucca, at my desire, to try to save a *man* from being *burnt.* The Spanish * * *, that has her petticoats over Lucca, had actually condemned a poor devil to the stake, for stealing the wafer box out of a church. Shelley and I, of course, were up in arms against this piece of piety, and have been disturbing every body to get the sentence changed. Taaffe is gone to see what can be done.

B.

1311.—To Percy Bysshe Shelley.

December 12, 1821.

My dear Shelley,—

Enclosed is a note for you from —. His reasons are all very true, I dare say, and it might and may be of personal inconvenience to us. But that does not appear to me to be a reason to allow a being to be burnt without trying to save him. To save him by any means but *remonstrance* is of course out of the question; but I do not see why a *temperate* remonstrance should hurt any one. Lord Guilford is the man, if he would undertake it. He knows the Grand Duke personally, and might, perhaps, prevail upon him to interfere. But, as he goes to-morrow, you must be quick, or it will be useless. Make any use of *my* name that you please.

Yours ever, etc.

1312.—To Thomas Moore.

I send you the two notes, which will tell you the story I allude to of the Auto da Fè. Shelley's allusion to his "fellow-serpent," is a buffoonery of mine. Goethe's Mephistofilus calls the serpent who tempted Eve "my aunt, the renowned snake;" and I always insist that Shelley is nothing but one of her nephews, walking about on the tip of his tail.

1313.—To John Cam Hobhouse.

Pisa,
December 16th, 1821.

Dear Hobhouse,—

I have waited several posts in the hope that you might perhaps stumble upon the papers I mentioned, the first act of a thing begun in 1815, called "Werner." If you can't, it don't much matter, only let me know it.

You will by this time, have received my very temperate answer to your very tipsy letter. I forgive you as a Christian should do, that is, I never will forgive you as long as I live, and shall certainly pay you in kind, with interest, the very first opportunity; but that need break no squares between us, as it hath been our custom for several years, the example being first set by yourself at Cambridge, and Brighton. "Don't you remember what happened seven years ago?"

Yours ever &c., B.

hyperbolical indecency. He himself says, that if 'obscenity' (using a much coarser word) 'be the Sin against the Holy Ghost, he must certainly not be saved.' These letters are in existence, and have been seen by many besides myself; but would his *editor* have been '*candid*' in even alluding to them? Nothing would have even provoked *me,* an indifferent spectator, to allude to them, but this further attempt at the depreciation of Pope.

"What should we say to an editor of Addison, who cited the following passage from Walpole's letters to George Montagu? 'Dr. Young has published a new book, etc. Mr. Addison sent for the young Earl of Warwick, as he was dying, to show him in what peace a Christian could die; unluckily he died of *brandy*: nothing makes a Christian die in peace like being maudlin! but don't say this in Gath where you are.' Suppose the editor introduced it with this preface, 'One circumstance is mentioned by Horace Walpole, which, if true, was indeed *flagitious.* Walpole informs Montagu that Addison sent for the young Earl of Warwick, when dying, to show him in what peace a Christian could die; but unluckily he died drunk,' etc., etc. Now, although there might occur on the subsequent, or on the same page, a faint show of disbelief, seasoned with the expression of 'the *same candour*' (the *same* exactly as throughout the book), I should say that this editor was either foolish or false to his trust; such a story ought not to have been admitted, except for one brief mark of crushing indignation, unless it were *completely proved.* Why the words '*if true*?' that '*if*' is not a peacemaker. Why talk of 'Cibber's testimony' to his licentiousness? To what does this amount? that Pope, when very young, was *once* decoyed by some noblemen and the player to a house of carnal recreation. Mr. Bowles was not always a clergyman; and when he was a very young man, was he never seduced into as much? If I were in the humour for story-telling, and relating little anecdotes, I could tell a much better story of Mr. B. than Cibber's, upon much better authority, viz. that of Mr. B. himself. It was not related by *him* in my presence, but in that of a third person, whom Mr. B. names oftener than once in the course of his replies.1 This gentleman related it to me as a humorous and witty anecdote; and so it was, whatever its other characteristics might be. But should I, for a youthful frolic, brand Mr. B. with a 'libertine sort of love,' or with 'licentiousness?' Is he the less now a pious or a good man, for not having always been a priest? No such thing; I am willing to believe him a good man, almost as good a man as Pope, but no better.

"The truth is, that in these days the grand '*primum mobile*' of England is *cant*; cant political, cant poetical, cant religious, cant moral; but always *cant,* multiplied through all the varieties of life. It is the fashion, and while it lasts will be too powerful for those who can only exist by taking the tone of the time. I say *cant,* because it is a thing of words, without the smallest influence upon human actions; the English being no wiser, no better, and much poorer, and more divided amongst themselves, as well as far less moral, than they were before the prevalence of this verbal decorum. This hysterical horror of poor Pope's not very well ascertained, and never fully proved amours (for even Cibber owns that he prevented the somewhat perilous adventure in which Pope was embarking), sounds very virtuous in a controversial pamphlet: but all men of the world who know what life is, or at least what it was to them in their youth, must laugh at such a ludicrous foundation of the charge of 'a libertine sort of love;' while the more serious will look upon those who bring forward such charges upon an isolated fact as fanatics or hypocrites, perhaps both. The two are sometimes compounded in a happy mixture.

"Mr. Octavius Gilchrist speaks rather irreverently of a 'second tumbler of *hot* white-wine negus.' What does he mean? Is there any harm in negus? or is it the worse for being *hot*? or does Mr. B. drink negus? I had a better opinion of him. I hoped that whatever wine he drank was neat; or, at least, that, like the Ordinary in Jonathan Wild, 'he preferred *punch,* the rather as there was nothing against it in Scripture.' I should be really sorry to believe that Mr. B. was fond of negus; it is such a 'candid' liquor, so like a wishy-washy compromise between the passion for wine and the propriety of water. But different writers have divers tastes. Judge Blackstone composed his *Commentaries* (he was a poet too in his youth) with a bottle of port before him. Addison's conversation was not good for much till he had taken a similar dose. Perhaps the prescription of these two great men was not inferior to the very different one of a soi-disant poet of this day, who, after wandering amongst the hills, returns, goes to bed, and dictates his verses, being fed by a bystander with bread and butter during the operation.

"I now come to Mr. B.'s 'invariable principles of poetry.' These Mr. Bowles and some of his correspondents pronounce 'unanswerable;' and they are 'unanswered,' at least by Campbell, who seems to have been astounded by the title: the Sultan of the time being offered to ally himself to a King of France because 'he hated the word League;' which proves that the Pa*di*shaw (*not Pacha*) understood French. Mr. Campbell has no need of my alliance, nor shall I presume to offer it; but I do hate that word '*invariable.*' What is there of *human,* be it poetry, philosophy, wit, wisdom, science, power, glory, mind, matter, life, or death, which is '*invariable*?' Of course I put things divine out of the question. Of all arrogant baptisms of a book, this title to a pamphlet appears the most complacently conceited. It is Mr. Campbell's part to answer the contents of this performance, and especially to vindicate his own 'Ship,' which Mr. B. most triumphantly proclaims to have struck to his very first fire.

"'Quoth he there was a *Ship;*
Now let me go, thou grey-haired loon,
Or my staff shall make thee skip.'

It is no affair of mine; but having once begun, (certainly not by my own wish, but called upon by the frequent recurrence to my name in the pamphlets,) I am like an Irishman in a 'row,' 'any body's customer.' I shall therefore say a word or two on the 'Ship.'

"Mr. B. asserts that Campbell's 'Ship of the Line' derives all its poetry, not from '*art,*' but from '*Nature.*' 'Take away the waves, the winds, the sun, etc., etc., etc., *one* will become a stripe of blue bunting; and the other a piece of coarse canvas on three tall poles.' Very true; take away the 'waves,' 'the winds,' and there will be no ship at all, not only for poetical, but for any other purpose; and take away 'the sun,' and we must read Mr. B.'s pamphlet by candlelight. But the 'poetry' of the 'Ship' does *not* depend on the 'waves,' etc.; on the contrary, the 'Ship of the line' confers its own poetry upon the waters, and heightens *theirs.* I do not deny, that the 'waves and winds,' and above all 'the sun,' are highly poetical; we know it to our cost, by the many descriptions of them in verse: but if the waves bore only the foam upon their bosoms, if the winds wafted only the sea-weed to the shore, if the sun shone neither upon pyramids, nor fleets, nor fortresses, would its beams be equally poetical? I think not: the poetry is at least reciprocal. Take away 'the Ship of the Line' 'swinging round' the 'calm water,' and the calm water becomes a somewhat monotonous thing to look at, particularly if not transparently *clear*; witness the thousands who pass by without looking on it at all. What was it attracted the thousands to the launch? They might have seen the poetical 'calm water' at Wapping, or in the 'London Dock,' or in the Paddington Canal, or in a horse-pond, or in a slop-basin, or in any other vase. They might have heard the poetical winds howling through the chinks of a pig-stye, or the garret window; they might have seen the sun shining on a footman's livery, or on a brass warming pan; but could the 'calm water,' or the 'wind,' or the 'sun,' make all, or any of these 'poetical?' I think not. Mr. B. admits ' the Ship' to be poetical, but only from those accessaries: now if they *confer* poetry so as to make one thing poetical, they would make other things poetical; the more so, as Mr. B. calls a 'ship of the line' without them,—that is to say, its 'masts and sails and streamers,'—'blue bunting,' and 'coarse canvas,' and 'tall poles.' So they are; and porcelain is clay, and man is dust, and flesh is grass, and yet the two latter at least are the subjects of much poesy.

"Did Mr. B. ever gaze upon the sea? I presume that he has, at least upon a sea-piece. Did any painter ever paint the sea *only,* without the addition of a ship, boat, wreck, or some such adjunct? Is the sea itself a more attractive, a more moral, a more poetical object, with or without a vessel, breaking its vast but fatiguing monotony? Is a storm more poetical without a ship? or, in the poem of *The Shipwreck,* is it the storm or the ship which most interests? both *much* undoubtedly; but without the vessel, what should we care for the tempest? It would sink into mere descriptive poetry, which in itself was never esteemed a high order of that art.

"I look upon myself as entitled to talk of naval matters, at least to poets:—with the exception of Walter Scott, Moore, and Southey, perhaps, who have been voyagers, I have *swum* more miles than all the rest of them together now living ever *sailed,* and have lived for months and months on shipboard; and, during the whole period of my life abroad, have scarcely ever passed a month out of sight of the Ocean: besides being brought up from two years till ten on the brink of it. I recollect, when anchored off Cape Sigeum in 1810, in an English frigate, a violent squall coming on at sunset, so violent as to make us imagine that the ship would part cable, or drive from her anchorage. Mr. H[obhouse] and myself, and some officers, had been up the Dardanelles to Abydos, and were just returned in time. The aspect of a storm in the Archipelago is as poetical as need be, the sea being particularly short, dashing, and dangerous, and the navigation intricate and broken by the isles and currents. Cape Sigeum, the tumuli of the Troad, Lemnos, Tenedos, all added to the associations of the time. But what seemed the most '*poetical*' of all at the moment, were the numbers (about two hundred) of Greek and Turkish craft, which were obliged to 'cut and run' before the wind, from their unsafe anchorage, some for Tenedos, some for other isles, some for the Main, and some it might be for Eternity. The sight of these little scudding vessels, darting over the foam in the twilight, now appearing and now disappearing between the waves in the cloud of night, with their peculiarly *white* sails, (the Levant sails not being of '*coarse canvas*' but of white cotton,) skimming along as quickly, but less safely than the sea-mew which hovered over them; their evident distress, their reduction to fluttering specks in the distance, their crowded succession, their *littleness,* as contending with the giant element, which made our stout 44's *teak* timbers (she was built in India) creak again; their aspect and their motion, all struck me as something far more 'poetical' than the mere broad, brawling, shipless sea, and the sullen winds, could possibly have been without them.

"The Euxine is a noble sea to look upon, and the port of Constantinople the most beautiful of harbours; and yet I cannot but think that the twenty sail of the line, some of one hundred and forty guns, rendered it more ' poetical' by day in the sun, and by night perhaps still more; for the Turks illuminate their vessels of war in a manner the most picturesque, and yet all this is *artificial.* As for the Euxine, I stood upon the Symplegades—I stood by the broken altar still exposed to the winds upon one of them—I felt all the '*poetry*' of the situation, as I repeated the first lines of Medea; but would not that 'poetry' have been heightened by the *Argo*? It was so even by the appearance of any merchant vessel arriving from Odessa. But Mr. B. says, 'Why bring your ship off the stocks?' for no reason that I know, except that ships are built to be launched. The water, etc., undoubtedly HEIGHTENS the poetical associations, but it does not *make* them; and the ship amply repays the obligation: they aid each other; the water is more poetical with the ship—the ship less so without the water. But even a ship laid up in dock is a grand and a poetical sight. Even an old boat, keel upwards, wrecked upon the barren sand, is a 'poetical' object, (and Wordsworth, who made a poem about a washing-tub and a blind boy, may tell you so as well as I,) whilst a long extent of sand and unbroken water, without the boat, would be as like dull prose as any pamphlet lately published.

"What makes the poetry in the image of the '*marble waste of Tadmor,*' or Grainger's 'Ode to Solitude,' so much admired by Johnson? Is it the '*marble*' or the '*waste,*' the *artificial* or the *natural* object? The 'waste' is like all other *wastes*; but the '*marble*' of Palmyra makes the poetry of the passage as of the place.

"The beautiful but barren Hymettus,—the whole coast of Attica, her hills and mountains, Pentelicus, Anchesmus, Philopappus, etc., etc.—are in themselves poetical, and would be so if the name of Athens, of Athenians, and her very ruins, were swept from the earth. But am I to be told that the ' Nature' of Attica would be *more* poetical without the 'Art' of the Acropolis? of the Temple of Theseus? and of the still all Greek and glorious monuments of her exquisitely artificial genius? Ask the traveller what strikes him as most poetical,—the Parthenon, or the rock on which it stands? The COLUMNS of Cape Colonna, or the Cape itself? The rocks at the foot of it, or the recollection that Falconer's *ship* was bulged upon them? There are a thousand rocks and capes far more picturesque than those of the Acropolis and Cape Sunium in themselves; what are they to a thousand scenes in the wilder parts of Greece, of Asia Minor, Switzerland, or even of Cintra in Portugal, or to many scenes of Italy, and the Sierras of Spain? But it is the '*art,*' the columns, the temples, the wrecked vessel, which give them their antique and their modern poetry, and not the spots themselves. Without them, the *spots* of earth would be unnoticed and unknown: buried, like Babylon and Nineveh, in indistinct confusion, without poetry, as without existence; but to whatever spot of earth these ruins were transported, if they were *capable* of transportation, like the obelisk, and the sphinx, and the Memnon's head, *there* they would still exist in the perfection of their beauty, and in the pride of their poetry. I opposed, and will ever oppose, the robbery of ruins from Athens, to instruct the English in sculpture (who are as capable of sculpture as the Egyptians are of skating); but why did I do so? The *ruins* are as poetical in Piccadilly as they were in the Parthenon; but the Parthenon and its rock are less so without them. Such is the Poetry of art.

"Mr. B. contends again that the Pyramids of Ægypt are poetical, because of 'the association with boundless deserts,' and that a 'pyramid of the same dimensions' would not be sublime in 'Lincoln's Inn Fields:' not *so* poetical certainly; but take away the 'pyramids,' and what is the *desert*? Take away Stone-henge from Salisbury Plain, and it is nothing more than Hounslow Heath, or any other uninclosed down. It appears to me that St. Peter's, the Coliseum, the Pantheon, the Palatine, the Apollo, the Laocoon, the Venus di Medicis, the Hercules, the dying Gladiator, the Moses of Michel Agnolo, and all the higher works of Canova, (I have already spoken of those of antient Greece, still extant in that country, or transported to England,) are as *poetical* as Mont Blanc or Mount Ætna, perhaps still more so, as they are direct manifestations of mind, and *presuppose* poetry in their very conception; and have, moreover, as being such, a something of actual life, which cannot belong to any part of inanimate nature, unless we adopt the System of Spinosa, that the World is the deity. There can be nothing more poetical in its aspect than the city of Venice; does this depend upon the sea, or the canals?—

"'The dirt and sea-weed whence proud Venice rose?'

Is it the canal which runs between the palace and the prison, or the 'Bridge of Sighs,' which connects them, that render it poetical? Is it the 'Canal Grande,' or Rial to which arches it, the churches which tower over it, the palaces which line, and the gondolas which glide over the waters, that render this city more poetical than Rome itself? Mr. B. will say, perhaps, that the Rialto is but marble, the palaces and churches only stone, and the gondolas a 'coarse' black cloth, thrown over some planks of carved wood, with a shining bit of fantastically formed iron at the prow, '*without*' the water. And I tell him that without these, the water would be nothing but a clay-coloured ditch; and whoever says the contrary, deserves to be at the bottom of that, where Pope's heroes are embraced by the mud nymphs. There would be nothing to make the Canal of Venice more poetical than that of Paddington, were it not for the artificial adjuncts above mentioned, although it is a perfectly natural canal, formed by the sea, and the innumerable islands which constitute the site of this extraordinary city.

"The very Cloacæ of Tarquin at Rome are as poetical as Richmond Hill; many will think more so: take away Rome, and leave the Tybur and the seven Hills, in the Nature of Evander's time. Let Mr. Bowles or Mr. Wordsworth, or Mr. Southey, or any of the other 'Naturals,' make a poem upon them, and then see which is most poetical,—their production, or the commonest guidebook, which tells you the road from St. Peter's to the Coliseum, and informs you what you will see by the way. The Ground interests in Virgil, because it *will* be *Rome,* and not because it is Evander's rural domain.

"Mr. B. then proceeds to press Homer into his service, in answer to a remark of Mr. Campbell's, that 'Homer was a great describer of works of art.' Mr. B. contends that all his great power, even in this, depends upon their connection with nature. The 'shield of Achilles derives its poetical interest from the subjects described on it.' And from what does the *spear* of Achilles derive its interest? and the helmet and the mail worn by Patroclus, and the celestial armour, and the very brazen greaves of the well-booted Greeks? Is it solely from the legs, and the back, and the breast, and the human body, which they enclose? In that case, it would have been more poetical to have made them fight naked; and Gulley and Gregson, as being nearer to a state of nature, are more poetical boxing in a pair of drawers than Hector and Achilles in radiant armour, and with heroic weapons.

"Instead of the clash of helmets, and the rushing of chariots, and the whizzing of spears, and the glancing of swords, and the cleaving of shields, and the piercing of breast-plates, why not represent the Greeks and Trojans like two savage tribes, tugging and tearing, and kicking and biting, and gnashing, foaming, grinning, and gouging, in all the poetry of martial nature, unincumbered with gross, prosaic, artificial arms; an equal superfluity to the natural warrior and his natural poet? Is there any thing unpoetical in Ulysses striking the horses of Rhesus with *his bow* (having forgotten his thong), or would Mr. B. have had him kick them with his foot, or smack them with his hand, as being more unsophisticated?

"'That not in fancy's maze he wandered long,
But *stooped* to Truth, and moralised his song.'

He should have written 'rose to truth.' In my mind, the highest of all poetry is ethical poetry, as the highest of all earthly objects must be moral truth. Religion does not make a part of my subject; it is something beyond human powers, and has failed in all human hands except Milton's and Dante's, and even Dante's powers are involved in his delineation of human passions, though in supernatural circumstances. What made Socrates the greatest of men? His moral truth—his ethics. What proved Jesus Christ the Son of God hardly less than his miracles? His moral precepts. And if ethics have made a philosopher the first of men, and have not been disdained as an adjunct to his Gospel by the Deity himself, are we to be told that ethical poetry, or didactic poetry, or by whatever name you term it, whose object is to make men better and wiser, is not the *very first order* of poetry; and are we to be told this too by one of the priesthood? It requires more mind, more wisdom, more power, than all the 'forests' that ever were 'walked for their description,' and all the epics that ever were founded upon fields of battle. The Georgics are indisputably, and, I believe, *undisputedly,* even a finer poem than the Æneid. Virgil knew this; he did not order *them* to be burnt.

"'The proper study of mankind is man.'

"It is the fashion of the day to lay great stress upon what they call 'imagination' and 'invention,' the two commonest of qualities: an Irish peasant with a little whisky in his head will imagine and invent more than would furnish forth a modern poem. If Lucretius had not been spoiled by the Epicurean system, we should have had a far superior poem to any now in Existence. As mere poetry, it is the first of Latin poems. What then has ruined it? His ethics. Pope has not this defect; his moral is as pure as his poetry is glorious.

"In speaking of artificial objects, I have omitted to touch upon one which I will now mention. Cannon may be presumed to be as highly poetical as art can make her objects. Mr. B. will, perhaps, tell me that this is because they resemble that grand natural article of Sound in heaven, and Similie upon earth—thunder. I shall be told triumphantly, that Milton made sad work with his artillery, when he armed his devils therewithal. He did so; and this artificial object must have had much of the Sublime to attract his attention for such a conflict. He *has* made an absurd use of it; but the absurdity consists not in using *cannon* against the angels of God, but any *material* weapon. The thunder of the clouds would have been as ridiculous and vain in the hands of the devils, as the 'villainous saltpetre;' the angels were as impervious to the one as to the other. The thunderbolts become sublime in the hands of the Almighty, not as such, but because *he* deigns to use them as a means of repelling the rebel spirits; but no one can attribute their defeat to this grand piece of natural electricity: the Almighty willed, and they fell; his word would have been enough; and Milton is as absurd, (and, in fact, *blasphemous,*) in putting material lightnings into the hands of the Godhead, as in giving him hands at all.

"The artillery of the demons was but the first step of his mistake, the thunder the next, and it is a step lower. It would have been fit for Jove, but not for Jehovah. The subject altogether was essentially unpoetical; he has made more of it than another could, but it is beyond him and all men.

"In a portion of his reply, Mr. B. asserts that Pope 'envied Phillips,' because he quizzed his pastorals in the *Guardian,* in that most admirable model of irony, his paper on the subject. If there was any thing enviable about Phillips, it could hardly be his pastorals. They were despicable, and Pope expressed his contempt. If Mr. Fitzgerald published a volume of sonnets, or a *Spirit of Discovery,* or a *Missionary,* and Mr. B. wrote in any periodical journal an ironical paper upon them, would this be 'envy?' The authors of the *Rejected Addresses* have ridiculed the sixteen or twenty 'first living poets' of the day, but do they 'envy' them? 'Envy' writhes, it don't laugh. The authors of the *R. A.* may despise some, but they can hardly ' envy' any of the persons whom they have parodied; and Pope could have no more envied Phillips than he did Welsted, or Theobald, or Smedley, or any other given hero of the *Dunciad.* He could not have envied him, even had he himself *not* been the greatest poet of his age. Did Mr. Inge '*envy*' Mr. Phillips when he asked him, 'How came your Pyrrhus to drive oxen and say, "I am *goaded* on by love?"' This question silenced poor Phillips; but it no more proceeded from 'envy' than did Pope's ridicule. Did he envy Swift? Did he envy Bolingbroke? Did he envy Gay the unparallelled success of his *Beggar's Opera*? We may be answered that these were his friends—true: but does *friendship* prevent *envy*? Study the first woman you meet with, or the first scribbler, let Mr. B. himself (whom I acquit fully of such an odious quality) study some of his own poetical intimates: the most envious man I ever heard of is a poet, and a high one; besides, it is an *universal* passion. Goldsmith envied not only the puppets for their dancing, and broke his shins in the attempt at rivalry, but was seriously angry because two pretty women received more attention than he did. *This is envy*; but where does Pope show a sign of the passion? In that case Dryden envied the hero of his MacFlecknoe. Mr. Bowles compares, when and where he can, Pope with Cowper—(the same Cowper whom in his edition of Pope he laughs at for his attachment to an old woman, Mrs. Unwin; search and you will find it; I remember the passage, though not the page); in particular he requotes Cowper's Dutch delineation of a wood, drawn up, like a seedsman's catalogue,[xiii] with an affected imitation of Milton's style, as burlesque as the *Splendid Shilling.* These two writers, for Cowper is no poet, come into comparison in one great work, the translation of Homer. Now, with all the great, and manifest, and manifold, and reproved, and acknowledged, and uncontroverted faults of Pope's translation, and all the scholarship, and pains, and time, and trouble, and blank verse of the other, who can ever read Cowper? and who will ever lay down Pope, unless for the original! Pope s was 'not Homer, it was Spondanus;' but Cowper's is not Homer either, it is not even Cowper. As a child I first read Pope's Homer with a rapture which no subsequent work could ever afford, and children are not the worst judges of their own language. As a boy I read

Homer in the original, as we have all done, some of us by force, and a few by favour; under which description I come is nothing to the purpose, it is enough that I read him. As a man I have tried to read Cowper's version, and I found it impossible. Has any human reader ever succeeded?

"And now that we have heard the Catholic reproached with envy, duplicity, licentiousness, avarice—what was the Calvinist? He attempted the most atrocious of crimes in the Christian code, viz. suicide—and why? because he was to be examined whether he was fit for an office which he seems to wish to have made a sinecure. His connection with Mrs. Unwin was pure enough, for the old lady was devout, and he was deranged; but why then is the infirm and then elderly Pope to be reproved for his connection with Martha Blount? Cowper was the almoner of Mrs. Throgmorton; but Pope's charities were his own, and they were noble and extensive, far beyond his future's warrant. Pope was the tolerant yet steady adherent of the most bigoted of sects; and Cowper the most bigoted and despondent sectary that ever anticipated damnation to himself or others. Is this harsh? I know it is, and I do not assert it as my opinion of Cowper *personally,* but to *show what might* be said, with just as great an appearance of truth and candour, as all the odium which has been accumulated upon Pope in similar speculations. Cowper was a good man, and lived at a fortunate time for his works.

"Mr. B., apparently not relying entirely upon his own arguments, has, in person or by proxy, brought forward the names of Southey and Moore. Mr. Southey 'agrees entirely with Mr. B. in his *invariable* principles of poetry.' The least that Mr. B. can do in return is to approve the 'invariable principles of Mr. Southey.' I should have thought that the word '*invariable*' might have stuck in Southey's throat, like Macbeth's 'Amen!' I am sure it did in mine, and I am not the least consistent of the two, at least as a voter. Moore (*et tu, Brute!*) also approves, and Mr. I. Scott. There is a letter also of two lines from a gentleman in asterisks, who, it seems, is a poet of 'the highest rank:'—who *can* this be! not my friend Sir Walter, surely. Campbell it can't be; Rogers it won't be.

"'You have *hit the nail in* the head, and * * * * [Pope, I presume] *on* the head also.

"'I *remain,* yours affectionately,
"'(Four *Asterisks*).'

And in asterisks let him remain. Whoever this person may be, he deserves, for such a judgement of Midas, that 'the nail' which Mr. B. has 'hit *in* the head,' should be driven through his own ears; I am sure that they are long enough.

"The attempt of the poetical populace of the present day to obtain an ostracism against Pope is as easily accounted for as the Athenian's shell against Aristides; they are tired of hearing him always called 'the Just.' They are also fighting for life; for, if he maintains his station, they will reach their own—by falling. They have raised a mosque by the side of a Grecian temple of the purest architecture; and, more barbarous than the barbarians from whose practice I have borrowed the figure, they are not contented with their own grotesque edifice, unless they destroy the prior, and purely beautiful fabric which preceded, and which shames them and theirs for ever and ever. I shall be told that amongst those I *have* been (or it may be still *am*) conspicuous—true, and I am ashamed of it I *have* been amongst the builders of this Babel, attended by a confusion of tongues, but *never* amongst the envious destroyers of the classic temple of our predecessor. I have loved and honoured the fame and name of that illustrious and unrivalled man, far more than my own paltry renown, and the trashy jingle of the crowd of 'Schools' and upstarts, who pretend to rival, or even surpass him. Sooner than a single leaf should be torn from bis laurel, it were better that all which these men, and that I, as one of their set, have ever written, should

> "'Line trunks, clothe spice, or, fluttering in a row,
> Befringe the rails of Bedlam, or Soho!'

There are those who will believe this, and those who will not. You, sir, know how far I am sincere, and whether my opinion, not only in the short work intended for publication, and in private letters which can never be published, has or has not been the same. I look upon this as the declining age of English poetry; no regard for others, no selfish feeling, can prevent me from seeing this, and expressing the truth. There can be no worse sign for the taste of the times than the depreciation of Pope. It would be better to receive for proof Mr. Cobbett's rough but strong attack upon Shakespeare and Milton, than to allow this smooth and 'candid' undermining of the reputation of the most *perfect* of our poets, and the purest of our moralists. Of his power in the *passions,* in description, in the mock heroic, I leave others to descant. I take him on his strong ground as an *ethical* poet: in the former, none excel; in the mock heroic and the ethical, none equal him; and, in my mind, the latter is the highest of all poetry, because it does that in *verse,* which the greatest of men have wished to accomplish in prose. If the essence of poetry must be a *lie,* throw it to the dogs, or banish it from your republic, as Plato would have done. He who can reconcile poetry with truth and wisdom, is the only true '*poet*' in its real sense, 'the *maker*,' 'the *creator*,'—why must this mean the 'liar,' the 'feigner,' the 'tale-teller.' A man may make and create better things than these.

"I shall not presume to say that Pope is as high a poet as Shakespeare and Milton, though his enemy, Warton, places him immediately under them.[xiv] I would no more say this than I would assert in the mosque (once Saint Sophia's), that Socrates was a greater man than Mahomet. But if I say that he is very near them, it is no more than has been asserted of Burns, who is supposed

> "'To rival all but Shakespeare's name below.'

I say nothing against this opinion. But of what '*order*,' according to the poetical aristocracy, are Burns's poems? There are his *opus magnum,* 'Tam O'Shanter,' a *tale*; the Cotter's Saturday Night, a descriptive sketch; some others in the same style: the rest are songs. So much for the *rank* of his *productions*; the *rank* of

Burns is the very first of his art. Of Pope I have expressed my opinion elsewhere, as also of the effect which the present attempts at poetry have had upon our literature. If any great national or natural convulsion could or should overwhelm your country in such sort as to sweep Great Britain from the kingdoms of the earth, and leave only that, after all, the most living of human things, a *dead language,* to be studied and read, and imitated by the wise of future and far generations, upon foreign shores; if your literature should become the learning of mankind, divested of party cabals, temporary fashions, and national pride and prejudice;—an Englishman, anxious that the posterity of strangers should know that there had been such a thing as a British Epic and Tragedy, might wish for the preservation of Shakespeare and Milton; but the surviving World would snatch Pope from the wreck, and let the rest sink with the people. He is the moral poet of all civilisation; and as such, let us hope that he will one day be the national poet of mankind. He is the only poet that never shocks; the only poet whose *faultlessness* has been made his reproach. Cast your eye over his productions; consider their extent, and contemplate their variety:—pastoral, passion, mock heroic, translation, satire, ethics,—all excellent, and often perfect. If his great charm be his *melody,* how comes it that foreigners adore him even in their diluted translations? But I have made this letter too long. Give my compliments to Mr. Bowles.

"Yours ever very truly, BYRON.

"*To John Murray, Esq.*

"*Post Scriptum.*—Long as this letter has grown, I find it necessary to append a postscript; if possible, a short one. Mr. Bowles denies that he has accused Pope of 'a sordid money-getting passion;' but, he adds, 'if I had ever done so, I should be glad to find any testimony that might show he was *not* so.' This testimony he may find to his heart's content in Spence and elsewhere. First, there is Martha Blount, who, Mr. B. charitably says, 'probably thought he did not save enough for her, as legatee.' Whatever she *thought* upon this point, her words are in Pope's favour. Then there is Alderman Barber; see Spence's *Anecdotes.* There is Pope's cold answer to Halifax when he proposed a pension; his behaviour to Craggs and to Addison upon like occasions, and his own two lines—

> "And, thanks to Homer, since I live and thrive,
> Indebted to no prince or peer alive;'

written when princes would have been proud to pension, and peers to promote him, and when the whole army of dunces were in array against him, and would have been but too happy to deprive him of this boast of independence. But there is something a little more serious in Mr. Bowles's declaration, that he '*would* have spoken' of his 'noble generosity to the outcast Richard Savage,' and. other instances of a compassionate and generous heart, '*had they occurred to his recollection when he wrote.*' What! is it come to this! Does Mr. B. sit down to write a minute and laboured life and edition of a great poet? Does he anatomize his character, moral and poetical? Does he present us with his faults and with his foibles? Does he sneer at his feelings, and doubt of his sincerity? Does he unfold his vanity and duplicity? and then omit the good qualities which might, in part, have ' covered this multitude of sins?' and then plead that '*they did not occur to his recollection*?' Is this the frame of mind and of memory with which the illustrious dead are to be approached? If Mr. Bowles, who must have had access to all the means of refreshing his memory, did not recollect these facts, he is unfit for his task; but if he *did* recollect and omit them, I know not what he is fit for, but I know what would be fit for him. Is the plea of 'not recollecting' such prominent facts to be admitted? Mr. B. has been at a public school, and, as I have been publicly educated also, I can sympathise with his predilection. When we were in the third form even, had we pleaded on the Monday morning that we had not brought up the Saturday's exercise, because 'we had forgotten it,' what would have been the reply? And is an excuse, which would not be pardoned to a schoolboy, to pass current in a matter which so nearly concerns the fame of the first poet of his age, if not of his country? If Mr. B. so readily forgets the virtues of others, why complain so grievously that others have a better memory for his own faults? They are but the faults of an author; while the virtues he omitted from his catalogue are essential to the justice due to a man.

"Mr. B. appears, indeed to be susceptible beyond the privilege of authorship. There is a plaintive dedication to Mr. Gifford, in which *he* is made responsible for all the articles of the *Quarterly.* Mr. Southey, it seems, 'the most able and eloquent writer in that review,' approves of Mr. Bowles's publication. Now it seems to me the more impartial, that notwithstanding that 'the great writer of the *Quarterly*' entertains opinions opposite to the able article on Spence, nevertheless that essay was permitted to appear. Is a review to be devoted to the opinions of any *one* man? Must it not vary according to circumstances, and according to the subjects to be criticised? I fear that writers must take the sweets and bitters of the public journals as they occur, and an author of so long a standing as Mr. B. might have become accustomed to such incidents; he might be angry, but not astonished. I have been reviewed in the Quarterly almost as often as Mr. B., and have had as pleasant things said, and some *as un*pleasant, as could well be pronounced. In the review of 'The Fall of Jerusalem,' it is stated, that I have devoted 'my powers, etc., to the worst parts of Manicheism;' which, being interpreted, means that I worship the devil. Now, I have neither written a reply, nor complained to Gifford. I believe that I observed in a letter to you, that I thought 'that the critic might have praised Milman without finding it necessary to abuse me;' but did I not add at the same time, or soon after (apropos, of the note in the book of Travels), that I would not, if it were even in my power, have a single line cancelled on my account in that nor in any other publication? Of course, I reserve to myself the privilege of response when necessary. Mr. B. seems in a whimsical state about the author of the article on Spence. You know very well that I am not in your confidence, nor in that of the conductors of the Journal. The moment I saw that article, I was morally certain that

"Lady Mary appears to have been at least as much to blame as Pope. Some of her reflections and repartees are recorded as sufficiently exasperating. Pope in the whole of that business is to be pitied. When he speaks of his 'miserable body' let it be recollected that he was at least aware of his deformity, as indeed deformed persons have in general sufficient wit to be.

"It is also another unhappy dispensation of Nature that deformed persons, and more particularly those of Pope's peculiar conformation, are born with very strong passions. I believe that this is a physical fact, the truth of which is easily ascertained. Montaigne has in his universal speculations written a chapter upon it more curious than decent. So that these unhappy persons have to combat, not only against the passions which they feel, but the repugnance they inspire. Pope was unfortunate in this respect by being born in England; there are climates where his Hump-back would have made his (amatory) fortune. At least I know one notorious instance of a hunch-back who is as fortunate as the 'grand Chancelier' of the Grammont. To be sure, his climate and the morals of his country are both of them favourable to the material portion of that passion of which Buffon says that 'the refined *sentiment* is alike fictitious and pernicious.'

"I think that I could show if necessary that Lady Mary W^{y} Montague was also greatly to blame in that ground, *not* for having rejected, but for having encouraged him; but I would rather decline the task, though she should have remembered her own line '*he comes too near that comes to be denied.*'

"I admire her so much, her beauty, her talents, that I should do this reluctantly. I besides am so attached to the very name of '*Mary*' that, as Johnson once said, 'if you called a dog *Hervey* I should love him,' so, if you were to call a female of the same species 'Mary,' I should love it better than others (biped or quadruped) of the same sex with a different appellation. She was an extraordinary woman. She could translate *Epictetus,* and yet write a song worthy of Aristippus. The lines

> "'And when the long hours of the Public are past,
> And we meet with Champaigne and a Chicken at last,
> May every fond pleasure that moment endear!
> Be banished afar both discretion and fear!
> Forgetting or scorning the airs of the Crowd,
> He may cease to be formal, and I to be proud,
> Till lost in the Joy we confess that we live,
> And he may be rude, and yet I may forgive.'

"There, Mr. Bowles, what say you to such a supper with such a woman? And her own description too? Is not her '*Champaigne and Chicken*' worth a forest or two? Is it not poetry? It appears to me that this Stanza contains the '*purée*' of the whole Philosophy of Epicurus. I mean the practical philosophy of his School, not the precepts of the Master; for I have been too long at the University not to know that the Philosopher was [...][xv] a moderate man. But after all, would not some of us have been as great fools as Pope? For my part I wonder that with his quick feelings, her coquetry, and his disappointment, he did no more, instead of writing some lines which are to be condemned if false and regretted if true."

(2) *Observations upon "Observations." A Second Letter to John Murray, Esq., on the Rev. W. L. Bowles's Strictures on the Life and Writings of Pope.*

"Ravenna, March 25th, 1821.

"Dear Sir,—

"In the further 'Observations' of Mr. B., in rejoinder to the charges brought against his edition of Pope, it is to be regretted that he has lost his temper. Whatever the language of his antagonists may have been, I fear that his replies have afforded more pleasure to them than to the public. That Mr. Bowles should not be pleased is natural, whether right or wrong; but a temperate defence would have answered his purpose in the former case—and, in the latter, no defence, however violent, can tend to any thing but his discomfiture. I have read over this third pamphlet, which you have been so obliging as to send me, and shall venture a few observations, in addition to those upon the previous controversy.

"Mr. B. sets out with repeating his '*confirmed conviction*,' that 'what he said of the moral part of Pope's character was (generally speaking) true; and that the principles of *poetical* criticism which he has laid down are *invariable* and *invulnerable*,' etc.; and that he is the *more* persuaded of this by the '*exaggerations* of his opponents.' This is all very well, and highly natural and sincere. Nobody ever expected that either Mr. B., or any other author, would be convinced of human fallibility in their own persons. But it is nothing to the purpose—for it is not what Mr. *B.* thinks, but what is to be thought of *Pope,* that is the question. It is what he has asserted or insinuated against a name which is the patrimony of Posterity, that is to be tried; and Mr. B., as a party, can be no judge. The more *he* is persuaded, the better for himself, if it give him any pleasure; but he can only persuade others by the proofs brought out in his defence.

"After these prefatory remarks of 'conviction,' etc., Mr. B. proceeds to Mr. Gilchrist; whom he charges with 'slang' and 'slander,' besides a small subsidiary indictment of' abuse, ignorance, malice,' and so forth. Mr. Gilchrist has, indeed, shown some anger; but it is an honest indignation, which rises up in defence of the illustrious dead. It is a generous rage which interposes between our ashes and their disturbers. There appears also to have been some slight personal provocation. Mr. Gilchrist, with a chivalrous disdain of the fury of an incensed poet, put his name to a letter avowing the production of a former essay in defence of Pope, and consequently of an attack upon Mr. Bowles. Mr. B. appears to be angry with Mr. G. for four reasons:—firstly, because he wrote an article in 'The L. Magazine;' secondly, because he afterwards avowed it; thirdly, because he *was* the author of a still more extended article in 'The Quarterly Review;' and, fourthly, because he was not the author of the said Quarterly article, and had the audacity to disavow it—for no earthly reason but because he had not written it.

"Mr. B. declares, that he will not enter into a particular examination of the pamphlet, which by a *misnomer* (in italics) is called 'Gilchrist's Answer to Bowles,' when it should have been called 'Gilchrist's Abuse of Bowles.' On this error in the baptism of Mr. G.'s pamphlet, it may be observed, that an answer may be abusive and yet no less an answer, though indisputably a temperate one might be the better of the two: but if *abuse* is to cancel all pretensions to reply, what becomes of Mr. B.'s answers to Gilchrist?

"Mr. B. continues:—'But, as Mr. G. derides my *peculiar sensitiveness to criticism,* before I show how *destitute of truth is this representation,* I will here explicitly declare the only grounds,' etc., etc., etc.—Mr. B.'s sensibility in denying his 'sensitiveness to criticism' proves, perhaps, too much. But if he has been so charged, and truly—what then? There is no moral turpitude in such acuteness of feeling: it has been, and may be, combined with many good and great qualities. Is Mr. B. a poet, or is he not? If he be, he must, from his very essence, be sensitive to criticism; and even if he be not, he need not be ashamed of the common repugnance to being attacked. All that is to be wished is, that he had considered how disagreeable a thing it is, before he assailed the greatest moral poet of any age, or in any language.

"Pope himself 'sleeps well,'—nothing can touch him further; but those who love the honour of their country, the perfection of her literature, the glory of her language—are not to be expected to permit an atom of his dust to be stirred in his tomb, or a leaf to be stripped from the laurel which grows over it.

"Mr. B. assigns several reasons why and when 'an author is justified in appealing to every *upright* and *honourable* mind in the kingdom.' If Mr. B. limits the perusal of his defence to the 'upright and honourable' only, I greatly fear that it will not be extensively circulated. I should rather hope that some of the downright and dishonest will read and be converted or convicted. But the whole of his reasoning is here superfluous—'*an author is justified in appealing,*' etc., when and why he pleases. Let him make out a tolerable case, and few of his readers will quarrel with his motives.

"Mr. B. 'will now plainly set before the literary public all the circumstances which have led to *his name* and Mr. G.'s being brought together,' etc. Courtesy requires, in speaking of others and ourselves, that we should place the name of the former first—and not '*Ego* et Rex meus.' Mr. B. should have written 'Mr. Gilchrist's name and *his.*'

"This point he wishes 'particularly to address to those *most respectable characters,* who have the direction and management of the periodical critical press.' That the press may be, in some instances, conducted by respectable characters is probable enough; but if they are so, there is no occasion to tell them of it; and if they are not, it is a base adulation. In either case, it looks like a kind of flattery, by which those gentry are not very likely to be softened; since it would be difficult to find two passages in fifteen pages more at variance, than Mr. B.'s prose at the beginning of this pamphlet, and his verse at the end of it. In page 4, he speaks of 'those most respectable characters who have the direction, etc., of the periodical press,' and in page 16. we find—

> '"Ye *dark inquisitors,* a monk-like band,
> Who o'er some shrinking victim-author stand,
> A solemn, secret, and *vindictive brood,*
> *Only* terrific in your cowl and hood.'

And so on—to 'bloody law' and 'red scourges,' with other similar phrases, which may not be altogether agreeable to the above-mentioned 'most respectable characters.' Mr. B. goes on, 'I concluded my observations in the last Pamphleteer, with feelings *not unkind* towards Mr. Gilchrist, or' [it should be *nor*] 'to the author of the review of Spence, be he whom he might.'—'I was in hopes, *as I have always been ready to admit any errors* I might have been led into, or prejudice I might have entertained, that even Mr. Gilchrist might be disposed to a more *amicable* mode of discussing what I had advanced in regard to Pope's moral character.' As Major Sturgeon observes, 'There never was a set of more *amicable* officers—with the exception of a boxing-bout between Captain Shears and the Colonel.'

"A page and a half—nay only a page before—Mr. B. re-affirms his conviction, that 'what he has said of Pope's moral character is (*generally speaking*) *true,* and that his 'poetical principles are *invariable* and *invulnerable.*' He has also published three pamphlets,— ay, four of the same tenor,—and yet, with this declaration and these declarations staring him and his adversaries in the face, he speaks of his 'readiness to admit errors or to abandon prejudices!!!' His use of the word 'amicable' reminds me of the Irish Institution (which I have somewhere heard or read of) called the '*Friendly* Society,' where the president always carried pistols in his pocket, so that when one amicable gentleman knocked down another, the difference might be adjusted on the spot, at the harmonious distance of twelve paces.

"But Mr. Bowles 'has since read a publication by him (Mr. G.) containing such vulgar slander, affecting *private* life and character,' etc., etc.; and Mr. Gilchrist has also had the advantage of reading a publication by Mr. Bowles sufficiently imbued with personality; for one of the first and principal topics of reproach is that he is a *grocer,* that he has a 'pipe in his mouth, ledger-book, green canisters, dingy shop-boy, half a hogshead of brown treacle,' etc. Nay, the same delicate raillery is upon the very title-page. When controversy has once commenced upon this footing, as Dr. Johnson said to Dr. Percy, 'Sir, there is an end of politeness—we are to be as rude as we please—Sir, you said that I was *short-sighted.*' As a man's profession is generally no more in his own power than his person—both having been made out for him—it is hard that he should be reproached with either, and still more that an honest calling should be made a reproach. If there is anything more honourable to Mr. Gilchrist than another, it is, that being engaged in commerce he has had the taste, and found the leisure, to become so able a proficient in the higher literature of his own and other countries. Mr. Bowles, who will be proud to own Glover, Chatterton, Bums, and Bloomfield for his peers, should hardly have quarrelled with Mr. Gilchrist for his critic. Mr. G.'s station, however, which might conduct him to the highest civic honours, and to boundless wealth, has nothing to require apology; bat even if it had, such a reproach was not very gracious on the part of a clergyman, nor graceful on that of a gentleman. The allusion to '*Christian* criticism' is not particularly happy, especially where Mr. G. is accused of having '*set the first example of this mode in Europe.*' What *Pagan* criticism may have been, we know bat little; the names of Zoilus and Aristarchus survive, and the works of Aristotle, Longinus, and Quintilian: but of 'Christian criticism' we have already had some specimens in the works of Philelphus, Poggius, Scaliger, Milton, Salmasius, the Cruscanti (versus Tasso), the F. Academy (against the Cid), and the antagonists of Voltaire and of Pope—to say nothing of some articles in most of the reviews, since their earliest institution in the person of their respectable and still prolific parent, 'The Monthly.' Why, then, is Mr. Gilchrist to be singled out 'as having set the first example?' A sole page of Milton or Salmasias contains more abase—rank, rancorous, *unleavened* abuse—than all that can be raked forth from the whole works of many recent critics. There are some, indeed, who still keep up the good old custom; but fewer English than foreign. It is a pity that Mr. B. cannot witness some of the Italian controversies, or become the subject of one. He would then look upon Mr. Gilchrist as a panegyrist.

"In the long sentence quoted from the article in 'The L. M.,' there is one coarse image, the justice of whose application I shall not pretend to determine:—'The pruriency with which his nose is laid to the ground' is an expression which, whether founded or not, might have been omitted. But the 'anatomical minuteness' appears to me justified even by Mr. B.'s own subsequent quotation. To the point:—'*Many facts* tend to prove the peculiar susceptibility of his passions; nor can we implicitly believe that the connexion between him and Martha Blount was of a nature so pure and innocent as his panegyrist Ruffhead would have us believe,' etc.—'At *no time* could she have regarded *Pope personally* with attachment,' etc.—'But the most extraordinary circumstance in regard to his connexion with female society, was the strange mixture of *indecent* and even *profane* levity which his conduct and language often exhibited. The cause of this particularity may be sought, perhaps, in his consciousness of physical defect, which made him affect a character uncongenial, and a language opposite to the truth,'—If this is not 'minute moral anatomy,' I should be glad to know what is! It is dissection in all its branches. I shall, however, hazard a remark or two upon this quotation.

"To me it appears of no very great consequence whether Martha Blount was or was not Pope's mistress, though I could have wished him a better. She appears to have been a cold-hearted, interested, ignorant, disagreeable woman, upon whom the tenderness of Pope's heart in the desolation of his latter days was cast away, not knowing whither to turn as he drew towards his premature old age, childless and lonely,—like the needle which, approaching within a certain distance of the pole, becomes helpless and useless, and, ceasing to tremble, rusts. She seems to have been so totally unworthy of tenderness, that it is an additional proof of the kindness of Pope's heart to have been able to love such a being. But we must love something. I agree with Mr. B. that *she* 'could at no time have regarded *Pope personally* with attachment,' because she was incapable of attachment; but I deny that Pope could not be regarded with personal attachment by a worthier woman. It is not probable, indeed, that a woman would have fallen in love with him as he walked along the Mall, or in a box at the opera, nor from a balcony, nor in a ball-room; but in society he seems to have been as amiable as unassuming, and, with the greatest disadvantages of figure, bis head and face were remarkably handsome, especially his eyes. He was adored by his friends—friends of the most opposite dispositions, ages, and talents—by the old and wayward Wycherley, by the cynical Swift, the rough Atterbury, the gentle Spence, the stern attorney-bishop Warburton, the virtuous Berkeley, and the 'cankered Bolingbroke.' Bolingbroke wept over him like a child; and Spence's description of his last moments is at least as edifying as the more ostentatious account of the deathbed of Addison. The soldier Peterborough and the poet Gay, the witty Congreve and the laughing Rowe, the eccentric Cromwell and the steady Bathurst, were all his intimates. The man who could conciliate so many men of the most opposite description, not one of whom but was a remarkable or a celebrated character, might well have pretended to all the attachment which a reasonable man would desire of an amiable woman.

"Pope, in fact, wherever he got it, appears to have understood the sex well. Bolingbroke, 'a judge of the subject,' says Warton, thought his 'Epistle on the Characters of Women' his 'masterpiece.' And even with respect to the grosser passion, which takes occasionally the name of '*romantic,*' accordingly as the degree of sentiment elevates it above the definition of love by Buffon, it may be remarked, that it does not always depend upon personal appearance, even in a woman. Madame Cottin was a plain woman, and might have been virtuous, it may be presumed, without much interruption. Virtuous she was, and the consequences of this inveterate virtue were that two different admirers (one an elderly gentleman) killed themselves in despair (see Lady Morgan's 'France'). I would not, however, recommend this rigour to plain women in general, in the hope of securing the glory of two suicides apiece. I believe that there are few men who, in the course of their observations on life, may not have perceived that it is not the greatest female beauty who forms the longest and the strongest passions.

"But, apropos of Pope.—Voltaire tells us that the Marechal Luxembourg (who had precisely Pope's figure) was not only somewhat too amatory for a great man, but fortunate in his attachments. La Valière, the passion of Louis 14th, had an unsightly defect. The princess of Eboli, the mistress of Philip the second of Spain, and Maugiron, the minion of Henry the third of France, had each of them lost an eye; and the famous Latin epigram was written upon them, which has, I believe, been either translated or imitated by Goldsmith:—

"Lumine Acon dextro, capta est Leonilla sinistro,
Et potis est forma vincere uterque Deos;
Blande puer, lumen quod habes concede sorori,
Sic tu cæcus Amor, sic erit illa Venus."

"Wilkes, with his ugliness, used to say that 'he was but a quarter of an hour behind the handsomest man in England;' and this vaunt of his is said not to have been disproved by circumstances. Swift, when neither young, nor handsome, nor rich, nor even amiable, inspired the two most extraordinary passions upon record, Vanessa's and Stella's.

"'Vanessa, aged scarce a score,
Sighs for a gown of *forty-four*.'

"He requited them bitterly; for he seems to have broken the heart of the one, and worn out that of the other; and he had his reward, for he died a solitary idiot in the hands of servants.

"For my own part, I am of the opinion of Pausanias, that success in love depends upon Fortune. 'They particularly reverence Celestial Venus, into whose temple, etc., etc., etc. I remember, too, to have seen a building in Ægina in which there is a statue of Fortune, holding a horn of Amalthea; and near her there is a winged Love. The meaning of this is that the success of men in love affairs depends more on the assistance of Fortune than the charms of beauty. I am persuaded, too, with Pindar (to whose opinion I subscribe in other particulars), that Fortune is one of the Fates, and that in a certain respect she is more powerful than her sisters.'—See Pausanias, Achaics, book 7th, chap. 26th, page 346. 'Taylor's Translation.'

"Grimm has a remark of the same kind on the different destinies of the younger Crebillon and Rousseau. The former writes a licentious novel, and a young English girl of some fortune and family (a Miss Strafford) runs away, and crosses the sea to marry him; while Rousseau, the most tender and passionate of lovers, is obliged to espouse his chambermaid. If I recollect rightly, this remark was also repeated in the Edinburgh Review of Grimm's Correspondence, seven or eight years ago.

"In regard 'to the strange mixture of indecent, and sometimes *profane* levity, which his conduct and language *often* exhibited,' and which so much shocks Mr. Bowles, I object to the indefinite word '*often*;' and in the extenuation of the occasional occurrence of such language, it is to be recollected that it was less the tone of *Pope* than the tone of the *time*. With the exception of the correspondence of Pope and his friends, not many private letters of the period have come down to us; but those, such as they are—a few scattered scraps from Farquhar and others—are more indecent and coarse than anything in Pope's letters. The comedies of Congreve,

Vanbrugh, Farquhar, Cibber, etc., which naturally attempted to represent the manners and conversation of private life, are decisive upon this point; as are also some of Steele's papers, and even Addison's. We all know what the conversation of Sir R. Walpole, for seventeen years the prime minister of the country, was at his own table, and his excuse for his licentious language, viz. 'that everybody understood *that,* but few could talk rationally upon less common topics.' The refinement of latter days,—which is perhaps the consequence of vice, which wishes to mask and soften itself, as much as of virtuous civilisation—had not yet made sufficient progress. Even Johnson, in his 'London,' has two or three passages which cannot be read aloud, and Addison's 'Drummer' some indelicate allusions.

"The expression of Mr. B., 'his consciousness of physical defect,' is not very clear. It may mean deformity, or debility. If it alludes to Pope's deformity, it has been attempted to be shown that this was no insuperable objection to his being beloved. If it alludes to debility, as a consequence of Pope's peculiar conformation, I believe that it is a physical and known fact that hump-backed persons are of strong and vigorous passions. Several years ago, at Mr. Angelo's fencing rooms, when I was a boy and pupil of him and of Mr. Jackson, who had the use of his rooms in Albany on the alternate days, I recollect a gentleman named B—ll—gh—m, remarkable for his strength, and the fineness of his figure. His skill was not inferior, for he could stand up to the great Captain Barclay' himself, with the muffles on;—a task neither easy nor agreeable to a pugilistic aspirant. As the bye-standers were one day admiring his athletic proportions, he remarked to us, that he had five brothers as tall and strong as himself, and that their *father and mother were both crooked, and of very small stature*;—I think he said, neither of them five feet high. It would not be difficult to adduce similar instances; but I abstain, because the subject is hardly refined enough for this immaculate period, this moral millenium of expurgated editions in books, manners, and royal trials of divorce.

"This laudable delicacy—this crying-out elegance of the day—reminds me of a little circumstance which occurred when I was about eighteen years of age. There was then (and there may be still) a famous French 'entremetteuse,' who assisted young gentlemen in their youthful pastimes. We had been acquainted for some time, when something occurred in her line of business more than ordinary, and the refusal was offered to me (and doubtless to many others), probably because I was in cash at the moment, having taken up a decent sum from the Jews, and not having spent much above half of it. The adventure on the tapis, it seems, required some caution and circumspection. Whether my venerable friend doubted my politeness I cannot tell; but she sent me a letter couched in such English as a short residence of sixteen years in England had enabled her to acquire. After several precepts and instructions, the letter closed. But there was a postscript. It contained these words:—'Remember, Milor, that *delicaci ensure everi succès.*' The *delicacy* of the day is exactly, in all its circumstances, like that of this respectable foreigner. 'It ensures every *succès*,' and is not a whit more moral than, and not half so honourable as, the coarser candour of our less polished ancestors.

"Page 12. produces 'more reasons,'—(the task ought not to have been difficult, for as yet there were none)—'to show why Mr. B. attributed the critique in the Quarterly to Octavius Gilchrist.' All these 'reasons' consist of *surmises* of Mr. B., upon the presumed character of his opponent. 'He did not suppose there could exist a man in the kingdom so *impudent,* etc., etc., except Octavius G.'—'He did not think there was a man in the kingdom who would *pretend ignorance,* etc., etc., except Octavius G.'—'He did not conceive that one man in the kingdom would utter such *stupid* flippancy, etc., etc., except—Octavius G.'—'He did not think there was one man in the kingdom who, etc., etc., could so utterly show his ignorance, *combined with conceit,* etc., as Octavius G.'—'He did not believe there was a man in the kingdom so perfect in Mr. G.'s "old lunes,"' etc., etc.—'He did not think *the mean mind* of any one in the kingdom,' etc., and so on; always beginning with 'any one in the kingdom,' and ending with 'Octavius Gilchrist,' like the word in a catch. I am not 'in the kingdom,' and have not been much in the kingdom since I was one and twenty, (about five years in the whole, since I was of age,) and have no desire to be in the kingdom again, whilst I breathe, nor to sleep there afterwards; and I regret nothing more than having ever been 'in the kingdom' at all. But though no longer a man 'in the kingdom,' let me hope that when I have ceased to exist, it may be said, as was answered by the master of Clanronald's henchman, the day after the battle of Sheriff-Muir, when he was found watching his chiefs body. He was asked, 'who that was?' he replied—'it was a Man yesterday.' And in this capacity, 'in' or out of 'the kingdom,' I must own that I participate in many of the objections urged by Mr. Gilchrist. I participate in his love of Pope, and in his not always understanding, and occasionally finding fault with, the last editor of our last truly great poet.

"One of the reproaches against Mr. G. is, that he is (it is sneeringly said) an F. S. *A.* If it will give Mr. B. any pleasure, I am not an F. S. A., but a Fellow of the Royal Society at his service, in case there should be any thing in that association also which may point a paragraph.

"'There are some other reasons,' but 'the author is now *not* unknown.' Mr. Bowles has so totally exhausted himself upon Octavius G., that he has not a word left for the real Quarterer of his edition, although now 'deterré.'

"The following page refers to a mysterious charge of 'duplicity, in regard to the publication of Pope's letters.' Till this charge is made in proper form, we have nothing to do with it: Mr. G. hints it—Mr. Bowles denies it; there it rests for the present. Mr. B. professes his dislike to 'Pope's *duplicity, not* to *Pope*'—a distinction apparently without a difference. However, I believe that I understand him. We have a great dislike to Mr. B.'s edition of Pope, but *not* to Mr. Bowles; nevertheless, he takes up the subject as warmly as if it was personal. With regard to the fact of '*Pope's* duplicity,' it remains to be proved—like Mr. B.'s benevolence towards his memory.

"In page 14. we have a large assertion, that 'the "Eloisa" alone is sufficient to convict him of *gross licentiousness.*' Thus, out it comes at last. Mr. B. *does* accuse Pope of *'gross* licentiousness,' and grounds the charge upon a poem. The *licentiousness* is a 'grand peut-être,' according to the turn of the times being. The grossness I deny. On the contrary, I do believe that such a subject never was, nor ever could be, treated by any poet with so much delicacy, mingled, at the same time, with such true and intense passion. Is the 'Atys' of Catullus *licentious*? No, nor even gross; and yet Catullus is often a coarse writer. The subject is nearly the same, except that Atys was the suicide of his manhood, and Abelard the victim.

"The 'licentiousness' of the story was *not* Pope's—it was a fact. All that it had of gross, he has softened;—all that it had of indelicate, he has purified—all that it had of passionate, he has beautified;—all that it had of holy, he has hallowed. Mr. Campbell has admirably marked this in a few words (I quote from memory), in drawing the distinction between Pope and Dryden, and pointing out where Dryden was wanting. 'I fear,' says he, 'that had the subject of "Eloisa" fallen into his (Dryden's) hands, that he would have given us but a *coarse* draft of her passion.' Never was the delicacy of Pope so much shown as in this poem. With the facts and the letters of 'Eloisa' he has done what no other mind but that of the best and purest of poets could have accomplished with such materials. Ovid, Sappho (in the Ode called hers)—all that we have of ancient, all that we have of modern poetry, sinks into nothing compared with him in this production.

"Let us hear no more of this trash about 'licentiousness.' Is not 'Anacreon' taught in our schools?—translated, praised, and edited? Are not his Odes the amatory praises of a boy? Is not Sappho's Ode on a girl? Is not this sublime and (according to Longinus') fierce love for one of her own sex? And is not Phillips' translation of it in the mouths of all your women? And are the English schools or the English women the more corrupt for all this! When you have thrown the ancients into the fire it will be time to denounce the moderns. 'Licentiousness!'—there is more real mischief and sapping licentiousness in a single French prose novel, in a Moravian hymn, or a German comedy, than in all the actual poetry that ever was penned or poured forth, since the rhapsodies of Orpheus. The sentimental anatomy of Rousseau and Mad^e de S. are far more formidable than any quantity of verse. They are so, because they sap the principles, by *reasoning* upon the *passions*; whereas poetry is in itself passion, and does not systematize. It assails, but does not argue; it may be wrong, but it does not assume pretensions to Optimism.

"Mr. B. now has the goodness 'to point out the difference between a *traducer* and him who sincerely states what he sincerely believes.' He might have spared himself the trouble. The one is a liar, who lies knowingly; the other (I speak of a scandal-monger of course) lies, charitably believing that he speaks truth, and very sorry to find himself in falsehood;—because he

> "'Would rather that the dean should die,
> Than his prediction prove a lie.'

"After a definition of a 'traducer,' which was quite superfluous (though it is agreeable to learn that Mr. B. so well understands the character), we are assured, that 'he feels equally indifferent, Mr. Gilchrist, for what your malice can invent, or your impudence utter.' This is indubitable; for it rests not only on Mr. B.'s assurance, but on that of Sir Fretful Plagiary, and nearly in the same words,—'and I shall treat it with exactly the same calm indifference and philosophical contempt, and so your servant.'

"'One thing has given Mr. Bowles concern.' It is 'a passage which might seem to reflect on the patronage a young man has received.' MIGHT seem!! The passage alluded to expresses, that if Mr. G. be the reviewer of' a certain poet of nature,'his praise and blame are equally 'contemptible.'—Mr. B., who has a peculiarly ambiguous style, where it suits him, comes off with a '*not* to the *poet,* but the *critic,*' etc. In my humble opinion, the passage referred to both. Had Mr. B. really meant fairly, he would have said so from the first—he would have been eagerly transparent.—'A certain poet of nature' is not the style of commendation. It is the very prologue to the most scandalous paragraphs of the newspapers, when

"'Willing to wound, and yet afraid to strike.'

'A certain high personage,'—'a certain peeress,'—'a certain illustrious foreigner,'—what do these words ever precede, but defamation? Had he felt a spark of kindling kindness for John Clare, he would have named him. There is a sneer in the sentence as it stands. How a favourable review of a deserving poet can 'rather injure than promote his cause' is difficult to comprehend. The article denounced is able and amiable, and it *has* 'served' the poet, as far as poetry can be served by judicious and honest criticism.

"With the two next paragraphs of Mr. B.'s pamphlet it is pleasing to concur. His mention of 'Pennie,' and his former patronage of 'Shoel,' do him honour. I am not of those who may deny Mr. B. to be a benevolent man. I merely assert, that he is not a candid editor.

"Mr. B. has been 'a writer occasionally upwards of thirty years,' and never wrote one word in reply in his life 'to criticisms, merely *as* criticisms.' This is Mr. Lofty in Goldsmith's *Good-natured Man*; 'and I vow by all that's honourable, my resentment has never done the men, as mere men, any manner of harm,—that is, *as mere men.*'

"'The letter to the editor of the newspaper' is owned; but 'it was not on account of the criticism. It was because the criticism came down in a frank *directed to Mrs. Bowles!!!*'—(the italics and three notes of admiration appended to Mrs. Bowles are copied verbatim from the quotation), and Mr. Bowles was not displeased with the criticism, but with the frank and the address. I agree with Mr. B. that the intention was to annoy him; but I fear that this was answered by his notice of the reception of the criticism. An anonymous letter-writer has but one means of knowing the effect of his attack. In this he has the superiority over the viper; he knows that his poison has taken effect, when he hears the victim cry;—the adder is *deaf.* The best reply to an anonymous intimation is to take no notice directly nor indirectly. I wish Mr. B. could see only one or two of the thousand which I have received in the course of a literary life, which, though begun early, has not yet extended to a third part of his existence as an author. I speak of *literary* life only. Were I to add *personal,* I might double the amount of *anonymous* letters. If he could but see the violence, the threats, the absurdity of the whole thing, he would laugh, and so should I, and thus be both gainers.

"To keep up the farce,—within the last month of this present writing (1821), I have had my life threatened in the same way which menaced Mr. B.'s fame,—excepting that the anonymous denunciation was addressed to the Cardinal Legate of R., instead of to Mrs. Bowles. The Cardinal is, I believe, the elder lady of the two. I append the menace in all its barbaric but literal Italian, that Mr. B. may be convinced; and as this is the only 'promise to pay,' which the Italians ever keep, so my person has been at least as much exposed to a 'shot in the gloaming,' from 'John Heatherblutter' (see *Waverley*), as ever Mr. B.'s glory was from an editor. I am, nevertheless, on horseback and lonely for some hours (*one* of them twilight) in the forest daily; and this, because it was my 'custom in the afternoon,' and that I believe if the tyrant cannot escape amidst his guards (should it be so written?), so the humbler individual would find precautions useless.

"Mr. B. has here the humility to say, that 'he must succumb; for with Ld. B. turned against him, he has no chance,'—a declaration of self-denial not much in unison with his 'promise,' five lines afterwards, that 'for every 24 lines quoted by Mr. G., or his friend, to greet him with as many from his unpublished poem of the "Gilchrisiad";' but so much the better. Mr. B. has no reason to 'succumb' but to Mr. Bowles. As a poet, the author of *The Missionary* may compete with the foremost of his cotemporaries. Let it be recollected that all my previous opinions of Mr. Bowles's poetry were *written* long before the publication of his last and best poem; and that a poet's *last* poem should be his best, is his highest praise. But, however, he may duly and honourably rank with his living rivals. There never was so complete a proof of the superiority of Pope, as in the lines with which Mr. B. closes his '*to be concluded in our next.*'

"Mr. Bowles is avowedly the champion and the poet of nature. Art and the arts are dragged some before, and others behind his chariot. Pope, where he deals with passion, and with the nature of the naturals of the day, is allowed even by themselves to be sublime; but they complain that too soon—

> "'He stooped to truth and moralized his song,'

and *there* even *they* allow him to be unrivalled. He has succeeded, and even surpassed them, when he chose, in their own *pretended* province. Let us see what their Coryphceus effects in Pope's. But it is too pitiable, it is too melancholy, to see Mr. B. '*sinning*' not '*up*' but '*down*' as a poet to his lowest depth as an editor. By the way, Mr. B. is always quoting *Pope.* I grant that there is no poet—not Shakspeare himself—who can be so often quoted, with reference to life;—but his editor is so like the Devil quoting Scripture, that I could wish Mr. B. in his proper place, quoting in the pulpit.

"And now for his lines. But it is painful—painful—to see such a suicide, though at the shrine of Pope. I can't copy them all:—

"'Shall the rank, loathsome miscreant of the age,
Sit, like a nightmare, grinning o'er a page.'

"'Whose pye-bald character so aptly suit
The two extremes of Bantam and of Brute,
Compound grotesque of sullenness and show,
The chattering magpie, and the croaking crow.'"

"'Whose heart contends with thy Saturnian head,
A root of hemlock, and a lump of lead.

'Gilchrist, proceed,' etc., etc.

"'And thus stand forth, spite of thy venomed foam,
To give thee *bite for bite,* or lash thee limping home.'

With regard to the last line, the only one upon which I shall venture for fear of infection, I would advise Mr. Gilchrist to keep out of the way of such reciprocal morsure—unless he has more faith in the 'Ormskirk medicine' than most people, or may wish to anticipate the pension of the recent German professor, (I forget his name, but it is advertised and full of consonants,) who presented his memoir of an infallible remedy for the hydrophobia to the German Diet last month, coupled with the philanthropic condition of a large annuity, provided that his cure cured. Let him begin with the editor of Pope, and double his demand.

"Yours ever, BYRON.

"*To John Murray, Esq.*

"*P.S.*—Amongst the above-mentioned lines there occurs the following, *applied* to *Pope*—

"'The assassin's vengeance, and the coward's lie.'

And Mr. B. persists that he is a well-wisher to Pope!!! He has, then, edited an 'assassin' and a 'coward' wittingly, as well as lovingly. In my former letter I have remarked upon the editor's forgetfulness of Pope's benevolence. But where he mentions his faults it is 'with sorrow'—his tears drop, but they do not blot them out. The 'recording angel' differs from the recording clergyman. A fulsome editor is pardonable though tiresome, like a panegyrical son whose pious sincerity would demi-deify his father. But a detracting editor is a parricide. He sins against the nature of his office, and connection—he murders the life to come of his victim. If his author is not worthy to be remembered, do not edite at all: if he be, edite honestly, and even flatteringly. The reader will forgive the weakness in favour of mortality, and correct your adulation with a smile. But to sit down 'mingere in patrios cineres,' as Mr. B. has done, merits a reprobation so strong, that I am as incapable of expressing as of ceasing to feel it.

"*Further Addenda for insertion in the letter to J. M., Esq., on Bowles's Pope, etc.*

"It is worthy of remark that, after all this outcry about '*in-door* nature' and 'artificial images,' Pope was the principal inventor of that boast of the English, *Modern Gardening.* He divides this honour with Milton. Hear Warton:—'It hence appears that this *enchanting* art of modern gardening, in which this kingdom claims a preference over every nation in Europe, chiefly owes *its origin* and its improvements to two great poets, Milton and *Pope.*'

"Walpole (no friend to Pope) asserts that Pope formed *Kent's* taste, and that Kent was the artist to whom the English are chiefly indebted for diffusing 'a taste in laying out grounds.' The design of the Prince of Wales's garden was copied from *Pope's* at Twickenham. Warton applauds 'his singular effort of art and taste, in impressing so much variety and scenery on a spot of five acres.'

"Pope was the *first* who ridiculed the 'formal, French, Dutch, false and unnatural taste in gardening,' both in *prose* and verse. (See, for the former, *The Guardian.*)

"'Pope has given not only some of our *first* but *best* rules and observations on *Architecture* and *Gardening.*' (See Warton's Essay, vol. 2^{d} 237, etc., etc.)

"Now, is it not a shame, after this, to hear our Lakers in 'Kendal Green,' and our Bucolical Cockneys, crying out (the latter in a wilderness of bricks and mortar) about 'Nature' and Pope's 'artificial in-door habits?' Pope had seen all of nature that *England* alone can supply. He was bred in Windsor Forest, and amidst the beautiful scenery of Eton; he lived familiarly and frequently at the country seats of Bathurst, Cobham, Burlington, Peterborough, Digby, and Bolingbroke; amongst whose seats was to be numbered *Stow.* He made his own little 'five acres' a model to princes, and to the first of our artists who imitated nature. Warton thinks 'that the most engaging of *Kent's* works was also planned on the model of Pope's—at least in the opening and retiring shades of Venus's Vale.'

"It is true that Pope was infirm and deformed; but he could walk, and he could ride (he rode to Oxford from London at a stretch), and he was famous for an exquisite eye. On a tree at Ld. Bathurst's is carved 'Here Pope sang,'—he composed beneath it. Bolingbroke, in one of his letters, represents them both writing in the hay-field. No poet ever admired Nature more, or used her better, than Pope has done, as I will undertake to prove from his works, *prose* and *verse,* if not anticipated in so easy and agreeable a labour. I remember a passage in Walpole, somewhere, of a gentleman who wished to give directions about some willows to a man who had long served Pope in his grounds: 'I understand, sir,' he replied, 'you would have

BYRON'S ADDRESS TO THE NEAPOLITAN INSURGENTS

A draft of the following Address, in Byron's own handwriting, was found among his papers. He is supposed to have entrusted it to a professed agent of the Constitutional Government of Naples, who had waited upon him secretly at Ravenna, and, under the pretence of having been waylaid and robbed, induced him to supply money for his return. The man turned out afterwards to have been a spy; and the Address, if confided to him, fell most probably into the hands of the Pontifical Government.

"Un Inglese amico della libertà avendo sentito che i Napolitani permettono anche agli stranieri di contribuire alia buona causa, ramerebbe l'onore di vedere accettata la sua offerta di mille luigi, la quale egli azzarda di fare. Già testimonio oculare non molto fa della tirannia dei Barbari negli stati da loro occupati nell' Italia, egli vede con tutto l'entusiasmo di un uomo ben nato la generosa determinazione dei Napolitani per confermare la loro bene acquistata indipendenza. Membro della Camera dei Pari della nazione Inglese egli sarebbe un traditore ai principii che hanno posto sul trono la famiglia regnante d'Inghilterra se non riconoscesse la bella lezione di bel nuovo data ai popoli ed ai Re. L' offerta che egli brama di presentare è poca in se stessa, come bisogna che sia sempre quella di un individuo ad una nazione, ma egli spera che non sarà l'ultima dalla parte dei suoi compatriotti. La sua lontananza dalle frontiere, e il sentimento della sua poca capacità personale di contribuire efficacimente a servire la nazione gl' impedisce di proporsi come degno della più piccola commissione che domanda dell' esperienza e del talento. Ma, se come semplice volontario la sua presenza non fosse un incomodo a quello che l'accetasse egli riparebbe a qualunque luogo indicato dal Governo Napolitano, per ubbidire agli ordini e participare ai pericoli del suo superiore, senza avere altri motivi che quello di dividere il destino di una brava nazione resistendo alla se dicente Santa Allianza la quale aggiunge l'ippocrisia al despotismo."

The following is Moore's translation:—

"An Englishman, a friend to liberty, having understood that the Neapolitans permit even foreigners to contribute to the good cause, is desirous that they should do him the honour of accepting a thousand louis, which he takes the liberty of offering. Having already, not long since, been an ocular witness of the despotism of the Barbarians in the States occupied by them in Italy, he sees, with the enthusiasm natural to a cultivated man, the generous determination of the Neapolitans to assert their well-won independence. As a member of the English House of Peers, he would be a traitor to the principles which placed the reigning family of England on the throne, if he were not grateful for the noble lesson so lately given both to people and to kings. The offer which he desires to make is small in itself, as must always be that presented from an individual to a nation; but he trusts that it will not be the last they will receive from his countrymen. His distance from the frontier, and the feeling of his personal incapacity to contribute efficaciously to the service of the nation, prevents him from proposing himself as worthy of the lowest commission, for which experience and talent might be requisite. But if, as a mere volunteer, his presence were not a burden to whomsoever he might serve under, he would repair to whatever place the Neapolitan Government might point out, there to obey the orders and participate in the dangers of his commanding officer, without any other motive than that of sharing the destiny of a brave nation, defending itself against the self-called Holy Alliance, which but combines the vice of hypocrisy with despotism."

BACON'S APOPHTHEGMS

On the last line of stanza cxlvii. of Canto V. of *Don Juan,* Byron has the following note: "It may not be unworthy of remark, that Bacon, in his essay on 'Empire,' hints that *Solyman* was the *last* of his line; on what authority, I know not. These are his words: 'The destruction of Mustapha was so fatal to Solyman's line, as the succession of the Turks from Solyman, until this day, is suspected to be untrue, and of strange blood; for that Solyman the Second was thought to be supposititious.' But Bacon, in his historical authorities, is often inaccurate. I could give half-a-dozen instances from his apophthegms only," etc., etc. The instances are those which follow.

BACON'S APOPHTHEGMS.	OBSERVATIONS.
91	
"Michael Angelo, the famous painter, painting in the pope's chapel the portraiture of hell and damned souls, made one of the damned souls so like a cardinal that was his enemy, as everybody at first sight knew it; whereupon the cardinal complained to Pope Clement, humbly praying it might be defaced. The pope said to him, Why, you know very well I have power to deliver a soul out of purgatory, but not out of hell.	"This was *not* the portrait of a cardinal, but of the pope's master of the ceremonies.
155	
"Alexander, after the battle of Granicum, had very great offers made him by Darius. Consulting with his captains concerning them, Parmenio said, Sure, I would accept of these offers, if I were as Alexander. Alexander answered, So would I, if I were as Parmenio.	"It was after the battle of Issus, and during the siege of Tyre, and *not* immediately after the passage of the Granicus, that this is said to have occurred.

158

"Antigonus, when it was told him that the enemy had such volleys of arrows, that they did hide the sun, said, That falls out well, for it is hot weather, and so we shall fight in the shade.

"This was *not* said by Antigonus, but by a Spartan, previously to the battle of Thermopylæ.

162

"There was a philosopher that disputed with Adrian the Emperor, and did it but weakly. One of his friends that stood by, afterwards said unto him, Methinks you were not like yourself last day, in argument with the Emperor: I could have answered better myself. Why, said the philosopher, would you have me contend with him that commands thirty legions?

"This happened under Augustus Cæsar, and *not* during the reign of Adrian.

164

"There was one that found a great mass of money digged under ground in his grandfather's house, and being somewhat doubtful of the case, signified it to the emperor that he had found such treasure. The emperor made a rescript thus: Use it. He writ back again that the sum was greater than his state or condition could use. The emperor writ a new rescript, thus: Abuse it.

"This happened to the father of Herodes Atticus, and the answer was made by the Emperor Nerva, who deserved that his name should have been stated by the 'greatest—wisest —meanest of mankind.'

178

"One of the seven was wont to say, that laws were like cobwebs: where the small flies were caught, and the great brake through.

"This was said by Anacharsis the Scythian, and *not* by a Greek.

209

"An orator of Athens said to Demosthenes, The Athenians will

"This was *not* said *by* Demosthenes but *to* Demosthenes by *Phocion.*

kill you if they wax mad. Demosthenes replied, And they will kill you, if they be in good sense.

221

"There was a philosopher about Tiberius that, looking into the nature of Caius, said of him, That he was mire mingled with blood.

"This was not said of Caius (Caligula, I presume, is in-tended by Caius,) but of *Tiberius* himself.

97

"There was a king of Hungary took a bishop in battle, and kept him prisoner; whereupon the pope writ a monitory to him, for that he had broken the privilege of holy church, and taken his son: the king sent an embassage to him, and sent withal the armour wherein the bishop was taken, and this only in writing—*Vide num hæc sit vestis filii tui?* Know now whether this be thy son's coat?

" This reply was *not* made by a king of *Hungary,* but sent by Richard the first, Cœur de Lion, of England to the Pope, with the breastplate of the bishop of Beauvais.

267

"Demetrius, King of Macedon, had a petition offered him divers times by an old woman, and answered he had no leisure; whereupon the woman said aloud, Why then give over to be king."

"This did *not* happen to Demetrius, but to *Philip* King of Macedon."

VOLTAIRE.

"Having stated that Bacon was frequently incorrect in his citations from history, I have thought it necessary in what regards so great a name (however trifling,) to support the assertion by such facts as more immediately occur to me. They are but trifles, and yet for such trifles a schoolboy would be whipped (if still in the fourth form);—and Voltaire for half a dozen similar errors has been treated as a superficial writer, notwithstanding the testimony of the learned Warton:—'Voltaire, a writer of *much deeper research* than is imagined, and the *first* who has displayed the literature and customs of the dark ages with *any degree of penetration* and comprehension.' For another distinguished testimony to Voltaire's merits in literary research, see also Lord Holland's excellent Account of the Life and Writings of Lope de Vega, vol. i. p. 215, edition of 1817.

"Voltaire has even been termed 'a shallow fellow,' by some of the same school who called Dryden's Ode 'a drunken song;'—a *school* (as it is called, I presume, from their education being still incomplete) the whole of whose filthy trash of Epics, Excursions, etc., etc., etc., is not worth the two words in Zaire, '*Vous pleurez,*' or a single speech of Tancred:—a *school,* the apostate lives of whose renegadoes, with their tea-drinking neutrality of morals, and their convenient treachery in politics—in the record of their accumulated pretences to virtue can produce no *actions* (were all their good deeds drawn up in array) to equal or approach the sole defence of the family of Calas, by that great and unequalled genius—the universal Voltaire.

" I have ventured to remark on these little inaccuracies of 'the greatest genius that England or perhaps any other country ever produced,' merely to show our national injustice in condemning *generally,* the greatest genius of France for such inadvertencies as these, of which the highest of England has been no less guilty. Query, was Bacon a greater intellect than Newton?"

i. Thus in the original, Byron having carefully erased three lines of writing.

ii. The rest of the letter is torn off.

iii. Thus in the original.

iv. In the original MS. these watchwords are blotted over so as to be illegible.

v. The rest of the letter is missing.

vi. Moore's translation of this of this extract is as follows:—

"You will see here confirmation of what I told you the other day! I am sacrificed in every way, without knowing the *why* or the *wherefore*. The tragedy in question is not (nor ever was) written for, or adapted to, the stage; nevertheless, the plan is not romantic; it is rather regular than otherwise;—in point of unity of time, indeed, perfectly regular, and falling but slightly in unity of place. You well know whether it was ever my intention to have it acted, since it was written at your side, and at a period assuredly rather more *tragical* to me as a *man* than as an *author*; for *you* were in affliction and peril. In the mean time, I learn from your Gazette that a cabal and a party has been formed, while I myself have never taken the slightest step in the business. It is said that *the author read it aloud!!!*—here, probably, at Ravenna?—and to whom? perhaps to Fletcher!!!—that illustrious literary character," etc., etc.

vii. Here about fourteen lines of the autograph are cut off.

viii. Byron gave Mawman a copy of the edition of Cantos III., IV., V. of *Don Juan*, and wrote the following inscription on the title-page:—

"to J. Mawman, Esqre
from the Author.

Septr 1st 1821.

"Mr. Mawman is requested to show this copy to the publisher and to point out the gross printer's blunders, *some* of which only the author has had time to correct. They did not exist in the MSS. but are owing to the carelessness of the printer, etc."

ix. Placed here as one of the inclusions mentioned in the previous letter; not sent at the time of writing.

x. The words following this point are erased, apparently not by the writer, and partly illegible.

xi. Here the manuscript ends.

xii. Of these there is one ranked with the others for his Sonnets, and *two* for compositions which belong to *no class* at all. Where is Dante? His poem is not an *epic*; then what is it? He himself calls it a "divine comedy;" and why? This is more than all his thousand commentators have been able to explain. Ariosto's is not an *epic* poem; and if poets are to be *classed* according to the *genus* of their poetry, where is he to be placed? Of these five, Tasso and Alfieri only come within Aristotle's arrangement, and Mr. Bowles's class-book. But the whole position is false Poets are classed by the power of their performance, and not according to its rank in a gradus. In the contrary case, the forgotten epic poets of all countries would rank above Petrarch, Dante, Ariosto, Burns, Gray, Dryden, and the highest names of various countries. Mr. Bowles's title of "*invariable* principles of poetry," is, perhaps, the most arrogant ever prefixed to a volume. So far are the principles of poetry from being '*invariable*,' that they never were nor ever will be settled. These 'principles' mean nothing more than the predilections of a particular age; and every age has its own, and a different from its predecessor. It is now Homer, and now Virgil; once Dryden, and since Walter Scott; now Corneille, and and now Racine; now Crebillon, now Voltaire. The Homerists and Virgilians in France disputed for half a century. Not fifty years ago the Italians neglected Dante—Bettinelli reproved Monti for reading "that barbarian;" at present they adore him. Shakspeare and Milton have had their rise, and they will have their decline. Already they have more than once fluctuated, as must be the case with all the dramatists and poets of a living language. This does not depend upon their merits, but upon the ordinary vicissitudes of human opinions. Schlegel and Madame de Stael have endeavoured also to reduce poetry to *two* systems, classical and romantic. The effect is only beginning.

xiii. I will submit to Mr. Bowles's own judgement a passage from another poem of Cowper's, to be compared with the same writer's Sylvan Sampler. In the lines "to Mary,"—

> "Thy *needles,* once a shining store,
> For my sake restless heretofore,
> Now rust disused, and shine no more;
> My Mary!"

contain a simple, household, "*indoor,*" artificial, and ordinary image; I refer Mr. B. to the stanza, and ask if these three lines about "*needles*" are not worth all the boasted twaddling about trees, so triumphantly requoted? and yet, in *fact,* what do they convey? A homely collection of images and ideas, associated with the darning of stockings, and the hemming of shirts, and the mending of breeches; but will any one deny that they are eminently poetical and pathetic as addressed by Cowper to his nurse? The trash of trees reminds me of a saying of Sheridan's. Soon after the "Rejected Address" scene in 1812, I met Sheridan. In the course of dinner, he said, "L. B., did you know that, amongst the writers of addresses, was Whitbread himself?" I answered by an enquiry of what sort of an address he had made. "Of that," replied Sheridan, "I remember little, except that there was a *phœnix* in it."—"A phœnix!! Well, how did he describe it?"—"*Like a poulterer,*" answered Sheridan: "It was green, and yellow, and red, and blue: he did not let us off for a single feather." And just such as this poulterer's account of a phoenix is Cowper's —a stick-picker's detail of a wood, with all its petty minutiæ of this, that, and the other.

One more poetical instance of the power of art, and even its *superiority* over nature, in poetry; and I have done:—the bust of *Antinous*! Is there any thing in nature like this marble, excepting the Venus? Can there be more *poetry* gathered into existence than in that wonderful creation of perfect beauty? But the poetry of this bust is in no respect derived from nature, nor from any association of moral exaltedness; for what is there in common with moral nature, and the male minion of Adrian? The very execution is *not natural,* but *super*natural, or rather *super-artificial,* for nature has never done so much.

Away, then, with this cant about nature, and "invariable principles of poetry!" A great artist will make a block of stone as sublime as a mountain, and a good poet can imbue a pack of cards with more poetry than inhabits the forests of America. It is the business and the proof of a poet to give the lie to the proverb, and sometimes to "*make a silken purse out of a sow's ear,*" and to conclude with another homely proverb, "a good workman will not find fault with his tools."

xiv. If the opinions cited by Mr. Bowles, of Dr. Johnson *against* Pope, are to be taken as decisive authority, they will also hold good against Gray, Milton, Swift, Thomson, and Dryden: in that case what becomes of Gray's poetical, and Milton's moral character? even of Milton's *poetical* character, or, indeed, of *English* poetry in general? for Johnson strips many a leaf from every laurel. Still Johnson's is the finest critical work extant, and can never be read without instruction and delight.

xv. A word or two here has been torn off with the seal.

xvi. The following passage on Keats, sent to Murray by Byron for insertion, was suppressed on account of Keats's death:—

"Additions to the passages from Keats.

"Further on we have—

> "'The hearty grasp that sends a pleasant Sonnet
> Into the brain ere one can think upon it,
> The Silence when some rhymes are coming out,
> And when they're come the *very pleasant rout*;
> The Message certain to be done to-morrow.
> 'Tis perhaps as well that it should be to borrow
> Some precious book from out its snug retreat,
> To cluster round it when we next shall meet.
> Scarce can I scribble on,' etc., etc.

"Now what does this mean?

"Again—

> "'And with these airs came forms of elegance
> *Stooping their shoulders* o'er a *horse's prance.*'

"Where did these '*forms of elegance*' learn to ride—with '*stooping shoulders*'?

"Again—

> "'Thus I remember all the pleasant flow
> Of words at opening a Portfolio.'

"Again—

"'Yet I must not forget
Sleep, quiet with his poppy coronet:
For what there may be worthy in these rhymes
I *partly owe* to *him,*' etc.

"This obligation is likely to be mutual. It may appear harsh to accumulate passages of this kind from the work of a young man in the outset of his career. But, if he will set out with assailing the Poet whom of all others a young aspirant ought to respect and honour and study—if he will hold forth in such lines his notions on poetry, and endeavour to recommend them by terming such men as Pope, Dryden, Swift, Addison, Congreve, Young, Gay, Goldsmith, Johnson, etc., etc., 'a *School of dolts,*' he must abide by the consequences of his unfortunate distortion of intellect. But like Milbourne he is 'the fairest of Critics,' by enabling us to compare his own compositions with those of Pope at the same age, and on a similar subject, viz. Poetry.

"As Mr. K. does not want imagination nor industry, let those who have led him astray look to what they have done. Surely they must feel no little remorse in having so perverted the taste and feelings of this young man, and will be satisfied with one such victim to their Moloch of Absurdity.

"Pope little expected that the 'Art of sinking in Poetry' would become an object of serious Study, and supersede not only his own but all that Horace, Vida, Boileau and Aristotle had left to Posterity, of precept, and the greatest poets in all nations, of example."